PERSONAL DEMON

PERSONAL DEMON

KELLEY ARMSTRONG

BANTAM BOOKS

PERSONAL DEMON
A Bantam Spectra Book / April 2008

Published by Bantam Dell
A Division of Random House, Inc.
New York, New York

Book design by Lynn Newmark

Bantam Books, the rooster colophon, Spectra, and the portrayal of a boxed "s" are trademarks of Random House, Inc.

Library of Congress Cataloging-in-Publication Data
Armstrong, Kelley.
Personal demon / Kelley Armstrong
p. cm.
ISBN 978-0-553-80661-8
I. Title.

PS3551.R4678P47 2008
813'.54—dc22
2007030334

Printed in the United States of America
Published simultaneously in Canada

www.bantamdell.com

10 9 8 7 6 5 4 3 2 1
BVG

To my sister, Alison.
Your assistance and unwavering support
has been more valuable—and more appreciated—than I can
convey with a simple "thanks."

ACKNOWLEDGMENTS

As usual, I need to thank those who make me look good . . . or at least do their damnedest with the material I give them! A huge thank you, once again, to my agent, Helen Heller, and my editors, Anne Groell of Bantam Spectra, Anne Collins of Random House Canada, and Antonia Hodgson of Warner Orbit.

This time, I want to offer a somewhat belated thanks to some people who helped me whip up a "series bible" I kept moaning about needing to write. Thanks to Ian O'Neill, Yan Ming, Genine Tyson, and Jennifer Thompson. I hate continuity errors and, with your wonderful help, I'll avoid (most of) them. And a big thanks to my beta readers, Laura Stutts, Raina Toomey, Xaviere Daumarie, and Danielle Wegner, who helped me avoid some of those nasty continuity errors with this one.

PERSONAL DEMON

HOPE

LUCIFER'S DAUGHTER

There was a time in my life when the prospect of watching a man die would have filled me with horror. Now, as I shivered beside the cenotaph, knowing death was coming, what I *felt* was very different.

Only knowing it was too late to stop what was about to happen kept me from screaming a warning as I clutched the cold marble.

"Did you bring the money?" the first man asked, his voice tight with an anxiety that strummed through the air. He wore dress slacks an inch too long, hems pooling around scuffed department store loafers. His old leather jacket was done up against the bitter March night, but misbuttoned. I could picture his fingers trembling as he'd hurried out to this midnight meeting.

The other man was a decade older, his jogging suit hood pulled tight around his red-cheeked face. Beside him, a Chow panted, the *chuff-chuff* filling the silence, black tongue lolling as the dog strained the confines of its short leash.

"Did you bring the money?" the younger man asked again as he glanced around the park, his anxiety sharp against the cold rage blowing off the other man.

"Did you really think I'd pay?"

The older man lunged. A blast of fear, so intense my eyelids quivered. Then a gasp, rich with shock and pain. Chaos rolled over me and moonlight sparked red against the knife blade. The stink of voided bowels filled the air as the younger man staggered back into a spindly maple. He tottered for a moment, propped against it, then slumped at its base.

The killer pulled his dog closer. The Chow danced, its chaos fluttering past me, confusion warring with hunger. The man shoved its head to the wound, steaming blood pumping. The dog took a tentative lick, then—

The vision broke and I reeled, grabbing the cenotaph. A moment's pause, eyes squeezed shut. Then I straightened and blinked against the bright morning sun.

At the foot of the cenotaph, a shrine had started, with plucked daffodils and scraps of paper scrawled with "We'll Miss You, Brian" and "Rest in Peace, Ryan." Anyone who knew Bryan Mills well enough to spell his name was still at home, in shock. The people hugging and sobbing around the shrine were only hoping to catch the eye of a roving TV camera, say a few words about what a great guy "Ryan" had been.

As I circled the crime scene tape, I passed the fake mourners, and their sobbing rose... until they noticed I wasn't carrying a camera, and fell back to sipping steaming coffees and huddling against the icy morning.

They might not have made me for a reporter, but the closest cop guarding the scene did, his glower telling me not to bother asking for a statement. I'm sure "Hey, I know what happened to your dead guy" would have been a guaranteed conversation opener. But then what would I say?

"How do I know? Um, I had a vision. Psychic? No. I can only see the past—a talent I inherited from my father. More of a curse, really, though I'm sure he thinks otherwise. Maybe you've heard of him? Lucifer? No, not Satan—that's a whole different guy. I'm what they call a half-demon, a human fathered by a demon. Most of us get a special power, like fire, telekinesis or teleportation, without a demon's need for chaos. But that chaos hunger is *all* I get, plus a few special powers to help me find it. Like visions of past trauma, which is why I know how your victim died. And I can read chaotic thoughts, like the one going through your head right now, Officer. You're wondering whether you should quietly call for the ambulance or pin me to the ground first, in case my psychotic break turns violent."

So I stuck to my job: reporting the news, not becoming it. I found a likely target—the youngest officer, buttons gleaming, gaze following the news cameras, shoulders straightening each time one promised to swing his way, then slumping when it moved elsewhere.

As I approached, his gaze traveled over me and his chin lifted to showcase a square jaw. A smile tweaked his lips. When I took out my notebook, the smile ignited, and he stepped forward to intercept me, lest I change my mind.

"Hello, there," he said. "I haven't seen you before. New at the *Gazette*?"

I shook my head. "I'm national."

His eyes glittered, envisioning his name in *Time* or *USA Today*. I always felt a little bad about that. *True News was* a national publication, though . . . a national supermarket tabloid.

"Hope Adams," I said, thrusting out my hand.

"Adams?"

"That's right."

A flush bloomed on his cheeks. "Sorry, I, uh, wasn't sure I heard that right."

Apparently, I didn't look like this officer's idea of a "Hope Adams." My mother had been a student from India when she met my dad at college. Will Adams, though, was not my biological father, and half-demons inherit their appearance from their maternal DNA.

As I chatted him up, a man lurched from behind the cenotaph. He peered around, his eyes wild behind green-lensed glasses. Spying us, he strode over, one black-nailed finger jabbing.

"You took him, didn't you?"

The officer's hand slid to his belt. "Sir, you need to step back—"

"Or what?" The man stopped inches from the officer, swaying. "You'll shoot me? Like you shot him? Take me away too? Study me? Dissect me? Then deny everything?"

"If you mean the victim—"

"I meant the werewolf."

The officer cleared his throat. "There, uh, was no werewolf, sir. The victim was—"

"Eaten!" The man leaned forward, spittle flying. "Torn apart and eaten! Tracks everywhere. You can't cover it up this time."

"A werewolf?" said a woman, sidling over as she passed. "I heard that too."

The officer slid a small "can you believe this?" smile my way. I struggled to return it. I *could* believe that people thought this was a werewolf; that's why *True News* had sent their "weird tales girl" to cover the story. As for werewolves themselves, I certainly believed in them—though even before the vision I'd known this wasn't one of their kills.

"Sorry about that," the officer said when he'd finally moved the conspiracy theorist on.

"Werewolves? Dare I even ask where that rumor came from?"

"The kids who found the body got all freaked out, seeing dog tracks around it, and they started posting online about werewolves. I have no idea how the dog got involved."

I was already mentally writing my story. *"When asked about the werewolf rumors, an officer on the site admitted he couldn't explain the combined signs of canine and human."* That's the trick of writing for a tabloid. You take the facts and massage them, hinting, implying, suggesting ... As long as no one is humiliated unfairly, and no sources are named, I don't have a problem giving readers the entertainment they want.

Karl would have found it entertaining too. If I'd been assigned this story a couple of months ago, I'd have been waiting for his next call, so I could say, "Hey, I got a werewolf story. Can I get a statement?" He'd make some sardonic comment, and I'd curl up, settling in for a long talk, telling myself it was just friendship, that I'd never be fool enough to fall for Karl Marsten. Kidding myself, of course. The moment I let him cross that line past friendship, I got burned ... and it was just as bad as I'd always feared.

I pushed memories of Karl aside and concentrated on the story. The officer had just let slip a lead on the kids who'd found the body— two girls who worked at the 7-Eleven on the corner—when clouds suddenly darkened the day to twilight. Thunder boomed, and I dropped my pen. As the officer bent to grab it, I snuck a glance around. No one was looking at the sky or running for cover. They were all carrying on as they had been.

The officer kept talking, but I could barely hear him through the thunderclaps. I gritted my teeth and waited for the vision to end. A storm moving in? Possible, if it promised enough destruction to qualify as chaotic. But I suspected the source was a Tempestras—a "storm" half-demon. One offshoot of my "gift" was the ability to sense other supernaturals through their chaotic powers.

I cast another surreptitious glance around. My gaze settled instead on the one person I hadn't noticed before. A dark-haired man, at least six foot three, with a linebacker's body ill-concealed by a custom-tailored suit.

He seemed to be looking my way, but with his dark sunglasses it was impossible to tell. Then he lowered them, pale blue eyes meeting mine, chin dipping in greeting. He walked over.

"Ms. Adams? A word please?"

HOPE

GODFATHER

I checked for chaos vibes and felt nothing. Still, any time a hulking half-demon stranger sought me out hundreds of miles from my home, I had reason to be alarmed.

"Let's head over there."

He nodded to a quiet corner under an elm. When we stopped, he shivered and looked up into the dense branches.

"Not the warmest spot," he said. "I guess that's why it's the one empty corner in the park. No sunshine."

"But you could fix that."

I braced myself for a denial. Instead I got a grin that thawed his ice-blue eyes.

"Now *that's* a handy talent. I could use that in my line of work."

"And that would be?"

"Troy Morgan," he said, as if in answer. "My boss would like to talk to you."

The name clicked—Benicio Cortez's personal bodyguard.

I followed Troy's gaze to a vehicle idling fifty feet away. A white SUV with Cadillac emblems on the wheels. Beside it stood a dark-haired man who could pass for Troy's twin. If both of Benicio Cortez's bodyguards were here, there was no doubt who sat behind those tinted windows.

My hastily eaten breakfast sank into the pit of my stomach.

"If it's about this—" I waved at the crime scene, "—you can tell

Mr. Cortez it wasn't a werewolf, so..." I trailed off, seeing his expression. "It isn't about the werewolf rumor, is it?"

Troy shook his head. Why else would Benicio Cortez fly from Miami to speak to a half-demon nobody? Because I owed him. The bagel turned to lead.

"Okay," I said, lifting my notebook. "I'm in the middle of a story right now, but I could meet him in an hour, say..." I scanned the street for a coffee shop.

"He needs to talk to you now."

Troy's voice was soft, gentle even, but a steel edge in his tone told me I didn't have a choice. Benicio Cortez wanted to talk to me, and it was Troy's job to make that happen.

I glanced at the crime scene. "Can I just get a few more minutes? If I can talk to one more witness, I'll have enough for a story—"

"Mr. Cortez will look after that."

He touched my elbow, gaze settling on mine, sympathetic but firm. When I still resisted, he leaned down, voice lowering. "He'd like to speak to you in the car, but if you'd be more comfortable in a public place, I can arrange it."

I shook my head, shoved my notebook into my pocket and motioned for him to lead the way.

AS I MOVED toward the curb, a passing car hit a patch of melting snow, throwing up a sheet of slush. I scampered back, but it caught my legs, dappling my skirt and nylons, the icy pellets sliding down and coming to rest in my shoes. So much for looking presentable.

I rubbed my arms and told myself the goose bumps were from the ice, not trepidation over meeting Benicio Cortez. I'm a society girl—meeting a CEO shouldn't be any cause for nerves. But Cortez Corporation was no ordinary Fortune 500 company.

A Cabal looked like a regular multinational corporation, but it was owned and staffed by supernaturals, and the unique abilities of its employees gave it a massive advantage over its competitors. It used that edge for everything from the legitimate (sorcerer spells to protect their vaults) to the unethical (astral-projecting shamans conducting corporate espionage) to the despicable (a teleporting half-demon assassin murdering a business rival).

I'd spent two years working for the Cortez Cabal. Unintentionally. Hired by Tristan Robard, who I thought was a representative of the interracial council, I'd been placed with *True News* to keep an eye on supernatural stories, suppressing or downplaying the real ones and alerting the council to potential trouble. My job soon expanded to helping them locate rogue supernaturals.

It had been the perfect way to guiltlessly indulge my hunger for chaos. The phrase "too good to be true" comes to mind, but I'd been in such a dark place—depressed, angry, confused. When you're that far down and someone offers you a hand back up, you grab it and you don't ask questions.

Then came my toughest assignment. Capturing a werewolf jewel thief during a museum gala. I'd been so pleased with myself...until that werewolf—Karl Marsten—ripped the rose-colored glasses from my eyes and proved that I was really working for the Cortez Cabal. When we escaped that mess, cleaning services came from an unexpected quarter: Benicio. My employment had been a secret operation of Tristan's, and his attack on Karl a personal matter, so in apology, Benicio had disposed of the bodies and provided medical assistance for Karl.

In return, we owed him. Until now, I'd never worried about that because I had a codebtor. Karl was a professional thief—capable of guiding me through whatever underworld task Benicio set us.

But now Benicio had come to collect, and Karl wasn't around to do anything about it.

MY SHIRT GAVE an obscene squeak as I slid onto the SUV's leather seat. If the man within noticed, he gave no sign, just put out a hand to help me.

As the door closed, the roar of morning traffic vanished, replaced by the murmur of calypso jazz, so soft I had to strain to recognize it. Gone too were the exhaust fumes, making way for the stench of stale smoke.

"Cigar," the man said, catching my nose wrinkling. "Cuban, though the expense doesn't make the smell any better. I requested a nonsmoking vehicle, but with high-end rentals, people think if they pay enough, they can do as they please."

Benicio Cortez. He bore little resemblance to the one Cortez I knew—his youngest son, Lucas. Benicio was at least sixty, probably no more than five eight, broad-faced and stocky. Only his eyes reminded me of his son—nice eyes, big and dark. The kind of guy you'd let hold your purse or take your son into the bathroom. Bet that came in handy when he was telling you he understood why you didn't want to sell your three-generation family business . . . while text-messaging a fire half-demon to torch the place before you got back from lunch.

"Do you mind if we drive?" he said. "If we sit here much longer, I'll be arguing my way out of a sizable ticket."

I was sure Benicio Cortez had more than enough cash in his wallet to pay for any ticket. I could say no supernatural likes drawing undue attention to himself, but I suspected he was testing my nerve . . . and maybe my naiveté, seeing whether I'd let him take me on a ride to parts unknown.

I said, "If you turn left at the lights, you'll hit construction, so you can make a very slow trip around the block."

"Perfect. Thank you."

A press of the button and the divider buzzed down. As he conveyed my directions to the driver, the passenger door opened and Troy climbed in, leaving the other guard behind, as if protecting his boss's idling spot.

Benicio raised the divider, then reached between our seats and pulled out a thermos.

"Another downside to rentals," he said. "No in-car beverage service. I'm spoiled, I'm afraid. I had this brewed on the jet, and I assure you, it's excellent, though the container might be somewhat off-putting." A rueful smile as he lifted the battered army-green thermos. "Ugly, but it does the job better than anything I've found."

The vacuum seal popped, filling the cabin with rich steam.

"I apologize for interrupting your work." He handed me a white china mug. "It wasn't a council concern, was it? My daughter-in-law would not be pleased." Lucas's wife was Paige Winterbourne, witch delegate to the council.

"It's not council work," I said. "But they'll expect a report from me—and my editor is expecting a story—so I need to get back before my sources wander off."

He filled my mug, then topped off his.

"I still feel responsible for the trouble you and Karl experienced with Tristan," he said finally. "I should have been aware of his activities. In recompense, I wanted to offer you and Karl a job—temporary, of course—and one particularly suited to your talents. You'd be paid, naturally, and I believe it would help you gain valuable skills for your work with the council. I hoped to talk to Karl first, but I have no way of getting in touch with him."

His gaze settled on me.

"I don't have his number," I lied, then added a truth. "Anyway, he's in Europe. Indefinitely."

"Indefinitely?"

"That's what he said."

"How unfortunate." He took a long sip of his coffee. "Have you had any experience investigating street gangs, Hope?"

I shook my head.

"Still you understand the concept—youths banding together at a time when they feel the need to belong, when they're eager to explore their power. As a young supernatural, you probably have some sense of what that's like yourself."

I didn't reply, waiting for him to get to the point.

"We raise our children to hide their powers and fit into human society, and that doesn't always sit well with them. Some form criminal gangs—mostly male, late teens to midtwenties, when they're coming into their full powers. They're better organized than human gangs—more focused and less casually violent, though not above using violence to achieve their goals."

Sounded like a youth version of a Cabal.

"These gangs tend to be most prevalent in Cabal cities, because there's a high concentration of supernaturals there and because they know we'll cover their indiscretions to protect ourselves. We could disband them, but we've decided it's wiser to let them have their fun, safely. They get the rebellion out of their system, and when they come looking for a job . . ."

"The Cabals are close by."

He nodded. "The problem is that every now and then, *their* tolerance for *us* wears thin. One of those gangs—a particularly well-organized one in Miami—has been the source of some rumblings. I need to find out what they're up to."

"So you want a ringer. A young supernatural with undercover experience who isn't well-known in the community. That's where I come in."

Even as I spoke, my pulse quickened, thinking of how it could be done, how much I'd learn, how much fun I'd have. The last thought threw on the brakes. I was imagining what it would be like to lap up all that criminal chaos guilt-free because, hey, I was only fulfilling a debt, maybe even helping avoid a violent confrontation between this gang and the Cabal.

For guilt-free chaos, I had to stick to my council work. With them I always knew I was working on the right side.

"I've never done deep undercover," I said. "I probably couldn't even *play* gang material. My background—"

"I know your background, Hope, and we'd work with that. You'd play a version of yourself. With Karl's help, you could pull this off easily."

"I'm still not seeing how Karl fits in. He certainly can't pass for college age."

"No, but he can protect you."

"I can read chaotic thoughts. I might not have werewolf strength, but if someone's about to pull a gun on me, I'll know it."

"You may need to break into an office or apartment..."

"Karl's taught me the basics."

Benicio eased back into his seat. "Perhaps you wouldn't need him, then. That would certainly be better. I'd rather not delay, tracking him down and jetting him back."

"No, I—I didn't mean I'd do it."

Benicio arched his brows as if to say "What *did* you mean then?" Even as denials sprang to my lips, the demon in my blood whispered "Why not? You owe him. Get it over with."

I set my mug in the holder. "No. I'm sorry. I'm flattered that you'd consider me for this, but I'm sure you need it done right away and I have a training session next week—"

"You'd be home by then. We'll fly to Miami now, you'll take the initiation test this afternoon and be in the gang tonight."

In the gang tonight... I wet my lips, then swallowed and managed a laugh. "Today? That seals it, then. There's no way I could leave to-day. I'm expected back in Philly tonight with—"

I glimpsed a transport passing on the left. We were on a four-lane major road.

"Where are we? I said to circle the block—"

"My driver is taking a longer route, giving us more time to talk."

I hesitated, but he'd left his other bodyguard at the park, meaning he wasn't shanghaiing me.

"As for your story," Benicio said. "I already have people investigating and they'll give you everything you need to write it. Then you can call *True News* later and tell them you're on the trail of a bigger, related story, the details of which I will also provide."

I plucked at the sodden hem of my skirt, saying nothing.

"As for Karl," he went on, "you're free to do this job without him, but I will insist on personally notifying Lucas and Paige, and having you speak to them to air any concerns. I'm not going behind my son's back. He's even welcome to come to Miami and supervise the operation."

I was out of excuses. I should have just said "Sorry, I don't want it," but I couldn't force the lie to my lips.

No matter what Benicio said, I owed him—and even if he never called it a debt, it gave him an excuse to keep making "offers." This would be an ideal way to get out from under the black cloud of this obligation. A week or less, starting immediately, all contingencies handled, with Lucas and Paige to ensure it was legitimate. I'd break not only the tie to Benicio, but my last one to Karl—the tie that bound us to this debt together.

It would also be the opportunity I needed to test myself. A year ago I'd had a scare that still gave me nightmares. Thrust into a situation surging with incredible chaos, I'd seen a friend in danger and had, if only for a moment, felt the urge to just sit back and lap up the vibes. I needed to explore my limits, push them, learn how to handle them.

I turned to Benicio. "I'll do it."

LUCAS

1

SOME PEOPLE ARE BEYOND HELPING. They've dug a hole so deep that no rope is long enough to throw to them and I have to say, "I'm sorry. There's nothing I can do."

I had the shaman's file on my desk, his number right there so I could tell him I wouldn't represent him in his case against the Nast Cabal. But I hated saying no, so instead I was organizing paper clips. I sorted them by size, then by color, as I listened to the tapping of Paige's keyboard across the office divider.

Why did we have so many varieties of paper clips, when most of our paperwork was electronic? Was it simply that you couldn't have an office without paper clips? Or did they serve a higher purpose—a frivolity to occupy the mind while one was supposed to be working?

I pushed the clips aside. Postponing the task wouldn't make it easier.

Just as I reached for the phone, the outside line lit up. Saved by the bell, which echoed down the quiet hall twice before I heard a drowsy "Good morning. Cortez-Winterbourne Investigations." Savannah, our eighteen-year-old ward and temporary executive assistant.

I waited for my line or Paige's to ring, but the light continued to blink. If it was for Adam, Savannah should realize he wasn't in. Unless we had something exciting on the schedule, he never showed up before nine-thirty.

Savannah appeared in the doorway. "The telephone is for you, sir," she said, and dropped a curtsey.

A deep sigh fluttered from the other side of the divider.

"Hey, he said I needed to conduct my secretarial duties 'in a more formal manner.'"

"He said more *businesslike,*" Paige's disembodied voice answered.

"Whatever."

Savannah marched over and perched on the edge of my desk, flipping her skirt over her knees. It'd been a struggle getting her out of blue jeans, but vanity had won out when she'd realized business attire suited her. She'd grown comfortable in the clothes, and in her role. Too comfortable, we worried.

When Savannah had decided to take a year off after high school and work at the agency, we'd presumed that once she discovered how dull secretarial work could be, she'd eagerly embrace college life. But the deadlines for college application were fast approaching, and the forms lay on her dresser, untouched.

As I reached for the phone, she said, "Oh, it's your dad."

My stomach executed a familiar flip-flop. Paige peeked around the barrier, green eyes and frowning mouth framed by long dark hair. She shooed Savannah out, followed her into the hall and closed the door behind them. Their footsteps tapped away down the hall until I was left with the hum of the computer and that blinking phone light.

I reached for my water glass and took a deep gulp. Yesterday's water—warm and brackish. I took another sip, then answered the phone. "Good morning, Papá."

"Lucas. This isn't too early, is it?"

"I've been in since eight."

"Good, good. How's Paige?"

And so it went for five minutes. How was Paige? How was Savannah? How was business? Was the new office working out? I had no objection to small talk with my father, but I knew it was only the preliminary step to some less pleasant subject. He'd called at exactly nine Pacific time—the earliest reasonable moment. That could mean it was important or just that he wanted me to think it was. With my father, either was equally likely, and equally a cause for concern.

"The reason I'm calling..." he finally said.

"Yes, Papá?"

"It's Hope Adams. I've offered her a week of contract work investigating a local gang, and she's accepted."

He went on to explain the situation, in far more detail than it warranted, hammering home the message that he wasn't hiding anything, which almost certainly meant he was.

"Is this in regards to the debt Hope and Karl owe?" I asked.

"They don't owe me anything, Lucas. I've told you that. This is an independent project."

"And Hope in no way feels obligated or coerced?"

"Absolutely not. She's here on the plane now. You can speak to her if you'd like."

I flicked a stray paper clip back into the pile. "This seems very sudden. I haven't heard any rumblings of an impending gang insurgence."

"They've been small so far, but they *are* there, and it's a problem best nipped in the bud."

"Particularly if 'nipping it in the bud' provides an excuse to test a young Expisco half-demon, evaluate her powers and demonstrate to her the benefits of Cabal employment."

He laughed. "I won't say I wouldn't love to have Hope on staff. But I know better than to poach her from the council."

"Perhaps you should speak to Paige, then. She's the council member, so she's the one who should be apprised—"

"Which is exactly what I hope you'll do."

There was no reason to go through me—he was on very good terms with Paige. So what was he up to?

"Are you concerned about the job, Lucas?" he asked after a moment.

"Frankly, yes. Hope is a capable young woman, but this could be a dangerous situation, particularly without Karl as backup."

"Having Karl would be ideal, but he's not available so..." He paused. "I know. Why don't you and Paige come to Miami? Finish up your work today and I'll send the jet for you tonight. You can provide Hope with backup and direct supervision."

I pinched my nose as I pushed my glasses up. I'd leapt straight into that one.

My father had done this before, calling with a case that would "benefit" from my attention. And while I was in Miami, he'd pester me to attend board meetings, client dinners, review recent organizational changes . . . anything to involve me in Cabal life.

"That won't be necessary," I said. "I'm sure you'll provide her with direct access to Cabal security. I'll oversee her investigation from here."

"If you change your mind . . ."

"I'll let you know. Now, if you'll give me a moment to update Paige, we'd like to speak to Hope."

HOPE

GOBLIN ROMEO

If the situation alarmed Lucas, there was no trace of it in his voice. He was his usual self—calm and serious, words chosen with care, as if he was addressing a courtroom.

Lucas confirmed everything his father had told me about the gangs. He agreed I was a good choice to infiltrate one and he saw nothing suspicious in his father's proposal. He would monitor the situation from Portland and, if I had any concerns or questions, he was only a phone call away.

Then Paige came on, and the tone changed. Was I comfortable with the job? How did I feel about it? Did everything *seem* okay? If the job bothered me at any point, even just a sense that something was amiss, I could call her, day or night—at home, at work or on her cell.

Not knowing the root of my powers—the chaos hunger was my guilty secret—they saw nothing odd about me taking this job. I was relieving myself of an obligation while gaining some experience, and that seemed perfectly reasonable to them.

Nor did they suggest the job might be more than I could handle. That would have been the first comment out of Karl's mouth. I chalked that up to age. Karl was at least fifteen years older than me—with a werewolf's slow aging, it was hard to tell exactly—but Paige was my age, and Lucas a year or two older. They could handle a job like this, so they knew I could.

When I hung up, I relaxed, my mind able to refocus on the task at hand.

"I need to know more about this gang," I said as Benicio sat across from me. "You said there were rumblings. Exactly what are we talking about? Causing more trouble than usual? Or planning a strike against the Cabal?"

"The latter, I suspect, though at this point, it *is* only rumblings. I doubt they're considering anything specific yet. You're only there to get a better idea of the situation."

He settled back in his seat and opened the window blind, as if that should be all I needed to know.

"So what *are* these rumblings?" I pressed.

He took a moment before answering. "This gang finds its recruits through an outside agent. That agent is also on my payroll, which is how I'll get you in. The gang leader, Guy Benoit, knows that this agent was an employee of mine, before an apparent falling out. Benoit has, of late, been asking him questions about the Cabal."

"Pumping your guy for information?"

The corners of Benicio's mouth twitched. "No, Benoit would never be so crude. He's a far cry from your typical street thug, Hope, and you'd do well to keep that in mind when dealing with him. Benoit is a brilliant leader. I sincerely hope to have him on my staff one day, but unfortunately he's not eager to embrace Cabal life."

A young woman stepped from the back room, phone in hand. Benicio motioned for her to take a message, then waited until she'd retreated before continuing.

"Guy Benoit is a sorcerer. His father started a small Cabal in Guyana twenty years ago. An ambitious project and one I would have been happy to support, if we hadn't run into a conflict of interest. The Benoit Cabal was disbanded and Guy's mother, a Vodoun priestess, fled with him to Louisiana. Five years ago, Benoit appeared in Miami and toppled the former leader of his gang in a masterful coup."

"Masterful?"

"Guy has a reputation for avoiding violence. Even his coup was bloodless. Ruthless, but bloodless. That's one reason I very much hope to hire him someday."

"After what you did to his family? If he's set up base in Miami, he's obviously looking for revenge, not a job offer."

Benicio only shrugged, unruffled by my bluntness. "In five years, Guy has given me very little trouble. Perhaps that was the calm before the storm—settling in and quietly getting the lay of the land—but he seemed to be happy to exact his revenge simply by lining his pockets at our expense, taking advantage of the Cabal's willingness to protect the gangs. It's only recently that he's begun asking my agent vague questions about our security force and our general organization. That must be significant. As for what it portends . . ."

"Finding out is my job."

He nodded.

FAITH EDMONDS WAS the undercover name Benicio had chosen for me. A rich college girl, Faith had quit school to enjoy a six-month stint of self-indulgence in Miami—parentally funded in exchange for a promise to return to her studies in the fall. The persona came with a South Beach apartment and a full set of ID, including platinum credit cards to buy a suitable wardrobe.

First, though, I had to pass the initiation. That afternoon, I'd meet a gang liaison who screened potential recruits. Benicio assured me the test would be only a formality. A rare Expisco half-demon would be a prize for any gang, and I was coming highly recommended by the recruiter on Benicio's payroll. The path had been groomed for me—I just needed to follow it.

ONLY IN MIAMI can you find a gang agent in a beach tent. Before I headed out, I bought suitable camouflage—bikini, sarong and sandals. In the store the bikini had looked lime green. Out in the sunlight, it turned neon. Another typical Hope Adams fashion disaster. I considered trying again, but a glance around the beach assured me I wasn't the most outrageously dressed. With a big pair of sunglasses, I blended right in. Even had the tan, though mine came with no risk of skin cancer.

I'd been to Miami before, but there's something deliciously surreal about standing on the sand under the blazing sun mere hours after being splashed with slush. While I knew I had a job to do, I couldn't resist taking the longer route, strolling along the beach.

As I wove through the carpet of rainbow-hued bikinis and umbrellas, I kept my face uplifted to the sky like a sun-starved flower, and almost tripped over a few outstretched legs. Sandals hanging over my arm, I scrunched through the hot sand to the shore, letting the ocean lap around my feet. When the breeze changed, the smell of empanadas broke through the heady mix of sea salt and sunscreen, and my stomach growled.

I paused by a vendor selling Latin sodas, drawn by the bright, unfamiliar labels, throat constricting as I eyed the sweaty, ice-cold bottles. But walking into this meeting casually sipping a soda wouldn't set the right tone. So I pushed on and quickened my pace until I saw the tent ahead.

A poster was plastered on the side: Spring Break Party Videos—Come On Girls, Show Us What Ya Got. A blond grinned out from it, her shirt lifted, a blackout banner with the company logo across her chest. I checked Benicio's directions again, in case I'd taken a wrong turn and missed the "Instructional Tai Chi" video tent where I was supposed to be. No such luck.

My contact was the dramatically named Caesar Romeo. He wasn't a gang member, just a supernatural they hired to weed through potential recruits sent by Benicio's agent. As for what kind of supernatural he was, either it wasn't important or Benicio thought I could figure it out. Doing so—safely—was my next goal.

I took my time sliding my sandals back on, then slowly walked along the side of the tent, but caught not so much as a vision flicker. My sense for supernaturals has about a 60 percent accuracy rating: the "weaker" someone's power is, the less likely I'd detect it. I'd been told I could hone this skill, but had no idea how except through practice and concentration. There were maybe a half-dozen other Expisco half-demons in the world and I had no idea how to find them, so I was stuck muddling through on my own.

Two girls stood at the tent flap, daring each other to go inside as a male friend egged them on. Typical students on a spring break, with burnt noses and bad dye jobs from a last-minute decision to test whether blonds really did have more fun.

"I hope she's not trying out for a spot," one girl muttered as I headed their way. "My fourteen-year-old sister has bigger boobs."

"She can practice her Kama Sutra on me anytime," the guy said.

I nodded to them as I passed, pretending I hadn't heard. Just like Mom would have done...though she probably wouldn't have added the mental "Fuck you."

I pulled the tent flap open a crack. A stomach-churning blend of pot and incense rolled out.

"Caesar Romeo?" I called.

"Who's askin'?"

"Faith Edmonds. You're expecting me?"

The dimly lit tent was divided into rooms. The front one was a reception area, complete with chairs and magazines—*Playboy* and *Penthouse*. Maybe for inspiration.

"Well?" the voice barked. "If I'm expecting you, what the fuck are you waiting for? Get your ass in here."

I followed the voice into a room that looked like a sultan's tent. Multicolored pillows carpeted the sand floor. A huge gilt mirror on a stand had been tilted at an odd angle—odd until I followed the reflection to the pillows.

Caesar Romeo perched on an ornate wood seat, so huge it looked like a throne. He was no taller than my five feet. His skin was wizened, and so darkened by the sun I couldn't guess his age or ethnic background. Beady black eyes glared out from deep-set sockets. A flame-red Afro, gold lamé shirt and tight white leather pants completed the look. If I believed in goblins, that's what I'd peg him as—one of the *pisacha* from my mother's tales.

His gaze crawled up me, then down, as cold and critical as a matron eying a slab of beef she wouldn't serve to her dog.

"Turn around," he said.

"I'm not trying out for a part," I said. "I'm Faith Edmonds. Ned Baker sent me."

Romeo waved a hand and I thought he was motioning at me, until I noticed a man smoking a joint off to the side, who was giving me a much more flattering appraisal.

"Felippe," Romeo said. "Go. Shoot those bimbos giggling at the door."

"Should I give them T-shirts?" Felippe asked.

"Don't waste the merchandise. They'll be lucky if they make the cut."

Felippe stubbed out his joint on a brass urn and left. Romeo's gaze followed him, and he listened as his assistant offered the girls a "role."

"Hear that?" Romeo said. "They'll flash their tits on film for nothing but the honor of being ogled by men they'd cross the road to avoid. Teasing little bitches. Like all you girls. Can't resist flaunting it at some guy who doesn't have a hope of touching."

Knowing I had to play nice, I settled for a noncommittal shrug.

"You disagree?" he said.

"I'm sure that applies to some women."

"But not all?"

"I can't speak for 'all.' Now, Baker tells me I need to pass some kind of test—"

"I suppose you think you're better than those girls, don't you? Smarter. More *dignified*." His lips curled in what I presumed was a smile. "Or maybe just more expensive."

"Maybe. Now, this test—"

"I have a better idea. There's another line of tapes I'm working on, high-end videos for more discriminating customers who want something more . . . exotic. The kind of girl they won't find humping poles. That sound more your style, princess?"

"I'm . . . flattered." I struggled to get the word out. I failed on the accompanying smile, though. "I'd rather just take the test."

He leaned back in his chair. "What if we skip the video? You undress right here, stretch out on the pillows . . . amuse yourself for a few minutes. No camera. No audience except me."

There was no lust in his eyes. No interest even. He didn't want to see me naked. Probably wouldn't even get a rise out of watching me masturbate. He just wanted to make me do it.

I smiled as sweetly as I could. "I'm afraid I'm pretty shy. My upbringing, the culture, you know . . ."

I tried to read him for chaos thoughts, but detected only a swirl of low-level negativity.

"What if I said there wasn't a choice? Do this or I tell Baker you failed the test?"

The chaos level rose. I shivered, but found little pleasure in it. My survival instinct ensures I don't enjoy chaotic impulses directed at me, thankfully.

I met his gaze. "Then I guess that's what you'll have to do."

I started to leave. Benicio had hired a spy, not a whore. He'd have to find another way to get me into the gang.

Romeo waited until I was almost out of earshot, then called me back.

"Take the fucking test. I was only trying to give you an easy way out. Just remember, when you change your mind, it'll take more than twiddling your knob to get a pass-card from me." He threw a scrap of paper on the floor. "An address. You're looking for a conch shell there. A tourist knickknack with Welcome to Miami and a girl in a bikini painted on it. Get it, bring it back, you get your pass."

I looked at the address. "Is this a house or a—"

"Could be a house. Could be a warehouse. Could be a fucking cemetery with the shell buried in one of the graves. Have fun, princess."

I kept my expression neutral and turned to leave.

"Oh, and did I mention it's a race?"

I stopped. "A race?"

"You think you're the only piece of pussy fancies herself a gangster? There's another girl out there with that same address, and there's only one spot to fill." He glanced down at his fake Rolex. "She left about an hour ago."

I FUMED THROUGH the entire cab ride. Was I surprised? I'd foiled that goblin's little game and I should have expected to pay for that. But how badly was he going to screw me over? *Was* there a competitor? Or was he just saying that, hoping I'd rush and make a mistake?

Even if Benicio found me another way into the gang, the failure would sting. Yes, Mr. Cortez, I know you tried to make it easy, but it wasn't my fault.

Whining. Complaining. Blaming someone else. I hate those traits in others, and I loathe seeing them in myself. Fate makes you a half-demon? Gives you visions of death and destruction? Makes you crave them like candy and cigarettes? Too bad. Suck it up and move on.

While I was damning myself for not handling Romeo better, I was heaping a generous dose of curses on his head too. My mother would have told me to look at the guy and imagine how many times he'd been rejected or laughed at by a pretty girl. Even if that didn't excuse his behavior, I should rise above it. But I couldn't. I wanted to win this race, drop the conch shell on his lap and guzzle the sweet chaos of his rage.

And I would. One way or another.

I CHANGED BACK into jeans and T-shirt, and had the cab drop me off in a tourist section that looked as if it'd been born in the fifties and untouched since. I stood in front of the Ocean View Resort, the kind of decrepit motel unwitting families book by name alone, only to arrive and discover they could indeed view the ocean—if they stood on the roof with binoculars.

Next door a soda fountain promised "authentic malt sodas." Having once tried a malt soda, this was not a selling point for me. On the other side was the ubiquitous Florida T-shirt shop. Three shirts for ten dollars. If they didn't survive the first wash after you got them home, you wouldn't fly back for a refund.

The address Romeo had given me was across the road. A souvenir shop with painted conch shells in the window. None had the markings he'd described, but the sign promised more designs inside.

This was too easy. I wasn't waltzing into that store until I'd taken a look around.

HOPE

SUNKEN TREASURES

I circled behind the store to a parking lot filled with compact rental cars and minivans with out-of-state plates. A narrow gravel path ran between the lot and the store.

I walked between the two minivans nearest the shop, my apartment key in hand, as if I was preparing to get into one of the vehicles. The solid wall of the store was broken only by a glass door that had probably once been a secondary entrance, dating from more prosperous days when the shop owned the parking lot. It was now blocked by a rack of cheap sunglasses.

Hoping to get a peek inside, I slipped to the front of the vans. As I reached the fence, I had a mental flash—a "light pop" like a camera flash had gone off. I backed up a few steps, then approached again. Sure enough, in the same spot, everything went white.

Sunken Treasures souvenir shop was protected by a spell.

About a year ago, while doing a job for the council, I'd realized I could detect security spells. With Paige and Lucas's spellcasting help, I'd learned to figure out exactly what kind of spell I was detecting. Like having an error box pop up on your computer screen—all you see at first is a basic warning message, but the details are there if you have the know-how to find them. Paige's analogy, not mine. Deep in my brain, a racial demonic memory knew what the spell was. And soon I had it: a perimeter spell to warn of one specific type of intruder—supernaturals.

A souvenir shop protected by a witch spell to detect supernaturals. Was the shop owned or staffed by a witch? Or was it part of the test—so someone would know when a recruit entered the store and could swoop in and make things very difficult.

Damn.

I idly watched a group of teens saunter through the lot. As one tossed a souvenir bag to another, I got an idea.

I FOUND MY target easily enough: a boy about thirteen, still young enough to be on vacation with Mom and Dad, but old enough to escape them when he could. He stood outside the T-shirt store, reading the off-color slogans.

As I approached, his face reddened as if he'd been caught doing something he shouldn't.

"Hey," I said, flashing a big smile. "Do you have a second?"

"Uh, sure."

I motioned to Sunken Treasures across the road. "There's something in there I want to get for my boyfriend, as a joke, but I'm, well, kind of embarrassed to buy it. It's a shell with a woman in a bikini on it."

To an adult, this would seem strange. But to a thirteen-year-old, all adults are strange, their motives inexplicable. I described the shell and gave him a twenty, with the promise of another when he returned.

Fifteen long minutes later, he was back, empty-handed.

"They have a rack of conch shells and some of them are painted, but none with girls in any kind of bathing suit."

"Huh. Must have been a different store, then."

I let him keep the twenty and he disappeared into the T-shirt shop.

My next mark was a fortyish man who sucked in his spare tire as I drew close. For him, I had a new story: I'd been in the store the night before with friends, some of whom had been drunk and made a scene. I really wanted this shell for my brother, but I was afraid the store owner would recognize me and kick me out.

He too returned empty-handed. "It's behind the cash register," he said, handing me back my twenty. "And it's not for sale. I tried, but the guy said a friend of his had painted it and it was only for display. Sorry."

TEN MINUTES LATER, I walked into the shop. It stank of cheap suntan lotion, not quite masking a smell that reminded me of Gran's attic, of dirt and dust and disuse. Most tourists probably never veered from the path between the door to the cash register, lined with T-shirt racks and baskets of cheap shells.

There was no bell over the door, but the clerk's head shot up as I walked in, setting off his spell. Middle-aged with blond shoulder-length hair, he wore a tank top, his flaccid triceps swaying as he moved to the counter. Behind him was the conch shell.

I made it two more steps before the vision hit. A deep voice chanted in my ear. Disembodied hands appeared, pale against the black. Fog swirled from the hands.

A sorcerer. My gaze went to his hands, which were safely folded on the counter. Sorcerer magic is cast by a combination of words and gestures, but the security spell suggested he might also know some witch magic. Better to keep an eye on his lips then, and duck if he started muttering.

I extended my hand. "Marietta Khan, special aide to the council. I work with Paige Winterbourne."

His eyes narrowed.

"You know who she is, then. Good. It has come to the council's attention that you're under surveillance by the Cortez Cabal, following reports of spellcasting in this neighborhood."

He paled, then straightened. "I've been broken into six times in the past year. I have the right to defend my property as long as I don't use excessive force."

"You're right."

"And if you people think—" He stopped. "I'm right?"

"I'm from the council, not the Cabal. Our job is not only to watch you, but to protect you against ungrounded Cabal prosecution. What I need from you is the paperwork."

"The . . . ?"

"Proof that you needed to cast the spells. I'll need incident numbers for the break-ins, insurance claims and a list of the spells you're casting. We'll take this to the Cabal, and unless they can prove you've cast something stronger, you're off the hook. In fact, if you have those papers and a copier here, I can take care of this right now."

"They're in the back."

"I'll watch the store while you get them."

I HIGHTAILED IT across the street, darting around slow-moving carloads of tourist gawkers, past the soda fountain, past the motel, past the empty shop. I ducked inside an alley and stopped, clutching my prize. My eyelids fluttered as I savored the chaos. Having caused it myself made it twice as potent. I closed my eyes, replaying the ruse and the theft—the perfect high: better than booze, better than drugs, better than sex. Well, better than *average* sex. A potent mix. And an addictive one.

That thought sobered me. I had the shell. If I wanted more chaos vibes, I'd have to wait until I handed it to Romeo. I opened my beach bag, wrapped the shell in a towel, then—

"Why don't you just hand that to me? I'll take good care of it."

HOPE

CANDY STORE

I glanced over my shoulder just in time to see hands rising in a knock-back spell. I dove. The spell caught me in the hip and spun me off balance, but I kept my grip on the bag and darted out of the way before my assailant launched a second one.

Ten feet away stood a young woman with spiky blond hair and so many piercings it'd take her an hour to prepare for a metal detector.

"My competition, I presume," I said. "Sorry about your luck."

"Oh, *my* luck's fine."

She cast again. I dodged the spell easily. Her lips tightened and her fury washed over me in delicious waves.

"Not used to casting against someone who knows what you're doing?" I said. "Lesson one: don't flail your hands."

Another cast. I feinted to the side, but from the look on her face, there'd been no need.

"Run out of juice?" I said. "Lesson two: don't spend it all in one place."

I reached into the side compartment of my purse, a little hobo-style handbag, designed for the young urbanite of the twenty-first century, with convenient compartments for sunglasses, cell phone, PDA and a concealed weapon.

The witch stared at the gun as if expecting me to light a cigarette with it.

"Sit down," I said.

After some prodding, she lowered herself to the ground, muttering about fair play. Among supernaturals, using weapons is considered an act of cowardice. But when your power package doesn't come with fireballs or superhuman strength, you need to even the playing field.

Once she was seated, I used another weapon—my penknife—to cut the bindings from a nearby stack of recyclable papers.

"It's called using what works," I said as I tied her. "You should try it. Starting with learning your own kind of magic. If you'd cast a witch's binding spell, I'd be the one sitting here, and you'd be the one with the conch shell."

She fumed and squirmed and glared. I closed my eyes and drank in her rage, then picked up my beach bag and walked away.

I WAS PREPARED for Romeo to give me a hard time about passing the test. He grumbled and glowered, and I got my chaos reward, but he didn't try to withhold the prize, probably for the same reason he hadn't let me walk out when I'd threatened to—he was well paid for this middleman job and wouldn't risk losing it.

He gave me an address and told me I was expected to show up there in two hours.

I HAD THE taxi do a drive-by of the gang's address before I returned to my apartment, and I was glad I did, because it told me a shopping trip was in order.

The taxi driver recommended Bal Harbour Shops and it was a good call. And a good thing I was using someone else's credit card.

Normally my frugal side would have kicked in, but I was still riding the high from besting the sorcerer, the witch and the goblin, so I was in the mood to treat myself. Considering that the test hadn't been the cakewalk Benicio promised, I felt justified using his cash.

ANOTHER CAB TOOK me to my temporary apartment. The driver made me for a tourist from the first word and tried to "treat" me to the scenic route. I might not know the layout of Miami, but I spotted that trick after two blocks and ordered him back on track.

As we neared my apartment, I marveled at a wrecking ball tearing through what looked like perfectly good single-family homes—big houses, luxurious even. But houses nonetheless, on valuable property that could hold a hundred times that many in luxury apartment condos. One glance over the Miami skyline, dotted with cranes and skeletal high-rises, told even the newest visitor that this was a city on the move. Out with the old, in with the new.

My apartment was what I would call new, though by Miami standards, it might be a few scant years from the wrecking ball. It wasn't to my taste—small, antiseptic and cold, painted in grays, whites and blacks, with spare modern furniture—but was in a trendy South Beach neighborhood and, for a girl like Faith Edmonds, location was everything.

I got back to the apartment just in time to change my clothes and place a few calls.

I phoned my editor first. Benicio had provided me with the details of a werewolf cult in Fort Lauderdale that I was supposedly investigating, possibly linked to the murder. His people would give me more later, so I could write the article. He'd booked a room at a Fort Lauderdale hotel in my name, with the phone forwarded to my cell. He was even having a young female employee drop by the room daily, to establish my alibi.

Normally "I've taken off to Florida chasing a story" isn't something you tell your editor, not without getting permission first, but I had a good relationship with my boss. I liked my job, gave it 100 percent and had no intention of vanishing at the first offer from a more respectable paper. In the world of tabloid journalism, that's employee-of-the-year material.

Naturally, he chewed me out. Then "get your ass back here" became "fine, but this is on your dime, Adams." By the end of the call, it had changed to "save your receipts, but if I get a bill for the Hilton, you're on proofreading duty for a year."

The next call I made was a dozen times harder. I hate lying to my mother, though it was nothing new. We'd always been close, and still talked for twenty minutes a day and met once or twice a week, but there were days when I felt like an impostor who'd replaced her youngest child. There was just too much I couldn't share with her.

She didn't know she had a half-demon for a daughter. She didn't know such a thing existed. I wasn't even sure she realized her ex-husband wasn't my biological father. My parents had separated around the time of my conception and everyone—my dad included—thought I was his. Did my mother have a postbreakup fling and kept it a secret? Or did she temporarily reunite with my dad after that fling and presume he'd fathered me? Or had Lucifer taken my father's form and returned for one last night together? All I knew was that I'd been raised as the youngest Adams child, treated no differently than my two brothers and sister.

But I had been different. As a child, I'd walk through a museum and stand transfixed before the weapons displays, seeing glorious visions of war and destruction. I'd stare at auto accidents, undoing my seat belt to turn and watch them until they disappeared, then pepper my parents with questions. They chalked it up to a vivid imagination and a taste for the macabre and, since I'd never done anything violent myself, they believed it was just a harmless personality quirk.

By the time I started hearing chaotic thoughts, I was a teenager, and smart enough to know it wasn't something to tell my parents. But it wasn't easy. After a breakdown in my senior year, I'd spent weeks in a private facility.

When I'd gone looking for answers, I asked enough questions in the right places for a group of half-demons to find me. I learned what I was and, with that, found some peace. As far as my family knew, though, I'd simply outgrown my problems. There were friends and extended family members who disagreed—I was a tabloid reporter in a family of doctors and lawyers, and after a brief stint in Los Angeles last year, I'd returned to the same small college town outside Philadelphia where I'd grown up, and lived in a condo owned by my mother. Not exactly a "success" by Adams family standards. But to my mother, I was happy and healthy and after the hell I'd gone through, that was all that mattered. And if she was satisfied, then there was no need to burden her with the truth.

So I called, gave her my story, canceled our lunch date and promised to phone again the next day.

DRESSED IN A deep orange cowl-necked top and flouncy tiered mini-skirt, I strolled up to an ugly rear service door and rapped, ready to present myself to my new associates.

Getting their attention wasn't that easy, as it turned out, and my knuckles were raw by the time the door swung open. But it was worth the wait.

I've never been one to swoon over hot guys, and I blamed it on elevation sickness from my new three-inch heels, but when that door opened all I could do was stare. He was average height, average weight, average build...and above-average gorgeous, with collar-length black curls, copper skin, deep-set, hooded green eyes and a grin that sucked my rehearsed introduction right out of my head.

I recovered after a split-second of gawking, fast enough to realize he hadn't noticed my reaction. He was too busy doing his own appraisal, that gorgeous smile making me as giddy as any chaos vibe.

"I hate to say it," he said, "but the club doesn't open for another hour, and you'll need to go in the front entrance."

"I'm here to see Guy."

"Oh?" Another notch on the smile. "In that case, come on in."

He moved back. As I stepped forward, though, he blocked my path, stopping so close I could feel his breath on the top of my head.

"Almost forgot. I'll need the password."

I looked up at him. "Password?"

He leaned against the open door. "Or handshake. I'm supposed to get the password, but I'd settle for the secret handshake."

"Let the girl in, for God's sake," said a voice behind him.

A woman appeared. Her tight black jeans and Doc Martens clashed with her Donna Karan blouse. Dyed black hair pulled back in a simple ponytail. Nostril and lip holes with no jewelry in them. Simple makeup, but a heavy hand with the eyeliner. She looked like a Goth trying to play it straight, and failing.

She waved me into the darkness beyond. "Ignore him. He's practicing for a new career as a comedian, which will come in handy when we kick his ass out of the door." She turned to him. "Go get Sonny and track down Rodriguez. Guy wants to talk to him."

His gaze hadn't left me. "Do I get an introduction first?"

"Later. If you're lucky. Now move." She led me through a curtain into a lit storeroom. "Speaking of introductions, you are...?"

I thought she'd know, but presumed she was testing me. "Faith. Faith Edmonds."

"The Expisco? Thank God. Guy almost had a fit when he learned we had a shot at an Expisco and might get a witch instead. But rules are rules, and the girl was the niece of a contact, so we had to give her a shot." She extended her hand. "Bianca, Guy's second-in-command."

She opened a door and we stepped into the club.

I know horror films always take place in dilapidated old mansions with creaky stairs and hidden passages, but for spooky places, I'd nominate a dance club before the doors open at night.

When the music's playing, clubs have an energy that's undeniable—the heat of strangers crowding together, the pulsing beat interrupted by the occasional squeal of drunken delight, the sometimes sickening blend of perfume and sweet drinks and hastily wiped up vomit. If you're not in the mood, it can seem like the ninth pit of Hell, but you still can't deny the life of it. Walking through this club now was like creeping through a cemetery.

My footsteps and voice didn't echo through the cavernous emptiness, but were swallowed by top-notch acoustics. Emergency lighting was the only illumination, too dim to even cast shadows. The over-amped air-conditioning raised goose bumps on my arms and legs. The smell of cleaning chemicals barely covered the mildew from drinks spilled on the carpeted upper level. The only sound was the slow *thump-thump-thump* of music in a distant room, thudding like a dying heart.

Bianca was saying something ahead of me.

"Sorry. I missed that."

"I said crew members don't officially work in the club, but you could be called on to serve drinks or help behind the bar if we're short-staffed. Everyone's expected to do their part. Is that okay with you?"

I could tell by Bianca's tone—friendly but firm—that this wasn't open to negotiation.

"Can't say I've ever waited tables, but there's a first time for everything."

"Good. Rodriguez is our tech guy and he'll set you up with an untraceable cell phone. You're expected to carry it at all times. If Guy wants you here, he wants you here *now,* whether it's 2 a.m. or lunchtime."

"Got it."

"You're expected to check in every day at five. He might not have anything for you, but he wants to see every face. So if you meet some hot Miami millionaire who asks you to join him for a three-day yacht trip to the Bahamas, the answer is no. Don't even ask Guy. It'll just piss him off."

"Got it."

"Speaking of hot millionaires, you'll be expected to hang out at the club and make them feel welcome. And, no, that doesn't include sleeping with them. Sometimes we pick a mark, ask you to get some information. Other times you'll just be hanging out, dancing, having fun and convincing people that this club is *the* place to be."

"Got it."

She motioned me to a booth under an emergency light. "A few final things before we meet Guy, and these are the ones you really need to pay attention to, so let's take a seat."

She waved at the room. "You're probably thinking that despite all these rules and responsibilities, this is a pretty sweet setup. But I'm warning you now, Faith, that if you're into the club scene, this is like being in a candy store with no money. I said we don't expect you to sleep with the patrons. Change that to 'you aren't allowed to.' No sleeping with them, no dating them, no giving them your number. You're limited to one drink a night, just so your breath will smell like booze. After that, you'll still order drinks but you'll be served soda and virgin cocktails. While you are here in the club, you'll be the model patron. If Guy so much as catches you smoking in the bathroom, your ass is on the line. If you do drugs, stop now. I don't just mean while you're here either. Guy expects you to be ready to roll at any moment."

"Harsh." None of it mattered to me—I wasn't about to get loaded and sleep with strangers—but I suspected Faith wouldn't be as strait-laced.

"That's the way Guy runs things. We have to stay under the radar. You can't get cozy with the marks. You can't get us investigated for breaking smoking bylaws. You can't get wasted and blow a job. We run this place squeaky clean on the outside. It keeps people from looking too closely." She smiled. "I tell Guy he should have been a drill sergeant, but the guy's a goddamn genius at this. He'll make you work your ass off, but if you stick it out, the rewards are pure honey."

From the way Bianca's eyes glittered every time she said Guy's name, I could tell she was no impartial judge.

"So, are you ready to meet your new boss?"

HOPE

THE FACE OF AN ANGEL

Bianca knocked on an office door, waited, then opened it. Behind the desk sat a man about my age, with a close-cropped Vandyke and short braids. He was running figures through a calculator, and his eyes stayed fixed on the result as we walked in. His suit coat hung on the chair behind him, and his white shirtsleeves were rolled up to reveal well-muscled dark forearms. Guy Benoit, the gang leader.

"Guy? This is Faith."

"The Expisco?"

"Yup."

He grunted something that could have been "good," then jotted down a figure before looking up. A cold-eyed evaluation, but unlike Romeo's, I couldn't tell whether I'd passed or failed. A second grunt and he returned to his accounting. I glanced at Bianca. She'd made herself comfortable, draped in a chair, long legs crossed in front of her, blue eyes fixed on Guy.

"I presume Bianca told you the rules of conduct?" he said, fingers flying over the calculator.

"She did."

"Thus ends your training, Faith. We expect our recruits to hit the ground running. Your crew mates will help, but don't expect anyone to hold your hand. If you don't work out, there are a dozen more to take your place."

"Yes, sir."

I added the "sir" instinctively, thinking even as the word left my mouth that he might take it as sarcasm. Had this been a job interview, I'd have been seriously considering how badly I wanted the position.

"I don't need to tell you the importance of being a loyal crew member. I'm sure the recruiter explained what happens to those who betray us, either intentionally or through carelessness."

"Yes."

"Then we won't need to discuss that ever again." He lifted his gaze to mine for a split second before returning to his work. "This club has a line every night yet it barely breaks even. For us, it's all about the marks. Miami is full of rich brats looking for a good time."

From the twist he gave "rich brats," I wondered whether the cover story Benicio gave me had been such a good idea.

"They have expensive tastes in everything, from women to booze to dope, and while that would be the easiest way to divest them of their trust funds, it's a fool's gambit. What we run here is a legitimate business, following every law right down to fire code regulations. There's more than one way to fleece a mark. If a young woman overindulges and passes out on our premises, it's our duty to see to her and make her comfortable. But we'll unload her apartment while she recovers. From your dossier, I believe that's the sort of thing you could help with."

I nodded. "I dated a professional thief a couple of years ago. I used to go on jobs with him. Just for kicks."

His lips tightened and I cursed under my breath. Benicio had screwed up. Or, at least, misjudged. Maybe most gangs were rebellious, undisciplined kids looking for easy money and a good time, but Guy took his job seriously, and expected his crew to do the same. A spoiled socialite looking for "kicks" wasn't welcome.

I tried to make up for lost ground. "I know how to use picks, torque wrenches, snap guns and shims. With the right tools, I can do impressions, but I'm still learning that. I can use a Slim Jim and hot-wire a car. I know the basics of safe drilling, but I've never opened one myself. I've disarmed simple security systems. What I've had the most practice at, though, is simple stealth skills—moving quietly, avoiding security cameras, foiling attack dogs, that sort of thing."

A grudging nod.

A rap at the door. Again Guy didn't answer, but the door opened after a few seconds. In walked a stocky young man, who looked no older than twenty.

"Rodriguez, this is Faith, the new recruit. She'll need a phone and pager, but that's not why I called you in. I want to talk about this next job."

Bianca stood and waved me to follow her. She made it two steps, then Guy said, "Bee? I need you here." He yelled something that sounded like "Jack," and the guy who'd let me into the club appeared. "You and Sonny take Faith to dinner. Make her feel welcome. Think you can handle that?"

The young man grinned. "I believe I can manage."

"Just don't talk her ear off. I want you both back by nine. You're on floor duty tonight. Oh, introductions. Faith, Jasper. Jasper, Faith."

The young man shot Guy the finger. Guy only smiled and shooed us out.

"Jaz, please," he said to me. "*No one* calls me Jasper. Not even my mother. The moment she recovered from her temporary insanity, it became Jaz on everything but official documents, and I plan to change those too, as soon as I can be bothered filling out the paperwork. Now to collect Sonny, wherever the hell he's hiding—"

"Right behind you," said a deep voice.

Behind us stood a young man, Jaz's size, but with straight dark blond hair to his shoulders, a deep tan and an angular face that wasn't ugly, but would never make it onto a billboard.

Jaz slapped him on the back. "Hey, bro. Guy just gave us another tough assignment. Gotta take Faith here out to dinner and chat her up. Faith, this is Sonny. Met him in preschool. Our first joint effort was putting worms in the sandbox and we've been together ever since." A wink my way. "Though the pranks are a little more serious these days."

He kept up a near steady patter all the way out of the club and down the street. He asked about my test, then told me about his and about Sonny's. Jaz had been with Guy's crew for a year now, with Sonny following him the next time a spot opened—they hadn't wanted to compete against each other. Jaz paused for breath only long enough to ask what kind of food I liked.

Normally, such nonstop chatter would have put me off, but in Jaz it didn't seem to be nerves or ego. It seemed like...energy. Endless energy, needing an outlet, and I could feel it, like low-level chaos rippling from him.

Over dinner, Jaz tried to let me do some of the talking, but considering that my life story was a fake, I was just as happy to let him continue.

He told me a bit about himself and Sonny. Nothing overly personal, just enough to be friendly. First, supernatural type. I hadn't been able to pick up vibes from either, and soon understood why. Both were the same minor type, magicians—a watered-down version of a sorcerer.

That they'd met in preschool was no coincidence. Their parents had worked in the St. Cloud Cabal satellite office in Indianapolis where they'd attended a school selected by the Cabal. An otherwise ordinary school. There was no risk in that—supernatural kids didn't come into their powers until their teens. They'd be encouraged to befriend those classmates whose parents worked with theirs—kids they'd see at Christmas parties and picnics and on the company's Little League team. Then, when they grew older, they'd already have someone who could share their supernatural coming-of-age experience, someone they could talk to and commiserate with. Watching Jaz and Sonny, seeing that easy camaraderie I'd lost with my human friends, I felt a pang of envy so sharp it was hard to eat.

They were younger than me, both twenty-three. They'd left home as teens and drifted about ever since. That wasn't surprising. I knew what it felt like, suddenly being different, with secrets to keep, powers to understand, searching for your moorings, for your identity, your place in this new world.

Jaz and Sonny seemed to have found an anchor in the gang. Neither had any complaints and that seemed genuine, not a put-on for the new girl. Jaz gave me a rundown of all the members: their races, positions and personalities. He certainly made my job of intelligence gathering much easier.

As dinner stretched well past the hour mark, I relaxed enough to take a closer, more critical look at Jaz. If I had a type, he wasn't it. The mop of curls to his jawline was longer than I liked. His eyes were too big, too soft. His mouth was too wide, too sensual. His build was slender, almost graceful. The overall picture was...I hate to say feminine, because there was nothing girlie about him, but there was a pretty-boy quality that was a far cry from—

I stopped myself. Karl wasn't my type either—too suave, too polished, too old.

But as for the puzzle that was Jaz, I solved it over dessert. When he twisted in his chair, the angle was just right to ignite a memory and I knew what he reminded me of: the angel Gabriel at my grandmother's church.

I'm sure there's something sacrilegious about having a crush on an angel, but I'd only been six or seven at the time. Gran was a proper society lady, one who had expected her son to grow up and marry a debutante. When he brought home an Indian girl from college, she hadn't been disappointed or angry, but simply, I think, confused. Like most women of her class and generation, this just wasn't a possibility she'd considered. But he was obviously in love, and the girl was as bright and beautiful as any debutante, so Gran gave her blessing.

She loved us as much as she did any of her grandchildren. Even after the divorce that didn't change. If there was any problem with Gran, it was only her need to make us feel we belonged. Hence the angel Gabriel.

When we visited, I always went to church with her because I knew it pleased her and it pleased my mother. Above the pulpit was this enormous painting of flaxen-haired, pale-skinned angels, and the artist had decided to single Gabriel out by making him dark-haired and brown-skinned.

To my grandmother, Gabriel served as proof for me that I was just as welcome in God's house as anyone, so she never failed to rhapsodize over how beautiful he was, and how being different from the others made him all the more special. A heavy-handed lesson, but her heart was in the right place. I spent many hours in that church staring at Gabriel with his soulful eyes and dark ringlets.

So the mystery of Jaz's attractiveness was solved. But it didn't make my heart patter any less when he turned *his* soulful eyes my way. The face of an angel covering a mind more inclined to devilry. Under the circumstances, it might be just what I needed.

———

AS WE LEFT the restaurant, Jaz said, "So you're an Exustio? Or is it Aspicio?"

"Expisco," I said.

"Exustio is fire," Sonny said. "Aspicio is vision."

"Damn half-demon names. All sound like Latin to me."

"Could that be because they *are* Latin?"

"Smart ass. Even Guy didn't know what an Exp—Expisco was. Had to get Bianca to look it up, and she had a hell of a time."

"It's a very rare subtype," I said.

"And a weird one." He glanced at me. "No offense, I just mean most of you get some elemental power or enhanced senses. Being able to sense trouble just, well, doesn't seem to fit."

"Full-blooded demons usually have special powers plus chaos sensors. Most half-demons get the powers without the sensors. I just get the sensors."

"Huh." He walked for at least ten steps in silence, which told me something was wrong. Before I could ask, he said, "The reason I'm bringing it up is that, well, Guy's . . . not convinced."

"That I am what I say I am?"

He nodded. "I wanted to give you a heads-up. He's going to test you, and soon."

HOPE

EASY RIDER

We cut through the pedestrian-only Lincoln Road Mall. The sun had set and the temperature dropped to a balmy seventy, though the humidity lingered. On the promenade, no one was pulling on warmer clothing. The barely-there bottoms, plunging necklines and bad boob jobs were on full display as the nightlife began to prowl, skirting the palms and umbrella tables as they zeroed in on their favorite club, hoping being early might get them inside.

Jaz kept up a steady travelogue, pointing out the sights along the way, including the drop-dead gorgeous guys lounging on tables outside Score, every one of them worthy of a magazine cover, and not one of them likely to return any female attention. There weren't as many gay bars in South Beach as there had been, Jaz said. They'd revitalized the area, made it the hottest place in Miami, then moved on. Many others had moved on too, and South Beach no longer had the cachet of a few years ago, but that didn't bother Guy. Less hip young things meant more tourists and wannabes, who made easier marks.

His club was a block off the Mall. Not prime real estate, but from the lineup outside, no one seemed to care. Jaz said Guy liked us to work the line a bit as we came in—find likely marks and let them in, earning an easy excuse for an introduction later. But since this was my first night, Jaz figured they could skip that, and we headed up the other side of the road, cutting across as we neared the front of the line.

We jogged across the road, dodging slow-moving cars, Jaz's fingers lightly resting on my waist to guide me. The smell of smoke wafted around us, some from exhaust, some from those in line getting in one last cigarette or cigar. A nervous laugh rang out over the murmur of the waiting crowd. Every voice seemed high-pitched, edged with forced fervor, as if they were trying to convince themselves that standing on the sidewalk was a very cool and fun way to spend an evening.

We approached the front of the velvet rope as a girl in a shockingly ugly gauze slip of a dress tried to convince the bouncer that she was the advance party for J. Lo and absolutely had to get inside right away because J. wouldn't stop by if her table wasn't ready. The bouncer listened, eyes never bothering to meet hers, his mouth barely opening enough to direct her to a club two blocks over, where they might believe J. Lo was coming and, better yet, care.

When the bouncer saw Jaz, though, his granite mask of ennui shattered into a wide grin, revealing a missing incisor. He slapped Jaz on the back and greeted Sonny, who edged the hopeful girl back, letting me through. Jaz lingered a minute, introducing me and making small talk as I felt the weight of stares on my back, and listened to the mutters of "Who are they?" in tones half curious, half contemptuous. Then the bouncer opened the doors and we stepped inside.

EASY RIDER WAS the club's name, and now I knew why. "Born to Be Wild" blasted from the speakers. Smoke swirled around a half-dozen pool tables. Two runways featured tattooed strippers with teased hair and torn fishnets. The female servers were clad in leather bikini tops and chaps; the guys got leather thongs and chaps. The tables were scarred and decrepit, the leather booths battered and torn. It looked like a biker bar, circa 1970.

It didn't take long, though, to see past the illusion. "Born to Be Wild" was a dance remix. The "smoke" around the pool tables was dry ice. Those tattooed strippers were gorgeous, and the tattoos probably came off with soap and water. The damage to the tables and booths was an artistic embellishment, not signs of age and misuse.

A club designed to make the young, wealthy and bored feel like they were wallowing in the grimy biker subculture without any danger of soiling their Pradas.

"Cheesy, huh?" Jaz whispered, his warm breath tickling my ear. "Works, though. They eat this shit up."

"I see that."

"Sonny? Can you take Faith to our table while I change?"

"Our table" was a booth with a view of the entire club. Bianca was there, with two guys she introduced as Tony and Max. Max was tall with a chiseled profile, a perfect tan and sun-bleached blond hair gathered in a small ponytail. Tony was about five six, compact and muscular, black hair cropped so short it was like a birthmark across his scalp. Both moved to give me room, Max shifting aside with a polite smile, Tony waving me in with a confident grin, as if I should be honored by the invitation. I slid in beside Max.

Having been to many clubs, I expected conversation to be impossible, but the booth must have been specially soundproofed. I still had to strain to hear, but could carry on a conversation.

Bianca set Tony and Max on a group of fortyish women trying hard to look twenty.

After they left, she turned to me. "Faith, I'd like you to—"

"Bee?"

Jaz appeared at her shoulder, dressed in a vintage wide-collared off-white dress shirt and black jeans.

"I thought I'd squire the lady around for a while. Introduce her to some people. Maybe take a tour of the dance floor."

Bianca looked from me to Jaz. "You two should catch some eyes. Make sure you do—have fun, play it up. You know the drill."

I soon understood why Jaz had made it into the gang despite his weak supernatural type. The guy had phenomenal people skills. As we circled the room, it was nonstop "How's the new job going?" and "Saw you in the paper last week" and "Hey, that girl you were checking out last time is here—without her boyfriend." Most people would sound smarmy and false, but Jaz had such an aura of bouncy good humor he pulled it off.

"Can I stop now?" he whispered as we left yet another group.

I choked on a laugh. "But you seem to be having such a good time."

"Not having a bad one but—" He shrugged. "Not my crowd, really. Any chance I can talk you into a break on the dance floor?"

"Done."

Jaz was a good dancer. Not fantastic, but decent enough that he didn't make a fool of himself, which summed up my own skills.

"Poor Max," he said during a lull in the pounding beat.

I followed his gaze to a corner where Max and Tony were chatting up the ladies Bianca had set them on. Every now and then Max's attention would wander.

"Not enjoying his assignment?" I asked.

"He's got the looks, so Guy makes him play the floor, but he doesn't care much for humans and has a hard time faking it. Like being gay and pretending you're interested in girls."

"He doesn't date humans?"

A genuine look of surprise. "Do you?"

I took advantage of an upbeat in the tempo to formulate my answer. Where I came from, if I didn't date humans, my social calendar would be very bare. Actually, it *had* been bare for about a year now, but that was another matter. Even calling nonsupernaturals "humans" seemed weird. The council sometimes used the word, but sparingly, as if it was borderline racist. To say, "I don't date humans" seemed like saying, "I don't date white guys."

But if I had the choice, wouldn't I prefer supernaturals? Not because I thought we were superior, but because they'd understand me better. Like if I moved to India, I'd probably date Americans.

I told the truth. "I don't have much choice where I come from but, if I did, I suppose I'd rather stick to supernaturals."

"It's not just the 'can't reveal my secret powers' thing. Not like *my* powers need much cover-up anyway. It's just more comfortable, you know? Like being in the gang. Hanging out with others like us. Helping each other." He glanced toward Max, then smiled and moved closer, lips to my ear. "Which gives me an idea. What do you say we preempt Guy's testing?"

"Hmm?"

"Guy wants to test you. Let's beat him to it. Help Max out and show Guy what you can do. The sooner he trusts you, the quicker he'll bring you in on the big jobs. And there's something in the pipe right now." His lips brushed my ear. "Trust me, you won't want to miss it."

WE JOINED MAX, Tony and the three women. I'd been reluctant—I couldn't see them welcoming a younger woman—but Jaz had insisted it'd be okay. He was right. I came with my own guy, so I wasn't competition. Having Max and Tony introduce them to friends seemed to waylay any suspicions that they were being played. And when I acted as if they were my age, it confirmed that the money they'd spent trying to look twenty again had worked.

We hung out with them for a couple of drinks. The guys had this down to a science. They took turns offering to buy a round, gathered orders, then returned with virgin versions for us and real drinks for the ladies, probably double strength.

The drunker the women got, the easier it was to pick up their negative thoughts. Once I had a few, I invited Jaz onto the dance floor. He took me to a corner partly obscured by a pillar, and where no one would notice we were doing more talking than dancing.

"So," he said, eyes glittering. "Could you pick up all their dirty little secrets?"

I laughed. "It doesn't quite work like that. I catch the chaotic thoughts—anything that might have negative connotations. Anger, sadness, jealousy...But it has to be an active thought. I can't hunt through their brains looking for secrets."

"Okay, okay. So'd you get something?"

He looked like a kid waiting for a present. I played it out, savoring his reaction.

"Two of the three are married," I said.

"Can I guess? Definitely the brunette—"

"Bzzz. Sorry. Divorced, and having a rough time of it."

"But she's the only one with a wedding band line."

"I suspect that's because the other two are more aware of theirs, and used tanner. The blond in blue is nervous. She didn't want to come along and she thinks she saw the daughter of a friend on the dance floor. The one in the red dress, Michelle, is definitely out to paint the town and get some revenge. Hubby is away for the week at a conference, and she knows he's taken his mistress with him."

When I finished, he was silent.

"If you don't believe me—"

"No, shit, I believe you. I'm just...speechless." He shook his head. "Holy shit. Now *that's* a power. Guy is going to love this."

"But there's nothing there we can use, unless it's blackmailing the husband over the mistress, but if the wife already knows..."

"Too complicated. Guy likes the short-term con and I think I know where he'll want us to go with this. Head back to Max and Tony. Tell them I'm in the john. I'll talk to Bianca."

WHILE JAZ WAS gone, Tony took a call. A simple "Yeah...yeah... okay...see you then." I guessed it was Bianca or Guy, telling him what was going on. He swung over to the other side of the woman in the red dress and started joking with her, subtly steering her closer to me.

When Jaz returned, he snuck up behind me and put his hands on my waist, tickling me. I jumped. He ducked out of the way, as if expecting a smack, then bounced back, goofing around, grabbing me around the waist, tweaking my hair, grinning all the while. I played along, twisting from his grasp, smacking his hands away and laughing. Finally, he caught me from behind and pulled me against him. His hands went to my thighs and slid under my skirt.

"Did I mention how hot you look tonight?" he said.

"Oh, please," Tony said. "Get a room, guys."

Jaz wrapped his arms around me, his chin resting on my head. "Exactly what I was thinking. You guys don't mind if we take off, then?"

"Go on."

Jaz steered me through a group, his arm around my waist, hand planted on my ass. Once we were out of sight of the others, he removed it and whispered, "Sorry. And thanks for not smacking me for real back there. I needed to create a distraction."

He opened his hand. In his palm lay a driver's license and keys on a unicorn-head fob.

"From the lady in red? Ah-ha. That's why Tony put her beside me...and why you put on that little show. Your hand slipped into her purse, didn't it?"

"We magicians may not get the fancy spellcasting, but when it comes to picking pockets, there's no one better."

———

HE TOOK ME into a room where Sonny and Guy were waiting with a key duplicating machine. I jotted down the address, then Jaz looked it up on MapQuest. When Sonny was done with the keys, Jaz left with the originals. A few minutes later, he returned.

"Okay?" Guy said.

"You need to ask?"

"Cocky bastard." Guy leaned back in his chair, gaze appraising us. "How about we put that self-confidence to the test, Jasper? You three will do the job."

"Without Bianca?"

"Think you can handle it?"

"You need to ask?"

"Sonny, you keep that ego of his in check. Faith, listen to Sonny. Now get your tools and go. You've got ninety minutes. Then I'm calling Tony and Max in for the night and the ladies go home."

HOPE

ADRENALINE

We used a crew vehicle to drive to the mark's address. I knew it wasn't right to call her "the mark." She was a woman with a name, one who was about to have her home violated and her possessions stolen just because she was out for the evening trying to take revenge on a philandering husband. But, like an undercover cop, I had to get my hands dirty in this job.

Shifting into the gang's mentality was easier than it should have been. I'd been hanging out with Karl too long and, while I often argued with him about the moral bankruptcy of thievery, I'd come to understand and accept it. He'd been raised by a thief, knew no other life, and he needed the adrenaline rush to work off the more uncivilized urges of a werewolf.

On an intellectual and moral level, I knew what I was about to do was wrong. But on a physical and emotional level? I couldn't wait to get started.

OUR MARK LIVED in a luxury high-rise. From Karl's lessons, I knew this would be tougher than breaking into a single-family dwelling. The only safe route in was through the patio door. Fortunately, with a third-floor apartment, that didn't require much skill or equipment. It helped that the balcony overlooked a tree-shrouded auxiliary parking lot. Once we'd donned our black hoodies and pants, we'd be invisible.

Jaz and Sonny agreed I should go up first and take a look while they stood guard. I made it to the balcony easily. The French doors couldn't be opened with the keys, but it was such a simple lock that a credit card would do the trick. It couldn't be that easy. I peered through the glass. Beside the front door, a light blinked on a security panel.

I pulled out the minibinoculars hoping I could identify the alarm type. When I did, I bit back a laugh. Cheap bastards.

A count to three, then I unlocked the door, threw it open and sprinted across the room. As I disabled the alarm, my heart sped from a canter to a full-out gallop.

I should have called Sonny up for a second opinion so if anything went wrong, I wouldn't shoulder the blame alone. But there was no time for that now. In less than a minute, this alarm would go off.

The pressure and the doubts should have made me fumble or hesitate. But the risk only added to the exhilaration. Then came those final few seconds, when I knew I was pushing the limit, either I'd succeed or I'd fail and I wouldn't get another chance because if I did fail, the alarm would sound and—

The blinking light turned off.

I leaned against the wall, trembling. Bliss. I smiled and closed my eyes, telling myself I needed to catch my breath but savoring every lick of chaos to the sweet end.

Then I waved Jaz and Sonny up and we set to work.

It quickly became apparent that these guys were no petty stereo-and-TV thieves. They knew what could be turned over fast, for the most profit, and they knew where to find it. Quick and clean—anything that didn't fit in the knapsacks stayed behind.

Most of what we took came from the safe. Like the locks and security system, it was a cheap one—a prop to scare off amateurs. It locked with a key, and we found one in our handful of duplicates.

I made a few suggestions, mostly about covering our tracks and leaving a tidy scene, so the owner wouldn't walk in to ransacked drawers—all tips from Karl.

Most of Karl's training had been theory, mingled with safe practice, like breaking into council delegates' homes with their consent. A flat line on the chaos monitor.

The theft with Jaz and Sonny couldn't have been more different. Sonny was enjoying himself, but Jaz was stoked—trumpeting every new find as if he'd discovered buried treasure, darting in to check our progress, prowling the apartment, peering out the windows for danger . . . and almost seeming disappointed when he didn't find it. He threw off chaos waves so strong and sharp I shivered each time he came near.

I found a dusty jewelry box on the top shelf of the closet—antique stuff that probably came from an estate. Sonny helped me sort through it, leaving the costume pieces behind. Then Jaz burst into the room.

"Got trouble, bro," he whispered to Sonny. "We're cutting it close to Guy's time limit and there's a couple fighting in the back parking lot. We'll have a helluva time getting off the balcony."

Sonny doused his flashlight, lifted the bedroom blind and looked out. "Shit."

"I know."

Jaz tried to keep his tone sober, but his eyes gleamed. I could feel the adrenaline pounding through him and turned my face into the shadows so he wouldn't see my response. When I glanced back at the guys, Jaz had *his* face averted, hands stuffed in his pockets, trying to play the cool professional. For my benefit, I presumed.

"Should we wait or go out the front?" I asked.

"Front's easier leaving than entering," Sonny said.

As we talked, Jaz rocked on the balls of his feet, saying nothing, as if knowing he couldn't be trusted to come up with the safest answer.

"They're still fighting," Sonny said after one last look out the window. "You guys got everything?"

We nodded.

"Then let's go."

I WENT FIRST, sprinting across the hall with my hood pulled up, face down. A survey of the stairwell showed only one camera, at the bottom and easy to pass unnoticed.

As Sonny shut the door behind them, I whispered a warning about the security camera. When he headed for the stairs, Jaz caught his arm and motioned up.

"No fucking way," Sonny said. "We're on a schedule and—"

Jaz caught my elbow. "Come on. I want to show you something." He leaned forward, eyes meeting mine, that infectious grin making my heart skip. "You won't regret it. I promise."

"Go," Sonny grumbled behind us. "Let's just make it fast."

HOPE

VIEW FROM THE TOP

As Sonny and I tramped past the sixteenth-floor landing, Jaz hit the last flight at a bound. By the time we arrived, Jaz had already picked the roof door lock. He looked out and murmured, "Perfect."

As Sonny strode ahead, surveying the roof for cameras or other trouble spots, I stayed by the door, letting my eyes adjust. Jaz came up beside me, his fingers touching my wrist above the glove, bare skin making contact. When I glanced over his gaze tripped away, smile unexpectedly shy. A quick squeeze of my gloved hand and he grabbed my elbow instead and steered me across the roof.

As we walked, his chaos vibes were light, teasing, barely enough to tap my radar. His eyes gleamed, like a boy getting into mischief. I tugged off my glove, then slid my hand into his. He grinned—so big and so bright that you'd think he was ten years old, a girl holding his hand for the first time. Seeing that smile, I knew I was going to fall for him.

For almost a decade now, anytime I'd met a guy and thought I could fall for him, I'd thrown up every barrier. I had too much to hide, too much else going on in my life, and I couldn't afford the ups and downs—and, yes, the pain—of romantic entanglements. But I looked at Jaz, saw myself falling and didn't care. Tonight I wasn't Hope Adams, didn't have all her problems, her insecurities, her responsibilities. Whatever this became, it couldn't last. No reason not to let myself enjoy the ride.

Jaz tugged me toward the edge, then let go, lowered himself to the roof and stretched on to his stomach, arms crossed under his chin, staring out at the city. After a moment, he glanced back at me.

"Well, come on." He waved for me to lie down.

I glanced at the ground.

"It's not that dirty. You're washable." He peered across the roof. "Yo! Sonny!"

Sonny appeared, sighed and shook his head, but sat down beside his friend, knees drawn up. I hesitated, then laid down.

The city stretched out before us, and it was breathtaking. A few blocks away, a bay glittered with the reflection of a hundred lights. Boats bobbed on the water like toy ships. Salsa music drifted on the brine-scented breeze. The humidity from earlier was all but gone, the night air pleasantly cool.

"People knock Miami, but they're just envious," Jaz said. "Look at it. Sand, surf, sun every day of the year. Goddamned perfect."

He went quiet for a moment, then stretched out his hand, pointing to the skyscrapers ringing the bay. "You see that one? Third left from the tallest? You know what that is?"

"No."

"Cortez Cabal headquarters. I bet if you had binoculars, you could see Benicio himself, up in his penthouse office, counting his billions."

I laughed.

"Can you imagine working there?" Jaz said. "A waterfront view from every window? How much does real estate like that even cost? And that's only the location. I hear they have marble floors in the damned bathrooms. The toilets probably run on Evian."

"Perrier, I think," Sonny said.

"You know what I mean. All that money. All that power. And where do the Cortezes get it? Not by casting their own spells, that's for sure. They use our powers to line their coffers. The supernaturals working for them think they've got it made. Like our parents, Sonny. Never a bad thing to say about the St. Clouds, no matter what the bastards did to them. They were just happy to have a job. Used them up and spit them out. Like slaves in the cotton fields, pouring out their lifeblood for the masters."

"You've been hanging out with Guy too long," Sonny said.

I knew we should be going, but neither seemed in any hurry, and sitting out here, when our mark could return anytime, set my heart tripping with a steady stream of chaos.

As I glanced at the distant Cabal headquarters, I found my excuse for staying longer: using the opening about the Cabals to get information.

"So Guy doesn't care for the Cabals?" I said. "I can see his point. They make life cushy for supernaturals—access to health care, special education for our kids, a community that understands us—but the employees pay for those perks. Still, it's not really much different from any corporation. They use your skills and give you a sweet benefits package in return."

"But in a corporation, if you screw up, they don't kill you. Unless you work for the Mafia."

"Which is what some say a Cabal really is. So that's what bothers Guy, then? The abuses of power?"

"More the concentration of power. The old-boys club, to the nth degree." Jaz waved at the building. "If you worked there, Faith, you wouldn't have a shot of getting to the upper floors unless you wanted to be a secretary. Not because you're a woman, but because you aren't one of them. None of us are. Maybe everyone on those upper floors isn't a Cortez, but you can bet your ass he's a sorcerer. No magicians or druids or half-demons. And if you were a werewolf or vampire? You couldn't get through the front door. Even Guy, who's a sorcerer, wouldn't rise very high, as smart as he is. He doesn't have the connections."

"Does he talk about this a lot?"

Jaz laughed. "You mean: are you going to have to sit through political sermons? Nah. He might talk about it now and then, but he's usually quiet."

"Except with Jaz," Sonny said.

Jaz shrugged. "He's got a lot of good ideas. I think it's just been bugging him lately, so he wants someone to talk to—someone he can sound off to about the stuff that's been happening."

"Stuff?"

"With the Cortez Cabal."

"There's been trouble?"

"This and that. Dustups."

Apparently there were a few details Benicio hadn't included in my debriefing. Surprise, surprise.

"Guy's been playing it down, but he's getting pissed off. I think he—" He tossed a pebble over the edge. Watched it drop. "Anyway, he's not the only one who's worried about the Cortezes. The mood isn't good, and I don't just mean in the gangs. The old man isn't getting any younger."

"Benicio? He's not that old."

Jaz shrugged. To him, sixty years old meant wobbling on the brink of a six-foot drop. Jaz was only a few years younger than me, but it had been a long time since I'd felt my age. Working for the council, hanging around with Karl, I'd been trying to act more mature even as I told myself I didn't care what he thought of me.

"You mean the succession question," I said.

Sonny snorted. "Question? According to Benicio Cortez, there is no question."

Jaz rolled onto his side, facing me. "That's the big problem, one that Guy says proves Benicio Cortez doesn't give a shit about his employees. He has three sons, all in the business. Oldest is what, forty? Been with the company all his life. Has what it takes to lead, everyone says. But who does Benicio name as his heir?"

"Lucas," I said.

"The illegitimate youngest son who wants nothing to do with the family business. Who's spent his adult life trying to fuck up the Cabals in any way he can. This is the guy Benicio Cortez wants to take his job."

I sat up. "Most people I talk to don't really think Lucas is the heir. They figure Benicio's just being wily, keeping his older boys in line." Lucas himself believed that.

"Guy thinks the old man's serious. And if he dies? If Lucas Cortez takes over the Cabal?" He shook his head.

"But if Guy thinks it means the end of the Cabal, isn't that a good thing?"

"It's not the Cabal *concept* Guy's against. It's the way they're run—the imbalance of power. He'd love to upset that balance, give some back to the little guys like us. But destroy the Cabal altogether, like Lucas Cortez would do? What would that do to supernaturals in

Miami? To people like our parents, with Cabal jobs? To the gangs? Guy wants reform, not annihilation."

So what, if anything, did Guy plan to do? I couldn't ask. Not yet. But I had my lead. Benicio was right—there was trouble brewing.

Dropping the subject was tough. The reporter in me could see the answers lying there, right under the surface. At least I could dig around the site, see what else popped up.

"You guys ever met Lucas Cortez?" I asked.

Sonny shook his head.

"I met a guy who went to college with him," Jaz said.

"Law school?"

"Nah, undergrad. This was back before Lucas got into his 'fight the power' shit. This guy knew who Lucas was because his dad worked for the Cortezes. Otherwise, he said, he never would have noticed him. A geek and a loner, the kind of kid you only talk to if you need someone to do your homework."

Sonny shook his head. "And this is the son Benicio wants to run the Cabal."

"I've met him," I said.

Jaz dropped the pebble he'd been playing with. "Lucas Cortez?"

"I was dating a thief who'd had trouble with Lucas. After we pulled one job, he came after us."

"Seriously?"

"*Seriously* would be overstating it. My ex got rid of him pretty easily. Like you said, he's a geek. A loser who fancies himself some kind of crusader." I sent up a mental apology to Lucas.

Jaz considered my words for a moment, then said, "Guy would like to hear this. Get your impressions. Would that be okay?"

Exactly what I'd hoped. I nodded and said I'd do my best, even call my ex if it would help.

CALL MY EX . . .

I'd spent the break-in trying to focus on Karl in the most neutral terms. My contact. My mentor. My friend. I'd called him my "ex" with Guy this afternoon and now with Jaz because that would be easy for them to understand. The truth was that "boyfriend" was the one word I couldn't pin on him, let alone "ex."

Karl Marsten...

A guy who should never have been part of my life, and there were days when I wished he never had been.

Karl, the werewolf jewel thief I was supposed to capture for Tristan, my bogus council contact. Karl, who'd shown me I was actually working for a Cabal, who'd introduced me to the real council and got me a job with them. Karl, who knew why I really worked for the council—my less than honorable motivation—and not only knew, but understood.

After that first meeting, almost two years ago, he'd kept coming around, his intentions murky. Chemistry we had, and sometimes even explored, but we both seemed more comfortable with friendship. He'd show up, let me poke holes through his ego, sometimes return the favor. We'd banter for a while, then slide into confessions and concerns neither of us shared with anyone else.

When he'd hinted about coming to one of my mother's charity galas, I'd teased that he was getting old and needing easier access to jewels. He'd joked that he wanted to meet my mother, see whether she approved of him. Then, at the Valentine's ball at my brother's Texas ranch, he'd shown up on the doorstep, ticket in hand.

If he'd been serious about wanting to come, we should have discussed the pros and cons of letting the supernatural side of my life seep into my family life. But the anger I'd felt on seeing him hadn't lasted.

Charm was Karl's specialty, but that night he'd used none of his usual too-clever charm that sent society matrons into vapors as he divested them of their jewels. My mother wouldn't have fallen for that. Instead, Karl had charmed her by being himself—or as close to it as he ever was around others.

When the party ended, I'd given him the grand tour of the grounds. The stable visit didn't go so well—his werewolf scent spooked the horses. When the groom had come down, wakened by the noise, we'd raced out like kids caught at a prank.

We'd stopped at the pool, tucked behind the gardens. I'd opened the gate.

He'd peered in. "I didn't bring my bathing suit."

"I can probably find one for you."

"Don't bother."

He'd stripped off his jacket and shirt, and I'd known, even as I let my dress fall around my ankles, that this was why he'd come. To take the step we'd been dancing around for two years.

Afterward, he scooped me up out of the pool, grabbed towels from the cabana and carried me into the woods.

As perfect a night as any romantic would want. Perfect even for a cynic like me.

I'd woken to see Karl on the edge of the clearing, his back to me, staring out at the dawn. I'd watched him and I'd felt . . .

But it didn't matter what I felt. What mattered, as I'd soon discovered, was how *he* felt because, with Karl, it was always about that. What he felt. What he wanted. And one night, no matter how wildly romantic, couldn't change that.

HOPE

HISTORY LESSON

I called Benicio the next morning. When he learned I had something to report, he asked me to meet Troy for breakfast and fill him in. In other words, he hadn't expected results so soon and didn't want them conveyed over the telephone.

I KEPT AN eye out as I left the building. No one in the gang knew where I was staying—even Guy hadn't asked. But I could see him putting new recruits under surveillance.

When the cab dropped me off, I saw Troy across the road, standing by a storefront, studying a map. His gaze flicked my way as I got out, but he didn't budge.

The restaurant was an anonymous little diner, the sort you can find anywhere. I took a booth at the back and had a full coffee cup before Troy came through the door.

He slid in across from me.

"Everything okay?" I asked.

"Yeah. The cloak-and-dagger stuff is just protocol."

He seemed in no rush to get down to business. We ordered breakfast and he asked how I was settling in, how the apartment was.

"You need anything, don't be afraid to call," he said. "When Mr. Cortez opens his wallet, take advantage. I do."

He gave me some pointers on the neighborhoods—recommending

shops and restaurants near my apartment and the club, along with ones to avoid. If I needed a break, he said he'd be happy to squire me around on his night off, maybe get out of the city, show me the area. The invitation was half flirtatious, half friendly, open for me to interpret as I wished.

When breakfast arrived, we shifted to business.

I told Troy what Jaz had said about Guy and his issue with the Cabal.

Troy snorted. "Same shit, different day. I've been hearing that crap since I was a teenager. Cabals are businesses, not charitable organizations. Sure, they use their employees. Doesn't every corporation? That's the point: use your resources to build your capital. And yeah, there are sides to Cabals that are just plain ugly. You won't catch me waving pompoms and spouting the party line, not even in front of Mr. Cortez. But you know what? As far as he's concerned I'm entitled to my opinions . . . as long as I don't share them with the stockholders. Whatever my beefs, you don't see me quitting either, and that's not because I'm afraid I'd be fitted for cement shoes. Maybe in the Nast Cabal or the St. Cloud or the Boyd, but where I am, Mr. Cortez doesn't want me here unless I want to be here."

"Makes sense."

"You want some guy watching your back if he's only doing it because he has to? I don't do this for a good medical package or to protect some Cabal ideology. I don't believe in that crap. But I do believe in the guy whose back I'm watching."

He speared a home fry and chomped it down before continuing. "That's what really burns me about some gang punk spouting that bullshit about Lucas, that naming him heir proves Mr. Cortez doesn't care about the Cabal."

"So it's true."

"It's true that Lucas is the *named* heir, but that's all anyone but Mr. Cortez himself can say for sure."

He slowly drained half his cup of coffee, as if deciding how to continue.

"You've never met Lucas's brothers, have you?" he said. "Hector, William, Carlos . . . ?"

"No."

"Let's just say that anyone who knows them and Lucas doesn't think Mr. Cortez's idea is completely crazy. Not that the others couldn't run the Cabal—Hector and William, that is. But the *best* person to do it?" He shook his head. "If Benicio Cortez didn't care about the Cabal, he'd pass it on to Hector and say, 'good enough,' and it'd run just fine. You know anything about Cortez Cabal history?"

"Not much. They were the first Cabal, and they're still the most powerful—"

"Not 'still.' They're the most powerful *again*." He leaned back, stretching until his leg brushed mine. "Now this is all way before my time, but I've heard the stories. When Mr. Cortez was growing up, the Cortez Cabal was locked neck-and-neck with the Boyds for third place, meaning they sometimes slipped to fourth out of four. And it wasn't because things had changed but because they *hadn't*. For a couple hundred years, the Cortez Cabal kept chugging along, doing what it always had, not changing with the times. Benicio Cortez changed that. And that means he's sure as hell not passing the Cabal over to Hector and saying, 'good enough.' It also means he's not going to hand it over to Lucas just to ... what, win over his rebellious son?" He laughed and shook his head. "You know Lucas. How would Mr. Cortez have a better chance of winning him over? Handing him the Cabal? Or promising never to bug him about it again?"

He was right. So in trash-talking Lucas, had I only added fuel to the fire? I told Troy what I'd said.

"You did the right thing. If you said any different, it would definitely put you on the 'no-invite' list when they're Cabal-bashing. If they ask you for more on Lucas, you should tell them—" He stopped. "No. Your instincts are good. Stick with them."

"Thanks. There *is* something you might be able to help me with. An incident with the gang that Mr. Cortez may have ... forgotten."

"Forgotten?" His lips twitched in a barely suppressed grin. "Or neglected to tell you?"

"Sorry. I'm not implying—"

"If you aren't, then you should be. The chances of Mr. Cortez *forgetting* to add something are near zero. Intentionally withholding information that he'd consider sensitive? I'd count on it. What seems to be missing?"

I told him what Jaz said about recent trouble between the gang and the Cabal.

"Dustups?" he repeated.

"Encounters, altercations—"

"I know what you mean, but I have no idea what *they* mean. Sure there are dustups. All the time. Always have been. They'll pull a job that gets too much attention or gets too close to our operations, and we'll flex our muscles, give their chain a tug, and remind them they *are* on a chain, operating in this city with the Cabal's permission."

"Has there been an increase in those sorts of encounters?"

"If there has been, I'd know about it. All security alerts come to me."

Troy promised to investigate further and I trusted he would. I was also inclined to believe him when he said that a sudden increase in Cabal-gang problems wouldn't be the kind of thing Benicio would keep from me. Yet, as I knew from experience, just because something doesn't cross Benicio's radar didn't mean it wasn't being done by a Cabal employee, using Cabal resources and the Cabal name. I'd have to work on Jaz some more.

TROY LEFT FIRST. I presumed he was watching my exit, but knew better than to look for him as I hailed a cab. I'd just given the driver my address when my cell phone rang, the gang one Rodriguez had given me.

"Faith? It's Jaz. I didn't get you up, did I?"

I checked my watch. I couldn't remember the last time I hadn't been up by ten—awake, showered, dressed, done breakfast and moving on with my day. Being in the gang, though, meant late nights and, probably, late mornings. Like being back in college. Well, being back in college for the kind of kids who skipped morning classes and stayed out at the bars all night, which hadn't been me.

"No, I'm awake."

"Good, good. You took off last night before I got a chance to ask your plans for today. I figured, being new in town, maybe you'd like some company. We have to be at the Rider by three, but—"

"Three? I thought it was five—oh, you mean you and Sonny."

"No..." A moment's pause, then, "Shit. Guy hasn't called you yet, has he? Better keep this quick, then, or I'll get hell for tying up the line. Short version is, you're in."

"In?"

"On the job tonight. The one I mentioned. I talked to Guy last night, told him how well you did."

"Great. Thank you."

A laugh. "While I'd love to claim credit, I don't have that kind of pull. Once he saw what you could do—that mind-reading stuff—he decided we could use you on the job. He was just double-checking with me, making sure everything went okay. So, you're in, but before that, I was wondering if you had lunch plans."

I didn't. We agreed to meet at the club.

HOPE

PLANS

At one, a cab dropped me off at Easy Rider. I was about to ring the side bell when a voice called from behind me.

"Hold up, Faith. I got it."

Footsteps thundered down the sidewalk. I turned to see Rodriguez jogging toward me, waving his key.

Rodriguez was the youngest member, no more than twenty. An average-looking guy, but there was a sweetness about him that made me want to fix him up with someone's little sister. Maybe it was the shy smile or the hair that flopped in his eyes or the big dark eyes that dipped away the moment they touched mine. When he'd given me my phone yesterday, he'd taken me through everything step-by-step, patient but never condescending, explaining everything in simple English—a far cry from most tech support guys I'd dealt with.

"Guy will give you a key soon enough," he said as he unlocked the door. "Until then, if no one answers the bell, ring Guy's office phone. The number's on your speed dial. He's usually in by noon."

He held the door open, then darted past me to the security panel and punched in a code.

"Even when someone's already here, this will be armed, and Guy expects you to rearm it after you come inside."

"Got it."

"Ask him for the code later. He should give you that, even if you don't have a key." He pressed the last button, then paused before shutting the panel. "That reminds me. You have some experience with alarm systems, right? Ex-boyfriend thief or something?"

I nodded.

"If you've got a second, would you mind taking a look at something? Jaz and Sonny ran into a system on a job last week that totally stumped them. It's not anything I've ever seen and I can't find schematics on the Web. They did some sketches for me."

"I'll take a look. If it's new and high-tech, I've probably seen it, but almost certainly can't crack it."

"No, that's fine. Just looking for an ID."

We'd gone three steps when his cell phone rang. He checked the number, hesitated, then motioned for me to wait.

"Did it come?" he asked as he answered. A pause, then he shifted his weight, one hand shoved into his pocket. "Okay, I'm ready. What does it say?" Another pause. Then a sharp laugh. "Haven't opened it? Are you trying to kill me, Nina? Come on, come *on*." A rueful look at me, then his eyes widened. "*¡Qué fuerte!* Seriously? Okay, okay. I gotta go. We'll talk tonight."

He hung up, grinning. "That was my sister. My college acceptance letter was late, and I was sure that meant I hadn't made it and . . ." His color rose. "And you have no idea what I'm talking about and I'm babbling like a moron. Sorry."

"No, that's great. You got in, I take it. Which college?"

The grin sparked again. "California Institute of Technology."

"Caltech? Wow. Congratulations."

"Thanks. I have to make a few calls. Oh, about that security system, are you going to be around later?"

"As far as I know. We'll look at it then."

He pointed me toward the front rooms. He'd just scampered off when the side door opened again. Bianca. I waited to walk with her.

As we cut through the dimly lit back rooms, she asked whether I'd been comfortable doing a job with Jaz and Sonny. From her tone, I gathered *she* hadn't been comfortable with it—a new recruit sent out with the next two newest members. I assured her everything had gone fine.

We found Sonny reading a novel in a near-dark booth.

"You strain your eyes, you won't be much good to us tonight, Sonny-boy," Bianca said, flicking on the lights for him. She turned to me. "If Sonny's here, Jaz won't be far."

"He's in the storeroom with Guy," Sonny said.

Bianca's lips pursed and she headed toward the back. I followed, leaving Sonny at his table.

Clearly Guy's friendship with Jaz wasn't something Bianca approved of. Did she think he was after her job? Anyone could see that Jaz's ambitions stretched no further than securing a place in the gang with minimal responsibilities, and burrowing in for as long as he could.

She asked about our lunch plans. Who'd suggested it? Was I going with Jaz and Sonny, or just Jaz? I wondered whether Guy had a policy about crew members dating, and Bianca was hoping to get Jaz in trouble.

In the storeroom, Jaz was counting boxes, Guy marking them down. Jaz was retelling some adventure, and Guy was laughing. It all seemed very normal, but there was a note in Guy's laugh, too rich and too loud, trying too hard to show his appreciation for the tale. And there was something in the way he was looking at Jaz, and the way he quickly glanced away when he saw us watching.

A laugh and a look didn't prove anything, but I wondered whether there wasn't a very different cause for Bianca's jealousy. That might also explain why she'd been so eager to know whether Jaz was taking an interest in the new girl. When Jaz saw me, though, his grin said that if Guy was interested in Jaz, it was a one-sided attraction.

"Is it—?" Jaz checked his watch. "Shit. Sorry, Faith. I meant to meet you at the door." He turned to Guy. "Mind if I skip out on the rest, boss? Got a hot lunch date."

Guy muttered something about being left with all the work, but waved us out good-naturedly. So maybe I was reading too much into a laugh and a look.

We were just stepping out the door when Tony barreled past, jokingly elbowing Jaz into the wall.

"Rod got his college letter," he said to Guy and Bianca. "Max and I are springing for pizza." He glanced back at us. "You guys in?"

Jaz hesitated, and I could tell he was torn. I reminded myself why

I was here. I couldn't turn down any opportunity to hang out with the gang, and get them talking about the Cabals.

"Uh, sure." I looked at Jaz. "If that's okay with you?"

"We're in," he said, then lowered his voice to me. "Rain check for tomorrow?"

I smiled. "Definitely."

WE ATE IN the bar, Max and Tony having dragged a small table over to a booth so we'd all fit. They'd brought the pizza, but Guy sprung for a twelve-pack of beer, taking it from the back and carefully noting it in his accounts. The beer was a local microbrew, Jaz said, and ribbed Guy about "springing for the good stuff for a change."

As for Rodriguez's news, Guy had known about his college hopes and seemed genuinely pleased for him, only joking that he'd better give him a special deal on technical consultation after he left.

"So when do we get to wager on how fast you'll be back?" Tony said, peeling a pizza slice from the box. "College was cool, but after one month sweating my ass off in a cubicle, I was so out of there. You don't get pizza and beer parties in a suit job."

"Once Rod's gone, he's gone for good," Jaz said. "If school doesn't keep him there, the California girls will." He winked at Rodriguez, then took a slug of his beer, his dancing eyes lifting to mine. "Though personally, I'm partial to East Coast girls." He leaned back. "But as for why anyone would give up this gig to go to college? Totally beyond me."

"I hear ya," Tony said, lifting his bottle. "To the sweet life. No worries, Guy. I'm not going anywhere."

Jaz and Sonny hoisted their bottles and chimed in their agreement.

"Great," Guy muttered. "Come fall, Bee and I will be stuck with all the loafers."

I turned to Max. "You're leaving too?"

He shrugged. "Probably following Rod out to Cali. That's the plan anyway. No college for me, though. I've got some other business out there."

"Five foot two with eyes of blue," Tony sang. "His girlfriend moved to L.A. last year."

"Ex-girlfriend."

"Yeah, the *ex* you still text ten times a day."

Max colored under his tan. "We're friends, okay? Sure, Jess is working in L.A.—"

"For the Nast Cabal," Tony interjected, to hisses and boos from Jaz and Sonny.

"Only until she gets her MBA," Max said.

"Like getting your education from the military. You gotta bet they're not going to let her waltz away when she's done."

Max shrugged. "She knows that. She'll pay her dues."

"And pay and pay and pay," Jaz said.

Tony nodded. "Face it, buddy, she's in and she's not getting out."

Max's eyes flashed, but Guy cut him off.

"Enough. Max knows what I think." Guy cut a look his way. "If Jess can pull it off, all the power to her, but Cabals don't give away free educations. As long as she knows that, and she's careful..." He shrugged. "Maybe it'll work out."

He passed around the pizza box as Jaz and Tony grabbed a second beer, and I could tell the conversation was going to shift away from Cabals.

"So if you work for a Cabal, they'll pay for college?" I asked.

"Uh-uh." Guy wagged a finger at Max. "See what you started?"

"Hey, *I* didn't start—"

"Yes," Guy said, twisting to face me. "A Cabal will pay for your degree, in return for years of indentured servitude slaving in their cubicles. If you decide you don't want to have Mommy and Daddy pay for your education, then we'll talk about extending your stay. You'd be better off earning your tuition here than getting yourself indebted to a Cabal. Working for me is a whole lot safer."

"And funner," Jaz said.

Sonny put his head in his hands and groaned.

"As you can see, there's at least one gang member who'll never leave me for college." Guy put his elbows on the table, leaning toward me. "Seriously, Faith, Cabal life isn't a route you want to take. Max's girlfriend—sorry, *friend*—is a shaman. They're a dime a dozen. If she's careful, she can probably quit after a few years, no hard feelings, no bounty for her scalp. But an Expisco half-demon?"

He shook his head. "If they get you, they'll never let you go. Employee for life."

"But if I'm so valuable, they'd pay me accordingly, right?"

"Have you got a price in mind? Proper compensation for your freedom? Your free will? Because that's what they'll demand. Yes, they'll pay—they'll pay for you as a commodity, not as a human being, because to them, that's all you—"

"Oh, God, please, no." Tony dropped his head to the table, then looked over at me. "You had to get him started, didn't you?"

Guy pegged him in the head with a bottle cap. "Okay, okay. It's Rodriguez's celebration. No more talk of Cabals. That's an order. You've got exactly ten minutes to goof off, then we need to get down to business and talk about tonight." To me, he added, "If you want to continue this conversation, today's a write-off, but grab me tomorrow. Don't even consider Cabal employment until you've talked to me, okay?"

"I will."

AFTER EXACTLY TEN more minutes of eating and drinking and joking around, Guy moved on to our plans for that night. I expected a larger scale version of what we'd done yesterday—maybe knock over a liquor store or hijack a transport, both common gang activities according to Benicio's notes. What Guy laid out though, made me realize why this gang, despite its size, was such a concern to Benicio.

His scheme was audacious. There was no other word for it. Clever, elaborate and mind-blowing in its boldness.

Bianca assigned us preparation tasks. I was put with Jaz and Sonny again, getting the equipment ready. As everyone filed out, Guy ordered me to wait.

"These marks tonight," he said when the others had left. "They're your kind of people, aren't they?"

Society people, he meant. I considered distancing myself right now—sure I come from that, but they aren't my people, not anymore. Too easy to see through that lie, so I nodded and said simply, "That's right."

He leaned back in his chair. "Any advice you can give? Potential problems I'm not seeing?"

After studying the plans, and rehashing his scheme, I ventured an idea to help him get away with it.

"Smart girl. I wouldn't have thought of that."

"The others might not be too happy. It'll cut into the profits."

He smiled. "Well, then, you won't mind if I take credit, will you?"

"Not at all."

LUCAS

2

I SWIPED MY KEY CARD at the office delivery doors and parked my motorcycle in the back hall. In this neighborhood, I wasn't leaving a 1929 Indian Scout in the alley. While it wasn't yet motorcycle weather, Paige had the car, so I'd brought the bike out of storage. I won't say I wasn't happy for the excuse.

I left my helmet on the seat and adjusted my glasses. For comfort, contacts are the preferred eye wear with helmets, but I couldn't be bothered inserting and removing them for a short ride. Savannah tells me that I could resolve the problem by exchanging my glasses for contacts permanently. I tell her contacts irritate my eyes. A lie. Glasses project an image and I've grown comfortable with that image. Investigating supernatural cases sometimes requires more than lobbing a few defensive spells, and I've won more than my fair share of fights simply because my opponent takes one look at me and presumes I won't throw the first punch.

Another key card swipe to get into the stairwell, then up to our second-floor offices where yet a third pass of the card is required. I'd grown up with such security measures at the Cabal offices, but I often overheard Savannah and Adam cursing as they fumbled to find their cards. No one complained, though. When it came to the building, we were still in the honeymoon phase.

Cortez-Winterbourne Investigations used to be housed in a cramped spare bedroom, and we hadn't dignified it with anything as formal as a name. It had been something to talk about in bed, late at night, how one day Paige would be able to quit her Web design business, I'd stop taking on commercial legal piecework and we'd run our legal-cum-investigative firm helping supernaturals full time, from an actual office. Now, some days, I walked around to the front door just to see the business name and reassure myself it was real.

Five years ago, I'd been a new lawyer, unemployed, no fixed address, chasing cases of injustice—and usually getting the door slammed in my face. No one slammed it harder than one infuriating, stubborn and absolutely bewitching young woman determined to protect her ward from the Cabals without any sorcerer's help. I'd gotten the case, though. And gotten the girl.

As I opened the door to the second floor, the smell of coffee hit me. I paused, still holding the door handle. No one should be here. Paige was at an appointment. Savannah and Adam were in Seattle, doing legwork for a case.

A pot left on the burner would mean burnt coffee, but this smelled fresh. Had Paige returned early? I smiled as I pulled off my jacket. Then I remembered the empty parking lot. If Paige's car wasn't here, neither was she.

I moved cautiously to the kitchenette door. A man stood at the coffeemaker, his back to me. His Rolex caught the light as his fingertips tapped the reservoir, waiting for the machine to finish brewing. He'd look at home in any financial district—the tailored designer dress shirt, pressed pants, polished leather loafers. Perfectly groomed, not a lock of dark hair out of place, not a shaving nick or rough patch to be seen. A man easily discounted as a soft urban professional. Just as one might presume that I'd caught him unawares.

I waited. He took two upside-down mugs from the shelf and flipped them over.

"Cream?" he asked without turning. "Sugar?"

"Black."

"I hope you don't mind that I helped myself."

"Not at all. I hope you don't mind if I ask for a refund on your work designing our security system."

Karl turned and flashed me a smile that could, despite the cliché, best be termed wolfish. "What kind of thief would I be if I can't break into a system I created? But if anyone else manages to do so, you're entitled to your money back." He filled the cups. "Or you would be, had you paid for my services."

"I tried to pay. You insisted on doing it pro bono. In return, one presumes, for some future favor. If you'd like, I can cut you a check right now."

"No, thank you."

I really would rather have paid. Karl Marsten wasn't someone I liked being indebted to. Clayton once told me, "Karl's first priority is Karl. And his second. And his third. Being Pack now won't change that." Which was to say that while Karl was a loyal new addition to the werewolf Pack, his loyalty extended no further than his self-interest. The same, presumably, went for his relationship with me. As long as I proved a useful ally, he could be trusted . . . though not, apparently, to ring the bell before entering.

"I presume this visit is in regard to the task my father gave Hope?"

He clanked the spoon against the edge of his cup and handed me my mug before we walked to my office. The smell of the coffee twisted my stomach. The mention of Hope's name didn't help. I'd spent the last two days wondering whether I'd done the right thing.

I didn't doubt there were rumblings of gang trouble, but I knew my father had another angle. I just couldn't decide what it was and, more important, whether it put Hope in danger.

If his ploy had been to get me to Miami to protect her, how carefully would he have evaluated the danger before setting her on the job? Was she in over her head while he bided his time, waiting for the panicked call from her that would bring me running? Something told me she'd never make that call, however bad things got.

Or was it all about Hope? His way of wooing her into Cabal life? If so, should I do something about it? Did I have the right to do anything about it?

My father had a knack for placing me in impossible situations. Damned if I acted, damned if I didn't. Only this time I feared Hope would be the one damned.

"So Hope *is* in Miami," Karl said as we sat. "I've been in Europe. I came back, had business in Philly and thought I'd take Hope to lunch. Her mother told me she was in Fort Lauderdale, pursuing an urgent story. When I heard 'Florida,' my first thought was your father. I'd hoped I was wrong."

"So you came to Portland to check? I'm sure a phone call would have sufficed."

"I had business here."

Similar, I'm sure, to the nonexistent business that had him in Philadelphia. But Karl's personal life wasn't my concern and I was happy to leave it that way.

I sipped my coffee. Stronger than I liked, with grounds peppering the surface. Not someone accustomed to brewing his own.

"Your father and I had a deal," Karl said. "He was not to call on Hope without notifying me first, and any debt we had, we'd repay together."

"Did Hope know that?"

He shook his head and set his cup down, untouched.

"I don't believe my father would put Hope in any real danger. He knows she's under council protection, and he brought this arrangement to my attention, which would suggest he isn't doing anything underhanded. I discussed the job with them both, and I'm convinced it's a task suited to her talents."

"What's she doing?"

As I told him, his face darkened. When I finished, he let out an oath, then sat there, not moving a muscle. His jaw was set so tight that, if I had werewolf hearing, I suspected I'd have heard his teeth grinding.

"I can't see that it's significantly different from the tasks Hope undertakes for the council," I said. "Except, perhaps, in scale. You don't have a quarrel with her council work—you were the one who brought her to them."

"Not the same thing."

"If you mean because she's committing criminal acts with this gang, she cannot be held responsible—"

"My point exactly."

"I don't understand."

"No, you don't, but I'm not sure I can say the same for your father. If he gave Hope this job, knowing what—" He rose. "I'm going to Miami. Put an end to this before it goes any further. Where's Hope?"

"First tell me what you plan to do, so we can discuss your options with regard to my father." Before he could argue, I went on. "As a member of the Pack, you represent the Pack. Any action you take against my father will be seen as the Pack acting against the Cabal. Is that the message you wish to send?"

His lips curled and parted, and I knew he was about to say that he'd send any message he damned well pleased, but he caught himself, realizing, perhaps, that such an approach would not be in his best interests.

"I'm getting Hope out of there," he said. "That's all I care about. Unless your father or his people interfere, there won't be any trouble. I'll deal with your father later—a civilized discussion about finding a civilized way to free Hope from our debt."

"It's my understanding that this isn't only about what she owes him. She's doing this of her own free will, and you might find she's not so easily dissuaded."

"Oh, she'll be dissuaded—if I have to pick her up and carry her out of Miami."

"Ah."

"Now where can I find her?"

I hesitated. While I was reluctant to send Karl tearing down there without knowing why he so urgently wanted Hope out, I knew I wasn't getting an explanation. Refuse, and he'd still fly to Miami, then make matters worse hunting her down himself.

"I don't have the address of the apartment where she's staying, but the gang owns a club called Easy Rider."

As he nodded, I saw Paige, still wearing her coat, in the open doorway, hand raised to knock. She greeted Karl, who exchanged a few impatient pleasantries with her before brushing past.

"Did I just hear him say he's taking Hope out of Miami whether she wants to leave or not?"

"So it would seem, but he was clearly not in the mood to discuss it further and I didn't want him racing around Miami looking for her."

"Should we call her? Warn her?"

I shook my head. "It would only make matters worse. As angry as Karl is, I trust him to be discreet." I paused. "But we should probably clear our schedules. Just in case."

HOPE

SWEET SIXTEEN

Our target was a sweet-sixteen party. When Guy first mentioned it, images of pillow-fighting, PJ-clad teenage girls sprang to mind, and the only profitable crime I could imagine was kidnapping, which would have had me on the phone to Benicio. But as he'd unveiled the plan, it became clear this was no slumber party, but a coming out worthy of a queen.

I'd heard of such parties in society circles, always described with the contemptuous horror the upper-crust reserved for the excesses of the nouveau riche. There was always a grand historical theme—Roman, medieval, Arabian. Tonight it was Egypt.

The party was held in a modest hall, one probably used mostly for weddings. Big enough to hold a couple of hundred guests, simple and security-free. This was obviously where they'd tried to cut costs, though it was the only place they had.

There were two Sphinxes—accuracy be damned—sculpted in ice and flanking the door. The pyramids were papier-mâché, and quickly relocated when guests realized how much dance floor space they took up. The mummies were, one hopes, also papier-mâché. Propped up in caskets, they wore masks and held trays of masks for the guests who wished to partake. Some of the young men and parents did, but few of the girls—there was no sense getting your makeup professionally done only to cover it.

The belle of the ball was a chubby, newly minted sixteen-year-old dressed as Cleopatra. On a litter borne by four young men in loincloths, she was carried through the crowd to the front, where her parents waited beside a silver bowl stuffed with envelopes. The guest of honor had requested congratulations in cash only, to fund a yearlong world tour before she went to college.

There was a single gift—a brand-new Jaguar convertible, rolled in through two huge rear doors as Daddy handed the keys to his squealing daughter. Watching the spectacle, I suspected those doors were the real reason her parents had rented the cheap hall. Having their daughter walk outside to see her new car just wouldn't have had the same impact as this tacky game-show moment.

The girl beamed as she was squired about the dance floor. She was Daddy's princess and nothing was too good for her. How would any other night—or any other man—ever compare?

We were about to make this night memorable for a very different reason.

I watched it all from a storage room above the hall. The crew had prepared for this days ago, after finding the party mentioned in the local society pages. There were four of these hidey-holes, each with a newly drilled spy hole, each manned by a crew member. Mine was a tiny room that stunk of stale cigarette smoke.

The party was in full swing when Jaz slipped in and crept over to sit beside me.

"So, did you get a sweet sixteen like this?" he whispered.

I laughed. "If I'd even suggested it, my parents would have sat me down for a long talk about the responsibilities of privilege. No one I knew got a party like this one. It's a different kind of 'society.' "

"Old money versus new?"

"Something like that. Debutante balls? Yes. Egyptian extravaganzas with papier-mâché pyramids and a bowl full of money? God, no."

"Debutante? You?" He grinned. "Say it wasn't so."

"What?" I waved at my T-shirt and jeans, grimy with storeroom dust. "I don't look like one? I'll have you know I can quickstep with the best of them, sir."

He laughed, earning a mock glare. "Sorry. I just can't picture you..."

The sentence trailed off as he watched the party below, then turned to me.

"No, actually, I can. You have that...I don't know. Aura, I guess." A small smile. "Even with dirt on your cheeks." His head tilted. "I bet you were something. Nothing like the rest of them."

"If you mean because I wasn't fair-haired and blue-eyed—yes, I did stand out a wee bit."

"Nah, not that." He shifted, sliding closer. "You'd still have stood out among all those—" he waved at the party below, "—empty girls. They might have been dripping in jewels, but I bet you shone the most."

My cheeks heated. I'm accustomed to flattery—the smooth, meaningless compliments that pass for greeting in the circles I'd grown up in and, later, the too-practiced, too-polished sweet talk of rich boys. But Jaz's words—so sincere in their inelegance—made me feel like I *was* sixteen again.

"I'd love to have been there," he said. "Of course, I'd have been serving champagne instead of drinking it."

"That's okay. There were a couple of times during my season when I ended up in the garden with one of the servers."

He grinned. "I can see that. Society guys really wouldn't be your type."

"Some of them are very nice but, in general, no."

"Well, if Guy had gone with his first plan, you'd have seen me in a snazzy little white jacket and bow-tie, with a tray in my hand." He winked. "Maybe bring back some memories."

"Guy wanted you on the waitstaff?"

"That was the original plan, before he decided it was too ballsy even for him." He slid over to sit beside me, leaning against my side, voice dropping another notch as his arm rubbed against mine. "To tell the truth, I was kind of hoping I would get to play waiter. Not just for the added buzz...though I wouldn't have minded that."

His head dropped forward, eyes a few inches from mine and, in that impulsive shared grin, I knew he'd guessed I enjoyed a "buzz" as much as he did. I didn't care. It felt good not to care.

"What I was really hoping for, though," he continued, leaning against me as he whispered, "was the chance to make a little extra on the side. Lift a pair of gold cuff links here, a diamond tennis bracelet there, maybe a—" He lifted a silver-banded watch and peered at the face. "Cartier. Damn, that's nice."

I glanced down at my bare wrist. "How'd you—?" I remembered him moving closer, rubbing against me, and I let out a laugh. "You're good."

"Thank you." He turned the watch over in his hands. "An older model, but in excellent condition. No scratches on the face. No engraving on the back. I bet I could flip this for two, three hundred."

"Try twenty bucks. It's a Cartier, but a cheap one. I got it for graduating high school."

"Must be nice. Know what I got for graduating high school? Well, I didn't actually graduate, but if I had, I'm sure there would have been a lovely Timex in it for me. I still say this is worth at least a hundred, for the name value alone, but I could be persuaded to let it go for less . . . to the right girl. Perhaps in exchange for a token of appreciation for my amazing talents?"

"Like a smack upside the head for stealing from me?"

His eyes glinted and he bared his teeth in a grin that sent a delicious shiver through me. "Perhaps next time. Tonight—" He waved at the party below. "Tonight is for genteel, civilized solutions. Tonight, you are the sixteen-year-old debutante and I'm the cad who swiped your watch and is holding it for ransom." He slid around to face me and dangled the watch between us. "So what would I get?"

"A smack upside the head."

He chuckled.

"But, if it's genteel solutions we're looking for . . ."

I leaned forward and kissed him. His lips parted against mine in a kiss as sweet as any I'd hoped for when I *had* been sixteen, fending off insistent hands and wet lips, dreaming of something a little more . . . genteel.

We kissed until a noise from the hall made me pull back. I opened the door and peeked out. It was just Max making his rounds of the second floor. An exchange of thumbs-up and he went on his way.

Jaz still sat where I'd left him. "I don't suppose you have any more jewelry I can steal."

I took back my watch. "I do, but you're not going to get it—or find it—that easily."

"No?" That devilish glint returned to his eyes. "Don't be so sure. I'm a master magician—"

My phone vibrated. I answered without speaking, as instructed.

"Five minutes to show time," Bianca said. "Is Jaz up there?"

I relayed the message to Jaz. He looked as if he was trying to decide whether we had time to pick up where we'd left off. I settled the question by laying on my stomach and peering through the peephole at the party.

Jaz stretched over me, his body grazing mine. "They have no idea what's coming. Supernaturals could take over the damned world if they wanted, and humans couldn't do a thing to stop it."

"Nah. Too much work."

"True. Let them keep the bureaucracy; we'll just reap the rewards."

Still crouched over my back, he moved his lips to my ear and used the excuse to brush along me, groin rubbing against my rear.

"See anything you like?" he whispered.

"Hmm?"

"Necklace, bracelet...new watch?"

I gave a soft laugh and shook my head.

"Oh, come on." He pointed to a fur-trimmed stole on a chair. "Dead animals?" His finger moved to a marble bust on the buffet table. "Butt-ugly statue?"

"No, thank you."

"No? How about the keys to that sweet new ride? Might be your only chance to trash a Jag. Say the word and it's yours."

I rolled over, still under him, looked up and knew he was only half joking. If I asked for something—for anything—he'd get it for me. Steal it for me. I fought a shiver of excitement.

His mouth moved down to mine—

My cell phone vibrated, bouncing along the floor.

"Time to move," he said with a sigh. A moment's hesitation, then he got up. "But I *am* going to get you something. A surprise."

WE SNUCK DOWN the rear stairs and met Guy in the back room with Sonny and Max. We five would be on the front line, while Bianca, Rodriguez and Tony worked from the wings.

"Outfits there," Guy said, pointing at a pile of staff uniforms as we walked in. "Masks over there. You have five minutes and counting. Pull 'em off and get 'em on. Faith, there's a closet for privacy—"

"Here's fine."

Sonny tossed me the smallest server uniform. I faced the corner, peeled off my T-shirt and pulled on the uniform top. It smelled of knockoff perfume with a faint touch of body odor. As for the former wearer, presumably she was tied up somewhere. Bianca, Max and Tony had been luring servers out for the past twenty minutes, getting their uniforms. It wouldn't be long before someone noticed a marked decrease in waitstaff.

"Sonny, here." Guy handed him one of the masquerade half-masks. "You and Max go. Your trays are right around the corner. Jaz, stop fussing with the damned tie, get out there and start charming. Faith—"

"Stay with you. I know."

He handed me my mask, and I put it on. It covered the top half of my face. I blinked, getting accustomed to it.

When the others were gone, Guy snapped on a mask, tugged at his tie, then rolled his shoulders. From the waves rolling off him, it wasn't anxiety he was fighting, but anticipation. There was probably no one in the gang who didn't get off on this, to some degree. That's why they were here—to exercise their powers for profit and, yes, for fun.

The swirl of chaos . . . about to turn into a maelstrom. I looked away so Guy wouldn't see my reaction.

"You ready, Faith?"

"Yes, boss."

He smacked a hand against my back. "You're doing just fine. We're about to give those talents of yours a real workout. You know what you're doing?"

"I'm your bodyguard against chaos."

A deep laugh, all traces of the reserved leader vanishing. This was Guy in his element.

"Ready to have some fun?"

"Yes, sir."

He put his hand against my back and guided me from the room.

HOPE

CRY HAVOC

The appearance of waitstaff in masks had caused little stir, even among the servers themselves. All were contract employees, and probably didn't even notice their coworkers had changed. The girls noticed, though.

Soon each of the guys was surrounded by a coterie of admirers, cajoling them to take off their masks. Even Sonny was playing it up, making motions toward his shirt and, I guessed, offering the teens the choice between having him remove that or the mask.

Jaz had the birthday girl in his circle and was doing an impromptu magic show complete with sexy smiles aimed her way. Her parents watched indulgently, whispering to each other, probably trying to decide what kind of tip the catering service should get for this unexpected extra.

"Stay close," Guy murmured as we headed for the front of the room, where the hood of the Jag protruded through the doors. A man stepped in front of us and fixed me with a sloppy grin.

"Did they save you for the second shift, cutie?" He waved his glass my way. "I'll take another Scotch. And there's a twenty in it if you just bring the bottle."

Guy flicked his fingers in a knockback spell and the man stumbled.

"Hey," he said, but it was halfhearted, as if he wasn't sure whether the booze or Guy was to blame.

We were hailed several more times as we crossed the room, but we ignored the summons and the huffs of outrage when we didn't stop. As we drew close to the car, Guy took a running leap and landed on the hood with a crack.

The room went silent as everyone stared at the masked server standing on the Jag's hood. Yet scarcely a chaos vibe rippled from the crowd, the guests certain there was a logical explanation.

"Ladies and gentlemen," Guy called. "I know some of you have already been enjoying the magic of our friends, but let me assure you, that's only a taste of what's to come."

Guy shifted and the car's hood cracked again under his weight. The general swirl of confusion swelled into anger. The birthday girl's father strode forward.

"Young man, get off that—"

Guy's fingers flew out in a knockback spell and the man staggered.

"I'm sorry," Guy said. "We must ask that there be no interruptions during tonight's performance."

Not a single cry of horror or disbelief greeted Guy's display. Instead, the anger wave subsided into murmurs and nervous giggles, as if the spell proved this was indeed a performance. The girl's father started forward again, face mottled with anger.

"I don't know what kind of stunt—"

He flew clear off his feet, sailing backward into the crowd. Now came the gasps, but scattered, most still convinced this was part of the show. What else could it be?

"And now, if my lovely assistant will help me get started . . ."

I walked toward the silver money bowl, aware of every eye on me. I concentrated on the vibes flowing past, searching for a clear, negative impulse directed my way. Out of the corner of my eye, I saw Jaz step away from his admirers, ready to jump in if anyone tried to stop me. No one did.

I reached the bowl.

One man strode forward. "What are you—?"

Guy hit him with a knockback. "I know she *is* lovely, but we must ask you to admire the performers from afar, for their safety . . . and yours."

I lifted the bowl. Jaz fell into step behind me. That wasn't part of the plan, but Guy's expression didn't change.

A buzz of unease rippled through the guests now. I caught the odd half-formed thought, weak and disjointed, the negativity too low for me to pick up more than snippets of "Is this...? Shouldn't someone...? What's going...?"

Guy took the bowl in one hand and offered me the other, helping me onto the car.

"Money." Guy's voice echoed through the hall as he lifted the bowl. "It makes the world go round. Or so they say. For folks like you, this—" he ripped open an envelope and pulled out a handful of hundreds, "—is the source of your power. Your only power."

A buzz of discomfort as some people glanced at their purses and pockets, thinking not of money, but of cell phones. No one took them out—they were just reassuring themselves that they were there, like sidearms, protecting them if this turned out to be more than a show.

"Where's our birthday girl?" Guy called.

Her friends parted around her.

"This is a lovely party, sweetheart. But if your daddy really loved you, he'd be giving you self-defense lessons instead of sports cars. Because this—" he flung the bills, "—doesn't protect you nearly as well as you think."

Now the phones came out. Guy wheeled on the closest woman to us, as she lifted one to her ear.

"Have a call to make? That's rather rude, but go ahead."

She pulled the phone from her ear and frowned at it.

"No signal? Handy things, reception blockers. Good for ensuring no annoying ring-tones interrupt a show. I'm afraid you'd need to step outside to use that, though I wouldn't recommend it. My performers hate to lose their audience."

One man strode toward the closest door. Guy waited until he was two steps from it, then hit him with an energy bolt that knocked him to his knees, gasping, as sparks flew.

When a group of teenage boys ran for the front door, a cloud of red smoke appeared in their path, twisting and writhing. A demon's head shot from the smoke. The boys fell back, screaming. A brave one raced for the next exit. Another red cloud. Then a huge dog's head lunged from it, snarling and slavering. Trip-wire illusions—sorcerer spells that activated when someone drew near.

Guy leaned down to me. "Cry havoc."

"And let loose the dogs of war," I murmured.

"And war it is, Faith," he said, barely audible over the screaming and shouting, as illusions sprang from every exit. "Never forget that. It's us versus them. They tell us not to make waves, to stay quiet, to buy peace by hiding." He met my gaze. "Do you like hiding, Faith?"

Without waiting for an answer, he spun and waved his hands, not murmuring his spell but shouting it. Sparks arced from his fingertips. Below us, Max cast and fog swirled through the room.

A vision flashed. A gun pulled from a pocket.

"Watch out!" I shouted to Guy as I spun, pinpointing the source. "There!"

The man didn't finish pulling out the gun before Guy hit him with an energy bolt. As he went down, Jaz tackled him. Another flash. This one auditory, little more than a snarl of rage. I yelled and pointed. Max flung a knockback spell at a woman as she ran for the buffet table, probably hoping to find a weapon there. Sonny took her down before the fog swallowed them.

Streamers started going up in flames as Bianca—dressed in black and nearly invisible—circled the room, setting them alight with her fingers. Guy and Max kept casting. Nothing more than special effects—fog and sparks and colored lights—but from the screams that filled the room, they thought the building was on fire, and ready to collapse around them.

I drank it all in—the horror, the panic, the terror. Chaos, sweeter and purer than any I'd ever known. For once, even the deepest part of me felt no guilt. As I watched the partygoers racing about, I saw the friends who'd abandoned me after my breakdown, when I'd first started seeing visions. In their screams, I heard adults who'd known me from childhood, whispering behind their hands "She was never quite right after that. Her poor mother..."

Guy tapped my arm, telling me it was time to move to the next phase. I stepped to the edge of the hood, ready to jump. Jaz swung over and extended a hand to help me.

"Like mice," Jaz whispered in my ear, gesturing at the partygoers. "See how they run. And for what? Fog and illusions and sparkly lights. Can you imagine what they'd do if we used real magic?"

His gaze met mine, sharp and hungry despite the lighthearted lilt in his words. Behind the mask, his pupils dilated and I could hear his breath quick and shallow as my own. Excitement. No, more than excitement. Arousal.

I looked up into those glittering eyes. Jaz stepped closer. His hand slid to the back of my head as he bent down, our masks rustling as they brushed, our lips—

A jolt and Jaz stumbled as Guy slapped his back.

"Save it," Guy said.

Jaz's head whipped around, eyes narrowing, lip curling as if ready to spit something at the interruption. Then he went still, his eyes half closing, the look fading.

"Yes, boss." He lowered his lips to my ear. "What a spoilsport, huh? Expects us to *work*." His finger slid up my jawline and tickled my earlobe. "Later?"

I twisted to look up at him and our gazes locked.

"Please," I said.

A sharp intake of breath and a final glimmer of frustrated lust. Then he dodged a second smack. We started forward, following Guy.

We found our target by the punch fountain. Cleo's father stood there, alone, fists clenched, glaring around the room, as if that could fix matters, too enraged to even think of protecting his daughter.

Jaz's hand slid from my waist and he was gone, circling wide around the man.

Guy stopped in front of the girl's father. Not so much as a glance around to make sure Jaz was in position, trusting he'd be there when needed.

"You!" The father waved a hand, as if clearing the fog. "You won't—"

"Get away with this?" Guy sighed. "So unoriginal. And, sadly, so wrong."

"The police are probably on the way right now."

Guy cocked his head. "I don't hear any sirens." His voice lowered conspiratorially. "Do you know why? Because we're using the best soundproofing money *can't* buy."

A thought flew from the father, as fast and sharp as a knife blade, and I only had time to start a warning, but Guy was ready and grabbed the man's hand as he went to throw a punch.

The man stiffened as the barrel of a gun dug into his lower back. He glanced over his shoulder at Jaz.

"So you know what that is?" Guy said. "We normally avoid guns. Too easy to misuse. But this one came courtesy of your guests. You really should have tighter security. These days, you can't be too careful."

"What do you want?" the man asked through gritted teeth.

"We already have what we want." Guy lifted the bowl he'd been casually toting in one hand. "Before we go, though, I wanted to congratulate you on raising such a philanthropic daughter."

The man's face screwed up. "What?"

"Philanthropic. It means—"

"I know what it means."

"Do you? That's not what I hear. Your family isn't known for sharing with the less fortunate, but that's about to change."

"What the hell are you—?"

"Tomorrow, in the *Miami Herald,* you'll find a small piece announcing your daughter's decision to donate half her sweet-sixteen party money to women's education in third-world countries."

"You're crazy. My daughter isn't going to—"

"Oh, but she is." He hefted the bowl. "You have my word that the charity will receive half the money in this bowl come morning... unless it's reported stolen."

"What?"

"If you report the robbery, I can't donate the money, can I? But that article will still run, saying your daughter intended to make the donation. That won't look good to the police—you saying someone 'stole' the money that your daughter promised to charity. They're going to think *you* took it, especially if they get an anonymous tip claiming you weren't happy with your daughter's plan."

"You—you can't—" he sputtered. "Everyone saw you take that bowl. I have over a hundred witnesses—"

"—to performance art gone horribly awry. You will apologize profusely to your guests and swear to put this troupe of actors out of business. Then you'll give your daughter her half of the money—from your wallet—and have a heart-to-heart with her on the obligations the wealthy have to support the less fortunate, which is why you contributed half the gift money in her name."

"That's crazy. I won't—"

Guy leaned forward as Jaz dug the gun in. "Oh, I think you will. You've seen what we can do, and that's only a taste. Trust me, you don't want the full lesson."

He cast two fog spells in quick succession, then strode toward the Jag, Jaz and me following. Another jump onto the hood, a quick walk over the roof and we were outside.

Guy called Bianca and told her to meet us back at the Rider. Then Jaz held the knapsack while Guy dumped in the envelopes.

"Party time, boss?" Jaz asked. He plucked out a handful of envelopes. Guy smacked his hand, and Jaz dropped all but one and stuffed it into his pocket.

Guy only laughed. "Yeah, it's party time."

HOPE

TEQUILA SHOTS

We dumped the getaway car, switched to a crew vehicle and met the others in the lot behind the Rider.

Jaz grabbed my hand, dragging me along as he jogged up behind Sonny. He draped his arm around his friend's shoulders.

"Party time, bro."

Tony looked over. "Seriously?"

Jaz hooked a thumb at Guy, still behind us. "Boss says so."

Bianca dropped back to walk with Guy. Jaz laced his fingers with mine and swung our arms. I laughed, almost expecting him to start skipping.

"Know what that means, Faith? Party time?"

"I have no idea."

"It means the Rider is ours. Open bar. No rules. No obligations."

Tony strode up on my other side. "No making nice to the tourists."

"No making eyes at forty-year-old humans," Max said.

Jaz grinned. "Nothing to do but party until the sun comes up."

"Then collect our share, go home and party some more."

Max and Tony threw open the doors and we walked in, the guys still laughing, so boisterous you'd think they'd already had a few hours at the open bar.

"Hey, boss?" Jaz called back. "You joining us?"

"Unlike some of us, I have responsibilities, Jasper. Money to count. A donation to make..."

"You're really cutting the take in half?"

Guy smiled. "More or less."

"I'll help you," Bianca said.

Tony dropped back beside her. "Do you have to, Bee? I was hoping you'd come play."

"Guy needs help—"

"No, I don't. You go, Bee. Boss's orders. Have fun. Get sloshed. Enjoy yourself."

After one lingering look at Guy, Bianca let Tony lead her into the club.

THERE WERE A handful of high tables next to the dance floor. The best seats in the house and always full. But when we strolled in, bouncers were already clearing two.

A server approached. "Mr. Benoit just called—"

"And said give us whatever we want," Jaz cut in. To me, "You drink tequila?"

I didn't, not straight, but I said yes. Hope Adams might not down tequila shots, but I was sure Faith Edmonds would.

Jaz ordered a bottle and Max asked for Scotch.

"Where's Sonny?" Jaz asked.

"Took off," Tony said. "Bathroom, maybe."

We settled in, Jaz, Tony and me at one table, Bianca, Max and Rodriguez at the other.

The server returned.

Jaz stared at the bottle of cheap tequila. "Holy shit, you trying to poison us? The good stuff. The *best* stuff."

Her gaze darted around the table. "Mr. Benoit didn't say—"

"Then call him. Or, better yet . . ."

He was lifting his cell phone when Sonny appeared, a bottle of Patron Silver tequila in one hand and Glenlivet single-malt Scotch in the other.

"I didn't trust them to fill the order right," he said.

"Bro, you are a lifesaver. Grab a seat—" Jaz looked at the three chairs, already taken.

He pushed his chair back and tugged my arm, patting his lap. I obliged as Sonny passed the Scotch to Max, then opened the tequila.

"Guy is going to kick your asses," Tony said, waving at the bottle. We glanced at Bianca, waiting for her to tell us to stop.

"Jaz can handle it," she said, mouth tight as she passed Max her glass.

"Sure, I can." Jaz grinned, the subtext—that Guy wouldn't chastise him for anything—flying over his head. "We deserve this." He handed me the first tequila shot. "*Faith* deserves this. When's the last time we pulled off a big job without a hitch? Without one scratch or one close call? We owe that to our newest recruit. The minute someone even *thought* of causing trouble, she knew it. How cool is that?"

"How fucking *useful* is that?" Rodriguez said, shaking his head. "Do you know how many times I could have used your power, Faith? Would have saved me a whole lotta time in juvvie."

"But then you wouldn't have gotten all that special high-tech training," Jaz said. "And put it to such good use."

A round of laughter. I glanced around, unaccustomed to talking so openly about my powers, but no one was close enough to overhear. With the booming music, we could barely hear each other.

Jaz lifted his shot glass and whispered, "Ready?" Then, ignoring the salt and lime on the plate, we downed them together. The tequila hit my gut like a fireball and I struggled not to gasp. Jaz's arms vibrated around me as he laughed, silently, not giving me away.

"So you really can read minds?" Tony asked as he finished his shot.

"Only chaotic thoughts. Sometimes."

Jaz shook his head. "*Most* times, judging by that demonstration at the hall."

Tony leaned forward. "So what am I thinking now?"

"Whatever it is, you don't really mean it. For example, you can think you'd like to strangle Jaz, but unless you mean it, I won't detect it."

"What if it's just wishful thinking?" Sonny said.

Jaz snatched the bottle from him and they parried insults for a minute.

"Cut it out, you two," Rodriguez called over. "I want to hear more about this power. How about we all think something bad, and see if Faith picks it up? We'll—"

I didn't hear the rest, caught up in the vision of a voluptuous redhead, writhing, bound to a bed. I followed it to a red-haired woman on the dance floor, then tracked it back to the source.

"Tony!" I shuddered. "Please. I think I need brain soap after that."

"What did you hear?" Jaz asked.

"Not hear. See. In living color." I glanced meaningfully at the red-head.

"Shit," Tony said.

"You doubted her?" Jaz smacked Tony's arm. "Dumb ass. I warned you. So what was he thinking about the girl?"

I shook my head.

Sonny waved the bottle. "Another couple of these and she'll tell us."

"Shit, guys," Tony muttered. "I was just joking."

"Uh-uh," Jaz said. "Remember what she said. If you aren't serious, she doesn't hear it. Or see it, apparently."

Sonny refilled our shot glasses. Tony gulped his, then took a second. I lifted mine.

"You don't have to drink it," Jaz whispered. "If you don't, I won't. No one will say anything."

My head was still spinning from the first, and I knew this one would take me over the edge. But I wanted to drink it. Hope Adams wouldn't. One shot—sipped and probably in a margarita—would have been her limit. But tonight I didn't want to be Hope. Didn't want to be twenty-seven years old, happy in my dead-end job, dumped by a middle-aged werewolf, struggling to make my family proud of me, staving off the demonic urges by sipping chaos, never satisfied, never full. Tonight, I wanted to be Faith Edmonds, twenty-one, no job, no responsibilities, chugging back chaos like tequila shots, getting sloshed in a nightclub, on the lap of the hottest guy in the room.

I downed the shot.

The room reeled. Jaz gulped his. His green eyes glittered with the buzz, and his arms tightened around me as he nuzzled my neck, hands sliding down my hips.

"Jesus," Tony said. "Not wasting any time with the new girl, are you?"

"He barely let her get in the front door before he pounced," Sonny said. "Making sure she didn't have time to check out her options."

"Jump before anyone else gets a chance, huh?" Tony said, kicking him under the table.

Jaz lifted his head from my neck. "After what she just saw in your head, I don't think you *had* a chance."

The others laughed and kept on Tony, razzing him, but Jaz's attention returned to me, his hands rubbing my arms, then sliding down my legs, his whispers telling me he was well on the way to being drunk. I leaned back against him and lapped it up.

"What time is it?" he murmured.

I sputtered a laugh. "Why? Is there someplace you need to be?"

"No, just wondering. I'd check myself but..." His fingers slid to the inside of my thighs. "My hands are busy."

I sighed and lifted my arm. There, on my wrist, was a sparkling new gold and silver Cartier.

"Holy shit."

"You said yours was a cheapie." He nibbled my earlobe. "You deserve better."

I lifted the watch, admiring it through the haze of tequila. "It's gorgeous."

"Yours is in your purse."

"Thank you."

"You're welcome." His nibbles moved down the side of my neck, making me shiver. "But I hope that's not all I get."

I twisted to kiss him over my shoulder.

"Uh-uh."

He put his hands under my armpits and lifted me from his lap and for a second, my fogged brain scrambled to figure out what I'd done wrong. Then he turned me around to face him.

"Ah." I swung my leg over his lap, straddling him. "Better?"

He put his hands on my rear and boosted me closer. "Much. Now, as you were about to do..."

I brought my lips up to his. Any other time, that would have been all I'd have done—a quick buss with a teasing promise that he'd get more later...when we weren't in a nightclub, on the edge of a crowded dance floor, sitting at a table surrounded by his friends. I'm a private person, and it doesn't get much more public than that. But my brain still buzzed from the tequila and my body buzzed from the heist.

I kissed him the way I would have kissed him back there, if Guy hadn't interrupted—a deep, hungry kiss, legs wrapping around his hips, body pressed against his, hands twining in his curls. He kissed me back as if this was exactly what he'd hoped for, his mouth crushing mine, tongue sliding in.

I dimly heard the catcalls of the others. "I'll have what he's having." "Get a room!" "Hell, no, stay here and we'll clear off the table."

Jaz just kept kissing me and rubbing against me, so hard I gasped and arched up, breaking the kiss. His hands wrapped in my hair and he pulled me in again, and everything around me disappeared, sucked into the vacuum of the unbelievable vibes pulsing off him, like nothing I'd ever felt before, not anger or hatred or anything I could put a name to, but pure, unadulterated chaos. When I looked into his eyes, I saw fire—beautiful, devouring flames of chaos and hunger and need, and something deeper that told me *I* was what he hungered for, what he needed and—

The world went black. A snarl echoed through the darkness. Fangs flashed. The smell of blood, then the splatter of it, thick and hot. The brush of fur against my skin, dark as the night around it.

I ricocheted from the vision, breaking the kiss. My gaze tripped over the crowd, searching for the face I knew was out there: Karl.

Jaz's hands slid to the back of my head, and he pulled my ear to his lips.

"Sorry," he whispered, breath coming hard, words disjointed. "Too fast. Not here. Got carried away."

"It's not—I thought I heard my parents' ring tone." I pulled my personal cell phone from my pocket and flipped it open. "Shit, shit, shit!"

Jaz rubbed my arm. "Pretend you didn't hear it."

"I can't. I'm supposed to check in every night. After last year, I'm on a very tight leash. I miss curfew, even down here, and I'm cut off."

"Better call back then . . . from someplace quieter. Come on. We'll find—"

"No," I said as I slid off his lap. "You stay. I'll be right back."

HOPE

HUNGRY

I crossed the road and slipped into a back alley. A blast of night air knocked away the last haze of tequila. Karl had seen me with Jaz, on his lap, drunk and making a fool of—

I rubbed my face. I was twenty-seven, single and entitled to go out, get wasted and get laid.

I sensed Karl's silent approach. I braced myself, and turned. And he was there, like so many times before, arriving unannounced, simply . . . appearing—in a parking lot, a grocery store, my living room. I'd glimpse the werewolf vision, look up and he'd be there, acting as if he'd just stepped out for a minute and returned.

As he strode down the alley, the shadows hid all but his shape. It didn't matter. His image was ingrained in my brain. I glanced at the shadow and saw that handsome face, jawline a little too strong, nose a little too sharp, but the flaws only adding an edge, a masculinity that belied the perfect grooming, the designer clothes. A wolf in banker's clothing, I'd tease, and he'd laugh and make a wry joke at his own expense, always the first to poke fun at the image he cultivated.

But tonight there was no laugh. No über-confident smile. His face was a stone mask, his gray-blue eyes as cold as if he'd been striding up to a stranger. I saw that, and my last glimmer of hope guttered out.

I tried to read him, but when he was angry, he kept his thoughts a swirl, no image or words concrete enough for me to pluck out.

"Sorry to tear you away," he said, each word clipped.

I forced a grin and plucked at my sweaty T-shirt. "That's okay. I could use a few minutes of fresh air."

"You're drunk."

"Because, naturally, that's the only explanation for being on a guy's lap in a nightclub. Actually, I'm not drunk. Working on it, though. What I was doing was following orders. Yours, if I recall."

"Orders?"

"Last thing you said to me. Before good-bye." I frowned. "Or did you say good-bye? Come to think of it, I'm not sure. But I know you did say you thought I should date other supernaturals, more my own age. He's a couple of years younger, but he is a supernatural, and half *your* age, so I figure that's close enough."

I wanted to stop. I imagined what my mother would do in this situation—and I wanted to be like her and to rise above it. But seeing him, I was back to that morning, in that grove, feeling his words like knives. And all I could think about now was stabbing him back.

I wished that night in the pool had never happened. I wanted things back the way they'd been, Karl back the way he'd been.

I imagined how this scene would have played out without that night. I could see it, Karl luring me off the dance floor, then slipping ahead and cornering me—literally cornering me, as he loved to do, backing me against a wall and getting so close all I could see, hear and smell was him and all I could think about was getting him close enough to feel him, to taste him.

He'd corner me, then tease me about the "boy" in the nightclub, daring me to give him five minutes and I'd forget there'd ever *been* a boy in a nightclub.

I could imagine his voice, arrogant and self-mocking at the same time, his tone light as if to say, "You can take me up on it if you want or we can pretend I'm only kidding."

I wanted that back—that banter, that lighthearted seduction, *that* Karl, not the cold, scowling man three feet away, his gaze shunting to the alley mouth as if counting the seconds until he could escape.

"Tell Benicio to find you another job," I said.

He frowned, brow creasing.

"I don't know how he got in touch with you; I didn't give him the number. I'm sorry if he dragged you back from Europe, but that's something you need to take up with him. You aren't needed here ... or wanted."

His shoulders tightened. Ego. That's all it was—all it ever was with Karl. He'd pursued me, caught me and dumped me, and now he was annoyed because I wasn't pining for him.

"Benicio didn't call me," he said. "I'm here because he *should* have. This is my debt."

"No, it's mine, and I have it under control."

"So I saw." His gaze slid in the direction of the club. "I suppose that's one way to get information from a man."

My fists clenched and I longed to smack him. Hit him as hard as I could, and make it hurt as much as he'd hurt me. But it wouldn't hurt him at all. Nothing did.

I managed to smile and shrug. "Whatever works. That's what you taught me. Go on home, Karl, wherever home is these days. This doesn't concern you. Nothing I do concerns you anymore. You made that clear."

He had the gall to look surprised. "I never said—"

"It was a long hunt, and probably not worth the reward, but you finally caught your prey. Congratulations, you're every bit the irresistible stud you think you are. Now leave me alone. Please."

I circled past him, heading back to the club. He grabbed my arm. "Hope—"

He stopped, head jerking around, following some noise I couldn't hear. His fingers tightened and he started down the alley, fingers still wrapped around my elbow. I dug in my heels. With his strength, it was the equivalent of a two-year-old balking, but the jolt was enough for him to realize I wasn't following willingly.

He shot me an impatient scowl, annoyed that I should object to being dragged deeper into a dark alley. As I looked back, a shadow stretched over the street-lit alley mouth. Someone *was* coming. I shook Karl off and brushed past him, getting farther down the passage on my own.

Two club-goers slipped into the alley. A noise from Karl that I knew he'd call a mutter, but was indistinguishable from a dog's low warning growl. He aimed a glare at the intruders, jaw tensing, and I knew he'd love nothing more than to stride down there and shoo them out—by the scruff of their necks if necessary. He was in this alley, therefore it was, for the moment, his territory. But, like the growl, he'd never admit to the impulse. He was a civilized man, not a half-wolf savage, and anyone who made that mistake would be quickly corrected.

So he settled for glowering at the intruders and pretending he felt no inclination to tear down there and kick their asses. They completed their transaction—drugs, I presume—and left. He watched them go, then turned to me, and when he did, the anger—all the anger—had faded from his eyes and he just looked tired.

"I need to discuss this with you, Hope, but it can wait until morning. Go back to your . . . friend."

I thought of returning to Jaz, but the evening's high had evaporated, and I wouldn't find it again.

"No, let's get this over with," I said.

I TEXT MESSAGED Jaz, saying I was in trouble with my parents and had to get back to my apartment. He wouldn't be happy, but I'd deal with that tomorrow . . . after I'd handled this and sent Karl on a fast plane home.

I told Karl what I'd done.

"I give him ten minutes to be at your apartment door."

"He won't."

Karl snorted. "You think he's just going to let it go at that? He—"

"He won't because he doesn't have my address."

"No?"

"No."

A grunt of something I couldn't make out. He led me into a lot and toward a trio of cars—a Porsche, a Ferrari and a Lexus. I glanced at the Lexus. Nothing sporty or eye-catching—just sleek, powerful and luxurious. A banker's car. I walked over to it. Not a rental sticker to be seen. I stopped at the passenger door. A blip of the key fob and the door opened. I got inside.

"This probably isn't something we should discuss in a public place," I said as he started the car. "Where's your hotel?"

"I don't have one. We can talk at your apartment."

I tried to think of a way out of this that wouldn't sound petty. When I couldn't find one, I gave him directions.

WE DROVE A couple of miles in silence, then Karl said, "Back there in the alley. What you said about that morning, about what *I* said . . . it wasn't like that."

"You didn't say it?"

He readjusted his grip on the steering wheel. "I meant that your interpretation wasn't my intent."

"How else does one interpret, 'I'm leaving and I want you to date other guys'?"

A moment of silence, then, "You're right."

That's all he said: you're right.

More long moments of quiet, stretching into minutes. I cleared my throat. "I know this is awkward and you're trying to make it less awkward, but that isn't necessary. We're going to bump into each other even after this business with Benicio. Maybe we'll even have to work together through the council. That's fine. I have no problem maintaining a professional relationship with you, Karl."

"Professional relationship?"

"Yes, I can behave professionally, as shocking as that may seem."

"That's not—" A pause. "So that's it then. You don't want me coming around anymore."

I wanted to scream, "What do you think?" But I knew what he thought. That whatever he'd done, when he showed up, his irresistibly charming self, I'd want him back. Not that I'd get him—he just liked to be wanted.

"No, Karl, I don't want you coming around anymore."

His jaw tightened and I expected it to stay locked for the rest of the trip, but after he turned the next corner, he asked, "Are you hungry?"

My stomach flipped; those words were so familiar. Werewolves have an abnormally high metabolism, meaning a normal restaurant meal is never enough. He'd often have one dinner at six and another at nine, just to avoid calling attention to himself by overeating. Tonight he probably hadn't eaten at all, so he'd be starving. But to admit to it? That would be to give in to the wolf, to concede that there were some instincts and drives he couldn't control.

So, when he was hungry, he'd ask if I was, and I'd long ago learned this was shorthand for, "Can we please get something to eat before I start gnawing on the furniture?" Sometimes I'd tease him, but usually I'd just play along and say yes. Then late one night, he'd come to my place hungry after the restaurants in town had closed, so I'd offered to cook for him. And after that, "Are you hungry?" became "Will you make me dinner?" And I always did because it was something I could do for him.

With Karl, taking wasn't easy. If he went to dinner with one of his Pack mates, he'd always pay, and I'm sure they thought he was being generous—or racking up brownie points to redeem later—but the truth was he couldn't stand to be indebted. So he'd visit me, he'd listen to me and he'd help me, but he'd never take anything in return . . . except home-cooked meals. So I did that for him—willingly and even happily.

And now, Karl was asking, "Are you hungry?" In some ways, that hurt more than all his jabs and icy glances.

"Restaurants are probably closed," I said finally. "Maybe a drive-through?"

He scanned the dark street. "It doesn't look promising. Do you have anything at the apartment?"

I shook my head.

"I see a convenience store at the next corner," he said. "They're bound to have groceries. I'll buy—"

"No." I took a quick breath. "No, Karl. I won't."

We drove the rest of the way in silence.

HOPE

DIPLOMATIC RELATIONS

I didn't offer Karl a drink at the apartment. Not even something non-alcoholic. I wasn't being petty—like I'd said, my cupboards were bare. Which was odd for me. Even traveling on business, one of my first stops was the local convenience store to get some drinks and snacks for my hotel room. A nesting instinct, I guess, to give myself a stable home base wherever I am. But here I'd been too distracted to even pick up bottled water.

Karl wasn't looking for details on the job. He already had them—courtesy of Lucas. What had him flying out to Miami was a breach of promise. Apparently, Benicio and Karl had an understanding that we'd repay this debt together. I tried to take the blame, telling him that Benicio had wanted to back out when he learned Karl was away.

"He *knew* I was out of the country. I left him a message before I went."

My mouth opened, ready with excuses—but when I took a moment to think it through, I knew the truth: I'd been played. Again.

I pulled my legs up under me on the sofa, squirming as if getting comfortable, gazing down until the first flash of humiliation passed.

"He wanted me on this job," I said finally. "He knew if he suggested waiting for you, I'd be offended and insist on taking it alone."

There was more to it than that. Benicio hadn't wanted someone older and more experienced taking a hard look at the job and warning me off. He'd seen that Karl and I were on the outs, and that I'd pounce on the chance to fulfill this debt alone.

"Lucas looked it over," I said, twisting my new watch. "He didn't see a problem with it."

"That's because he doesn't have all the facts." Karl met my gaze. "About you."

"But neither does Benicio. There's no way he'd know—"

I stopped, hearing my naiveté. Just because Lucas didn't know about an Expisco half-demon's chaos hunger didn't mean his father didn't.

"It's no different from my work for the council," I said. "I need this. You're always the first to tell me I need it—get my fill of chaos in a way that doesn't hurt anyone."

"No, not that doesn't hurt *anyone*. In a way that doesn't hurt *you*. If you can look me in the eye and tell me this doesn't feel any different than chasing rogue half-demons and sorcerers, I'll leave. But if you can't . . . ?" His fingers tapped against the chair arm. "I've already spoken to Lucas. If you walk away now, he'll handle this for us."

"What if I don't want to walk away?"

His mouth tightened a fraction before he smoothed it out. "I'm asking you to reconsider, Hope. Whatever you think of me right now, remember all the times you did take my advice, because you knew it was in your best interest. This is the one arena in which you cannot accuse me of self-interest. I'm thinking of you and what I think is best *for you*, knowing you as well as I do."

I glanced away. Angry—even sarcastic retorts—flitted past, but I didn't pursue them. Couldn't.

"I can do this job."

"Yes, you can. The question is: should you?"

I lifted my gaze to his. "I think I should."

His fingertips massaged the leather arm. "This is about last year, isn't it? About what happened with Jaime?"

For a moment, I was back in that room, lying on the cold concrete. The killing room. I felt the unbelievable chaos of those horrible deaths swirling around me. I heard the fear in Jaime's voice. Heard the clomp of footsteps outside the room. Knew they were coming for her, death was coming for her and, for just the briefest moment, felt an undeniable thrill of anticipation. It had only lasted a second, but I hadn't trusted it to stay gone, hadn't trusted myself not to do something to make the situation worse so I could feed off the chaos. So I'd told her to knock me out.

I shook my head. "This has nothing to do with—"

"—with testing yourself? Seeing how far you can push it? How far you can *control* it?"

"We've been through this and—"

"And you're not going to discuss it. Fine. But tomorrow morning, Hope, I'm going to talk to Benicio. You don't need to be there, but if you want to have your say, you're welcome to join me."

"I will."

"Good." He checked his watch. "It's too late to check into a hotel—"

"Just sleep on the damned couch, like you planned to."

I pushed to my feet, strode into the bedroom and tried not to slam the door.

I WENT TO bed, but didn't sleep. The tequila and the chaos highs had worn off and now, alone with nothing to occupy my brain, my thoughts slid back to the heist. Unlike my adventures on behalf of the council, there was no second wave of chaos bliss to be found in the replay. I thought of how many people we'd scared—blameless people, terrified by us, just for kicks.

I reminded myself it was a job, like my council work. No matter what I thought of the Cabals and their methods, a crisis with the gangs would ripple throughout the supernatural community. Brokering a peaceful deal—or, at the very least, one with minimal bloodshed—was a just cause.

But the guilt came not from participating in the heist, but from enjoying it. No, *reveling* in it. I thought of that sixteen-year-old girl, what we'd done to the biggest night of her life, and I recalled what I'd thought—that we were, in fact, doing her a favor. I remembered that, and I was disgusted.

In the morning, the guilt wouldn't be as sharp, the edge dulled by acknowledging that, yes, I'd made a mistake; yes, I wasn't proud of myself; and yes, I wouldn't let it happen again. But now, in the dark of night, lying alone in bed, there was nothing to do but think about it.

If I had the apartment to myself, I'd have gotten up—read a book, watched TV, done whatever would distract me until morning. But with Karl in the next room, I wouldn't even turn on my bedside light to read, desperately wanting him to think I was sleeping soundly, my conscience as free as his would be after a heist. So I lay there, staring at the wall, watching the clock tick through the hours.

I waited until six-thirty, the earliest I reasoned I could pretend to wake up. I showered and dressed, dragging it out past seven before I finally emerged.

Karl was already at the table, reading the *Wall Street Journal* and drinking coffee from one of the china mugs supplied with the apartment. On the opposite side of the table was a take-out cup of coffee, a bakery box, a newspaper and a pharmacy bag.

He didn't say a word as I walked in, just slid over a mug and plate from the center of the table, and resumed his reading.

I opened the bag. Inside was a tiny bottle of eyedrops. I looked from it to the extra-large coffee and knew, as silent as I'd been, that I hadn't tricked him and I'd been a fool to think I could.

It didn't matter that Karl had probably never passed a sleepless night after a heist. He knew me. As much as I hated to admit it, the proof lay here before me, not just in the eyedrops and caffeine, but in everything. The coffee, double cream, no sugar. Inside the bakery box, a blueberry bran muffin. The paper: *USA Today*. Even the eyedrops were my brand, and the "sensitive eye" formulation I used. There were married couples who didn't know each other as well as we did.

It was a quiet meal. Not like us at all. Usually, even while reading our different papers, we'd exchange a steady volley of comments and quips about the articles. Newspaper reading as a joint activity, like so many other things we did together—each doing our own thing, maintaining our independence and yet finding a way to share it.

That morning there was no anger in the silence, though. It felt almost . . . cautious, as if fearing that opening our mouths would lead to a fight, and this joint meal—albeit a silent one—was as close to comfortable as we could manage.

After breakfast, I called Benicio for my daily check-in. I said nothing about the heist or about Karl, but did mention that I might learn something later and, if I did, could I call him? He said he'd be at the office all morning.

We left at eight thirty.

THE FIRST HALF of the trip was as silent as breakfast. Then Karl mentioned he'd checked in at Stonehaven after coming back from Europe, and I asked after Elena and Clayton and their eighteen-month-old twins. And there we found the perfect neutral topic: babies.

I asked how the little ones were doing and how they were growing and what milestones they'd reached since I last saw them. As adorable as children were, neither of us had the slightest interest in them, but it was a subject we could discuss without fear of it devolving into a fight. So we stuck with it for the rest of the trip.

WE WALKED IN the front doors of the building that Jaz had pointed out the other night: Cortez Cabal headquarters. I'd wanted to keep our entrance low key, but should have realized things were never low key when Karl was around.

Every female eye turned his way as we entered the lobby. Karl is rarely the best-looking man in a room, but when he walks in, you can be forgiven for thinking he is. He has that proprietary confidence usually only seen in men like Benicio Cortez. In Karl, though, it tipped over into an "I know you're watching me" arrogance that made it even harder to look away.

Karl ignored the women, but if any man looked my way, Karl met each furtive glance with a level stare. Establishing territory. It didn't mean anything. He'd do the same with any woman at his side— friend, lover or acquaintance. The wolf peeking out.

The lobby itself was spectacular but not ostentatious, and that's not an easy look to achieve, no matter how much money you spend. The foyer was large without being cavernous. Dark doors blocked the sun and good soundproofing muffled the street sounds, plunging the visitor into a peaceful oasis, complete with two walls of aquariums, a ten-foot-square "sand garden" with a half-toppled castle, a wall fountain, driftwood benches and a handsome young man gliding about with a tray of iced water.

Those milling about the foyer were mostly tourists. Human tourists, probably here to check out the nineteenth-floor observatory. All good public relations. To them, Cortez Cabal was simply Cortez Corporation—a huge company like any other.

As Karl veered toward the front desk, I excused myself to get a closer look at one aquarium. I knew how Karl planned to get past the receptionist and a man's charm is always more effective when he doesn't have a woman at his side.

Before I could leave, his grip tightened on my elbow, holding me back as he surveyed the area—his gaze touching on and evaluating everyone in the lobby. Again, typical werewolf, however much he denies it.

As I admired the fish, I watched Karl's reflection in the aquarium glass. He was talking to the receptionist, doing nothing as blatant as flirting, simply giving her his undivided attention. She fell for it. They all do. Of course, I'm not one to talk.

A few minutes later the receptionist sent us, with a security guard escort, to a private elevator. We stopped on the top floor. Judging by the generous use of marble and the bank of receptionists and secretaries, I guessed it was the executive level.

"This man insists on speaking to Benicio Cortez. He wouldn't state his business."

The receptionist on duty there glowered at the guard, as if to say that we should never have gotten past the front desk. The guard pretended not to notice, probably already preparing his "I did what I was told" defense when this breach of protocol was investigated. Blame would fall on the lobby receptionist, and I felt bad about that, but if she could be so easily swayed by a good-looking charmer, she shouldn't be in charge of the main gate.

The receptionist turned to Karl. "And you would be . . . ?"

"An emissary, here on behalf of my Alpha."

"Alpha? You mean—"

The receptionist exchanged a glance with the guard, who took a slow step back from Karl before stopping himself. Karl's lips twitched, fighting a smile.

"Hector Cortez is in," the receptionist said. "That's Mr. Cortez's—"

"I know who Hector Cortez is. I doubt you want me returning to my Alpha telling him I was granted an audience with the second-in-command. Mr. Cortez understands the importance we place on hierarchy, which is why he always speaks to the Alpha himself."

The receptionist looked to the others behind her. A cry for help that no one answered, all busying themselves with their tasks.

"You can check on that by calling him, can't you?" Karl said. "If I'm wrong, he'll send Hector."

An exchange of looks, then a few murmured words from the receptionist, and the guard escorted us through a pair of doors.

I PRESUMED WE were in a waiting room, but there were no year-old magazines or battered chairs to give it away. It looked more like a home office—the kind you see in magazines, with deep leather chairs, a recessed bookcase and twin oak desks. Pastries rested on a silver platter topped with a glass lid, a dainty container more suited to petit fours than the chocolate chip muffins within. Beside the door was a built-in coffee and cappuccino machine.

The guard left after receiving a call, probably telling him it would be impolite to hover over a werewolf delegate. That didn't mean we were left alone. Every few minutes an employee found a reason to come to the waiting room, some pausing outside the door, the more daring entering and filling their cups at the coffeemaker.

"Getting a glimpse of the beast," I whispered.

"All I need is a cage to pace in."

"It's your own fault. Benicio would have granted you an audience without involving Jeremy."

"I know."

"But that wouldn't have been nearly as entertaining, would it?"

He smiled and leaned back, stretching his legs and crossing them at the ankles. "They'd be gawking at you too, if they knew what you were."

"That's the difference between us—I avoid the limelight; you jump in with both feet."

"No, I simply tire of clinging to the shadows. Now and then, it's nice to step out."

I shook my head and got a glass of water, then sat down again.

"Speaking of shadows, how was business in Europe? Profitable, I presume?"

Karl shrugged. "Profitable enough."

I waited for details, but they didn't come. Usually he loved regaling me with tales of his escapades, knowing that I loved imagining myself climbing over those rooftops, narrowly escaping detection. I shivered just thinking about it.

"Getting restless?" he said after a moment. "How about a self-guided tour?"

"I doubt that's allowed."

"Think anyone will stop us?"

HOPE

LEARNING FROM THE MASTERS

Karl waited until the hall was empty, then we slipped from the room. He led me to the left, picking up speed as voices turned the corner at the other end.

We spent the next ten minutes prowling the executive floor of Cortez Cabal headquarters—probably second only to major government buildings for security—and no one even noticed.

We slid easily back into our old roles. Karl as the ever-patient, ever-entertaining teacher, instructing not with lectures but by example. Me as the eager student, lapping it up—both the lessons and the chaos, that steady low-level thrum that set my heart thumping but left my brain clear.

I watched and took mental notes. Paid attention to how he could predict where every security camera would be. Noted how he avoided people just as deftly, not darting out of their way, but turning so they saw only his back and passed, intent on their work, presuming he belonged.

If trapped between a group approaching from either end, he always chose to walk past the suits rather than the clerical staff. He'd square his shoulders, his usual gliding walk shortening to a self-important strut saying to me something like, "And to the left are the photocopiers..."

This seemed the riskier choice, exposing himself to a VIP over a secretary, but soon I understood. Clerical staff knew names and faces, so they could easily run a file down to "Jones in accounting," and they'd have known Karl didn't belong. But the executives? They caught a glimpse of a guy in a suit showing a new hire around, and they presumed he belonged there.

We turned yet another corner, and found ourselves in a long narrow hall of unmarked doors.

Karl leaned down to murmur, "Now this looks like a place where they might keep a few things worth stealing. But which door?"

I glanced at each as we passed. "Stockrooms, but nothing important. Nonconfidential files, cleaning supplies, miscellaneous storage . . ."

I stopped at one with dual locks. "Ah, here's something."

Karl slanted a look my way. "You think so?"

"You don't?"

"I'm willing to make a wager on it."

"Twenty bucks."

A small smile. "Twenty it is."

He didn't even glance around to make sure no one was coming. He'd hear footsteps. He picked the locks, opened the door and flicked on the light.

"Office supplies?" I stepped in. "No way. There must be something else. They're using the supplies as a blind."

"A good idea, but if there was anything more valuable, there'd be more than locks on the door. I think this is all you'll find. Office supply theft is a serious problem in every business."

"Guys making a quarter-million a year are going to pilfer—" I reached into the nearest box, "—stick pens?"

"Not just any stick pen." He took it from me and flourished his hand at the lettering. "An official Cortez Corporation stick pen." He tucked it into my pocket. "A memento."

There were boxes of engraved silver pens—probably corporate gifts—right beside it, but his gaze passed them by, knowing if he gave me something of value, I'd feel guilty. A stick pen I could live with, and enjoy a residual chaos surge every time I used it.

"Guess I owe you twenty bucks," I said as we walked from the room.

"I was being a gentleman, and refraining from the 'I told you so's.' "

"There's nothing of value on this floor, is there?"

"All the critical files, rare spellbooks and bearer bonds are likely in a vault somewhere. But there is something of moderate value in there."

He gestured at a door we'd passed, as plain as the others, the smooth handle suggesting it didn't even have a key lock.

"Ha-ha," I said.

His brows arched. "You doubt me?"

"God forbid."

He took hold of my shoulders and propelled me toward the door. When we were about two feet away, I caught a telltale flash.

"Security spell." I glanced back at him. "How'd you know?"

"About the spell? Just a hunch. What caught my attention was a less mysterious security measure. Do you see the metal plate running along the door frame? There's an electronic lock of some sort, probably attached to that." He pointed to a wafer-thin slot beside the door, then said. "We should get back."

WE'D JUST TURNED the final corner back to the waiting room when two men approached from the opposite side, one strolling a few paces behind, making no effort to match the other's brisk stride.

For a moment, I thought the leader was Benicio. He had the same stocky build, dark hair and rounded face, but when we drew closer I saw his dark hair was less gray-streaked and his face was less lined.

The man lagging behind was about a decade younger, also Latino, but taller and well built. I could see similarities in the features, but where the older man was average looking, bland even, the younger was worth a double-take ... though I tried not to make mine too obvious.

"Looking for us?" Karl said as we neared them. "My apologies. You keep the restrooms well hidden, it seems."

The lie came blithely, accompanied by an air that said he really didn't give a damn whether they believed him or not.

Karl extended a hand to the older man. "Karl Marsten."

"Hector Cortez. This is my brother, Carlos."

Carlos ignored Karl and took my hand. "I'd guess this lovely young lady is Hope Adams, but I don't think I could be so lucky."

He flashed a smile meant to be as charming as his words, but both carried a smarmy note that set my teeth on edge.

Hector and Carlos Cortez, two of Lucas's three half-brothers. I'd been wondering whether Benicio himself would come to collect us or would send someone instead. When it came to Cabal relations with werewolves or vampires, every nuance would be noticed and analyzed by the entire corporation.

Only in the last decade had the werewolves reentered the larger supernatural world. As evidenced by the way Karl had been treated, they were still viewed with a combination of curiosity and trepidation. Some weren't happy that Benicio had initiated contact with Jeremy Danvers, the werewolf Alpha. Sending his sons to meet us was a small step back, but perhaps the politically shrewd move.

"Karl. Hope."

Footfalls sounded behind us and we turned to see Benicio approaching from the other end of the floor, Troy behind him.

"Meetings never run on schedule, do they? Come along then. We'll talk in my office."

As we followed Benicio, I couldn't help smiling. A deft move. In accompanying Karl personally, Benicio could not be accused of any slight against a werewolf envoy. Yet those who didn't want to see their leader treating the Alpha—via his proxy—as an equal would argue that Benicio had sent his sons but, after an accidental hallway encounter, the only civil thing to do was take us himself. Another lesson learned.

BENICIO LED US through a tiny reception area, then dismissed Troy to an adjoining room.

We entered what was—from the photos on the desk—clearly Benicio's private office, but it wasn't much larger than the waiting room. Still it certainly was the best real estate in the building, overlooking Biscayne Bay, with an amazing floor-to-ceiling window that showcased the view.

"You must be here to discuss my arrangement with Hope," Benicio said as he waved us to chairs. "But I'm not sure this was wise, bringing her in when she's supposed to be undercover."

"No?" Karl settled into his chair. "Then I guess you'll have to abort the mission."

My knees locked before I could drop into my chair. I shot a look at

Karl, certain now that he'd invited me along because he knew it could mark the end of my job.

"Did you introduce her to anyone on your way in?" Benicio asked.

"Of course not. I simply presented myself as a Pack envoy, except to your sons, who also figured out who Hope was. But I presume they'll be discreet."

I relaxed. While Karl might have hoped this "indiscretion" would force the end of my mission, he hadn't done anything that would put me at risk.

"I presume you want to join Hope in repaying this debt?" Benicio said.

"I'm considering it."

And that was it. No accusations of reneging on a deal. It was as if both men acknowledged what had happened, and were mutually agreeing to move past the pointless blame and recriminations stage to get down to business.

"First, though," Karl continued, "I want to know what you're withholding from Hope."

Benicio walked to a table with a pitcher of iced tea and glasses. Stalling? Or subtly reminding Karl of civilities?

I accepted the tea; Karl did not.

Benicio handed me my drink, then sat with his own. "If you're referring to the problems Hope mentioned to Troy, we're still looking into that." He glanced at me. "Were you able to get any details?"

"I tried yesterday, with the guys who originally mentioned them. They assured me everything was under control and I didn't need to worry. I'll press for more when I can."

"Is there anything else?" Karl asked Benicio.

"In that matter, we were withholding nothing, so no, there's nothing *else*. You have my assurance that this job is exactly as I outlined it to Hope."

They locked gazes. I tried to read vibes, but picked up nothing to suggest Benicio was lying. Of course, knowing my powers, he wouldn't be foolish enough to let an incriminating thought form.

After a moment, Benicio said, "If my assurance isn't enough, Karl, then consider that the Cortez Cabal is on better terms with the werewolf Pack than it ever has been, and certainly on better terms with it than the other Cabals are. That's an advantage I intend to keep. I'd gain nothing by endangering it, which is what I'd do if I deliberately misled a Pack member."

A moment's consideration, then Karl said, "I want in, then. In light of these allegations by the gang and their obvious antagonism toward the Cabal, I think you'll agree that Hope's task is more dangerous than you expected."

"Perhaps."

"I presume you have a tracking device on her? In the identification cards you gave her?"

I looked over sharply. Benicio nodded.

"Good," Karl said. "I'll want a GPS linked to that transmitter. I also want Hope to have a panic button, connected to me. Disguise it as something a young woman might carry in her pocket at all times— a coin, a mirror, lipstick, anything that won't look suspicious."

"Done."

"I also want your assurance that if, at any time, I feel—" a glance my way, "—Hope and I feel she's in imminent danger, she can abort and the debt is paid."

I expected Benicio to balk, since there was nothing to stop us from pretending I felt endangered, but he simply said, "Agreed." Maybe he trusted me. Or maybe Karl was right and Benicio knew I got more from this mission than the satisfaction of relieving a debt.

Benicio and Karl hashed out specifics. Then Benicio made a call downstairs to have us outfitted with Karl's technological demands.

HOPE

BRUSH-OFF

As the technician explained to Karl how the GPS worked, I took a trip to the restroom. Coming back, I was waylaid by Carlos. He didn't make any excuse for being in the laboratory wing, probably thinking I'd be flattered that he'd tracked me down.

He tried the same routine Troy had—I was new to the city and he could show me around. From Troy, though, the offer had been casual and friendly. If I'd taken him up on it and wanted nothing more than an escort, he'd be fine with that. With Carlos, there was no such subtlety.

"I'll give you my card," he said. "You want to go out, you call. I'll show you a good time. Guaranteed."

He extended the card. Before I could take it, it was snatched by a hand appearing around me.

"She's not interested," Karl said.

"I think she can tell me that herself."

"She doesn't need to. I just did. Now, if you'll excuse us . . ."

Karl put his arm around my waist and led me away. When we reached the elevator, I slipped from his grasp.

"I thought you want me dating more supernaturals. What's wrong with that one? He's closer to my age, wealthy, gorgeous—"

"—with a reputation for leaving girls in worse shape than he finds them. And with your powers—"

"—he's hoping I'd get off on it. I caught a few vision scraps, enough to know his reputation is warranted, which is why I stood for your 'hands off my property' routine."

Karl grunted.

"Given the choice between insulting a Cabal son and letting him think I'm otherwise engaged, I'll go with option B. But if you try that with anyone else, you'll get a very different reaction."

I said it lightly, teasing him, and expected a retort, but he just watched the floors of the elevator count down, then stepped off when the doors opened.

"YOU DIDN'T GIVE me much of a choice in there," I said as we walked down the street. "I didn't want to argue in front of Benicio. But I don't need—"

"—protection. I believe I've heard this before."

I kept my tone even. "If you want to repay the debt, that's fine. You go off and do your thing, I'll hang out here and do mine, and we'll say you protected me. No one will be the wiser."

He turned a corner so sharply that I went another three steps before realizing he wasn't beside me, and had to backtrack.

"I'm just saying you don't need to protect me. I don't need it, and I don't really want it."

"And you think I do? You think I like having to drop everything and fly out to Miami to see what kind of trouble you're getting into this time? You think I'm looking forward to spending the next few days skulking in shadows keeping an eye on you?"

I stumble-stepped, stunned, then stopped.

"You don't have a choice," he said, back to me, still walking. "And, apparently, neither do I."

He jaywalked across the road and strode away. I stared after him, unable to believe what I'd heard. I'd never asked for his protection. He was the one who chased after me, fretted about me and hovered over me. I wanted to go after him. To pound on his back and shout, "How dare you!"

Self-centered, arrogant bastard.

What a shock.

I turned and headed back to the main road, managing a graceful exit, should he turn to see it. But I knew he wouldn't.

―――――

I HADN'T FOUND a cab yet when my cell phone rang. I scrambled to grab it, eager even when I didn't want to be. Then I realized it was the gang phone.

"Hey," Jaz said when I answered.

"Hey, yourself," I said with a genuine smile. "I was going to call you this morning, but I don't have your number."

"It should be on your phone. Rodriguez—"

"—programmed it in. Okay, I feel like an idiot. I completely forgot."

"No problem. I'd have called earlier, but I didn't want to wake you. Figured you might be a little rough after the tequila."

"A little."

"Anyway, uh, I wanted to call and say I'm sorry about last night."

"You? If apologies are due, they should come from me. It's just— well, after the problems with my folks, I freaked out."

Pause. My heart started hammering. Did he doubt my story? I instinctively tried to read his vibes but, of course, I couldn't over the phone.

"I'm sure there was a problem with your parents," he said finally. "I know what that's like. But, well, I wouldn't blame you if you went outside last night, got some fresh air, cleared your head and realized that going back in wasn't what you wanted."

"No, that's not—"

"I was pushing it. Pushing hard. I could tell the tequila was going to your head, and I took advantage of that. I was riding high, not just on the booze. After a big job I get . . . pumped, I guess you'd say. I got carried away."

"You weren't the only one. In fact, I'm pretty sure I started things. But, yes, it was a little . . . public, after I thought about it."

"Which is cool with me. Would a private lunch be more your style, then?"

I smiled. "It would."

He gave me an address where I could meet him in an hour, just enough time to change, put on the watch he'd given me and slide back into being Faith Edmonds.

―――――

JAZ TOOK ME to an upscale tapas bar with the assurance, as we walked in, that he was buying. Obviously, Faith could afford a nice meal, but he seemed to think it was only polite to announce that he was paying when he'd made an expensive choice. From the way he grinned as we walked in, his arm around me, he was happy to be taking me to a place he considered more my style.

Had he not been flush after collecting his share from Guy, this would be a luxury he couldn't afford. From the clues I'd picked up, Jaz's and Sonny's parents had worked menial jobs for the Cabal. They'd grown up in working-class lives that had dipped dangerously close to the poverty level after they left home. To them, joining the gang was like winning a lottery, and as much as I'd love to tell Jaz to keep his money, I knew this was important to him. I kept my mouth shut, ordered a moderately priced meal and enjoyed it.

As we ate, I knew I should ask more about the gang-Cabal encounters, but I wasn't eager to remind myself I was here under false pretenses. When conversation did circle to the gang, Jaz started it. He'd talked to Guy that morning. It seemed the police hadn't been notified about the heist. The *Herald* had run a tidbit about the contribution after Guy's tip-off, and he'd delivered the money, via courier, to the agency.

"Guy might not say it, but he was really pleased with your idea about the charity. He said it was brilliant."

I must have looked surprised.

He laughed. "Yeah, he let it slip that it was your idea. But only to me. As far as everyone else knows, it was his. Which is for the best. Saves you from getting crap from the others, who don't appreciate handing over a cut of their share to charity."

"Are you okay with that?"

"Sure. With Guy's original plan, the robbery would have been reported. That's not a big deal—Guy knows his stuff and we haven't had the cops sniff around since I joined. The big concern, though, is the Cabals. The minute it showed up in the paper—hell, the minute it went out on the police scanner—the Cortezes would know it was us. Then they'd make sure we know they have us covered."

"In other words, letting you know they're watching."

"And, even if we don't need their help, we're—" He chewed as he searched for a word. "—obligated to them. Reminds me of this guy I knew in school. His uncle was a politician who'd always take his nieces and nephews aside and tell them, if they ever got in any trouble with the cops, even a speeding ticket, just come to him. Well, my friend never got a single ticket, but when his uncle needed help campaigning, you can bet he called the 'debt' in. With the Cortezes, they don't call in the debt. They just let it hang over our heads, which drives Guy crazy."

"I'm sure it does." A sentiment voiced with complete sincerity, having lived with just such a ticking bomb for two years.

"Your scheme, though, meant it was never reported to the cops, meaning the Cabal won't be on Guy's back about it. So he's grateful."

And here was my chance, as much as I hated to take it. "I suppose he's especially sensitive about that now, after the recent problems..."

"Yeah."

Jaz took a drink of his beer. I struggled against the urge to let it drop, and tell Benicio I couldn't get anything more. I reminded myself why I was here and felt a prickle of unease that I needed the reminder.

"Is that what it's been about?" I pressed. "These dustups? About the gang owing the Cabal for its protection?"

"Some of it. Normally, like I said, the Cabal just lets us know we're covered, maybe raps our knuckles if we call too much attention to ourselves. But the last big job we pulled?" He shook his head. "They went all Sopranos on our heads."

"What happened?"

He hesitated, as if he shouldn't go on, but the urge to talk won out. "It was the next afternoon. Sonny and I collected our share, and we were heading back to our place, goofing off, buzzed by the windfall. Sure, we had our guard down but, shit, it was the middle of the day, and South Beach isn't exactly downtown Miami. But on this back road, we get jumped by four guys. Two in front, two behind, cutting us off. A magician's powers are nearly useless in a fight. And, I gotta admit, I'm not much of a brawler. Sonny neither. Just not our thing. So we see these four guys surrounding us and we didn't put up any resistance. They must have been disappointed, 'cause one smacks me into a wall. When Sonny jumps in to help me, he gets a pistol in the temple."

"Shit."

"And they say *we're* the thugs. You should have seen these guys. Wearing golf shirts and slacks like they're off for a day on the course. Only time they swing a club is to bash someone's head in. Anyway, Sonny and I, we're down for the count, barely conscious and I'm looking at these guys in their nice shirts and slacks and dress shoes, probably ten years older than me, and I'm not getting it, you know. I'm still thinking this is just a mugging, or maybe a case of mistaken identity.

"Then the leader starts yammering on about the gang, and how we're overstaying our welcome, getting too big for our britches— whatever clichés he could come up with. It takes me a while, 'cause I'm still out of it, but finally it clicks: shit, these guys are from the Cortez Cabal."

"Did they say so?"

He nodded. "They went on about how we were pissing off Mr. Cortez, and we needed to remember our place or he'd show it to us. Then they took our cut and left us there."

"They robbed you?"

"Can you believe it? Shit, they probably pull in that much a week. I figure they were just being jerks, but Guy says they took the money to say that everything we earn, we owe to them. He says that sounds like Benicio."

The message, yes. But the delivery? No.

I'd heard of other Cabals pulling stunts like this. The Cortezes were no less ruthless, but such thuggery wasn't Benicio's usual style. Maybe he thought that was the only language the gang would under- stand. But from what Benicio said about Guy, he knew he wasn't a dumb brute. To maintain a level of respect, Benicio would approach him in a more civilized way. This sounded more like rogue elements in the Cabal.

I considered raising the possibility, but my position was too pre- carious to start defending Benicio Cortez. Brokering peace was a job best left to the professionals. For now, I'd gotten a little more infor- mation and could push duty aside, relax and enjoy lunch with Jaz.

HOPE

REBOUND

As we were leaving, Jaz grabbed my hand and ducked into a side hall. At the end was a locked door. A flick of a credit card and we were inside an intimate private lounge.

Only two security lights lit the room and we had to pause just beyond the door. After a minute, I could make out a few tables and a small bar.

Still holding my hand, Jaz led me into a darkened nook beside the bar. Then, without a word, he pulled me to him in a kiss. I could feel his heart hammering. From the thrill of the break-in, I presumed, but when he pulled back, there was trepidation in his eyes, lifting only when I leaned in for another kiss.

"Whew," he breathed.

"Not so sure of your welcome?"

"I wanted to make sure last night *was* about being in a public place, not about me."

"It definitely wasn't you."

Another kiss, starting slow. My head spun again as that delicious aura of chaos swirled from him. Soon we were on the floor, my legs wrapped around his hips, his hands in my hair, kissing me hard enough to bruise my lips, but I didn't care.

We writhed against each other, his hands on my rear, then my breasts, but making no move to slide under my clothes, rough gropes mingled with tender caresses, making my head spin all the more.

Frustrated lust coursed through me, the kind I hadn't felt since I was a teenager, making out with a guy in his backseat, waiting for him to take the next step.

"Sure you're not leaving?" he whispered, voice ragged.

"You're teasing me, aren't you? Payback time."

An almost sheepish look. "Nah."

"Oh, no?" I slid my hand down his shirt and rubbed his crotch. A soft moan as he shifted to make it easier. "I wouldn't blame you if it was payback. Not a nice thing for me to do."

"I survived." He opened one eye. "But, yeah, I was pretty revved up. Ran outside after I got your message, hoping I could catch up with you before you left."

"Can I make it up to you?"

He chuckled. "Pretty sure you could."

"How?"

The chuckle turned to a laugh, then a groan as I slid my fingers under his waistband. "Better not leave it too open-ended for me."

"It *is* open-ended. Anything you want."

He entwined his fingers in my hair. "If I was a typical guy, I suppose I'd do this..." He tugged my hair, pulling me down his chest, then stopped. "Is that what you had in mind?"

"It would be... if you were a typical guy."

A laugh loud enough that I glanced at the door.

"You're right. No one's ever mistaken me for a typical guy. Meaning, if you make that offer, I may ask for something a little atypical."

"Go ahead."

His gaze searched mine, as if considering how I might react. A quick grin, then he put his hands on my back, flipped us over, laid me on the ground and backed away.

"Undress for me."

"You want me to...?"

"You heard me."

I smiled. "Just checking."

He'd backed up to a spot a few feet away, and sat there, eyes on me, waiting.

I stood and started with my sandals, taking a moment to get past that first blast of embarrassment and recapture the chaos vibes still circling around us.

"If you don't want to ..." he said.

I met his gaze. "No, I want to."

I did want to. I wanted Jaz and everything he promised to be—a giddy, passionate affair that would remind me what such a thing could be, and help me move past Karl.

I reached for my skirt next, then stopped and, instead, pulled off my panties, tugging them down my thighs, aware of Jaz's gaze following every move. I pulled them off one leg, then kicked them off the other. Not the most graceful kick, but Jaz didn't seem to notice.

My halter top tied in the back, and my fumbling with that was also less graceful than I would have liked. Once untied, I let the shirt fall and Jaz let out a hiss, seeing I wasn't wearing anything under it. He shifted, inching closer.

"Just one piece left," I said, tugging at the skirt. "Sure you don't want to do the honors?"

"Go ahead. Please."

This time I did drag it out, slowly writhing out of the skirt until I stood there, naked. And he didn't move. Just stared, which was better than any compliment he could have paid me. After a moment, though, as if realizing he should say something he said, "You're gorgeous." A blush darkened his cheeks. "I mean, you were gorgeous already, but now you're ... damn."

I laid down, arms beneath my head, stretching languorously, his admiration making me bold.

"So now what do you want me to do?" I said.

A deep chuckle. "Oh, I could think of a few things, but if you do, this is going to end very quickly." He slid his hand down to his crotch and stroked himself through his jeans, no hesitation, no embarrassment. His brazenness—and the sight—made a fresh wave of heat course through me.

"Your turn, then," I said. "Take it off for me."

He grinned. "An order I would love to obey, but ..." He slid over to me. "I think I'd better leave them on awhile, to slow me down."

He moved over me, clothes brushing my bare skin, light enough to send shivers through me. Then he lowered himself, mouth coming down to mine in a kiss so hard I gasped, as I wrapped my arms and legs around him, his clothes rough against my bare skin. I could feel him hard against me, his jeans chafing me in places I probably wouldn't want to be chafed tomorrow, but right now, it felt amazing.

"Still want me undressed?" he whispered against my ear.

"Not necessary," I said, and reached for his fly.

I was still getting the button undone when his cell phone rang. He grabbed it from his pocket and threw it across the room, where it gave one strangled ring before dying.

"What if it's Guy?" I said.

"It is. Fuck him. I'll deal with it."

I undid his button. Then my cell phone started and Jaz let out a string of curses venomous enough to make me jump. He lifted off me and hovered there, then backed away.

"Better get it."

In other words, he'd take his punishment from Guy, but wasn't going to let me.

It was indeed Guy, and in a foul mood, demanding to know if Jaz was with me. Jaz must have overheard, and took the phone. After a minute, he hung up, scowling.

"Some Cabal bullshit. Wants us there in twenty minutes."

Even the promise of more Cabal information wasn't enough to keep me from thinking *It's a ten-minute cab ride, fifteen tops, so that leaves us five minutes* ... But it was too late. The mood was broken.

When I asked Jaz what he wanted to do, he gave a humorless laugh. "What I want to do obviously isn't what I'm going to do. And I'm not rushing this." He leaned over, lips brushing mine. "It's too important to rush. We'll have time afterward. Maybe I can manage a bed for you, like a gentleman."

"I don't want a gentleman."

A grin. "Let's get this damned meeting over with, then."

EVERYONE WAS ALREADY in Guy's office when we arrived. Jaz led me over to where Sonny was leaning against the wall.

"Glad you could join us," Guy said.

Jaz's silence—when he'd usually make a good-natured comeback—had Guy eyeing him, then glancing at me.

"Everything okay?" Guy asked.

"Peachy, boss. So what's up?"

"What's up" was indeed a Cabal problem, though not urgent enough to warrant such a sudden meeting . . . but that may have been sexual frustration talking.

Guy had received information that identified one of the men who'd robbed and beaten Jaz and Sonny. From his contact, Guy knew the target spent most evenings out, and kept a home office. Where there's an office, there's paperwork, or at least the electronic version. A break-in might tell us why the Cabal suddenly felt the need to smack down Guy's gang. If that failed, then they could wait until the man returned and get the information direct from the source.

As Guy talked, Jaz's annoyance with the meeting fell away, until he was fairly squirming in his seat, shooting grins my way.

"Sounds like we're going to have another exciting night," he whispered to me, then called to Guy, "I'm out for interrogation duty, boss. Not my style. But I'm there for the break-in. Faith should come along— she can scout for trouble and she's a damned good thief, so—"

"I appreciate your enthusiasm, Jasper, but that's not the plan."

Jaz glanced at me. "But that power of hers—"

"—is invaluable in a sensitive break-in. I agree. Of course she's in."

"He means *you're* out," Bianca said.

"You and Sonny will stand down tonight," Guy said. "For cat burglary, you can't be beat, but tonight we're looking for information, not valuables."

"But—"

"No buts. I need Rodriguez for the computer and Faith for trouble detection and Bianca for searching. I'll be hunting too, and that's a full house. You other four will patrol the perimeter, with Tony and Max coming in later if we need muscle for questioning."

Guy talked for a few more minutes, then adjourned the meeting. Jaz stared straight ahead, gaze blank, uncharacteristically thoughtful. Then he squeezed my hand and winked.

"I'll fix this."

I could have said it was hardly the end of the world if he missed tonight's break-in. But it wouldn't matter. In some ways, Jaz was like a child—he wanted what he wanted, and he wanted it now. It sounded like immaturity, but there was no real selfishness behind it, nor any tantrums to be thrown when he didn't get his way. Like last night. While he'd admitted to being frustrated, he'd waited until noon to call, in case I had a hangover, then had taken me out to lunch. With Jaz, "I want it and I want it now" seemed almost an...innocence. A purity of impulse.

As the meeting broke up, he rocked on his heels, a greyhound at the starting gate.

Guy looked up from a conversation with Bianca to call, "Jaz, Sonny, over here. Got an errand for you."

Jaz leaned against me, hand brushing my rear. "Shit. That's not what I wanted to hear."

His fingers toyed with the hem of my miniskirt, eyes glittering, mouth coming down to mine, once again forgetting everything around us. A throat clearing from me stopped him.

"It's your fault." His gaze met mine, those sexy hooded eyes dark with desire. "If you were a witch, I'd think you'd cast a spell on me."

Coming from anyone else, a corny pickup line. From Jaz, it made my heart skip. When he got close to me, the world vanished, lost in that swirl of his aura, that chaos vibe, and I suddenly knew where it came from—that childlike part of him that saw what it wanted, and grabbed for it, free of guilt and self-doubt.

I tilted my head back, lips parting as he—

"Jaz," Guy barked. "Are you listening to me? Get down here."

A flicker of anger, but it evaporated before I caught more than a spark. Propelling me forward, he headed toward Guy.

"Sorry, boss. I thought you were still talking to Bee. Got a job for us, you said."

"For you and Sonny. I need Faith here."

"Damn." He turned to me. "I'll call you as soon as I'm done. We'll meet up for—"

"For nothing. This is work time, Jaz, not social time. You seem to be having some trouble distinguishing the two lately."

Not an unwarranted accusation, but from the way Jaz stiffened, I could tell he didn't like being reprimanded.

"We're fine," I said. "When you called, we had to leave lunch, so we'd planned to grab something to eat together later, but obviously that's not going to work, which is understandable under the circumstances."

"All right then. I'll make sure you get fed before tonight, but a tête-à-tête is out of the question. This is going to be a delicate operation and I need you both on task. Completely on task."

"We will be."

"Good. Take five minutes, Faith, while Bianca and I talk to these guys, then I want you back here."

"Yes, sir."

I WAS COMING back from the restroom when I saw Jaz pacing outside Guy's door.

"All done?" I said. "Then it must be my turn."

He reached for me before I could pass. "Don't worry. I'm not going to spirit you off into a corner. Guy's already miffed, so I won't make it worse. I just wanted to say..." He looked around, then pulled me closer. "I just wanted to say I'll make it up to you."

I grinned. "I'm counting on it."

I expected him to grin back, but his face stayed serious, eyes meeting mine. "I mean it, Faith. I've screwed up, and I know that. Getting ahead of myself. I...do that a lot. I can't help it. But when this is over, I'll make it up to you." He paused. "Ever heard of Nikki Beach?"

I shook my head.

"It's a bar on a private beach with beds and teepees. When this is done, that's where I'm taking you. Dinner, dancing, relaxing on the beach, then off to the best damned hotel I can find. No more making out on a bar stool or a restaurant floor. I'm going to do it right. Make it special."

I shivered, lifted onto my tiptoes and brushed my lips across his. "I can't wait."

HOPE

DILEMMA

Guy wanted to discuss the job. He and Bianca would be doing most of the searching, but as long as I was there, I would help, meaning I needed to know what they were looking for. So I thought I'd at least find out the target's address, maybe his name.

Not a chance. Guy told me what I'd be looking for, and that was it. Even my reporter tricks didn't get more out of him. He trusted his gang, but never liked to test that unnecessarily. He made the plans, and we carried out our end. To most, like Jaz, this was the perfect arrangement—minimal responsibilities for maximum reward. But it wasn't terribly helpful when you were a spy, and the gang you'd just infiltrated was making plans to rob—and possibly torture—the employee of the man you worked for.

I had a responsibility to tell Benicio. Yet I had time to consider the matter on the cab ride to my apartment, and I began to wonder whether informing Benicio really was the obvious choice.

If, as I believed, Benicio hadn't orchestrated the attack on Jaz and Sonny, then he'd have no idea who this employee might be. What if he overreacted? Did I want to see Jaz, Guy, Sonny and the others arrested and possibly tortured because of a rogue Cabal agent?

What if I was wrong about Benicio's involvement? In that case, might he not set a trap for the gang and end up with the same outcome as scenario one: everyone taken into Cabal custody? The Cabals were known for torturing those who withheld information. It might not even get that far—an "accident" while taking them into custody would be a convenient way to get rid of an inconvenient problem.

If I feared the Cabal's reaction, I should call Lucas. Yet if I did, with no proof that his father was about to do anything wrong, would I be crying wolf? Make matters worse?

What I really needed was a sounding board. Someone whose opinion I trusted, someone with no allegiance either way. As much as I hated to admit it, I wanted to talk to Karl. But at the thought of asking for his help, I shuddered.

If he was at the apartment, I'd tell him what was happening. Then, if he chose to offer advice—and I couldn't imagine Karl not throwing in his two cents—I'd listen.

He wasn't at the apartment.

I headed for the shower, hoping a shot of cold water would clear my thoughts.

I CAME OUT of the bathroom, wrapped in a towel, and nearly smacked into Karl. Of course, I didn't know it was Karl at first—my gaze down, thoughts elsewhere, walking out of the bathroom to find a man standing there. I yelped and stumbled back, heart in my throat.

"Goddamn it, Karl—"

"I need to talk to you."

"Great. Try the buzzer in the lobby. Or, better yet, the phone to let me know you're coming over."

"I rang the buzzer. You didn't answer."

"Which gives you the right to break in?"

"I need to talk to you. Get something on."

I thought of Jaz that afternoon, asking me to undress, watching me as I did, the look on his face telling me I was beautiful even before he said the words.

And then there was Karl... "Get something on." As if I'd strutted out here in a towel just to annoy him.

I strode into my bedroom and slammed the door.

———

TEN MINUTES LATER, he shook the bedroom door handle. It didn't have a lock, but he made no move to open it, just rattling to get my attention. God forbid he should knock like a normal person.

"I'm not dressed yet."

A low growl. "You're stalling, Hope."

"No, I'm dressing."

Or I would be, once I figured out what to put on. It wasn't a big deal—I could change before I saw Jaz again—but I stared at my choices, brain frozen, unable to consider the options much less pick one, too busy thinking about how to deal with Karl. Or, better yet, how to *avoid* dealing with Karl.

The door banged against the frame, then rebounded, as if Karl was giving it a test push. I could sense him hovering, waiting for the door to open so he could pounce.

"I don't know why you're here, Karl, but—"

"I'm here about your mission tonight."

I paused, silk tank top in hand. "How'd you—?"

"The security on that nightclub leaves much to be desired."

"Oh."

"You weren't going to call me, were you?"

"Was I supposed to?"

Silence, then a rustle, as if he'd brushed against the door. Walking away? No, I could still sense him hovering, the anger vibes muted but clear.

"You won't ask for my help."

"I don't need—"

"Of course you don't."

I picked a plain T-shirt and yanked it on. "I can handle—"

"Of course you can. The fact that you're about to do a potentially difficult and dangerous break-in and you have a professional thief nearby to offer advice is irrelevant, isn't it? Because you can handle it, and you sure as hell aren't going to ask me for help."

I realized then he was offering to help with the break-in, not insinuating I couldn't make the decision about telling Benicio on my own. Which, in this case, I couldn't... but I didn't need him knowing that.

"I'm sure the gang can handle—" I began.

"In L.A., you encouraged Jeremy to call me for help on a break-in."

"Because he should. He's your Alpha."

"You wouldn't call yourself, would you?"

I passed over the skirt options and tugged on jeans, then opened the door. He was right there, so close I was surprised he didn't fall in.

"I did call you about that," I said.

"For advice, not help. I offered help and you refused, putting the onus on me to come down to L.A. and watch over you."

"You said you came to watch over Jeremy."

He didn't answer.

"Let me get this straight. You don't want to help me. You don't want to watch my back. But now you're complaining because I never ask you to?"

"It's not that I don't want to help. I don't want to want to."

I brushed past him. "For a man whose best weapon is words, you're either having a really bad day or you're talking circles around me."

I sat on the sofa and looked back to see him still by the bedroom door.

"When I was in Europe, you wouldn't have called me, would you? Wouldn't have called after I got home. If I didn't take the first step, you would have just . . . left things."

"*You* walked away, Karl. Was I supposed to chase after you? If a guy dumps me, I don't try to change his mind. I have more self-respect than that."

"I didn't dump—"

"You told me to date other guys!"

"I was—" He shook his head and strode into the living room. "Whatever circumstances I leave under—good or bad—it's always up to me to make contact again."

"I give you space and you're complaining? The guy who made it clear from the start that this relationship—if we can call it that and really, you'd rather we didn't—"

"That's—"

"Unfair? Maybe it is and, if so, I apologize. The point is that you made it clear *you* were in charge, that all contact would be under your conditions. It took almost a year for you to give me your phone number."

"No one outside the Pack has my number, Hope, and they only have it because Jeremy insisted. You're the only person I've ever willingly given it to."

I didn't know what to say to that, and the fight cooled into awkward silence, me sitting on the couch, gaze down, Karl standing in front of me, looking more uncomfortable than I'd have imagined possible.

"I *could* use your help, Karl," I said quietly. "Not with the break-in—I don't know anything about the place, so I have to trust the gang on that. But there's something..." I glanced up at him. "I really need some advice. Your advice."

HOPE

GONE

When I finished, I said, "I know I'm probably making too big a deal out of it."

"You're not. Benicio put you in a difficult situation, with no guidelines for what to do should trouble arise, probably because he didn't expect any."

"It's a sham, isn't it?" I said, walking to the window and looking out. "The job, I mean. Yes, there is grumbling in the gang, but that was only an excuse to call me in. To put me through my paces, see what I can do."

"And give you a taste for what you could be doing."

I balled up my hands, fighting to keep from raising them to my mouth. Chewed nails wouldn't become Faith Edmonds. It was a habit I'd finally broken six months ago, but had never been so tempted to restart as I'd been in this past month.

Tricked by the Cortez Cabal again. This wasn't just about testing me; it was about tempting me.

I wanted to say, "Maybe that's his plan, but he's not succeeding." A lie. Karl had seen it in my face last night. Drunk on chaos, chugging it back and paying for it in the morning. As with booze, though, if I kept at it, my tolerance level would rise and the guilt hangovers would disappear. I'd end up in the place I fought so hard to stay out of.

"So your advice?" I asked carefully.

"Don't call. If he complains later, it was my decision. You won't like suggesting I have the final say, but as progressive as Benicio is, he's old enough that he won't bat an eye at the implication that you'd defer to someone older and, yes, male."

I managed a snort. A smile touched Karl's eyes, though it didn't reach his mouth.

He continued. "Proceed with the break-in as planned. Later, we'll inform Benicio of the findings. If, however, you discover nothing, and they plan to interrogate this employee, notify me, discreetly, and I'll call Benicio."

"I can text you with the name and address."

He paused.

"Text messaging," I said. "On your cell phone."

"Right. Yes. Of course."

I tried not to smile. As technologically savvy as Karl was, I'd bet he'd never once used the text message option. For him, the phone was a one-way tool, to make hotel reservations or call a source. And his number always appeared as blocked.

I continued. "If you do contact Benicio, you should ring Lucas too, as a heads-up. He asked to be kept in the loop in case anything turns ugly."

"Agreed. So—"

My gang-supplied cell phone rang.

"Sorry," I said as I retrieved it from the kitchen. "It's probably Jaz."

"Jaz?" He said it as if it was a foreign word.

"Jasper. The—"

"Boy."

"He wanted to hook up—"

"I'm sure he did."

I gave him a look. "I don't mean—" Well, actually, that *was* why Jaz wanted to get together. I answered the phone.

"Hey."

"Faith?" It was Guy. "Is Jaz there?"

"Uh, no. I haven't seen him since he and Sonny took off on that errand. Hasn't he come back yet?"

"He did. About an hour ago. They were heading to their place to get ready for tonight. I called to ask them to swing by early, but I'm not getting an answer."

"Ah, well, Jaz . . . dropped his phone earlier . . ."

"I called him after you left, and it was working fine. Sonny isn't answering either. I'm concerned. Jaz can be high strung, and I know he wasn't happy at being left out tonight, but to ignore my calls . . ."

"Even if he did, Sonny wouldn't."

"I'll check with the others, then maybe head to their place." He hesitated. "If I do, I could use a second pair of eyes, if you're free."

My chest constricted. If Guy wanted "a second pair of eyes" he'd pick one of the others. Asking me meant he wanted a service the others couldn't provide: chaos detection.

He thought something had happened to Jaz and Sonny.

"Sure," I said, keeping my voice steady. "Give me a call and I'll be there."

I disconnected and slumped into a chair. Karl didn't ask what had happened—he wasn't one to avoid eavesdropping or pretend he had.

"Maybe they're just out of the cell-service area," I said. In Miami. Right. "Or they could be someplace that's blocked reception—a restaurant maybe. Yes, that's probably it. Guy can be a little paranoid."

"Not a bad trait in a leader, particularly when it comes to the safety of his subordinates."

My phone rang again. Guy calling back. He'd contacted Bianca, then Rodriguez—who was with Tony and Max. None of them had seen or heard from Jaz or Sonny since the meeting. Guy gave me an address. I said I'd be there in twenty minutes.

JAZ AND SONNY'S place was what I'd expected: a well-kept walkup in a neighborhood that straddled the line between dubious and dangerous. They could afford better, but this was decent enough, and they probably didn't spend much time here.

People who've gone through rough times financially seem to have two responses when their fortunes change. Some spend the money as fast as they can, treating themselves to everything they missed. Others are careful, determined to have some left over if the flow ebbs. At first glance, you'd peg Jaz and Sonny as type one. But they weren't as careless as they seemed, especially Sonny.

Security was like the building itself—decent, but nothing special. Guy broke into the apartment effortlessly. As we stepped in, I braced for the worst. While I'd convinced myself they were just out of phone contact, I kept thinking back to their encounter with the Cabal goons. Those guys hadn't targeted Jaz and Sonny at random. They weren't only the newest gang members—they were also the least supernaturally powerful. And let's face it, one look at them and they were clearly guys who liked to resolve their disputes over beers, not broken heads.

So I braced myself to see a ransacked apartment, stepped into the living room and let out a sigh of relief. I wouldn't call the place tidy, but there was no sign of a break-in or a struggle. A basket of dirty laundry waited to be taken to the cleaners. Sonny had tossed his jacket on the sofa. Sections of the *Miami Sun* were spread about, left wherever they'd been read. Breakfast dishes were stacked in the sink. It looked like my apartment when I was busy and didn't expect visitors.

I removed my shoes—a lesson from my mother embedded deep enough to be instinct—then headed for the tiny kitchenette. I learned only that someone liked Cheerios and someone preferred Froot Loops, and I could probably guess who was who. With a smile, I moved toward the bedroom. As I entered the hall, I stepped on a wet patch of carpet.

I turned toward the open bathroom door. The light was on, and a towel on the floor. I've been known to drop and leave towels, my mother's lessons being less concerned with housekeeping than etiquette. But there was water on the floor, trailing into the hall, suggesting whoever got out of the shower hadn't toweled off.

I heard the steady trickle of water, the shower dripping fast. Clothing was draped over the closed toilet—Jaz's from earlier. I picked up the towel. Dry and haphazardly folded. Unused. Someone jumping out of the shower, leaving the bathroom dripping wet and—

And what?

I closed my eyes and concentrated. No visions popped up. As I opened my eyes, I looked at the counter, and saw Jaz's wallet, with his keys, cell phone and a scattering of coins. Emptying his pockets before he took off his pants.

I opened up the wallet. Jaz's driver's license, a few frequent customer cards, three twenties, a ten and two fives.

Where would Jaz go in such a hurry, without his cell phone, keys and wallet?

I fought the rising panic. This was Jaz—impetuous Jaz. Sonny could have called him, he hopped from the shower, talked to Sonny, said "dry enough," dressed and went out for a bite to eat, trusting Sonny to have a phone and wallet.

"Faith?"

Guy walked into the bathroom, holding a cell phone and a set of keys. "I found these under Sonny's jacket."

I stared at the keys. "But the front door was locked, right?"

"It was."

We both headed for the patio door. It had looked closed, but now we could see that it wasn't shut far enough to lock, as if someone had haphazardly pulled it shut behind him.

I looked outside. The sun had been down for over an hour now. Risky for a balcony break-in, but not impossible.

I glanced at Guy. "The money. Their share from last night—"

"After last time, they left it in the safe. They each took a couple hundred."

Jaz had eighty dollars in his abandoned wallet, which meant—after lunch and cab rides—nothing was missing. Had someone broken in looking for more money? But who would know we'd pulled the job? I hadn't told Benicio. A mole in the gang... besides me? Not impossible. But why not wait until the guys were gone on tonight's break-in? Unless the robbery was less important than the message.

And that message was...?

I looked around the empty apartment and tried to rein in my galloping heart. No visions plus no vibes equals no chaos. I calmed myself with this mantra and set about helping Guy search.

Despite outward appearances, the place *had* been ransacked. The intruders had been careful to stuff things back in the drawers and close them, but it only took one glance inside to know someone had been hunting for something. The money? Maybe.

When we finished, I did a more thorough chaos reading. I did pick up snatches of visions, but when they came clear, I realized they were old images, from other tenants—a child being beaten, a date being raped. Images that would sneak back from my subconscious to torment me later, the thrill of chaos set against a backdrop of horror, a setting for sleepless, soul-searching nights.

For now, I had to concentrate on Jaz and Sonny, and none of my visions featured them.

"Maybe it's not chaotic enough for me to pick up," I said. "Maybe there's a . . . logical explanation."

We both fell silent, knowing how unlikely that was.

"The break-in is off, obviously," Guy said finally. "So you have a free night. I'll go back to the club, in case they show up."

"Can I help?"

"Go home and try to relax. With any luck, Jaz will call you. If not, we'll come back tomorrow, see if you can pick up any traces once you get some distance."

HOPE

BONUS POINTS

I left the apartment in such a daze that I was climbing into a cab before I noticed a dark Lexus idling down the block. Karl. Not hiding, just staying away so Guy wouldn't notice him.

Protecting me, as was his job. He could have asked me for the address instead of following my GPS signal. I knew why he hadn't. However much it made sense to have backup, I'd have argued.

I felt a twinge of guilt. He'd had a point earlier. I never called him—not for help, advice or just to say hello. Part of it was fear of relying on someone. Fear of needing someone. After my powers appeared, I'd struggled for years, off-balance, self-reliance gone. And so many people had failed me, nearly everyone except my family, who'd stood by, in pain, watching me suffer. When I found my balance, part of me had to prove I could stand alone . . . and part of me feared ever again relying on anyone to catch me if I stumbled.

With Karl, that need was coupled with my determination never to be just another woman who'd fallen for him. I'd wanted to be different, so I'd gone completely the other way, acting as if he could walk away tomorrow and I wouldn't care. Surprising that he hadn't said "screw this" and left.

Or, I suppose, that's exactly what he'd done . . .

———

THOUGHTS OF KARL kept me distracted until we met up at the apartment. Then I had to tell him everything, which ignited the fears I'd tamped down so well. By the end my hands were shaking, and I stuffed them into my jean pockets so Karl wouldn't see. There was nothing I could do about my quavering voice.

"It's probably just a misunderstanding," I said. "Right now, they might be strolling into the club, ready for duty. I've left my condo without my cell phone and wallet—when I'm running out to the corner store or the coffee shop. There's nothing to say they don't have another set of keys."

"We should notify Lucas."

"Why?" My voice squeaked and I cleared my throat. "I'd sound as if I was overreacting."

I moved to the sofa, grabbing every support along the route.

Something had happened to Jaz.

I dropped onto the sofa, one hand clutching the arm as though I might slide off.

I hadn't seen a chaos vision. Hadn't felt a vibe. If something serious happened in that room, I'd know it.

Wouldn't I?

I was always the first to say my powers were far from perfect.

Karl sat beside me. Hands on his thighs, back straight. Then he reached over and patted my leg, a horribly awkward tap, like one you'd give a stranger in distress, while praying you wouldn't be called upon to do more.

He glanced my way. Our eyes met and I saw . . . panic. Like I might throw myself into his arms and start sobbing. I looked away fast.

"I—I'm going to take a bath. Try to relax."

I waited, hoping for him to say, "No, stay and talk about it." But he mumbled, "Good idea."

I pushed from the sofa and hurried to the bathroom.

FIFTEEN MINUTES LATER, Karl rapped on the door.

"May I come in?"

"I'm still in the tub."

"So . . . no?"

A few hours ago, he'd coldly refused to talk to me in a towel, and now he wanted to come in when I was bathing?

"If you want to, I guess," I said, words coming slow, with obvious reluctance.

The doorknob turned. I arranged a washcloth over my breasts. Yes, he'd seen them before, but damned if I was putting on a show that he clearly didn't want.

He shut the door behind him, as if we might be disturbed. For the second time that night, he looked uncharacteristically uncomfortable, hair ruffled, as if he'd run his hands through it.

"Yes, Karl?"

His gaze slid to me for the first time, then quickly turned away. "I thought...I could help. If you'd like. I can go to their apartment and—" His jaw worked, chewing over the next words, then he spit them out, as if making some embarrassing confession. "I could sniff around. See if there are any signs of . . . violence."

"Blood, you mean."

"And I can look—sniff—for trails, maybe find out where they went."

I wanted to scream, "Yes, please!" but studied his expression, trying to gauge how genuine the offer was, how much he was hoping I'd say, "No, that's okay."

"I should, Hope," he continued. "I can find some answers for you. You can stay here and wait—"

"No, I'll come."

WHEN WE ARRIVED at the apartment, I was in a strange mood, almost giddy. Now I would know what had happened. If I'd thought of it earlier, I'd have asked Karl, but he worked so hard to suppress his werewolf side, it was easy to forget what he could do.

He wouldn't find a murder scene. If they'd been killed, their bodies would still be there. I should have realized this, but had been so determined not to consider the possibility, that I hadn't allowed myself to think it through.

If the Cabal *was* involved, they had Jaz and Sonny. Maybe not in the best of shape, but they'd be alive. Their kidnappings would be for negotiation or a show of force.

In this frame of mind, the specter of Jaz's death all but banished, I could relax. Karl would help me solve this puzzle, and then, if it was a kidnapping, we'd have proof to take to Benicio and demand answers.

The building door, as earlier, was unlocked, but Guy had relocked the apartment door.

Karl took out his picks.

"May I?" I asked.

"Of course."

It would be quicker if he did it, but the hall was empty. Karl handed me his gloves—sheer fabric that let me feel and grip objects, but wouldn't leave prints.

I shifted so my body would block anyone's view from the right. Karl took up position on my left.

"You're blocking my light," I said.

"You can't pick locks in the dark?"

"You still need to teach me."

"That's what I'm doing."

He stayed where he was, shadow cast over my hands. I closed my eyes and worked by feel. Overkill, but my heart was already picking up speed and I wasn't averse to adding an extra layer of challenge... and danger.

After a minute, his hand closed around mine. My eyes flew open.

"Keep them shut," he murmured. When I did, he straightened my fingers, guiding them. "Now, you can feel the..."

He led me through it. I struggled to pay attention, but the feel of his fingers through the thin fabric, the warmth of his breath, the overwhelming awareness of him, standing inches away... Let's just say the chaos buzz of the lock-picking wasn't the only thing making my pulse race.

Finally, we got it unlocked. I opened the door.

"Do you still have those locks I gave you for practice?" he asked.

"I do."

"You should work on them in different light conditions."

"You mean I'm not perfect yet?"

"Shockingly enough."

He propelled me through the hall, then circled the room, sniffing discreetly.

"I don't think that's going to do it," I said.

"I'm just starting."

"You mean you're working up to the undignified part."

A snort, but he didn't disagree, just kept circling.

"Just get down on the carpet," I said. "I swear I won't take photos."

He crouched, then cast a surreptitious glance my way.

"Oh, good God, just get down already." I turned my back to him and crossed my arms. "Better? I swear, Karl, even in Miami, you win bonus points for vanity."

Another snort. Another noticeable lack of disagreement. After a few minutes, I said, "When Elena and I worked a council job together, she said her sense of smell is better when she's in wolf form."

"Humph."

"I'm just saying..."

"Elena's sense of smell is better than mine in any form."

"And you admit it?"

"Only because it isn't a skill I care to excel in." A pause. "But you're right. I should Change."

"I was kidding, Karl. I know it's not like snapping your fingers—"

"No, I should. I'm already overdue."

"Ah, that's why you've been so grouchy."

"Yes. It has absolutely nothing to do with you."

I spun but only got a view of his back a split second before he closed the bedroom door. He'd want privacy for his Change and that *wasn't* vanity. I'm curious about many things, but witnessing the human-to-wolf transformation isn't one of them.

"I'm going to try picking up visions," I said. "So try to keep the screams of agony to a minimum, okay?"

A muttered epithet. I grinned and walked to the sofa.

HOPE

THE SCENT OF TROUBLE

While Karl Changed, I worked on summoning chaos visions. To automatically detect chaos, it has to be strong—either very recent or very chaotic. To find more, I need to pop up my antenna by concentrating. The problem is that then I get too many signals, all competing for air time in my brain.

I caught flashes—a raised hand, an angry shout, a muffled plea—with no context to place it in. Having Karl Changing in the next room didn't help. There was no chaos from it—pain doesn't count unless it's accompanied by an emotion, and Karl was beyond that. Still, I knew he was undergoing something agonizing, to help me, so I couldn't stop feeling twinges of guilt.

Finally there came the noise I'd been waiting for, the bump-bump of Karl moving around the bedroom, sniffing. After a moment, silence. Then a grunt of canine frustration.

I walked to the bedroom door . . . and laughed.

"Problem, Karl?"

A black nose appeared at the narrow opening of the almost-shut door. He tried wedging his muzzle into it to fling it open, but couldn't get leverage. Another grunt, annoyed now. The nose withdrew. I could picture him sitting on his haunches, out of my sight, pondering the predicament.

"If you scratch at the door, someone will probably let you out."

A huff.

I pushed open the door. Karl was sitting exactly as I'd pictured him. He fixed me with a look, then stalked out.

Before I met Karl, I'd wondered what a changed werewolf looked like. Not an all-consuming topic of curiosity, but I *had* wondered. I'd heard stories, but no eyewitness accounts. I had my curiosity satisfied that first night.

Admittedly, having little experience with wolves, I'd thought he looked like a big dark-haired dog. Later, I'd found a picture of a black wolf with snow on its muzzle, giving the photographer an imperious "I most certainly was *not* playing in the snow" glower. The wolf—and its expression—reminded me so much of Karl that the picture now hung in my home office. He hated it. Threatened to abscond with it every time he visited, but of course, he never did.

Karl worked his way around the apartment with his nose to the floor. Not wanting to hover, I went into the living room, sat cross-legged on the floor and concentrated.

After a few minutes, a vision came that I hadn't seen before—a spray of blood. Heart hammering, I pulled back from the vision, took a deep breath, then chased it, trying to untangle it from the other threads. Finally, by concentrating on just that image, I was able to tug it to the forefront.

I struggled to pull my mind's eye away from the blood and see the rest of the scene. The screen was very small, focusing only on the event, as usual. Blood sprayed. Then, in the next iteration, I made out a flash of motion. Then a flash of flesh. Finally, a flash of fist. That was it.

The blood came from a punch, maybe to the nose, not even a hard punch at that, the spark of chaos coming from surprise. A playful jab that made contact? Sonny and Jaz goofing around? A previous tenant? I couldn't see either actor, but whatever the explanation, this wasn't a truly chaotic event.

Karl walked behind me, so close his fur tickled my neck. I leaned back and he stopped, letting me rest against him. We stayed like that for a moment. Then he pressed his cold nose against the back of my neck, making me jump, and gave a growling chuckle before moving on.

"Not getting anything?" I asked.

I didn't know whether he could understand me. He glanced my way, but that might only have been a reaction to my voice.

"Have you gone through the bathroom yet? That's where it seems to have started, whatever *it* was."

A soft grunt, and he walked that way. So he *could* understand me.

I started following, then heard the squeak of the front-door knob. Karl's head swung up, ears swiveling.

I grinned. "Seems like someone's home and we've all been worrying for nothing."

The door opened. I started forward. Karl lunged and grabbed my hand in his teeth, fangs pressing into the skin, but careful not to break it. When I looked over at him, he flared his nostrils. I was about to pull away, when he flared them again, making a show of sniffing the air.

Whoever was in that hall wasn't Jaz or Sonny. I was about to dive into the bathroom with Karl when a voice called, "Faith? Is that you?"

I pulled away from Karl. He snapped to get my attention. I shook my head and started to close the door behind me. He lunged into the opening. Then he backed up, leaving a paw in the gap as I pulled shut the door.

Guy walked in. He wore a blue paisley shirt and smelled of cologne, as if he'd been heading out to hit the clubs, take a break from worrying about Jaz and Sonny.

"It is you," he said. "I thought I heard your voice."

Karl's paw vanished into the bathroom. I left the door as it was, so he could get it open, and moved into the living room.

"I heard someone coming in and thought it might be the guys."

"Sorry," he said.

"I know I probably shouldn't be here, but I thought maybe it would be easier to pick up a vision when I was alone."

"Was it?"

I moved to the sofa, making him turn his back to the bathroom door. "I caught flashes. Nothing relevant. But I'd like to keep trying."

He didn't take the hint, just told me to go ahead and he'd poke around looking for clues he might have missed. A dark shape passed the partly open bathroom door, Karl changing position to keep an eye on Guy.

Guy checked under the sofa.

"So no one's heard anything, I take it?" I said.

He shook his head and moved to the entertainment stand, searching it. I crossed to the door, struggling to think of a way to get him out of here. When I turned, he was in the middle of the room, looking around. His gaze fell on the bathroom door.

"I suppose I'll take off, then," I said. "Try to get some sleep."

I was about to ask him to walk outside with me, claim the neighborhood made me nervous, but he beat me to it, adding, "I should probably go too. This isn't helping. It's just..." He rolled his shoulders. "Making me feel useful, I guess."

I nodded. "Same here. Better to rest and clear our heads."

We headed downstairs. I planned to call for a cab, then circle the block in it and return for Karl.

But Guy, surprisingly, wanted to talk. Obviously he was worried and tense and, like many people under stress, he reacted by talking. He explained what the others were doing to hunt for Jaz and Sonny, then he told me some of their theories, then gave more details on their recent attack by the Cabal goons. Any other time, I'd have made the most of his loquacious mood, but all I kept thinking was *How do I get out of here?* before Karl shot out the front door after me. When Guy finally did pause enough for me to say, "Oh, I should call that cab," he put out a hand to stop me.

"I'll give you a lift."

"Oh? Uh, sure. Where are you parked?"

"Just down the road."

He put his hand on my elbow and started leading me along the darkened sidewalk. "I want to stop by the club first, grab my stuff."

"Sure."

"We could probably use a drink too." A smile my way. "On the house."

Shit. In other words, Guy still wanted to talk. I knew I should take advantage, but my brain was spinning with worries about Jaz, and worries about Karl now too, whether he'd know where I'd gone, whether he'd remember to sniff the balcony and under it.

So how to say no to Guy without sounding like I was giving him the brush-off?

"Miss?"

I turned to see Karl approaching. He wore an ill-fitting blazer, shoulders straining the seams—a jacket meant for a thinner man, probably from Sonny's closet. He dipped his head deferentially.

"You wanted me to wait with the cab, miss?"

His accent was a Deep South drawl, copied from Clayton, if I was any judge.

"Uh, no," I said. "I didn't say that, but if you've been waiting, I guess I should—"

"Hold on." Guy took a couple of twenties from his pocket. "There. Go."

Karl took a hard look at Guy, then his gaze slipped to me. "This man bothering you, miss?"

"Yeah," Guy said, words sharp. "I'm a black guy in a bad neighborhood. Of course I'm bothering her. Now, beat it, asshole, or—"

"I was just asking, son. No need to get your back up."

Guy took a step toward Karl. "I'm not your son—"

I jumped between them, which was what Karl was hoping for. Rile Guy up and give me an excuse to get flustered.

I turned to Guy. "Please don't. Not tonight. I—I should just go, okay? I'll see you tomorrow."

Guy protested, but I made it clear I didn't want trouble and he stood watch as Karl led me back to the Lexus.

"Seems someone was hoping for a little company tonight," Karl mused. "Some mutual comforting perhaps in the wake of the crisis?"

"Trust me, Guy's not interested in the opposite sex."

Karl backed the car out. "Oh, I'm quite certain you're mistaken."

"Have a sixth sense for these things, do you?"

"No, but I have an excellent sense for signs of sexual attraction. It's difficult to lure a woman someplace quiet and divest her of her jewels without them."

"At the risk of being sexist, I'll suggest your radar works better on women than men, Karl. I've had enough attention since I got to Miami that my self-confidence is flying pretty high, and I'm telling you, Guy's not interested in me."

He muttered something under his breath, but didn't answer, just circled the block, then returned to check beneath the balcony.

"Too bad Guy interrupted," I said as we snuck around the rear of the building. "Otherwise, I could have just walked you down here before you changed back."

His look said he wasn't dignifying that with a retort.

"I always wanted a dog," I said, nearly running to keep up with his long strides. "My brothers were both allergic. Have I told you that?"

"Once or twice."

"Maybe, someday, you could humor me and—"

"Don't finish that sentence."

I grinned and jogged ahead, found the right balcony, then waved him over. "Up in the apartment, you didn't find any blood, did you?"

He shook his head and crouched.

"And scent trails? You could make out Jaz and Sonny, right? Oh, and now you know what Guy smells like—"

"Cologne. Which—" he glanced up at me, "—most men don't wear to go hunting for lost friends."

"Well, he didn't wear it for me, considering he didn't know I was at the apartment. Maybe he *was* hoping for company—heading out for some club-hopping to clear his head. But you could still smell his scent, couldn't you?"

"Vaguely."

"Well, then you have your four baseline scents including mine. Was there anyone else—"

He pressed a finger to my lips. "No, there wasn't. Now, may I finish what I'm trying to do here? Before someone hears us?"

"Sorry, I'm just—"

"Anxious. I know." As he ducked, I thought he brushed his lips across the top of my head. "Just a few minutes, and I'll have your answers."

He sniffed the ground without asking me to turn away. Then he tossed me the keys. "You go back to the car. I'll finish up here."

A few minutes later, he climbed into the driver's seat. "Nothing."

"No sign of Jaz or Sonny?"

"Almost no sign of anyone. There's little reason for anyone to walk that way *unless* they were planning a break-in—there are no ground-level patios and it isn't a shortcut to anywhere. The only trails I found were faint."

"Meaning old."

He nodded.

"And upstairs? Only the four of us?"

"That's harder to tell. Obviously far more traffic and it's hard for me to distinguish a day-old scent from an hour-old one. But I'm reasonably certain no one else was in that apartment today. And I'm absolutely certain no one climbed up or down that balcony. If the door was cracked open, it's because one of those boys opened it, and didn't close it right."

"Damn it, this doesn't make sense."

"No, it doesn't."

HOPE

MATING INSTINCT

We returned to my apartment. As we walked into the building, I said, "Thank you, Karl."

He hesitated, hand on the door.

I touched his arm. "I mean it. Thank you."

He nodded. As we walked through the lobby, Karl cleared his throat. "I'm sure it might be busy for you tomorrow, but if you can find the time, I'd like to take you to dinner."

"Dinner? Uh, sure."

"It's my birthday."

The admission was so unlike Karl that I was silent until we reached the elevator.

"I'd ask how old you'll be, but I know I'll never get it from you."

"Fifty."

I thanked God he picked that moment to push the button, leaving no chance to glimpse my reaction. I'd always guessed Karl was in his midforties, and fifty wasn't much older, but it *seemed* a lot older.

I could say it didn't matter—werewolves age slowly, so physically, Karl's no more than midthirties, but all that means is that when I'm walking down the street with him, I won't be mistaken for his daughter. In terms of life experience, he *is* fifty and that's what counts.

The elevator arrived and we stepped on.

"Is your birthday tomorrow? Or today?" I asked.

He checked his watch. "Oh, I see. Today, then."

I stood on my tiptoes and brushed my lips across his. "Happy birthday, Karl."

Before I could step back, he leaned down. His kiss was almost as brief as mine, but firm. Like his hands on my hips, pressing, but not pulling me to him, making me strain forward, hoping for more. But I only got that one brief kiss. When he pulled away, I found myself arching onto my tiptoes, prolonging the contact until the last possible moment. Then I jolted back onto flat feet.

I thought about what I was doing, the door I was reopening. Was I trying to reopen it? And if I was, did that mean I was closing another? I tried to remember Jaz, but his image wouldn't form. All I could think about was Karl.

My gaze down, I laid a tentative hand on Karl's chest. I listened to his breathing, felt the rise and fall of his chest and the warmth of him through his shirt, sensed his gaze on the top of my head, waiting for me to look up. But I couldn't.

"I hate this, Karl," I whispered. "Who'd have thought we'd come to this? You and me, snipping and snapping at each other. I hear us doing it, and I can't believe it. Not us."

"I'm sorry."

"You?" I managed a laugh, harsh to my ears. "I've been just as bad."

"But you had a reason to be angry."

I looked up, finally meeting his gaze. "And, maybe, so do you."

He inhaled. Exhaled. And looked away.

The elevator climbed another floor.

"Hope..."

His voice was so soft I wasn't sure I heard him, and I looked up. He touched my chin, fingers gliding up my jaw, so light that when I closed my eyes, I couldn't feel it. When I looked, his eyes were right there, inches from mine. He tilted my chin up—

The elevator dinged. As the doors opened, we both looked over. In unison, our gazes shunted to the button panel.

"That 'stop' button looks pretty good," I said.

He made a noise in his throat that sounded like agreement. "Unfortunately, if it stops for more than a couple of minutes, we'll be rescued by the building super."

"Had some experience with that, have you?"

He gave me a look. "On a job."

"That's what I meant. Seducing the marks in an elevator. How dé-classé."

A growl and he grabbed for me, but I quickstepped out of his reach and darted through the doors. He swung in front, caught me and slammed me against the door opening. His mouth crushed against mine, knocking the breath from me. The door bounced against my back, but he only pushed me into it, hands going to my rear, fingers digging in as he boosted me up, pushing between my legs until I straddled his hips.

I wrapped my hands in his hair, legs clasped around him, pulling him closer as he pressed into me, fierce and insistent. My brain whirled, a high made all the richer because there wasn't a chaos vibe to be found. It was all him. The smell of him, the taste of him, the—

The alarm buzzed right behind my head. The elevator, warning us that its door was blocked.

Karl snarled at it, and I laughed, and he turned the sound into a harrumph, with a glare that said I hadn't heard what I thought I heard. His lips went back to mine, punishingly hard, and my brain reeled, body arching into his, the ache so sharp that he could have taken me there and I wouldn't have noticed where we were. Noticed or cared.

He pulled back, my lip caught between his teeth. I shuddered and squirmed against him, and he let out a low growl, then swung me around, in two steps pressing me into the opposite wall, next to my apartment door. He thrust me against it, hard enough that he could let go with one hand and tug the keys from my pocket. Once the door was open, he tried to swing me through, but stumbled, and we crashed to the floor.

When I laughed, he gave me another "pretend you didn't notice that" glower. I closed my eyes, braced for another bruising kiss, but his lips brushed mine, feather light. I shivered. When I opened my eyes, he was right over me, and in his face was everything I'd seen that Valentine's night and later convinced myself I hadn't.

I inhaled sharply and the shock hit me, like a whiff of smelling salts. That morning after flashed back. All the pain, the humiliation. My hands shot between us and I tried to scramble back, but his grip tightened. He leaned down to my ear.

"I won't hurt you again, Hope."

He kept his lips at my ear, his breathing shallow, caressing my jaw as he pushed back a lock of hair.

"Never again," he whispered. "I promise."

My heart skittered. This was what I wanted to hear. What I'd dreamed of hearing. That it had all been a big misunderstanding.

But it hadn't been. He'd said so himself. There was no other way to interpret what he'd said.

His lips moved to my neck, gliding along my pulse, registering my reaction. He moved to my throat, light kisses that sent my pulse racing, but I stayed stiff in his arms.

He rose, face coming to mine. "I didn't walk away from you that morning, Hope. I ran. Turned tail and ran. *My* problem. But it won't happen again." His hand moved to the side of my face, fingers brushing my cheek. "I came back, and I'm staying."

His mouth came down to mine. The kiss started slow, almost tentative, as if testing his welcome. When my hands went to the back of his head, it was like a watershed breaking. He grabbed me, and rolled us over, moving on top of me, his weight crushing in the most delicious way.

When I gasped, he thrust against me, all smoothness gone as he fumbled with the front of my jeans. He cursed, as if undoing a simple button was beyond him, as lust-clumsy as any teenage boy, and I was thrown back to that night in the pool, that first kiss igniting, Karl pulling back, struggling to be suave, to be gentle, to be a perfect lover, only to be swept up again and finally giving up, slamming me against the side of the pool. Brutally passionate and unforgettable.

And how many nights since then had I spent trying to forget it?

How many nights would I spend trying to forget this one?

When I broke the kiss, he hung there for a moment, panting. Then he looked down at me and blinked, and I knew he saw the truth, that I didn't trust him. His lips curved in an oath.

He cupped my face, lowering his until he was so close I could see only his eyes. "It won't happen again, Hope. It was *my* problem."

"And that problem was...?"

"Later. I'll explain it all later." He brushed his lips against mine. "I need you. Now. Please."

I shivered, eyelids fluttering. God, how many times had I dreamed of hearing that? I could look into his eyes, and see it. He wanted me. Desperately. And I had to talk about it first? Was I crazy?

I squeezed my eyes shut. If I said yes, I'd never get that explanation. Right now, he might honestly intend to give it, but come morning, he'd brush me off with a, "Don't worry, it wasn't about you." That would be that.

Every morning after, if I went to sleep beside him, I'd worry he wouldn't be there when I woke, because I didn't know what drove him away the first time.

I opened my eyes. "I need to know now."

"No."

"No?"

"Not now?"

A tightness in his voice turned the words into a query—or maybe a plea—and I sputtered a laugh.

He growled. "You have no respect for a mood, do you?"

I eyed him. Considered my options. Realized there was only one way I was getting my answers, as much as I hated to use it.

I grabbed the back of his head and pulled him down in a kiss. His hands went to my shirt, and he had it out of my jeans and over my head so quickly, I barely realized we'd broken the kiss. A snap of the front clasp on my bra, then his thumbs tickled over my breasts as he pushed it aside.

His shirt started to follow, but I caught his hands and whispered, "Let me. Please." I took hold of the hem, met his gaze and said, "Right after you tell me why you left."

He let out an oath on a blast of chaos so sharp I arched my head back and shuddered.

"Like that, do you?" he said.

I grinned. "You know I do."

"Damn you."

"Mmm." I nibbled the side of his neck. "Tell me more...like what you meant that morning."

A growl and another string of obscenities.

I writhed under him. "Not bad. But it needs a little more venom. Say it like you mean it."

"I wish I could. You have no idea, sometimes, how much I wish I could."

He grabbed me in a kiss so hard, so rich with frustration, that had he reached for my jeans again, I wouldn't have stopped him. Instead, he broke it off and sighed.

"You're right," he said.

"Hurts, doesn't it?"

"Damn you."

A moment's silence. Then he rolled off me and propped his head up on his arm. I twisted onto my side to face him.

"This is going to take a while."

"I've got all night."

A noise, half sigh, half growl. "All right then. When I went to Europe, I planned to take you with me. I'd make it sound like a whim. A lark. Light and casual. Then morning came, and I realized you'd *know* it wasn't a spur-of-the-moment decision, and if I was telling *myself* it was light or casual..."

He shook his head. "I wanted to forget about it, but I couldn't. So I told myself I'd mention the job, see your reaction when I said I was leaving."

"See how crushed I was?"

A muscle in his cheek twitched at the coolness in my voice, but after a moment he nodded.

"And when I wasn't upset enough, you had to keep pushing. See what did upset me. Not just flying off to Europe for a few days, but indefinitely...and maybe I should date other guys while you were gone. See if anything dug in enough to hurt."

"Yes."

I scrambled up. "You bastard."

"Hope—"

"No." I backed away. "You want brownie points for being honest? You hurt me just to see if you could, just to prove that I have feelings for you?"

He shook his head. "I didn't want to see if I could get a reaction. I *wanted* a reaction. I wanted you to think exactly what you did—that you'd been seduced, that I was just as cold and self-serving as you've always suspected. I wanted to walk away and close the door. *Slam* it, so I could never come back."

"I don't understand."

"I'm not sure I do either."

He pushed to his feet and looked around, then settled onto the couch. I stayed on the floor, arms around my knees.

"I've never understood it," he continued. "What happened that night at the museum. Why I helped you get away from Tristan and why, after I had helped, it was so hard to walk away. Why, even when I did, I couldn't *stay* away."

He shifted to see me better around the coffee table. "Not that I couldn't understand the attraction. You're beautiful. You're smart. You're fun to be around. But I've been with beautiful women, smart women, fun women, and there wasn't one I didn't walk away from in the morning. I only ever felt a twinge of regret if I had to leave a piece of jewelry behind. At first, I told myself it was because you were a challenge. You weren't interested in me and I wanted to change your mind. But even when I knew I *could* change your mind, I didn't. Because, if I seduced you, then I'd have no excuse for coming back, and..." A pause. "I wanted the excuse."

I hugged my knees, wondering if I should say something, but feeling like I wasn't supposed to.

"I've been having dreams. For a few months now..." Another pause, his jaw working, as if trying to figure out how to word something. "I don't dream very often. It's usually...wolf. If I postpone my Change, I dream of Changing. If I haven't hunted, I dream of hunting. I'm reminded, prodded. Lately, I've been dreaming of you. Of us. Of..."

He fell silent, jaw tensing again.

"Cabins," he spat finally, as if making some terrible confession. "I dream of forests and cabins and us, and no one else. I dream of taking you someplace, holing up, making love and making—" He clipped off the last word.

"Making what?"

He met my gaze and his lips twitched. "From that look on your face, you know what I was about to say. Let me remind you, emphatically, that it's a dream. When I wake, I'm as horrified as you."

"Thank God."

He arched a brow. "Can you honestly see me living in a cabin? It's a symbol, obviously. An impulse. Not to carry you off into the woods and raise a pack of squalling brats. Just to...be with you."

"The instinct to mate."

He gave a low growl, and I braced for an argument, but he only turned his gaze toward the window, as if he'd already figured out what the impulse was, and just hated hearing it put into words.

"It's understandable, isn't it?" I said. "You're fifty years old with no children. The animal instinct to reproduce is sure to kick in—"

"So I start having caveman fantasies about the first woman in prime childbearing years to cross my path? In some ways, I wish to hell that's all it was. A biological imperative that randomly fixed on an appropriate target."

He stood and walked to the window, his back to me.

"I used to hear other werewolves talk about it," he said. "The problems of living solitary lives. Fighting the urge to find a mate and settle. I'd commiserate, if it was to my advantage, but even as I was listening I was calling them fools. Weak. Convincing themselves it was an instinct because they didn't have the balls to admit the truth— that they wanted a wife and kids and a picket-fence life. I'd never felt the urge to stay with a woman until morning, let alone for life, so I was living proof there was no mating instinct. The truth was, it seems, that I just hadn't met..."

He let the sentence fade, and stared out into the night. The silence dragged out past seconds into minutes.

"Damned inconvenient, isn't it?" I said finally. "That's the problem."

He glanced my way. I got up and perched on the edge of the coffee table.

"You've been on your own since you were sixteen," I said. "Since your father died. There hasn't been anyone. No lovers. No friends. No one you couldn't cut ties with in a heartbeat...and wouldn't kill if they got in your way. Then you joined the Pack, but you're still ambivalent about that and tell yourself it's a business arrangement and keep social contact to a minimum. Now you have me. Someone who might expect some kind of commitment from you in return, a commitment you might—horrors—want to give. Damnably inconvenient."

He gave a hoarse laugh. "You can't resist, can you? Even this you can turn into 'Karl thinking about himself again.' "

"Am I wrong?"

He met my gaze, then turned back to the window. "Damn you."

I crept to him, stood on tiptoes and kissed the back of his neck—or that was my goal, though I barely reached his collar. He glanced over his shoulder in surprise. I put my hands on his sides and leaned in, laying my cheek against the middle of his back.

"Remember when we met? Before you left, you said you were going to make a fool of yourself over me. That's still what you're worried about. That you'll find yourself doing things you never dreamed of doing, things you laughed at in others, and you'll make a fool of yourself."

A sigh rippled through him. "You never cut me any slack, do you? You can't find some unselfish motive, like that I don't want to hurt you. Or even a romantic one, perhaps that I'm worried about having my heart broken."

"A broken heart is just a fancy way of saying you've been made a fool of—that you opened up, let someone in, and they took advantage. As for hurting me, I'm sure that's in there somewhere, but it's not the driving factor."

"Dare I ask what is, in your opinion?"

"That a relationship with me would not only be inconvenient, but potentially humiliating. After all these years of being happy on your own, why risk that for a relationship that might not work out?"

"Sounds like you're trying to dissuade me."

I kissed the back of his shirt. "If you can be dissuaded, I think you should be."

"No. I don't think I can."

He turned, pulled me to him and kissed me. Then he waited. After a moment of silence, he sighed. "My grand confession, my soul laid bare, and you aren't even going to throw me a scrap, are you?"

"If you're waiting for me to say that the idea of being a werewolf's chosen mate is incredibly romantic, maybe swoon at your feet . . ."

"Perish the thought."

"Granted, my mother would be thrilled to see me hook up with someone, but a fifty-year-old werewolf thief might not be her idea of the ideal partner."

"We won't tell her about the thief part. Or the werewolf part." A pause. "Or the fifty-year-old part."

"If you ask *me* whether a fifty-year-old werewolf thief is *my* ideal partner, in my idealized life . . ."

"I suppose not."

"Sorry." I looked up at him. "But if you ask me whether it's what I *want,* my answer might be different. No guarantees. But there's a strong possibility."

"I can live with that."

He scooped me up and carried me into the bedroom.

LUCAS

3

I WAS IN BED, waiting for the alarm to ring. Paige lay on her side, facing me, the blankets pushed down to her waist. She'd been naked when we'd gone to bed last night, but must have risen at some point, putting on a short nightgown to go downstairs. Now the nightgown was twisted, and one breast peeked from the curtain of long curls, straining to be free, thwarted only by that last half-inch over her nipple. It needed only a tweak of the silk folds to finish its escape. Most mornings I would have completed the rescue, then turned off the alarm and found a less jarring way to wake her. But last night we'd worked on a new spell, and while that might not seem the obvious excuse for my hesitation, Paige's methods of spell practice are far from obvious.

Paige is as voracious a student of the art of spellcasting as I am. But that doesn't stop her from livening it up with an extra twist. Last night's added attraction had been a personal favorite of mine: strip spellcasting. Fail to cast the spell, lose an item of clothing. Given that it was a new and difficult spell, that first stage hadn't lasted long, leading us—naked—to the second, in which at any sign of a successful cast, the "winner" receives a service from the "loser." By the time we felt confident in our ability to cast the spell, we were exhausted, barely able to find our way to bed, and six hours later, I still wouldn't consider myself fully recovered. That did not, however, keep me from enjoying the sight of Paige and even feel the first twinges to suggest I wasn't as tired as I'd imagined.

She rolled onto her back, covers twisting until she was nearly free of them. The hem of her gown rode up one thigh, granting me a peek at the red lace panties beneath. The bodice had pulled even tighter, her breast now straining all the more to be free, her nipple poking against the fabric and making me decide that, indeed, I was quite recovered.

A gentle tug and the trapped breast was free, full and firm, the nipple still erect, begging for attention. First, though, I tugged the other side of the skirt up, until it was around her belly, the bright red panties on full display. I took a minute to enjoy the view.

My wife has a body worthy of the attention. Full, soft and generously rounded everywhere a woman should be rounded. I'm not usually aware of such things, but even on our first meeting, I'd noticed. At the time, if a fortune-teller had told me that one day I'd waken to this sight every morning, I'd have demanded my money back. So I can be forgiven if I do, now and then, like to wallow in my good luck.

I saw the clock preparing to flip to six and tapped off the alarm. Then I leaned down, tongue tickling over that waiting nipple. Her response was instantaneous, a low moan of pleasure. I took her nipple between my teeth, my tongue—

My cell phone blared so loud we both jerked up . . . fortunately without injury.

"Ignore it," I said, pulling her back.

"No." She reached over me, breast brushing my lips, then handed me my phone. "You answer. I'll keep things going."

With a grin, she kissed my chest, then moved lower. An order was an order, so I answered.

"Lucas? It's Karl. We have a problem."

Paige heard and stopped, scant inches from her destination. She glanced up at me, a question in her eyes that I really didn't want to answer. I considered accidentally hitting the disconnect button. She read my mind and gave a soft laugh, kissed my stomach, then rolled from bed with a mouthed "later."

I cursed Karl Marsten, sat up and gave him my almost complete attention.

I WAS STILL on the phone when a cup of steaming coffee appeared by my hand, slid discreetly across the desk. I'd moved into the tiny office adjoining our bedroom and was jotting down notes as Karl talked. I motioned for Paige to stay, but she gestured something I couldn't decipher, and slipped from the room.

"Jasper Davidyan?" I said. "That's D-a-v-i-d-y-a-n?"

"Yes, but Hope suspects the surname is phony, and I'd agree. It comes from the license in his wallet, which is definitely a forgery."

"You said he goes by Jaz. Is that one z? Two? Or an s?"

A snort, clearly contemptuous of the moniker in general and not about to speculate on the specifics.

I continued. "So Hope found no sign of chaos at the apartment, and you discovered no extraneous trails or blood—"

"No, I said I told *her* that."

"Ah." I sipped my coffee and waited. It took a few moments, but he finally went on.

"There was blood under an armchair that, judging by the marks in the carpet, had been moved to cover it. And there was a bloody rag in the bushes below the balcony."

"But you kept this from Hope?"

His tone frosted. "It was spatter under the chair. Just enough to make a mess and there wasn't much more on the rag, meaning no one's dead or seriously injured. If Hope knew, she'd worry and she's already worrying enough."

I took the rest of the details, then signed off.

I was jotting down a list of steps to pursue when Paige appeared, this time bearing toasted and buttered English muffins for two, and a coffee for herself. I took the plate and mug and filled her in.

"I don't think your father's involved," she said finally.

That was, as she knew, my first question and the one I least trusted myself to answer.

"I'm not discounting the possibility—" she said.

"Always wise," I murmured.

"—but, unless I'm missing an angle, I can't see the advantage for him. He hired Hope to infiltrate the gang. Granted, he's also hoping to woo her to the dark side, but he's a practical man, and he'll want value from the job, so there's no sense sending her in if he plans to squash any whiff of rebellion three days after she starts."

"Agreed."

"Has she spoken to your dad since?"

"She was supposed to check in this morning, but Karl turned off her alarm and made the call himself. Probably wise. He's better equipped to gauge my father's reaction."

She nodded. "When it comes to bullshit detecting, Karl's a natural."

"He told my father that Hope had been on a job with the gang the night before and was still sleeping and, according to Karl, my father gave no indication that this was a surprise or that he was expecting anything else. He told Karl she could call later if she wished, or wait until tomorrow's check-in."

"Any chance these guys took off?"

I tore a piece of my muffin. "Hope says they were happy with the gang, even after being beaten and robbed. And Karl concurs. They weren't going anywhere from what he could see."

"So what are their theories?"

"Hope suspects rogue elements in the Cabal."

"Like what happened to her."

"Precisely. Karl is looking at an inside job, specifically the gang leader. He wants me to investigate him."

"The leader has a beef with the Cortezes so he takes out his own guys and blames the Cabal? Devious. Not surprised Karl came up with that one. What does Hope think?"

"He hasn't mentioned it to her. He's also not telling her about the blood, which, admittedly, I don't understand. Hope's hardly the sort to fly into histrionics at the supposition that these young men met with violence."

"She's involved with one of them."

I frowned.

"Hope's involved with one of the guys. Probably this Jaz." She set down her coffee cup. "Karl doesn't want to tell her about the blood, meaning she's more attached to them—or one of them—than a casual acquaintance would imply. Karl doesn't know them, but he's certain they didn't up and leave town. And, from the way Karl spoke of them, he has some issues with this Jaz. Why would Karl have a problem with a young man whose disappearance has Hope so worried? One word. *Sex.*" She picked up her coffee and sipped, considering. "Or, at least, sexual jealousy. There was a relationship or the threat of one."

"I missed that completely."

"I could be wrong. But if I'm not, then we have to consider another suspect."

"Karl."

LUCAS

4

PAIGE SETTLED AT HER COMPUTER, preparing to run investigative searches on the gang members. As moral as Paige is, she's also an experienced hacker from her college days, and sees no reason not to use those skills in pursuit of a just cause.

The concept of breaching ethical boundaries to reach a morally acceptable goal is something Paige struggles with more than I do, though it's always an issue in our line of work. But if the breach leaves no obvious victims, and only puts Paige herself at risk, then she doesn't hesitate to do it.

It was now seven—or ten in the East—making it a reasonable hour to begin placing calls. I was reaching for the phone when a call came in for Paige from Gillian MacArthur, one of the students in her "Sabrina School." Paige mentors a small group of young witches, long distance, those without ties to others. Life can be difficult for witches. Their primary institution, the Coven, is more interested in hiding a witch's powers than in strengthening them.

The witch-sorcerer divide doesn't help matters, not when the Cabals are run by sorcerers. Witches and sorcerers are historical enemies, a ridiculous prejudice that carries over to this day. According to the witches, they took the less powerful sorcerers under their wings, taught them stronger magic and were rewarded by being thrown to the Inquisition—getting them out of the way so the male spellcasters could rule the supernatural world unopposed. More specifically, it is the original Cabal—the Cortezes—whom they blame as the instigators. Our sorcerer version tells us that witches did indeed help us better hone our innate abilities, but when we became too powerful, they turned us over to the Inquisitors, and we retaliated by doing the same to them. I suspect the truth lies somewhere in the middle.

With an impotent American Coven and exclusion from the Cabals, witches lack a strong place in the supernatural world, something Paige is trying to change. Her Sabrina School is one step in that direction. Today, though, she kept the call short, promising to phone back, then handed the receiver to me.

I dialed the number from memory. It took six rings for someone to answer. This wasn't unusual, in a household where no one was ever in any rush to make contact with the outside world and trusted that if the caller was a friend, he'd know to stay on the line.

A woman answered, her greeting friendly but distant, as if she had better things to do, but given that no one else was going to pick up the phone, it had fallen to her, as it usually did.

"Elena, it's Lucas."

Her tone brightened. "Hey, Lucas."

We chatted for a minute, then I asked to speak to Clayton. He was outside with the children, and it took a few minutes before he made it to the phone.

"What's up?" he said.

No pleasantries exchanged this time. Not even an introductory hello. In anyone else, it would be a sign that my call was unwelcome. With Clay, there was no such subtext. Why bother with hello when I'd know he was there as soon as he started talking? Why ask after Paige's health, or mine, or Savannah's, when he knew if we were unwell, he'd already have heard it from Elena? The point of civilities was lost on Clay, and I must admit, it's sometimes pleasant to get straight to business without wading through five minutes of social conventions.

"I have a hypothetical question to put to you regarding Karl Marsten."

"What's he done now?"

"If he felt some attachment to a woman and she began to form an attachment to another man, could his reaction be . . . violent?"

"We're talking about Hope, right?"

"Not necessarily. I'm posing it as a—"

"Hypothetical question." The line buzzed as he moved, probably thumping down onto the sofa, getting comfortable. "If it's not Hope, then the answer is no, because Marsten doesn't 'feel some attachment' to any woman—hell, to any person—except that girl. But if we are talking about Hope, which I presume we are, then the answer is different."

"All right, it's Hope."

"So she's getting cozy with another guy, and you're asking whether he could get violent? Toward her? No."

"I was thinking of the other party."

"The competition? Yeah, he could. Not saying he would, but he could."

"How violent are we talking?"

"Look, just tell me what's going on. Yeah, yeah, client privilege or whatever, but you know I'm not about to go blabbing to anyone—including Marsten. Only person I'd tell is Elena, but that goes without saying."

I explained the situation.

"Shit," he said when I finished. "So you're asking whether Marsten would take out his competition permanently? Wish I could cut back your list of suspects and tell you no." A rustle, as if he was changing position. "You know Marsten attacked the Pack, right? Six, seven years ago? Because we wouldn't give him territory unless he joined?"

"You've told me, yes."

"Well, because he couldn't hold territory, what he'd do is settle in a city for a few months and unofficially declare it his. Any other mutt showed up, he'd track them down and take them out to a fancy dinner. Buy them whatever they wanted, foot the bill, chat them up, be as gracious a host as only Marsten can be. Then he'd tell them they had until dawn to clear out. If they didn't leave? Elena would get a call or a letter telling her she could remove that mutt from her dossiers."

"He killed them?"

"Hell, yeah. Marsten's not stupid. He knows you don't quash a threat by tossing out warnings, maybe break a bone or two. Kill a few mutts and word gets around: don't tread on Karl Marsten's territory."

"And in this case, Karl's territory would be Hope."

"But killing these kids doesn't send a message to anyone except Hope and, as cold as that bastard can be, I can't see him doing that. Could he have gone to scare the kid and things got out of hand? Maybe. Or if he felt that he could lose Hope to some kid she just met? Doesn't sound likely, but who knows. You aren't asking me if I thought he did it, but whether he could. Short answer: hell, yeah. Now, about this job Hope's doing. Does Elena know? 'Cause she'll feel out of the loop if—"

A whisper. Elena.

"One sec," Clay said.

He didn't bother covering the receiver.

"Time to go," I heard Elena say. "Parent and tot swim starts this morning, remember?"

Clay let out an obscenity.

"Is that a no?"

"That's a 'why the hell can't we just buy a pool?' "

"We can, but this has nothing to do with swimming lessons and everything to do with social interaction."

Another, stronger epithet.

I considered hanging up, but if I did, Clay would call me back, annoyed, never understanding that I'd consider it rude to be privy to a private conversation.

"They love being around other children," Elena continued. "Did you see them at the playground last week, Kate toddling after the older kids?"

"She was stalking them."

A sputtered curse, from Elena this time. "She's eighteen months old! She was not—"

"Classic stalking behavior."

"And I suppose Logan hiding in the bushes was part of the ruse. She'd steer them into the trap, then he'd spring out—"

"Shit, I never thought of that."

An exasperated groan, then a sharp "Hey!" from Clayton, probably as he got a poke or pinch. The phone line crackled.

"Lucas?" It was Elena. "Please excuse Clay's rudeness, again."

"That's quite all right. Tell him I'll talk to him later."

"I'll have him call you back...if spending an hour in a pool crowded with humans doesn't traumatize him too much."

"It makes me uncomfortable," Clay said in the background. "It does not—"

"Bye, Lucas."

"Good-bye, Elena."

The line went dead.

HOPE

BIRTHDAY PRESENTS

I woke alone, and flashed back to that Valentine's "morning after." This had better not be another case of next-day jitters. While his explanation of that next day made the memory less painful, I wasn't enduring round two.

As I pushed off the covers, the door opened. Karl walked in with coffee. Hot and fresh—from the same place he'd bought it yesterday. Even if there'd been a coffeemaker and supplies, he'd have gone out. Having tasted his coffee, I was grateful.

I took a sip and closed my eyes. "Mmm."

"I bought a few groceries. Eggs, bacon, bread—presuming there's a toaster."

"You're going to make me breakfast too? Wow."

He gave me a look. "You know I don't cook."

"Well, I sure hope this means you plan to try. Expecting me to cook breakfast isn't a good way to sell this mate business."

"Does that mean I should cancel the offer on the cabin in the Poconos?"

I laughed and swung my feet out. "I'll make you breakfast, Karl, but only because it's your birthday . . . and because, in comparison to the cabin and baby-making, it seems relatively benign. First, though, I'm having a shower—" The rumble of his stomach cut me short. "Okay, first breakfast."

"Thank you."

I headed toward the closet, but Karl tugged me back. "You don't need that."

"If you're asking me to cook you breakfast in the nude then, yes, it is your birthday, but no. Bacon spatter is very, very hot."

He handed me the button-down white shirt he'd worn the night before.

"Oh, you want me to wear your shirt. Little show of property rights?"

"You can't just humor me and put it on without comment, can you?"

"At least I didn't accuse you of wanting your scent on me."

He helped me into the shirt. "I believe I've already accomplished that."

"Which is why I suggested a shower . . ."

"I wasn't complaining. In fact—"

"Don't say it. Please." I looked down at the half-buttoned shirt. "Do I at least get to put on panties?"

"It's my birthday."

"Gonna milk that for all it's worth, aren't you?"

"Gonna try."

I STARTED FRYING bacon and making toast. The toast would go cold before I put the eggs on, but this was only the first batch. Even without Karl's grumbling stomach, his pacing would have told me he was starving. So I fed him two slices and that seemed to be enough to let him turn his attention to other matters . . . like getting his hands under my shirt as I stood at the stove.

At first he just moved his fingers over my thighs and rear, stroking and tickling. Then he eased his fingers between my legs. I flipped the bacon and shifted, and his fingers slid in. I stood there, spatula raised, bacon forgotten . . . until the stink of burning pork reminded me.

"Distracted?" he said as he pushed his fingers in deeper.

I bit back a moan. "Maybe. But you're the one who wants breakfast, so if I burn it . . ."

"Not your fault."

I arched onto my toes and wriggled. Then I felt something that definitely wasn't his fingers. I leaned forward, lifting up—and caught a spray of bacon grease in the face.

He pulled me back, then leaned down to murmur, "Sorry. It won't work very well anyway. Not unless we get you a stool."

"You calling me short?"

"Petite."

He turned me to face him, and perched me on the edge of the low section next to the stove. Then he slid the shirt up over my thighs, pulling my legs around him, and pushed into me.

I gasped. "Having sex with a woman *while* she's cooking your breakfast? Your fantasies are showing your age, Karl."

"Is that a complaint?"

"An observation."

"Ah."

"But if I overcook the bacon..."

"My fault. Risk noted." He thrust into me. "And accepted."

OVER BREAKFAST, KARL wanted to talk about Jaz and Sonny's disappearance. I'd rather have not. The mention of Jaz's name made my stomach churn. I was worried about him and desperately wanted to find him, to make sure he was safe. And then what? How would I explain this?

Thank God you're back, Jaz. Er, but about that special night you had planned...

Yes, I'd initially wanted a fling with Jaz *because* of Karl, to wipe him from my mind, but it hadn't been a casual hookup. I liked Jaz, cared about him, and that only made it all worse.

But if I did care, then I had to put my own feelings of guilt aside and concentrate on figuring out what had happened to him. Karl raised the possibility that Jaz and Sonny's disappearance was an inside job. I think he was shocked when I agreed it was a possibility. Did he expect me to jump to the defense of people I'd met only days ago? We weren't dealing with a Boy Scout troop.

When he told me whom he suspected, though, I *did* disagree. Could I see Guy killing a crew member to further his agenda? Possibly. But it wouldn't be Jaz.

We decided the next step was to get into the club and take a look around while everyone else was sleeping off a late night hunting for Jaz and Sonny. It was unlikely we'd find a "why I kidnapped my crew mates" note hidden in the back closet. But if Guy kept any records of those Cabal dustups they'd be at the club.

YESTERDAY, KARL HAD huffed about poor security at the club. Seems that had been his ill humor talking. The security was well above anything I could breach, and even Karl had to work to get us in.

Once inside, we split up to check the building and ensure we were indeed alone. Karl would take the office; I'd look through the club and back storerooms.

Walking through the club reminded me of the first time I'd cut through with Bianca. Now, alone, that unnatural hush and shadowy darkness was even worse.

I felt my way around the pool tables as I circumvented the dance floor. Ahead I saw those floor-side tables where we'd partied after the sweet sixteen heist. I stared at the chair where I'd sat on Jaz's lap.

If Jaz hadn't disappeared, would last night have been different? No. If Karl and I had managed to find another route past the anger, I'd be here now worrying about what to tell Jaz.

Had I used him?

In a way, yes. I'd seized a genuine attraction to try and get over Karl.

But that attraction... Part of me wanted to say it was purely physical. He was young and hot and interested—the perfect recipe for chemistry. To admit there'd been more felt like a disloyalty to Karl, that buried romantic in me wanting to say that Karl was everything I'd ever wanted.

But with Jaz there had been a connection. Had there been no Karl, then I think we could have had something.

"How did you get in here?"

I jumped at Bianca's voice. But when I spun around, I couldn't see her.

"I asked you a question," Bianca said.

Her voice was sharp. I felt her anger ripple through me as I peered around the club.

"You have five seconds to tell me who the hell you are, or I'm escorting you to the front door. After I call security."

A man's laugh, then a voice, unfamiliar. "There's no one here but us, Bianca."

"Do I know you?"

"Don't you?"

The voice grew closer, and a dash of fear seeped into her anger. I closed my eyes and circled, stopping when I felt a mental twinge that said "this way to the chaos buffet." When I opened my eyes, I was staring at the door to the stockrooms.

"What do you want?" Bianca said.

"Uh-uh. Keep your distance, babe. Third-degree burns aren't on my agenda."

I slid my gun from my purse and hurried to the hall door.

HOPE

TASTE OF DEATH

I slowly turned the knob, then opened the door a crack. Light flooded out. I listened. All was silent. A peek through. Four doors, all closed. If I remembered right, the first two were for janitorial supplies and technical equipment, and the last pair for bar stock.

"One last time," Bianca said. "What do you want?"

Her voice echoed, simultaneously heard in my head and, muffled, from down the hall. I raised my gun and took a slow step forward, testing the floor against my shoes, seeing how easily they'd squeak on the painted concrete.

"I want you to take a message to your boss," the man said. "From Benicio Cortez."

I broke into a jog, moving as quickly and silently as I could.

"What is it?" Bianca asked.

"Here, catch."

I stumbled back, hit by a lash of chaos so strong it left me blinking, blinded.

I squeezed my eyes shut, brain screaming, knowing what was coming and fighting to stop—

Bianca's face. Her horror. Reduced to pants-wetting terror as she saw the gun lift, the gunman's finger on the trigger, and knew she couldn't escape, couldn't scream, wouldn't have time. The bullet spit from the gun, near silent, hitting her square in the forehead. I heard her last thought, a mental scream of defiance. *No! Not me! Not now!* Then . . . silence.

I could see Bianca's horror, recognize her horror, be horrified by it and yet, I *felt* none of it, consumed as the chaos flooded me, leaving me trembling and panting and . . . Oh, God. Wanting more.

The first time I'd felt someone die, that night I'd met Karl, it had been too strong, like my first shot of hard liquor, leaving me reeling, no pleasure to be taken. And I'd been relieved. So relieved. However screwed up my lust for chaos, at least I was never going to enjoy *that*. I'd soon realized I'd been wrong. Like liquor, it was only the first hit that stung.

As the vision dimmed, I saw a man bend over Bianca's body. Average height, dark-haired, late thirties, Latino, with a heavy jacket and loose pants.

The gunman checked Bianca's pulse. No chaos vibes emanated from him. With nothing to keep the vision going, it continued to fade.

The door swung open. The gunman strode into the hall and, for a second, I couldn't move. Then the man wheeled, gaze going to mine, eyes widening in shock and I realized, with an oddly calm clarity, that I was standing twenty feet from the man who'd just shot Bianca. Chaos still buzzed through my head, numbing my reflexes. If he had lifted his gun and fired, I don't know if there'd have been anything I could have done about it.

But he just stared at me, as if in shock himself. I felt the weight of my gun in my hand, but before I could unthinkingly lift it, I realized he had the advantage. My gun hung at my side, fingers grasping it awkwardly, my readiness thrown off by the chaos blast.

I wheeled and ran.

The door was only a few steps away, but I zagged to it rather than taking a straight path, recalling my defense lessons against spellcasts. My brain tripped ahead, laying out a memory map of the club and showing me places to hide.

Hide was what I had to do. All the exits were at least fifty feet away, and no amount of zigging and zagging would get me that far without a bullet through my back.

Escape wasn't on my mind anyway. I had a gun, and I wasn't letting Bianca's killer walk away.

I slammed the door behind me. Then I ducked and ran around the bar. A flash of light told me the gunman had opened the hall door. I dropped to the floor and gripped the gun. When I closed my eyes, I could feel his vibes, not anger but anxiety, his thoughts a mental loop of "Shit, where'd she go?"

My target was in place. All I had to do was peek over the bar, raise the gun and shoot him. At the thought, my heart tripped faster, but not from excitement.

I'd never killed anyone.

I could have laughed at the thought, almost a guilty admission, like saying I'd never driven a car. In the normal world, not having killed people is a perfectly acceptable "missed life experience." Desirable, in fact. But in the supernatural world, at least in the type of work I did, it's a given that at some point it will come down to kill or be killed.

Karl told me once that he couldn't remember the faces of every man he'd killed. It wasn't that there were scores of them, but enough that they no longer stood clear in his mind. He hadn't said it with regret, but nor had he been bragging. He was simply making a thoughtful statement during a discussion of risk and death in the supernatural world.

I could look on this the same way: kill or be killed. But was I in danger? The gunman hadn't fired at me in the hall. Now he wasn't putting out any vibes of anger or threat.

Could *I* justify leaping from behind the bar, gun blazing, taking down a stranger who hadn't made a move on me?

Still crouching, I retreated into the shadowy corner between the bar and the wall, my back protected, gun raised. I wasn't letting him walk out of here. He had answers, and Karl could get them from him.

While it would be nice to take the gunman down alone, I stood a better chance of success if Karl helped. I reached for my panic button, then stopped. Push it and Karl would come running—into a room with an armed killer.

I flipped open my phone and began a text message. I got as far as "bar gunman" when a rubber sole squeaked on the floor. I glanced at the glowing cell phone, shut it quickly, then scrunched back against the wall.

I was too exposed. I saw that now. I was relying on dim lighting, a shadowy corner and dark clothing, which was fine for a casual glance, but if he walked around that bar, searching, he'd see me. To get to either exit, he *had* to walk around the bar.

He slid into view. Less than twenty feet from me, gun up, gaze sweeping the room with every step.

Heart hammering, I readied myself. If he saw me, I'd have to—

His gaze swung my way . . . and kept going. I exhaled a long, shuddering breath. If he was giving off any chaos vibes, I couldn't detect them—they were too low to penetrate my own anxiety.

The gunman kept moving away, heading toward the back hall.

The back hall . . . where Karl was . . .

I fumbled for my phone. How could I open it without turning on the backlight? Damn it, I should know this!

The gunman walked along the wall. Ten feet above his head was the second tier, a wide ledge lined with the dark shapes of tables. I decided he was far enough that I'd risk the phone's backlight, and was opening it when one dark shape on that second tier moved. A man's figure swung over the low railing.

Karl landed square on the gunman's back, his drop so soundless the man let out a startled yelp. The two men went down. I ran to cover Karl. As I passed the bar, I caught another motion, out of the corner of my eye. A figure on the top tier across the room, dressed in black, with something on his shoulder, long and—

"Karl! Partner!"

As the words left my mouth, I wished I could suck them back, say something clearer and I was about to yell "gun" when that gun swung my way. I dove, and Karl did the same, flinging the man off him and going for cover.

I scrambled under the nearest pool table, then scampered around the centerpiece, putting it between myself and the second gunman. I flattened out on my stomach, gun raised.

Something thumped against the table beside me. A soft sound, barely enough to carry. I swung my gun toward it.

"Stay," Karl hissed.

While I could have slugged him for not "staying" himself, for taking the risk getting to me, I couldn't deny a dart of relief when his dark figure dropped beside me.

"Shhh," he said.

Again, I wasn't the one who needed the warning, but I turned my attention to the path I'd been watching.

Karl slid closer, lips moving to my ear.

"They're retreating. Heading for the side door. Two sets of footsteps." He hung there, breath warm against my ear. "Still going. Still... The door. Open. Closed. Silence. Footsteps down the back hall. Receding. We'll wait. Be sure."

He stayed where he was, pressed up against me. After a minute, he rubbed a hand over the back of his neck.

"You okay?" I whispered. "That drop—"

"—was nothing. But I think I wrenched my neck when you yelled."

"Better than catching a bullet."

"True. And you? I don't smell blood, so I presume you're okay?"

"He killed Bianca. The guy you jumped. I... saw it."

His gaze swung to mine. He didn't ask "are you okay?" because he knew I wouldn't be, and it had nothing to do with the horror of watching someone die. His arm went around my back as he leaned toward my ear and whispered, "We'll talk."

"After we get the hell out of here, right? Before someone discovers the body and finds us hiding under the pool table."

A small smile. "Preferably."

I pushed up as he backed out from under the table. I was getting to my feet when he pushed me back under and dropped beside me.

"Footsteps."

A door slapped open, and Tony's voice wafted in. "—goddamn cleaners. Just like the last time. Guy freaks out, certain the Cortezes broke in. I say, 'Hey man, couldn't the cleaners have forgotten to re-set the alarm,' but no... Gotta be a conspiracy."

"Bianca's supposed to be here for deliveries," Max said. "Could have been her."

"Bee's going to forget to rearm the system? As if."

"Looks like she's still doing inventory. The hall light's on. We should tell her about the alarm."

"And get shanghaied into helping count boxes? Enjoy. I'm heading around back, see whether Guy's here, if he has any news about Jaz and Sonny."

We waited until Max and Tony stepped through their respective exits, then hightailed it out.

LUCAS

5

PORTLAND IS A CITY of many charms. Primary among them is the geography—almost as far as I can get from my father and his Cabal without leaving the continental U.S. As the saying goes, though: act in haste, repent at leisure. I suggested that Paige and I settle in Portland during a particularly dark period between my father and myself, and I have, in some ways, come to regret it. The distance may be comforting, but if trouble arises in Miami, it takes me a while to get there.

While Paige had the insight to pack overnight bags and print out the flight schedule after Karl's call, it was still late in the day by the time our plane crossed the Florida border.

A trip to Miami is never something I undertake lightly. It is the seat of the Cortez Cabal, and when I am there, I cannot forget who I am.

It's not that I consider Cabals evil entities. I wish I could. Early life conditions us for a fairy-tale world of good and evil, of wicked witches and beautiful princesses, hideous trolls and stalwart knights. You are good or you are evil and there's no in-between, no "extenuating circumstances."

We don't like extenuating circumstances. They make things messy. We want evil to hide behind a dark mask—cold and faceless. If the villain is not evil, how do you hate him?

If your father is not evil, how do you hate him?

I grew up in a world where the Cabals were clearly on the side of virtue. My family founded the first Cabal in Spain, after the Inquisition. We saw our people—supernaturals—persecuted by a society that didn't understand that we were *not* evil, and we gave them a place where they could be safe, and raise their children in safety, and freely use their powers and prosper from them. We didn't just give them jobs; we gave them a way of life.

I grew up believing in that family mythos. When my father led me through his offices, I saw happy people who smiled and bowed to him as if he was a beneficent king. I was a prince—petted and pampered. Outside those walls, though, I was the son of an unwed schoolteacher, living in a modest home up the Florida coast, where the name Cortez only meant I was "another damn Mexican." Is it any wonder I clung to the fantasy as long as I did? Right into high school, to the summer I went to work for my father and walked in on him dictating execution writs as casually as if he were ordering more toner for the copy machines.

I could have plugged my ears and told myself I'd misheard. But my father raised me to never turn my back on a question until it was answered. So I did my due diligence, and found that my palace was built on the bones of the dead. And those happy, smiling faces I'd seen since childhood? I'd play the smiling, happy employee for my boss too, if crossing him meant he'd send fire demons to burn my family alive.

The truth had seemed clear. Cabals were evil. Cabals must be destroyed.

I made a vow, that I'd do whatever it took to bring the Cabals down. A foolish, arrogant vow that only a sixteen-year-old could make, based on a clear division of good and evil that only a sixteen-year-old can see. I delved ever deeper into Cabal culture and counterculture, no longer a prince but an outsider. Instead of galvanizing me to action, the distance only brought the picture into sharper focus. And with sharper focus, I began to see the gradients of black and white.

Cabals do provide scores of supernaturals with a world in which they belong. One cannot underestimate the importance of that for people who otherwise spend their lives hiding. People who have to look at their bleeding child and evaluate the risk of taking him to the doctor. Of those people who smile and nod at my father every day, 90 percent are truly grateful and free of fear.

If they betray the Cabal, the punishment will be execution—horrible execution—but they have no intention of doing so. Yes, they've heard stories of families being murdered, but those are other Cabals. Yes, they've also heard of Cortez Cabal employees being killed after leaving the organization, but that is the price you pay for reaping the benefits. One of those benefits is security, and if the Cabal must kill a former employee to safeguard its secrets, so be it.

So is a Cabal evil? No. Is there evil within a Cabal? Absolutely. That's what I fight—the greed and the corruption that arises from an environment where all you have to do is cry "security issue" and you can get away with murder. Yet the world still looks for black and white. In me, supernaturals want to see a meddler or a savior. I am neither, so I disappoint.

I refuse to work for the corporation or take part in Cabal life, and yet I maintain a relationship with the CEO. By naming me heir, my father offers me the chance to take over the Cabal itself, to institute my reforms from within, and yet I refuse. Simple things, one would think. Simple decisions. If you hate the institution, turn your back on it completely. If you want to change it, take it over. Black and white.

Even by coming here today, I'll displease both sides. To some, I'll be meddling in Cabal affairs, without even a client as my excuse. To others, I'll be letting my father sweep me into his world again, on the pretext of helping manage a crisis, as he had with the Edward and Natasha problem four years ago. I've learned long ago that this is what I should expect anytime my path crosses my father's in a professional capacity. It can't be helped. But that doesn't make it any easier.

PAIGE AND I walked into the terminal. I carried two overnight bags; she had her laptop case.

We waded through a throng of friends and relatives greeting arrivals. Twenty feet away, Karl sat reading a newspaper, alone on a bank of chairs. Despite the shouts and crying around him, he never even glanced up.

As we emerged from the crowd, he snapped the paper shut, rose and strode into the terminal . . . away from us. Paige arched her brows at me. Was Karl simply being cautious? Or did he suspect he'd been followed? After less than a dozen paces, he stopped, wheeled and shot us a "Well, are you coming?" glower. He barely let us catch up, then was off again.

"We should find someplace with a modicum of privacy," I said. "I know several—"

"Here's fine."

He veered into a bar packed with commuters fortifying themselves for the flight—or the drive home. It hardly seemed the place to discuss matters of a supernatural nature, but a crowded public place was more secure than an empty one, where words could carry and neighbors might be bored enough to eavesdrop.

"Where's Hope?" Paige asked as Karl pulled out her stool, the action seeming more reflex than courtesy.

"After the girl died, Benoit—the gang leader—called her in. He has them hunkered down at the club, planning their next move. No one leaves."

That explained his brusqueness then. He was eager to get this over with so he could return. His haste was warranted. Should Hope push her panic alarm now, it would be a half-hour or more before he could respond.

Karl pulled a manila envelope from his folded newspaper and removed a sheaf of photos. Eight-by-ten shots, all grainy, the resolution poor.

"Hope used her cell phone to take pictures of the originals, then sent them to me," he explained.

The top photograph was of two young men. Both sat bound to chairs, bowed forward, as if so exhausted that their bindings were all that was holding them upright. The dark-haired one bore an ugly cut across his cheekbone, his cheek coated with a layer of dried blood. The fair-haired young man had a black eye and a swollen lip.

"Jaz and Sonny, I presume?"

He nodded. "The original was left beside the girl's body."

"Was any note attached?"

"Three words on the back: more to come."

That could mean anything from "more information forthcoming" to "more mistreatment of the prisoners" to "more victims to follow." Intentionally cryptic, leaving the recipient hoping for the best while imagining the worst.

"And her killer claimed to be delivering a message from my father, not only with the picture, but the young woman's death? The Cortez Cabal rarely utilizes kidnapping. The outcome is fraught with uncertainty. If it fails, you must kill the victims. If it succeeds, you have living witnesses. If it succeeds *and* you kill the witnesses, your credibility as a negotiator is irrevocably damaged. To send such a blatant message, and leave evidence of his complicity..." I shook my head. "It's not—"

"—your father."

"No, I was going to say it isn't my father's style."

Karl's fingers drummed against the tabletop. "Same thing. The point is—"

"No, pardon the interruption, but it is not the same thing. If my father wishes to commit a criminal act that may later damage his reputation, he has been known to choose a method that is deliberately out of character."

When Karl frowned, Paige explained, "So when he's accused of it, even his enemies will say 'that's not Benicio Cortez's style'...ergo, it couldn't be Benicio Cortez."

Most people would be shocked by such duplicity. Karl looked as if he was taking notes.

I said, "You may not wish to raise the possibility to Hope, but it's very likely these young men are no longer alive. There's nothing in the photograph to indicate when it was taken. Usually, if proving that a kidnap victim is alive, his captors—"

"Put a newspaper in the picture."

Karl himself had been involved in a kidnapping—a brutal one of Clayton during his strike against the pack—and as he turned his gaze to watch passersby, I wondered whether there was a touch of discomfiture in his straying attention.

He flipped the photograph behind the stack. Next was a black-and-white security camera shot, showing a man walking down a hall.

When I saw the man's face, my heart sank. As quick as I was to agree that my father could be involved in this, such assertions were born more of self-preservation than of conviction. Saying my father would never do such a thing was a direct route to humiliation.

"I take it you recognize him?" Karl said.

"Juan Ortega, head of the Cortez Cabal private security division."

"According to the gang, this is the same man who beat and robbed the kidnapped boys," Karl said. "He's the one whose home they were going to break into last night, before the boys disappeared."

"Could he be moonlighting for someone else?" Paige asked.

"Unlikely. If he was caught, he'd be executed. An employee who is willing to work for an outside interest might be persuaded to sell information to that interest."

"What if he wanted to leave the Cabal and this was his way to do it?"

"Blackmail? Let me leave or I'll kill these boys and pin it on you? My father would agree, wait until the danger had passed, then devote all his excess manpower to hunting Ortega, whereupon he'd be tortured as a lesson to others. Ortega would know that." I pushed the photo back to Karl. "I'm not saying Ortega's involvement proves my father is behind this, but it lends credence to the theory."

Karl flipped to the next photo. A tall light-haired man with a scar by his mouth. My heart dipped a little more.

"Andrew Mullins," I said before Karl could ask. "He's in security too, under Ortega. I don't know him as well. I'm presuming this is the second gunman?"

Karl nodded.

"Then leave these with me and go back to Hope. I'll call when I know something."

HOPE

FEAR AND LOATHING

The room blurred. The gun barrel flashed under the harsh light. I squeezed my eyes shut, but the gun kept rising. The finger moved on the trigger. The gun flared. Bianca's eyes widened in horror. The bullet—

Goddamn it, stop!

Guy had bustled me from the war room while they planned the strike against the Cabal. I presumed that meant he didn't trust me yet, but I'd be naive if I wasn't considering the possibility that they knew I was a spy.

If he suspected, though, he wasn't doing a very good job of imprisoning me. Max hadn't activated the storeroom lock. I'd detected only a security spell across the doorway, which would warn them if I left.

As for why Guy picked this room, I wondered whether he knew more about Expisco half-demons than he'd let on. Being here, with such a strong source of chaos nearby, prevented me from listening in to their distant thoughts and conversation.

I'd now watched Bianca die twenty-one times, and no matter how hard I fought, the ending was always the same. The bullet hit and I gasped, struck by a bolt of indescribably delicious chaos.

This last time, the gasp was more a mewl, my overstimulated nerves protesting, my body shaking with exhaustion. But that didn't block the charge of pleasure—or the wave of self-loathing. And, finally the questions.

I'd known she was in trouble and hurried into the back hall to help. Had I tried hard enough? Had I run fast enough? I'd seen her killer raise the gun and I'd stopped running, hit by the chaos wave. As the scene replayed, that split-second of inaction seemed to stretch into long minutes, during which I stood in that hall, doing nothing, overwhelmed by the chaos.

"—need to strike at—" Tony's voice in my head, penetrating the chaos fog.

I strained to hear more. I needed to focus on finding out what they were planning so I could warn Benicio.

But *should* I warn him? It looked as if he'd kidnapped Jaz and Sonny, and had Bianca killed. What obligation did I have to tell him anything? I didn't have enough information, didn't know who was really the aggressor and who the defender. That's why Karl had insisted on letting Lucas decide our next move. Whatever allegiance Lucas felt to his family, his allegiance to truth was greater.

"—I just don't think—"

"—then walk away—"

I strained to pick up more, but the chaos ebbed and surged as the gang members' moods veered between grief-fueled outrage and anxiety over whatever they were planning.

"—get past security—"

"—trust me—"

Were they going to break in somewhere?

"—will be the toughest—"

"—once in, though—-"

The room wobbled, then went black. The gun rose—

Not now! I pressed my hands against my eyes, but the images kept flashing. I couldn't stay here. If I was going to figure out what was happening, I needed to—

As the bullet struck Bianca, my cell phone beeped, warning me of an incoming message. Had I not been clutching it, I'd never have noticed.

I fumbled with the phone and let out a whoosh of relief as I saw Karl's number. It was a simple "I'm back" message. I responded by sending the one I'd pretyped, explaining the situation in the most succinct, least alarming language.

Ten seconds later, my phone rang.

"What the hell do you think you're doing?" Karl blasted before I could say hello. "Get out of that room now, Hope. Goddamn it, I can't believe you're sitting there—"

"I'm not sitting here," I hissed under my breath. "I'm doing my job. If I leave this room, my cover's blown—"

"Blow it! For all you know, they're figuring out how to kill you."

"Then why leave me without a barrier spell to keep me in? They—"

"You can't take the chance. Get out of there or I'll—"

"Stop yelling and listen, Karl. The gang is planning a break-in. They're in the same room I was in yesterday. When you get here, you can eavesdrop. Find out what's happening."

He paused, then asked, calmer, "Where are you? In case I need to find you."

"The room Bianca was killed in."

"Get out of there, Hope. You—"

"I need to learn how to handle it."

He let out a string of curses and let me know what he thought of me torturing myself in the name of Expisco education. After a moment, he said, "If anyone comes to get you, hit the panic button. I don't care if you think they're bringing you coffee and doughnuts, hit that button. If it's nothing, I'll slip away and no one will be the wiser. But you *will* hit that button."

"I will."

LUCAS

6

ᴀᴛ ꜱɪx-ᴛʜɪʀᴛʏ I walked into Cortez Cabal headquarters. There was no question that my father would still be there. For him, the day didn't end for another hour or so. That was a lesson he'd taught me—that if you expect your employees to work nine to five, and your executives eight to six, then, as CEO, you need to be there even longer. Whatever my father's faults, he treats everyone from the janitors to the board of directors with consideration and respect...at least when he doesn't need them tortured, maimed or executed.

I hadn't notified my father of my arrival...or that I was coming to Miami at all. I wanted to see his reaction without giving him time to prepare his defense. I do not enjoy the subterfuge. I can't say the same for him.

The lobby doors had barely shut behind me before a receptionist and a guard flanked me. Did I need a cab driver paid? A car taken to the executive lot? A coffee? A cold drink perhaps—it was quite warm today. Was I here to see my father? Was there anyone else they could call for me? Would I like a member of the clerical staff on hand for my visit?

Paige urges me to find the humor in this, and it is almost sublimely ridiculous. But I can't laugh it off—at the root of it is my father's biggest machination, his grandest scheme: naming me heir.

By naming as his successor the only son who does not want the job, he ensures peace among my three brothers, and safety for himself.

The latter says something about his relationship with them—and the real possibility that they would commit patricide to hasten their inheritance. It is a truth my father recognizes. Name me heir, and my brothers must stay their hands and work hard, hoping to persuade the board of directors that they would run the company successfully, should the board wish to exercise its influence on my father and convince him to change his inheritance plans.

Where does that leave me? In the worst situation of all, made worse by my father's refusal to acknowledge that this is a ruse at all. I have asked—once even pleaded—for him to admit, just to me, that it's a political ploy. He will not.

The receptionist fell back to her station as the guard escorted me to the executive elevator. That was awkward for all. Considering my anti-Cabal efforts, my guide might look more like an armed escort, though he was only trying to accord me due respect.

The dilemma was resolved when the parking garage elevator opened and out stepped my half-brother, William. On seeing me, he hesitated, as if considering his chances of hastily retreating. Normally, I'd have let him go, but given the choice between discomfiting the guard or William, I decided my brother could handle it.

"William, how are you?" I walked forward, hand extended.

Every employee in the lobby had stopped to watch.

"Lucas."

He gave my hand a fleeting shake.

"I was just going upstairs to speak to Father. If you were headed that way, we can ride up together."

He couldn't escape gracefully, so he said, "Yes, of course."

The guard relinquished me to him.

Of my three half-brothers, I get along best with William, which is not to say he was going to invite Paige and me to Sunday dinner anytime soon, but he'd never tried to kill me—a sign of resignation, if not acceptance. On the elevator, I asked after his wife and infant son. Another nephew whom I suspected I'd never meet. Hector's two boys—now teenagers—didn't even know they had an Uncle Lucas. When they were younger, I'd send birthday and Christmas gifts, but after a few years of having them returned, I'd realized to continue would be mere stubbornness . . . and an expenditure I could ill afford.

Once off the elevator, aware that others could be watching,

William struggled to show a polite return interest in my life by asking about Savannah's educational plans.

"Well, well, well," a voice sang out behind us. "If it isn't the geek crusader. What horrible crime have we committed this time?" Carlos slid past me, planted himself in my path and held out his wrist. "Here, baby brother, get it over with."

"Hello, Carlos."

He made a show of looking around. "Where's the little witch? Is it just my imagination, or do you lock her away whenever I'm around?"

"She's otherwise occupied this evening, but I'm sure you'll see her later."

He flashed his teeth. "Oh, I'll make sure of it."

I tensed, but tried not to show it. Let Carlos know he'd struck a nerve and he'd never let up. Paige always repelled his attentions, but with Carlos, rejection only served to whet his appetite.

"If you'll excuse me, William, Carlos—"

My father's office door opened and Hector came out.

When my eldest brother steps into a room, the hairs on my neck rise and icy dread settles into the pit of my stomach. William and Carlos dislike me, but Hector hates me—a hatred so pure it vibrates between us. Can I blame him? He's the oldest son. He's been a hard-working, vital part of the Cabal since before I was born. Yet he has to suffer the humiliation of my father pretending he'll hand the business to me.

"What the hell are you doing here?" Hector advanced. He's at least four inches shorter than me, but it took all I had not to shrink back.

"Got your bags packed, Hector?" Carlos said. "Because I think you're about to be sent on a little trip."

"Lucas."

I tore my gaze from Hector as my father brushed past him to embrace me. Even as I returned the hug, he started pummeling me with questions. Where was Paige? When did we arrive? How was our flight?

My brothers might as well have been invisible. The temperature around us seemed to plummet, but my father was oblivious. He ushered me into his office, still asking questions.

When it came to his family, my father was as blind as King Lear, blithely fostering jealousies among his offspring, then seeming shocked when they turned against him. Sometimes it was as calculated as naming me heir. But more often, it was the thoughtless slights, like ignoring them in my presence or prominently displaying on his desk a photo of me as a child...with my mother beside me. How did my half-brothers feel, seeing that? Their own mother's picture was farther back, displayed more from duty than from desire. My father would say that they were grown men and knew he hadn't lived with their mother for years, remaining married only because he couldn't afford the divorce. Yet it was the emotional impact that mattered, and that he couldn't see.

"Paige did come to Miami with you, didn't she?" he said as he closed the door.

"She's at the hotel, unpacking."

"Which hotel?"

"The South Continental."

"Why don't I have you moved—"

"Paige likes the Continental."

"I was going to suggest you stay at my house."

I stifled a sigh. I thought I'd preempt him by refusing his upgrade offer, but I'd only pushed him to something more difficult to decline.

"I'll discuss it with her. But, having just unpacked, I doubt she'd want to—"

"Tomorrow then. I'm sure she'll be busy with the case you're working on so I'll have my staff stop by the hotel and pack for her."

Two questions framed as a statement. If I didn't argue the presumption that I was staying longer than a day and working a case, he'd know both were true.

"We may not be here that long, Papá, and I'm not visiting in an official capacity."

I waited for his face to fall, disappointed that I'd avoided his trap. Instead, he clapped me on the back and laughed, and I realized I had indeed been trapped...into proving how well I assimilated lessons I pretended to ignore.

"She'll join us for dinner, though, won't she?"

I could point out that I hadn't received, much less agreed to, any dinner invitation, but that would be petty. Sometimes it was easier to play the game and let him win the small victories, reserving my strength for the larger battles. I said yes.

I took Karl's envelope from my satchel. I felt my father's gaze on me and resisted the urge to glance up.

I removed the photographs and, before he could see them, flipped to the second—the security camera picture of Ortega. Then I laid the stack facedown on my lap.

"Does Juan Ortega still work for you?"

"Yes, of course."

"Did he work for you today?"

"I said he still—"

"But *today*. Was he at work today?"

He pushed a button on his desk. An adjoining door opened and Troy walked in. He smiled when he saw me.

"Hey, Lucas."

My father cleared his throat.

Troy bowed his head, mock-obeisant. "Mr. Cortez, I mean."

A sigh from my father. "Was Juan Ortega at work today?"

As my father's primary bodyguard, Troy would be apprised of all irregularities involving security, including absenteeism. For a division head like Ortega, he'd know whether he was absent without checking his daily log.

"No, sir. He called in sick this morning."

"Could you follow up on that, please?"

A nod as he stepped back into his office.

"Troy? One moment please." I turned to my father. "I'd like to follow up myself, with a personal visit."

"Of course. Find the address, please, Troy. We'll be leaving within the hour."

"One more thing." I plucked the second man's photo from the stack and held it up, showing it only to Troy. "Is this Andrew Mullins?"

"Yep. Second-level officer, works under Ortega." He paused, then pulled out his PalmPilot and checked. "Also off today. Seems we have an epidemic."

I thanked Troy. My father waited until he was gone, then said, "I presume your visit has something to do with this epidemic?"

I placed the photograph of Ortega on his desk. "This was taken at 11:21 this morning, at the Easy Rider. Ortega told Guy Benoit's second-in-command that he was there to deliver a message from you, then he shot her in the head and left this photo—" I turned to the one of the young men, "—next to her body with the words 'more to come' written on the back."

I resisted the urge to study his reaction. Shock and consternation were expressions my father had mastered decades ago, along with the ability to mask those reactions. After a moment, he shook his head.

"Whoever brought this to you is lying, Lucas. They have a vendetta against me or the Cabal, or they have chosen to blame an easy target."

"Hope Adams brought it to me. She was outside the room when Bianca was killed. She saw it in a vision, then saw Ortega himself come out of the room, carrying the murder weapon. He and Mullins chased her before Karl's arrival apparently made them decide she was a problem they could deal with later. We have the security photographs, and two eyewitness accounts. That hardly seems like a fabrication designed to frame the Cabal and tarnish your reputation."

"Lucas, I did not—"

"This first picture, if you're interested, is of two members of the gang, who have been missing since last night. Earlier this month, after a lucrative heist, these same young men were beaten and robbed by a man matching Ortega's description, again bearing a warning from the Cortez Cabal."

"I did not kill this girl or kidnap these boys—"

"I didn't say you did. You have underlings to do that for you."

"Yes, these men are my employees and, yes, if Hope says she saw Ortega kill that young woman, then I have no doubt he did. But they were not acting under my authorization or any authorization that I have knowledge of. While I'd hope that my word would be enough, I know it isn't and I know that's my fault. So I'd suggest we pay Ortega and Mullins a home visit and check on their health."

HOPE

PANIC BUTTON

Bianca died twice more before Karl sent me a message. Three words: get out now.

I messaged him back, asking whether I should try to maintain my cover.

One word: abort.

Had Karl been able to find the exclamation mark, I suspected he would have used it. I considered his command. Yes, he was prone to blowing things out of proportion where my safety was concerned, but however strong his instinct to protect, he always backed down if he was overdoing it.

I sent back "Are you sure?" and got a profanity in response.

I stood just inside the door and mentally ran through my escape route. Once I breached Max's spell barrier, I couldn't stop. I threw open the door and started down the hall at a quick march. If they caught me running, I was doomed.

Through the club, into the front hall—

"Faith?"

Tony stood in the doorway between the club and the hall.

"Oh, thank God," I said. "You guys are still here. I called Guy to say I needed to use the bathroom, and no one answered. I thought I'd been left behind."

"Nah, we're just finishing up. Guy was going to send Max to get you in a minute. I'll take you to him."

A dark form appeared behind Tony. Three slow, silent steps, and Karl was close enough to breathe down Tony's neck.

As he reached out, I gasped, eyes going wide. "Tony!"

Karl grabbed him by the back of the shirt and flung him into the wall with a crack that sent plaster flying. As Tony dropped, I hurried over to check his pulse. Karl grabbed my arm. With my free hand, I lifted Tony's eyelids, making sure they weren't dilated. I started for the door, but Karl swung me around, nearly flipping me off my feet, and dragged me back toward the club.

"What—?" I began.

"Shhh!" A quick glance and discreet sniff around, then he pulled me behind the coat check and toward the side closet. I was about to tell him the door was kept locked, but saw it was ajar, and realized this was where he'd been waiting.

He pulled me inside. As he closed the door, the room went dark, and his hand stayed on my wrist, gripping hard enough to make me wince.

"What the hell were you doing?" he whispered. "You almost gave me away."

"It was too late for Tony to react. But when he comes to, he'll tell the others that I tried to warn him, which will make it seem as if my disappearance wasn't voluntary."

"So you can go back and pick up where you left off? It's over, Hope. Your job is done, and you need to stop worrying about—"

"About whether they'll realize I'm a spy and change the plans you presumably overheard?"

He went quiet.

"My wrist?" I whispered.

He slackened his grip, and rubbed the spot with his thumb, then pulled me into the darkest section of the closet. I lifted onto my tiptoes to whisper in his ear, but still had to tug his shoulder to get him to bend.

"Can I ask why we're in here when the exit was twenty feet away?"

"I didn't want to exit."

"Then why call me—?" The answer hit. "You son-of-a-bitch."

I slipped my arm from his grasp. His hand went around my waist before I could step away.

I continued. "You want them separated, looking for me, don't you? I'm not in danger. You just wanted to sound the alarm—and use the excuse to blow my cover so we can leave Miami."

"I wanted them out of that room so I can get something in it. And, yes, I want *you* out of Miami."

"You told me I was in danger, and I trusted you."

A moment of uncomfortable silence, then, "They have plans in that room. Blueprints—"

"Which you could have gotten without blowing my cover."

At a sound from outside the room we both went silent. It was Guy and Rodriguez. They'd found Tony. I heard Guy phone Max and tell him Tony had been knocked out. He wanted Max to meet Rodriguez at the front door, then go after me while he tended to Tony.

Rodriguez helped Guy carry Tony away, still unconscious. Once we were sure they were gone, we slipped from the closet.

I followed Karl. I tried to focus on the task, but my nerves were frayed from almost two hours of watching Bianca die.

Why did I insist on trusting a man everyone warned couldn't be trusted? Maybe I *did* enjoy the chaos of my own suffering, and I was just too deluded to see it.

"Hope? I need you to stand guard here. Are you going to be able to do that?"

"Of course I can." I snapped the words, then rubbed my face. "Sorry. Yes, I'm fine and I can handle this."

"Are you sure?"

I nodded. Karl's gaze darkened and I could feel chaos strumming from him. Anger? Frustration? Impatience? Impossible to tell.

He said, "We're getting you out of here. As soon as I'm done."

"I don't need—" I bit off the sharp words and managed a softer, "I'm fine, Karl. Really. Just go."

His look said he expected me to collapse from chaos overdose the moment he turned his back.

"Go," I said between my teeth. "I'm fine."

He left. I rubbed my arms, struggling to stay alert. Fight the fatigue. Experience it, learn from it, then push it aside.

"We need to move now," a voice said. "Go to the warehouse, get the equipment and strike."

I was ready to bolt, my tired brain misidentifying the sound as something I was hearing with my ears, not my mind. When I realized otherwise, I closed my eyes and concentrated.

"But if they took Faith after they knocked me out—" Tony's voice.

"All the more reason to move." Guy.

"I tried calling her—"

"Her phone switches straight to voice mail. Whoever took her must have it and turned it off."

Where were they? I couldn't tell. No, wait, if I couldn't hear them with my ears, then they weren't that close.

I took out my panic button, just in case.

"Are you up for it?" Guy asked. "How's the head?"

"Pounding like a son-of-a-bitch, but those Tylenols should kick in soon. I'm not backing out, if that's what you're asking. Those bastards have three of our guys, and we're getting them back. I'd love to know what attacked me, though. What's that strong? Werewolf?"

"The Cabals don't hire werewolves."

The voice faded. I hurried to the end of the hall, hoping to pick them up again, but either they were too far away or the chaos had faded from the exchange. I ran back and found Karl shuffling through a filing cabinet.

"They're leaving," I said. "Did you find what you wanted?"

He smacked the drawer shut in response.

"They must have taken it," I said. "I'm going to follow them. If you want to keep looking—"

He strode past me and waved for me to fall in behind him. As much as I longed to lead, I couldn't argue with the logic of putting the guy with superhuman hearing and strength in front.

Guy and Tony—and presumably Max and Rodriguez—were gone. That meant Karl had to track them by scent. Easy enough inside. Once outside, though, even if he'd been comfortable sniffing the ground, he couldn't do it without attracting a lot of attention. So it was slow going. When the sidewalk branched, he had to stoop and tie his shoe to figure out which way they'd gone. Finally, the trail ended . . . in the delivery lane where Guy usually parked.

He paced, stopping every few steps to sniff the ground, as if hoping he was mistaken about the obvious answer.

Finally he straightened and said, "Gone."

"From what I heard they're going after their target now. You saw blueprints. Office? Private residence?"

"A couple of office floor plans, plus one or two that could have been homes. It was too far to see." He took out his cell phone. "Lucas might recognize them, if they're Cabal."

LUCAS

7

WE PICKED UP PAIGE on the way to Ortega's house, so we could head out to dinner right after . . . and because her witch spells might come in handy. Troy's partner, Griffin, had gone home, leaving Troy as my father's bodyguard for the night, as usual. We also brought two security guards.

Paige and my father chatted on the ride—casual conversation, unrelated to the task. My father raised me to see witches as simply another supernatural race, one with which we have an unfortunate history. Yet, our Cabal, like the others, has only one token witch employee and when business partners mock witches, he'd never defend the race.

He will come to Paige's defense, though. Whatever problem a business contact might have with a Cortez marrying a witch, he'd best not voice it within my father's hearing. That's more about defending Paige as the wife of his son, but I'm grateful for it.

His affection for her appears genuine. He certainly takes more interest in her than he does in Hector's or William's wife . . . a fact that also does not go unnoticed by my brothers.

WHEN WE GOT to Ortega's house, my father sent the guards around to cover the back while Troy escorted us to the front door and rang the bell. After the third ring, Paige said, "We really should get a look inside. Lucas and I can come back after dark..."

Her words trailed off as my father took two small envelopes from his pocket, opened one and emptied a key ring into his palm.

"You have keys for all your employees' homes?" Paige said.

"Management level and those with security clearance only."

"I don't want to know how you get them, do I?"

He smiled as he handed the keys to Troy. "Legally, as shocking as that might seem, though some would argue we're taking advantage of our employees' vulnerabilities to justify violating their civil rights."

"I've never agreed it was legal either," I murmured, then explained to Paige. "Included in Ortega's contract is a stipulation that he allow his home to be refitted with locks and an alarm system. Most employees realize this means the Cabal will retain a set of their keys and alarm override codes, but that is not—" I looked at my father "—explicitly stated."

"But as long as they know and don't argue..."

"They don't argue because they're supernaturals, and they rely on the Cabal for more than mere employment, therefore they too readily permit you to violate—"

"Can you tell we've had this discussion before?" my father said to Paige. "And it's not one we should be having on the front stoop. Troy?"

"The dead bolt's sticking, sir. Just a— There it is."

When Paige tried to follow Troy into the house, my father caught her arm.

"Troy will disarm the system and perform a cursory search."

Troy's voice floated back. "So if Ortega's set a tripwire bomb, I'm the only one who'll go ka-boom. This is why you have a Ferratus half-demon on staff, sir."

"Griffin is with his children. You don't have any."

"In other words, no one will care if I go ka-boom."

"I'd care. I hate training new bodyguards."

My father's eyes twinkled as Troy tossed a few choice words back. A Tempestras half-demon was an odd choice for a bodyguard—being able to affect the weather isn't terribly useful as a defense mechanism—and more suitable guards regularly applied for Troy's job, but my father would never consider replacing him. When a man is at your side almost every day, from waking to sleeping, there are more important qualifications than supernatural abilities.

After a few minutes, Troy returned with the "all clear," and we went inside.

Ortega wasn't there. His house was tidy, his luggage was missing and his closets contained less clothing than one would expect a man of his income and position to possess. Most damning of all—his safe had been emptied and left open. It looked as if he'd left quickly and of his own free will.

We searched the house, but Ortega wasn't foolish enough to leave any clues. The computer hard drive had been removed. The filing cabinet was empty, as was his desk. There weren't even papers on the refrigerator door.

As I fingered an empty kitchen hook, where a calendar had probably hung, I said to my father, "It would appear he's made a clean—"

"Got something," Paige called from the living room.

We found her kneeling before the fireplace.

"I never thought I'd see this outside a movie, but he's burned some papers," she said. "And he was in such a hurry there are still pieces left."

Black ashes and gray bits of paper lay in an otherwise pristine fireplace. In Miami, fireplaces were the sort of thing builders added purely for the emotional impact—a potential buyer sees it, pictures romantic nights by the fire or a faithful dog dozing before the flames, and only later realizes the impracticality of such dreams when the temperature rarely drops below sixty.

I retrieved tweezers from the bathroom, removed the largest scorched pieces and laid them on a blank sheet of paper. The edges were charred, but I could make out a few words in the middle.

"That's the club address, isn't it?" Paige said.

I nodded. The partial address was visible, and below it "11 AM–invent—"

"It's telling him when to expect Bianca to be there doing inventory," Paige said. "It must be a scheduled time—maybe when stock arrives."

The rest was mostly random phrases: "—must be complete—" "—absolutely no one—" "—message that we—"

I carefully gathered the fragile pieces and put them into a bag for lab analysis.

"We should speak to the neighbors," Paige said. "Ortega lived alone, right?"

My father nodded. "He's been divorced for about ten years, with no children."

"And, as far as we can see, no long-term girlfriend, which means it would be easy for him to cut and run. But it also gives me an excuse for talking to the neighbors."

She went to the neighbors and introduced herself as Ortega's new girlfriend, concerned because she hadn't heard from him in two days and he wasn't answering his phones. The couples to the right and across the road couldn't help. Though Ortega had lived here since his divorce, they knew nothing about him. That wasn't uncommon—avoiding unnecessary contact with neighbors is another way for supernaturals to hide what we are.

But the neighbor to the left was a divorcée in her forties who'd probably been eyeing Ortega, and who took one look at Paige and couldn't resist breaking the bad news—that Ortega had been home and probably avoiding her calls. She'd last seen him at nine-thirty that morning, which she recalled because it struck her as unusual for him to be leaving for work so late. Then, seeing him putting suitcases in his trunk, she'd presumed he was on vacation. He'd driven off, alone.

HOPE

SECURITY CLEARANCE

Karl tried to relay over the phone what he remembered of the blue-prints, but Lucas insisted—quite rightly—that it should be done in person, so Karl could draw them. He agreed, with great reluctance.

"You wanted to dump it on them and walk away, didn't you?" I said when he hung up.

"What do you want me to do, Hope? Lie to you again?" He turned on his heel and set out toward the rental car. "I suppose if I really cared about you, I'd watch you suffer and do nothing about it. But you're not suffering, are you? You're *learning*."

"I need to learn to handle it, Karl. You've said so yourself. You en-couraged me to join the council—"

"—because I knew you needed a safe way to enjoy chaos while do-ing some good. And, yes, I encourage you to expose yourself to more. In small doses. Like walking across burning coals to toughen your feet. But your idea of learning to withstand burning is to throw your-self onto the pyre and grit your teeth, because by God you're going to prove you can do it or die trying."

"Karl, I—"

He threw open the passenger door. "Get in and let's finish this."

It was a silent trip to the hotel where Lucas and Paige were staying.

Karl didn't understand why I had to push so hard, and it was wrong of me to expect him to. He believed I was in danger with this job so, to him, there would be no reason to continue. Why should we care what happened to these people? I'd done my duty, paid my debt, and now I should be free to go home. To protect me, he had to lie, because he knew I'd never walk away otherwise. Wrong-headed, but right-hearted.

WHEN I'D FIRST heard about the council, I pictured a group of gray-haired politician types. There wasn't a gray head in the bunch, which wasn't surprising when you considered they had to get out there and resolve problems themselves. The younger, more dynamic council is a fairly recent development, after the council had to face, unprepared, a true and serious threat.

Paige's mother, the council leader, had died fighting that menace and Paige had been thrust into her position. So even before meeting Paige, I'd seen her as a potential friend. Someone just as young, confused and overwhelmed as I was.

And when I saw her for the first time, that feeling only intensified. Paige had "friend" written all over her. A cute and zaftig young woman with green eyes that sparkled with good humor—the sweet, unpretentious girl next door.

Paige *was* sweet and unpretentious. But behind that smile was a razor-sharp mind, and the kind of confidence I could only dream about. Paige knew what she wanted from life, and she was going to get it, by sheer force of will and the sort of energy that would make you a millionaire if you could bottle it.

I've known ambitious people, and they're often driven by the kind of self-interest that would make Karl look altruistic. But what Paige wanted was a better life for *others*. Lead the council into a new era of reform. Help her husband protect the rights of wronged supernaturals. Open a long-distance spellcasting school for young witches without social support systems. And do it all while making a living, maintaining a household, raising the orphaned teenage daughter of a black witch, and being married to the rebel son of the most powerful Cabal leader. Paige gave new meaning to the superwoman cliché. While we got along fine, I'd been too daunted to pursue that imagined friendship.

Paige had the hotel room door open as I was still rapping. She hugged me, greeted Karl, then ushered us inside. Lucas was on the phone.

When I'd discussed Lucas with Jaz and Sonny, I'd called him a geek. To be brutally honest, that had been my impression when we first met. He was Karl's height, but maybe half his build. I knew he was more wiry than skinny, but with his usual three-piece suits, he looked scrawny and introspective. He had short black hair, dark eyes and a face that was, well, plain. The glasses didn't help. Nor did the perpetually somber expression. The only time I ever saw him smile was when Paige was around.

The room was modest and comfortable, which I expected from them. A bed, a city view and a small desk, with Paige's laptop and stacks of papers, as if they'd been working here for days instead of hours. Taped to the wall was what looked like a list of investigative steps, written in Lucas's precise hand. Paige had added a few: *eat, sleep, compensate for this morning's untimely awakening by—*

Paige untaped the sheet. "Sorry, I was goofing around. You know Lucas and lists."

Lucas hung up and greeted us with firm handshakes and quiet hellos. His tie was slung over the chair back, and he quickly pulled it off before waving us to the seats and perching on the edge of the bed.

As I sat, I caught Paige's frown of concern. When she asked whether I'd eaten, I insisted I was fine.

"I could use something," Karl said. "Let me call down—"

"You two talk to Lucas," Paige said. "I'll call room service and get sandwich platters and appetizer trays for all of us."

A deft way of making sure I ate, and I didn't miss Karl's discreet nod of thanks.

Karl mapped out sketches of the blueprints he'd seen, blank in some spots and uncertain in others. He finished as room service arrived.

"This is an office floor at Cortez headquarters," Lucas said, pointing to one of the drawings as we ate. He picked up another. "And this looks like the executive level. Not to slight the gang's abilities, but breaking in there would be extremely difficult."

"He means impossible," Paige said. "He's just leaving himself some wiggle room, should the unthinkable happen and he's wrong.

You were on that floor yesterday, Karl. What did you think of the security?"

Most people on the council were wary of Karl, but Paige saw no need to be cagey about his occupation. He seemed to appreciate the candor, and gave a complete evaluation, admitting that he doubted even he could break in without inside help.

"Which you wouldn't get," Paige said. "That's considered treason, punishable by the highest penalty."

"Execution?" I said.

"Too lenient."

"With a breach that severe, an example must be made," Lucas said. "Which isn't to say that the gang wouldn't be able to find someone willing to risk it for a high enough reward. We're already searching for Juan Ortega, who may have committed treason, acting under someone else's authority and killing Bianca. But no single person outside the family would have enough clearance to bypass all the security required to access the executive level after hours. Finding enough people willing to take that risk?" He shook his head. "That, even I would admit, does approach impossible. Still, I'll notify my father."

He picked up the other two sketches. "As for these, they appear to be house plans, though I don't recognize either. This one could be a high-ranking Cabal employee, given the size. The other looks like an apartment. I should fax them to my father." He glanced at Paige. "Is there a fax in the building?"

"I didn't see one. The front desk would probably do it. Or if you want privacy, there should be a twenty-four-hour print shop somewhere nearby."

She was reaching for the phone book when he said, "It would be easier to drop them off," and picked up his cell phone again.

I anticipated a strained conversation—business-like at best—but it sounded like any son talking to his father. Lucas explained what we had, asked about dropping by and Benicio seemed to readily agree. Then Lucas glanced at Karl, who didn't pretend he couldn't hear the other side of the discussion, and shook his head.

"They've had a very taxing day, Papá," Lucas said. "They want to get back—"

Pause.

"Yes, perhaps it would but—"

Another pause, then he covered the receiver. "My father would like you and Hope to accompany us. He wants to ask you about the plans directly."

Karl hesitated.

"Once that's done, your part will be over," Lucas said. "You can head to the airport from there if you like."

Karl nodded.

WE TOOK SEPARATE cars. Karl had no intention of hanging around any longer than he had to. The moment we were done, we'd be heading to the airport.

Benicio lived on Key Biscayne, a secluded island south of Miami Beach, accessible only by a long toll causeway that had Karl muttering, looking in his rearview mirror as if trying to judge how far we were from the airport. It wouldn't be more than a thirty-minute drive, but the closer we drew to the island, the more distant Miami seemed. The island was gorgeous, heavily wooded with white-sand beaches glittering under the remains of a perfect sunset.

If I worked in Miami, I'd want to live on Key Biscayne, though as we started passing houses, I knew I could never afford it. There were probably less expensive areas, but I didn't see a house that would sell for under a million. Even the hotels looked out of my price range.

Benicio lived on the waterfront, of course. The homes on the large, secluded lots weren't mansions, but I was sure it had to be one of the most exclusive neighborhoods in Florida.

Lucas pulled into the drive of a house set back and partially obscured by forest. The eight-foot fence looked merely decorative, but Lucas stopped to talk into a tree, which I presume discreetly held an intercom.

After a moment, he glanced at Paige, as if saying something. Karl rolled down his window as Lucas turned back to the intercom.

"Is he having trouble?" I asked.

"No one's answering."

I put my window down and inhaled. It even smelled different than Miami, the warm air not quite so humid, the smog gone. A breeze fluttered past, rich with the scent of some heady tropical flower. It was so still and quiet I could hear water lapping against the beach, at least a quarter mile down the winding drive.

Lucas got out of the car. We joined him as he examined the intercom. Karl took a look, but it wasn't his area of expertise, so he focused on something that was—the secured gate.

Paige got out too, waving her cell phone. "No answer from your father, but he might just be busy."

"I'll call the duty guards," Lucas said.

"Is the gate usually guarded?" I asked Paige.

"It isn't manned, but there are guards who patrol the yard. One during the day. Two at night. That's who Lucas is calling."

The distant symphonic ring of a cell phone started. We peered into the darkness, trying to pinpoint the sound.

"It's near the house," Karl said as he walked back. "The gate's still secured."

The ringing stopped.

"Voice mail," Lucas said as he hung up. He looked more puzzled than concerned. My first thought was that *this* was the gang's target. But Lucas would have recognized the blueprints, and the locked gate meant no one had broken in.

"Is the fence electrified?" I asked.

Lucas shook his head. "My father prefers to handle intruders more discreetly. It's wired to an alarm system that would alert the guards."

As he headed back to the car, Paige said, "Please don't tell me you're going to ram the gate."

A tiny smile. "Nothing so dramatic."

He pulled the car up alongside the fence.

"Ah, a step stool," Paige said.

Lucas went first, then helped Paige down on the other side. As I crested the fence, a vision flashed and I nearly toppled over. The sudden movement snapped me from the vision, and I let Karl help me down, then closed my eyes, trying to recapture the vision. After a moment, I heard a voice.

"About time. How long does it take you—" The man swallowed the last words. "Jesus, Frank, what are you—?"

"Hands where I can see them," a second voice hissed.

I struggled to see faces, but could make out only shadowy figures against a black backdrop.

"Have you lost your mind?" the first man said. "Whatever you're doing—"

"How do I get in the room?"

"Room? What—?"

The vision snapped as abruptly as before. As it faded, I felt a faint lick of chaos. Lucas, Paige and Karl all stood around me, waiting.

"Someone with a gun. Someone named Frank. He was asking about a room. How to get into a room."

"What room?" Paige asked.

"I don't know. I couldn't—" I gave an angry shake of my head. "I'm sorry. That's not enough, I know. Let me try again—"

"No," Karl said. "We're here now. Quicker to look ourselves. The cell phone sounded from just over there."

Lucas handed Karl his phone. "Hit redial if you need it. Paige and I will head to the house. If anyone's in the yard, we can warn the guards inside."

"Any problems, call my cell," Paige said.

Karl turned to me. "Stay close."

I nodded.

"I mean it, Hope."

"I know."

HOPE

DEATH INTERRUPTED

Security spotlights lit up the house, but most of the yard was dim and shadowy, and the perimeter black. It was still so quiet I could hear the waves.

Karl stuck to the dark edges. He had me walk beside him—on the fence side, where presumably he thought it was safer, but was also tough for anyone not blessed with a werewolf's night vision. I switched my chaos sensors on full.

As we passed between the fence and a small stuccoed outbuilding, Karl tugged me closer and I snapped from my reverie. Before I could reorient myself, a blinding light made me stumble back.

"For Christ's sake, Nico, do you mind?"

A flash of darkness as the man shielded his eyes against the light. But it moved closer, a halogen beam, so bright that the figure holding it was only an outline.

"Can I get a little privacy here? I'm taking a—"

The *pffttt* of a silenced shot.

I reeled, the vision fading. Karl gripped my forearms to hold me steady. I tugged free and followed the vibes to the outbuilding.

He caught up in two long strides, and I braced myself to be pulled back, but he only took my arm and whispered, "Gun?"

I thought he was asking about the vision—what kind of gun the man had. A testament to how tired I was, I guess. After a moment I realized he meant, "Do you have your gun and if so, get it out."

When I did, he motioned for me to head around the building one way while he went the other.

I hugged the wall. I could sense Karl behind me, watching to make sure I was alert enough to do this. Once reassured, a soft crunch of undergrowth told me he was moving, then all went silent.

I made it around the first corner before the vision hit again. It was the same scene from the same angle. I bit back my frustration. There had to be a way to train myself to at least change the viewing angle. Another reason why I'd love to speak to another Expisco.

Three more steps brought me to the next corner. The main house was fifty feet ahead, but I tried to ignore it and concentrate on this building. Presumably the door was on the next wall. I stopped, listened. I could feel only low-level chaos, which might be coming from Karl.

When I reached him, he had the door cracked open, face against the gap, sniffing. When he looked at me, I knew what I'd seen wasn't some random or past vision. Someone had been shot inside.

"Will you wait?" he whispered.

I shook my head. The low strum of chaos rose to a steady beat. I touched his arm and lifted my lips up to his ear.

"I'll see it anyway, whether I go in or not."

His chin dipped in a nod and that drum of chaos subsided.

He opened the door and stepped into the dark room, his head up, nose working. I could make out a dinette table and chairs, a small fridge and microwave, a sofa and a bank of maybe a half-dozen lockers. A staff lounge for the guards.

Karl's gaze moved to a closed door. Light shone under it.

"Stay right—" He bit the words off, chewed them over, then said, "Cover me."

I followed, gun ready, as he stopped outside the door, head tilted to listen as his nostrils flared. He turned the handle, then threw open the door.

A figure sat on the toilet, and my first impulse was to back out, apologizing. Then I saw the blood.

The man was slumped against the back of the toilet, mouth open. Male and under forty were the only characteristics I noticed, and not because of the extent of his injuries, but because I couldn't tear my gaze from those injuries long enough to notice anything else.

He'd been shot twice in the face, at close range. The first bullet had shattered his cheek. The second left his nose a mangled flap of gore, dripping blood.

I remembered the blinding flashlight beam and the shot. Had he seen death coming? Had he felt the bullet? Had he suffered at all? I hoped not, but somewhere from within me came an altogether different wish, not that the man suffered horribly, but that maybe, just a little spark of something, a flare of chaos that I could—

I swallowed hard and rubbed my hands over my face.

"It must be—" I whispered. "One of the guards. Paige said—"

The man's eyes opened. I fell back with a yelp.

Karl hauled me toward the door.

"What are you—?" I began. "He's alive. We have to—"

My words came out shrill and jumbled. I fumbled for my phone, but my fingers were shaking so badly I dropped it. As I wrenched against Karl's grasp, the man gave a low moan. My gaze flew to his.

His eyes were so blank and empty, I was certain that groan had been his last, that I hadn't reacted fast enough, that I should have—

His lips parted, a bloody froth bubbled and I stared, transfixed.

"He's gone, Hope."

"Gone? Are you crazy?" I tried to pull away. "He's alive. Can't you see?"

I wrenched around, saw those blank eyes and knew Karl was right. Not a lick of chaos emanated from the man—no fear, no pain, just emptiness. But I kept struggling to get to him, because there was the off-chance I was wrong and I would not walk away. The impulse to help was still there, not yet buried under that lust for chaos, and I clung to it with everything I had.

Karl pulled me to the door. I could see him talking, but his words floated past unheard. Then came two that didn't: Paige and Lucas.

I reached for my phone. "We have to call—"

He took the phone, stuffed it into my pocket and caught my hands when I went for it again.

"You won't stop me from warning them, Karl. I won't let—"

His grip went tight enough to hurt now, face coming down to mine.

"That guard is still bleeding, Hope. That means he was just shot, and whoever shot him was taking him out before going after Benicio—before heading into the house."

"Which is why we have to warn—"

"And set off Paige's cell phone? Yes, we have to warn them. But not that way."

He scooped up my gun, which I hadn't even realized I no longer held. When I reached for it, he held it just out of reach. His gaze searched mine then, without a word, he handed it back and we hurried from the building.

LUCAS

8

I TOLD MYSELF I was overreacting. Laughed as I imagined what I looked like, slinking through the shadows under cover of a blur spell.

Were the guards watching me from the darkness of the yard, struggling not to laugh? Or inside, at the monitor station, busily taping the footage to pass around a Cabal e-mail loop: look at the guy, he's so paranoid he can't even walk up to his dad's front door without hiding under a spell.

No one could have broken into my father's house.

Paige had joked earlier that I hated to use the word *impossible,* in case I was proven wrong. But this situation came as close to impossible as I could imagine.

The front gates couldn't be operated without a signal from within the house, and anyone climbing the fence would set off an alarm, notifying two patrolling guards, the house guard and Troy. But *we'd* climbed the fence . . . and no one was rushing out to stop us.

I pushed back the thought in favor of the hope that I was making a monumental fool of myself.

My father was fine.

Even if someone breached the fence, he couldn't get into the house. My father refused to employ illegal or supernatural security methods in the yard—he couldn't risk having a drunken teen scale his fence and slam into a barrier spell. But with the house, he had no such compunctions.

Even the Cabal vaults—which contained not only a fortune in bearer bonds, but all the powerful spells and supernatural secrets accumulated in centuries of Cabal-hood—were not as carefully guarded as this house. My father was more valuable to the Cabal than any bond or spell. Lives had been sacrificed to provide the highest security the supernatural world knew.

There was only one door, which had to be opened by the guard within. Once inside, the visitor found himself in a completely secured concrete box. To get into the house proper required another door to be opened, which could only be done by my father or Troy.

There was another way through the front door. Should my father be in the yard or on the beach, he'd hardly want to knock at his own door, so a retinal scanner allowed him access. It was also set to recognize one other person: me. As for why I might need to get inside without him, he never said, only that I'd find out if the need arose.

After motioning for Paige to stay back, I stepped in front of the camera and waited. If, by chance, the perimeter security was malfunctioning, and all was well inside, the guard would spot me and open the door.

I counted sixty long seconds. Paige stayed where she was, asking nothing.

I activated the scanner.

A whir as the lock electronically opened. I cracked open the door and cast a sensing spell, checking for signs of life. It came back negative.

The room within looked like any vestibule. Even the guard's desk was decorative teak, with the LCD security screens inset in frames.

The guard sat in his chair, head on his arms, which were folded on the desk, as if he'd fallen asleep. Only the spilled take-out coffee cup told me otherwise. Paige brushed past me, her fingers going to the man's neck.

"Dead," she said. "But what...?"

She let the sentence trail off, knowing I'd be asking the question already. There was no blood or other sign of trauma. He seemed simply to have laid his head down and gone to sleep.

Paige bent to sniff the spilled coffee, and I knew her conclusion before she voiced it.

"Poison."

That made no sense. None of it did. But questions flew from my head as I turned and saw the interior door propped open with a pen. As I stared at that crude instrument, brain insisting I make sense of it, Paige pointed to a pencil by the main door. Half a pencil, the other half presumably outside, after it failed its purpose in keeping the heavy door—

The interior door was open. The guard dead. My father inside.

It took all I had not to throw open that door and run in. I cast another sensing spell, then slid through the interior door. I heard her cast a cover spell, and quickly did the same, annoyed that I'd lacked the forethought to do it without prompting.

The cover spell let us stay hidden, as long as we remained still. I looked around the living room. There was nothing that I couldn't scan in an instant and say "yes, that belongs there."

Paige tapped my arm and motioned toward the kitchen, meaning she'd check in there. While part of me wanted to keep her close, another part knew that if my father was in danger, every moment was critical.

It didn't take long to search the house. It was only a couple of thousand square feet, my father being the sole inhabitant and not inclined to entertain. Paige met me next door to my father's bedroom suite, in a small room where Troy slept. To get to my father's, an intruder had to pass through here, adding an extra layer of security.

Paige cast a privacy spell, though I now doubted the precaution was necessary. We'd cast sensing spells and if someone was here, even hidden or unconscious, we'd know it.

"If Troy realized someone broke in, and he got your dad out, they'd call so we wouldn't walk in on a killer. If they took your dad, they'd leave Troy behind." Dismay touched with guilt crossed her face. "Troy..."

"No," I said. "Yes, it may be a logical explanation—Troy kills the guards with poisoned coffee and kidnaps my father—but no. Not Troy."

"Maybe not willingly," she said slowly. "But if he was blackmailed. Or someone in his family was threatened..."

"He doesn't have any family. No long-term girlfriends. No children. No vices that he could be blackmailed with. He is, in short, the perfect bodyguard."

As I defended him I wondered how much it was rooted in affection, rather than conviction.

"I cannot believe he'd do it," I said. "But, in light of no other obvious explanations . . ." I couldn't finish the sentence.

"Is there anyplace else your dad could be? On the property? I know there's no basement, but—"

My head jerked up. "The panic room."

LUCAS

9

"I CANNOT BELIEVE I FORGOT—" I strode into my father's bedroom. "It's accessed through the bedroom. Where, I don't know. But surely it's equipped with a method of communicating with the outside world. He should have been able to call for help."

I walked around the walls, lifting paintings, mirrors, anything that could conceal a panel. Or would it be as small as a latch? I crouched at the dressing table and began examining the underside.

"Um, the door can't be in here," Paige said.

I turned sharply, irritated in spite of myself. "It is. He said it was accessed through the bedroom."

"The bedroom? Or the bedroom suite? Because there's no way there's a hidden room behind any of these walls, Lucas."

Two sides were exterior walls, the third ran the length of the adjoining bath and the fourth was the length of Troy's sleeping quarters. Not enough space for a panic closet, much less a room.

I cursed. Thinking before I acted. That had never been a problem before.

Paige was already in the bathroom, mentally taking measurements. She pulled open the door to the walk-in closet. A flick of the light and "Yes! Here, the east wall. Behind it is the kitchen, but there's plenty of room—"

She stopped, looking down. A sharp inhalation, then she disappeared into the closet, moving fast. I hurried to the doorway.

The closet was in disarray. Someone had haphazardly yanked clothing off hangers, dumped shoes on the floor.

I remembered what Hope had said. A voice, asking how to get into "the room." The panic room.

Paige was pushing aside hangers, frantically hunting for the door. A stifled gasp. She lifted fingers smeared with blood. There, on the sleeve of a gray suit coat, was a bloody handprint. And at Paige's feet, a stain on the carpet. More blood smears crossed to the door and likely continued outside, where the dark wood in the bedroom and black marble in the bath had hidden the traces.

Finally, I found the trigger—several buttons recessed into the rear of the lower clothing rod. Those buttons would need to be pressed in sequence. An access code. Perfectly logical—why have a panic room if anyone can get in—but how would *I* get in? My father was inside, too injured to call for help, and I was stuck out here, pressing the damned buttons—

Call the Cabal.

I was lifting my phone when the rack moved with a hydraulic whoosh. Paige stumbled back out of the way. Before I could get around the door to see within, I heard my father's voice, starting a spell.

"Papá!"

I swung around the door and pulled up short. He stood there, his shirt front covered with blood. His lips moved, but I could hear nothing, could only see the blood.

Damn it, move! Help him! He needs first aid, an ambulance . . .

I couldn't budge, brain insisting this was impossible. Paige rushed past me and past my father. I opened my mouth to call her back, then saw a body lying in a pool of blood. Troy.

As she dropped beside him, I strode to my father, finding my voice at last.

"Are you okay? There's blood—"

"It's Troy's. I'm fine."

I saw my cell phone still in my hand and lifted it. "Have you called—?"

He took it from me, fingers flying over the keypad. I knelt beside Paige. Troy had been shot in the chest and was unconscious. Blood soaked his shirt. There were more bloodied clothes on the floor, where my father must have tried to stanch the flow.

Paige was ripping off Troy's shirt. I leaned in to help.

I could see the shot now, an exit wound just below his heart. There was so much blood...

My father bent beside Paige. "What can I do?"

She asked him to bring cold cloths.

A minute later, he returned with wet towels. "The ambulance should be here in five minutes. This damned room..."

"Built before the cellular age," I murmured as I cleaned the blood from Troy's chest, looking for other injuries. "And never tested for reception later, because it had a land line. But a land line can be cut."

He nodded. "When the guards didn't call the office for their hourly check-in, the security office would have been alerted. It always seemed that would be fast enough..."

Unless you had a man dying on the floor, and the gunman possibly right outside the door.

My father mopped Troy's brow, then looked at Paige. "Is he as bad as—?"

He stopped and shook his head, realizing he didn't want an answer. Troy was too pale. His breathing was too shallow. As skilled as Paige and I were at first aid, this was beyond us.

"He was talking to someone," my father said after a moment. "I was in my room. I couldn't make out who he was talking to, but nothing seemed to be wrong, and I thought it was you, that I'd misunderstood and you were already on your way when you phoned. I was heading to the door when Troy walked in. That startled me—he didn't knock first. I think he knew something was wrong and was trying to warn me, but as he walked through that door—"

My father blinked. No outward sign of emotion, but that blink told me everything, as did the slight catch in his voice. "They shot him in the back. He tried to tell me something, but he passed out before he hit the floor. I managed to get the door closed and cast a barrier spell. I should have looked first, seen who—" He shook his head. "All I could think about was getting him into this room and calling for help. Then, too late, I realized I couldn't." A pause, then he looked up sharply. "The ambulance. It'll be here any minute. You should—"

"I'll open the gates," I said as I got to my feet.

"Hope and Karl," Paige called after me. "They'll be—"

"I'll call them."

———

KARL WAS AT the front door, trying to find a way in after discovering that the outside guards were dead. Had he attempted to break a window, he or Hope could have been seriously injured by the protection spell. I should have warned him about that. Another unacceptable oversight.

Who had been on duty tonight? I almost certainly knew them, had talked to them, inquired after their families, who would be expecting them home in a few hours . . .

I shook it off and told Karl and Hope about my father, pointing them to the panic room, then opened the gates. I was partway up the drive when the ambulance arrived. I climbed in and updated them on the situation.

As the paramedics and I got close to the panic room, I heard Karl and my father arguing, and broke into a run.

HOPE

CHAOS-CRAZED

I stood in the panic room, my brain a swirl of perfect chaos.

Paige's thoughts were loudest, a frightened jumble of self-doubt. *Did I do that right? Am I missing something? What if I'm making it worse? Where's the ambulance?*

Benicio's thoughts were too muddled to distinguish, one intense wave after another. Under that, I could pick up Karl's steady throb of anger and distress.

Then there was the man on the floor. Dying...His soul, slipping from his body, the grief and anxiety and fear of the others swirling around him, a cocktail more potent than anything I ever dreamed of. I drank it in, oblivious to my surroundings. I couldn't remember how I'd gotten in there. Couldn't remember why I was there. Couldn't even remember who this man was, lying on the floor, dying. All that mattered was that he *was* dying and when he did, the reward would be beyond imagining.

Karl was yelling about getting someone to leave. Not me. He wouldn't do that—wouldn't pull me away, not when death was so close, hanging in the air...

This was what I was made for. This was where I belonged, in the center of the whirlwind, drinking it in...

"You need to get her out of here." Benicio's voice.

"You don't think I'm trying?" Karl's snarl.

The room spun, pulling me under.

"It's the chaos." Benicio. "She's—"

"I know what's happening." Karl. "And apparently you do too."

His anger spiked and I shuddered. So delicious, so perfectly—
Hands went around my waist. Lifted me. I lashed out with everything
I had. The arms only gripped tighter and carried me, kicking and
punching and screaming, from the room, out two doors, into the
bright glare of a white room.

The chaos lifeline snapped under the glare of those bathroom
lights. I looked up and saw my reflection—a nightmarish version of
myself, my hair wild, lips pulled back in a snarl, face contorted with
pure animal rage.

The face of a demon.

Karl carried me into the bedroom. He lowered me onto the bed,
and as I gulped air, my throat raw from screaming, I struggled to
block the memory of my reflection, telling myself it'd been some hell-
ish trick of my mind.

The last five minutes flooded back. What I'd felt in that room.
What I'd thought. All of it as alien as that horror in the mirror and
yet, like the reflection, recognizable.

"K-K-Karl . . ."

I looked up, my eyes filled with tears of shame, and could see only
a watery figure. I felt his arms around me as he crouched, pulling my
face against his chest.

"Shh, shh, shh."

"I-I-I—"

"Shhh."

I forced my head up, to find his face, to look him in the eyes.

"I wanted him to die, Karl. I couldn't even remember who he was.
A man I know, I like, and I wanted him to die so I could feed off—"

My head jolted forward, gorge rising, and before I could stop it, I
threw up on him.

"Oh God, oh God, I'm so—"

He took my chin and lifted it, looking me in the eye. "It's okay,
Hope."

With his free hand, he deftly unbuttoned his shirt, peeled it off and
tossed it on the bed, never breaking eye contact. Thinking of that—
throwing a vomit-covered shirt onto Benicio Cortez's Egyptian cotton

sheets—I had to bite back a surge of hysterical laughter. My eyes filled at the same time and I started shaking so badly I couldn't breathe.

My mind was back in that room, wallowing in the chaos, gulping it down, seeing Troy . . .

A sudden vision shoved the memory aside. I was peering through bushes, watching a dark-haired young man on a restaurant patio, eating a burger with one hand, writing with the other, gaze fixed on a book. Something about him looked familiar.

The vision faded and I saw Troy again, dying. Then I saw him sitting across from me, laughing and flirting, and I was thinking what a nice guy he was, how he was someone I'd like to know better, someone I . . .

Wanted to watch die?

My stomach heaved, but there was nothing left.

Karl pulled my face back to his. I struggled to understand him.

"Focus on me, Hope. On what I'm showing you."

His face swam in front of me, then vanished, and I was behind the bushes again. I could see my hand, holding back a branch as I peered through. My fingers were long and slender, masculine but smooth, not a child's but not yet a man's.

"Hey!" a voice boomed. "So this is where you're hiding."

The dark-haired man at the table lifted his head, lips curving in a crooked smile that finally made the recognition click. Jeremy Danvers, the werewolf Alpha. Another young man, thickset and muscular, grabbed him in a headlock, leaned over, snatched Jeremy's drink, took a swig and made a face.

"Get this man a beer," he called to two others stepping onto the patio.

"Next year," Jeremy said. "When I can legally—"

"Stop being so damned proper. It's hot. I'm buying you a beer. You're drinking it."

The man swung a chair around and plunked down.

"Please, sit, Antonio," Jeremy said. "No, you aren't interrupting my work at all."

They continued bantering as the other young men joined them, but the conversation faded under the swirling emotions from the watcher. Envy. Longing. Loneliness. His fingers whitened on the branch as he strained to listen, lapping up the camaraderie from the patio, caught up in his feelings. Then others overlapped—those of an adult looking back on the memory. Regret, grief and guilt, as intense as the chaos of the panic room, and it swept me along, giving me something to feed on, a rich substitute devoid of moral consequences.

After a moment, though, it wasn't enough and the shaking started anew, my chest constricting, breathing ragged—

"Focus, Hope. Focus on me."

Another vision. This one black emptiness. Only voices. One I knew, but much younger than I'd ever heard it.

"You don't understand, Dad."

"Yes, I do. You're the one who doesn't. The Pack isn't for us."

"It's for werewolves, isn't it? And we're werewolves. That's how it's supposed to be—living like that, with others, others like us. I *feel* it—"

"It's an instinct. You have to fight it. Rise above it. It's not a club with a special handshake, Karl. They won't let us in. They'd kill us."

"How do you know that if you've never tried?"

"I know. We have to stay out of their way. We have to—"

Run. Always running. The coward's way.

Are you calling your father a coward?

No, of course not. I'd never . . .

The thoughts disintegrated into a muddle of rage and guilt. I drank it up, knowing it was a memory, something Karl was offering me, a gift . . .

When my stomach stopped churning, I rubbed my hands over my face.

"I—I think I'm okay now," I said. "Can we—?"

"Leave?" He got up from his crouch and rolled his shoulders, working out the kinks. "I plan to."

I saw the back of a paramedic who'd just passed through with the stretcher. I got up, wanting to ask how Troy was, but my knees wobbled and Karl had to catch me.

Paige appeared in the doorway. She managed a wan smile, and motioned for Karl to sit me back on the bed. As she checked my pulse, I flashed back to the panic room, to how I'd left it, over Karl's shoulder, flailing like a chaos-crazed demon. Paige had seen that. They saw, and now they knew my secret.

But as shame flooded me, I remembered how they knew. Not from

Karl, who'd never betray my secret. From Benicio. Who'd told Karl to get me out of the room. Who had thrown me into a chaotic situation, knowing I'd thrive on it and, like a junkie, want more.

He'd used me just as much as Tristan had. There was a difference between seducing a prospective employee with promises of huge bonuses and preying on her weaknesses, feeding her the drugs she wants, knowing she'll become addicted.

Lucas walked in, but my gaze went past him to Benicio. Then I looked away. I didn't want to lay the blame on him. So what if he'd tempted me? I wanted to be above temptation. In control. Responsible.

"I'll be at the hospital," Benicio said to Lucas. "I want you and Paige—" A sharp intake of breath. "Your brothers."

"I'll warn them."

"I should have thought—"

"I'll look after it, Papá. You go with Troy. I'll have guards meet you at the hospital."

After Benicio left, I looked up to see Lucas lost in thought as Paige walked over to him. He murmured something to her, then turned to Karl.

"I hate to ask . . ." he began.

"Then don't," Karl growled. "We've done more than enough already and Hope has paid more than—"

"What do you need?" I cut in. I met Karl's gaze. "Please."

"No."

My insides twisted, and I had to swallow to keep from heaving again.

He laid his hand on mine, cupped in my lap. "You've done enough, Hope."

"I haven't," I whispered, too low for the others to hear. "I need to help. To finish this by doing something good."

A moment's silence as he studied me. Then he turned to Lucas. "One last favor. And I *do* consider it a favor."

"It is," Lucas said. "I need to find my brothers—"

"And what, you want us to make phone calls? Get your Cabal flunkies out of their beds—"

"No. We need to track them down and warn them. In person. Just find them, please, Karl. Then you can go."

WE DROVE KARL'S rental, following Lucas as he made calls, trying to locate his brothers. Karl continued to grumble—why did we have to find them when a direct phone call would give them quicker warning? I agreed, but in Lucas's defense, put forward possible explanations. Karl was having none of it. Not only was he worried about me, but playing tracking dog for a thirty-year-old sorcerer chafed. He had enough trouble obeying his Alpha.

The reminder of Jeremy brought back the memories Karl had shown me, and I longed to ask what they meant. This wasn't the time. I wasn't sure there'd ever *be* a time. Karl had only shown me that in a desperate attempt to yank me out of a dark place.

We'd just left the neighborhood when Lucas called my cell.

"Hector is at home," he said. "Paige and I will visit him. Carlos is out for the evening, and will be difficult to locate, so I'm going to ask you two to go see William, who was apparently working late. My father's other bodyguard, Griffin, will meet you at the office and escort you inside."

"Okay . . ."

I could understand why Lucas wouldn't want a security team swooping in and alarming Hector's family at home, but this made no sense. If William was in the office, there was an entire security division on site to check on him and take him into protective custody.

"Why don't we find Carlos?" I said. "If he's harder to track, Karl would be perfect."

"We know where the others should be. So I'd like to handle them first."

Karl shot me a look. "As long as he doesn't expect me to track Carlos *after* we talk to William."

"I heard that," Lucas said. "Tell Karl no. Once you've found William and turned him over to Griffin's care, I won't ask any more of either of you. If William isn't at the office, though, I'd like Karl to try to ascertain, by scent, whether he was there recently. And, Hope, if you could check for any visions . . ."

In other words, he suspected William might have been kidnapped . . . or worse.

"If he *is* gone," Lucas said. "Please ask Karl to track him as far as possible, then contact me."

LUCAS

10

"SO HAVE I COMPLETELY LOST MY MIND?" I asked as I drove.

Paige gave a tiny smile. "Not yet." She directed me around a corner, following the instructions the Cabal had given. "For your father's sake, I hate to say it, but your reasoning is sound. I just hope you're wrong."

"As do I."

I glanced in the rearview mirror as a dark car pulled in behind us. A flash of its headlights told me it was the guards I'd requested. "Am I wrong to keep my suspicions from Hope and Karl?"

A pause this time. Choosing her words with care, she finally said, "It's . . . not ideal. But you already know that."

I nodded.

"If you tell Karl the truth, he won't help, but the only way to answer your questions about your brothers is with his tracking abilities and Hope's visions."

"So I'm employing questionable means to achieve a goal I believe is in the best interests of the majority. Sounds like my father."

"It isn't the same."

Isn't it?

AT HECTOR'S HOUSE, the Cabal guards pulled in behind us.

I was about to see family members I'd never met. Family who didn't know I existed.

No matter how sound my justification, Hector would say I was just using a shrewd excuse to undermine his authority. Proof I was becoming a threat.

Paige took my elbow and rubbed her thumb across the back of it, pimpled with goose bumps despite the warm night air.

"Is there any other way we can do this?" she asked.

I shook my head.

Someone had walked into my father's house, bypassing security without raising alarms, someone familiar enough that the door guard not only accepted poisoned take-out coffee from him, but didn't feel it necessary to clear his admittance with my father. Someone Troy would chat with, unperturbed, in his bedroom.

There were four people who could get into Benicio Cortez's home without question: his sons. Only one did I deem capable of orchestrating such a complex, coldhearted and technically brilliant scheme. A plot that required not only intelligence but patience. First, he needed to have Cabal security harass the gang members, causing noticeable friction between the two groups. Then kidnapping and murder, done by employees who probably believed they were working under Cabal auspices. The gang, incited to violent retaliation, would make the perfect scapegoats for murder.

Only Hector could pull it off. But that didn't mean the others weren't involved. This was why I couldn't phone my brothers. They had to be surprised, their whereabouts confirmed by myself or someone whose impartiality I trusted.

I turned to Paige. "Perhaps you should wait—"

"No," she said. "And don't ask again."

CABAL FAMILY SORCERERS are expected to marry human women and keep their supernatural side a secret, which means there is an entire side of their lives—a critical side—they cannot share with their life partner. Yet they rarely challenge the custom. Men like Hector and my father are raised to believe in the archaic tradition of the noble classes, where wives are chosen for political connections and their suitability as gracious hostesses and loving mothers.

A modern wife like Paige might expect to be a full partner, influencing the workings of the business. That is unacceptable. One could blame it on sexism, but it is more a matter of race.

The upper echelon of a Cabal is staffed entirely by sorcerers, who are, by default, male. We rule the Cabals as if by divine decree. To allow a member of another race to have a say in the workings of the business would be dangerous. Ask any Cabal family sorcerer and he'll rationalize the prejudice by saying that sorcerers have always been in charge and have done a fine job so far, and therefore there is no need to appoint a member of another race to the board. The truth, though, is rooted in fear.

Marry a supernatural woman and she will, by necessity, be a race other than sorcerer. If she is truly her husband's partner, she may be equally ambitious, with an eye toward the executive offices and an eventual seat on the board. Most of the time, a supernatural wife would have no such designs, but the Cabal will not take that chance.

So, my brother's wife was human, and that made what I was doing all the more difficult. It did, however, mean that getting access to their house was simple. All security had to be human in origin—it would be difficult to explain away a trigger illusion to a wife who knew nothing of the supernatural. It also had to be as unobtrusive as possible. Even the most trusting wife, if forced to live in an armed camp, will eventually start suspecting her husband's business isn't as legitimate as he claims. That meant there was only common external security, but everyone from the butler to the gardener to the maid was a trained Cabal security officer.

Hector's butler had been expecting us, and had the front door open as soon as we walked up the steps.

"He's in his office," he whispered.

"Has he been in there long?"

"Since returning from work shortly after eight."

"And the family?"

"Mrs. Cortez is discussing tomorrow's menu with the chef. I told him to keep her occupied. The boys are in bed, so you shouldn't be disturbed."

We followed the butler. The two guards brought up the rear. We were passing a darkened living room when a woman's voice came from the doorway just ahead.

"Hello? Oh. I didn't hear the bell ring."

The butler stepped sideways, as if blocking me from her sight. An unnecessary precaution. Bella, Hector's wife, had never met me. I presumed that was the petite blond woman who stood in the semidark doorway.

She was well dressed and attractive, a combination that usually indicated self-confidence, yet she paused a few feet from us, as if uncertain she had the right to question the appearance of strangers in her home.

"I'm sorry, Mrs. Cortez," Paige said, stepping forward. "We asked your butler not to disturb you. We're from the office, on a matter that I'm afraid can't wait until morning."

Bella cast a nervous glance from us to our guards. "Is Hector expecting you?"

"It's quite all right, ma'am," the butler said. "I'll vouch for them, as will Mr. Cortez."

"But he doesn't want to be disturbed. Carlos made that very clear."

"Carlos Cortez?" I said.

"Yes, his—" She colored. "Of course you know who Carlos is. I'm sorry. Yes, that Carlos."

"When was Carlos here?"

She checked her watch. "An hour—no, I'm sorry, I mean he left an hour ago, so he arrived perhaps twenty minutes before that. He wasn't here long."

Which meant both Carlos and Hector had been here when Troy was shot. So neither could be responsible. William as the mastermind? Much less plausible, which is why I'd felt safe sending Hope and Karl after him.

"I'll call Hope," Paige murmured, as if reading my mind.

"Carlos made it very clear Hector didn't want to be disturbed," Bella went on. "And when he says that, he means it."

Paige shot a pointed look at me. Bella's nervousness had nothing to do with the late-night arrival of strangers—she was afraid of upsetting Hector. Very afraid from the way her hands trembled.

"I'm sorry, Mrs. Cortez," Paige said. "We know this is an inconvenience to both you and your husband, and we wouldn't have come without calling again if his father hadn't insisted. If you'd like to phone Mr. Cortez..."

Paige intended to calm Bella with the assurance that we had my father's blessing, but the fear in the woman's eyes only grew. Afraid of arousing Hector's anger by calling my father? Or fear of my father himself? Because my father refused to name Hector heir, Hector insisted he was robbing his grandchildren of their birthright and therefore deserved to play no significant role in their lives. So they had little contact with him. A decision that hurt my father like nothing else Hector could have done. As for Bella's fear, I could only imagine what stories he told them to keep his sons from wanting to know their grandfather better.

"Mom?"

Stockinged feet appeared on the steps, then a stocky youth dressed in jeans and a T-shirt.

"Emilio," the butler mouthed to me.

My sixteen-year-old nephew.

"What's wrong, Mom?" Emilio said as he came down.

"I'll call Hope," Paige murmured, and backed away.

Emilio stopped at the bottom of the stairs. He looked at me, then the guards, then back to me, his face registering not an iota of recognition.

"They need to speak to your father," the butler said. "They're from the office and they'll be gone just as soon as they can."

I fought to hide my growing frustration. Hector was probably less than fifty feet away. We could check on him and be gone in five minutes.

"Who's this?" Emilio said, jutting his chin at me.

"He works with your father."

"Yeah, you said that." He looked at me. "I've never seen you before."

"No," I said softly. "You haven't. I work in the Pacific Northwest. I'm sorry, Emilio, but I need to speak—"

"How do you know my name?"

"He works for the company, sir," the butler said, now openly struggling with his exasperation.

Emilio looked at me. "Then it's not Emilio to you. It's *Mr.* Cortez."

I felt a flicker of true impatience, and maybe something more, but said, calmly, "As you wish." I turned to the butler. "Now, the office is—"

"I really don't think—" Bella began.

"I've got it, Mom," Emilio said, with a snap in his voice that, at his age, would have earned me a five-hundred-word essay on the nature of respect for one's parents.

Bella didn't reprimand him. In fact, I swear I saw her flinch.

"Go see Ramon," Emilio said to his mother. "He was looking for his gym uniform."

With that, Bella hurried off up the stairs. I felt that familiar chill down my spine as I looked back at Emilio.

"Lu—" Paige began, then stopped herself, just in case. "We really should hurry."

As she spoke, she kept her gaze down, which seemed odd—Paige never avoids eye contact. Then I realized why she'd stepped away so quickly.

"Yes, right," I said, then to Emilio, "I'm sorry. Please excuse—"

He jumped into our path so quickly it startled Paige, and she looked up. Their eyes met. His went wide in shock. Then his lip curled.

"A witch?" He turned to me. "You brought a witch into our house?"

"No, I brought my wife." The words came out before I could help myself. I took Paige's arm. "If you'll excuse—"

"No, I don't excuse you, and she is not welcome in my house."

Under other circumstances, Paige wouldn't have stood for that. But Emilio was young, and it was not the time to educate him on the follies of prejudice, so she laid her fingers on my arm and said, "I'll be in the car."

With a nod to the guards, who parted to give way, she started forward, then stumbled, feet flying out, hands going up to brace against a fall. As I scrambled to grab her, I saw Emilio's fingers raised, and knew she hadn't tripped.

"Walk faster, witch," he sneered, and lifted his hand in another knockback spell.

I wheeled on him and caught his hands so quickly he yelped.

"Don't," I said.

"You—"

Emilio froze, caught in Paige's binding spell.

"Go," she said. "I'll keep him."

Her expression was annoyance mingled with regret—this was a step she'd rather not have taken.

I strode behind the butler, who seemed not at all perturbed by his young employer's predicament . . . and perhaps somewhat amused to see the boy trapped by a witch's spell.

One guard followed at my heels. The other, after a motion from me, stayed with Paige.

LUCAS

11

THE BUTLER PAUSED at the wooden door.

"I have to knock, sir."

This was one routine he didn't dare break, even at my father's bidding.

The butler rapped. From within I could hear a rock ballad that predated my musical experience, from the seventies perhaps. When I frowned at the lack of response, the butler said, "He probably hears us. Mrs. Cortez was right, sir. He really doesn't like to be disturbed."

"Then I'll take responsibility for doing so."

I tried the door. Locked but with nothing complicated. I removed a card from my wallet and, ignoring the butler's fidgeting, swiped it through the crack.

The office was everything one would expect from a Cabal CEO . . . or a man who expected to become one. Wood was the primary decorating material, and the air reeked of lemon cleaner. The room was at least five hundred square feet, with a cavernous feel, as if Hector had declared this was the size of office befitting his station, then hadn't known how to adequately fill the space. The lack of clutter made it easy to see that it was unoccupied.

I walked to the bathroom. Empty.

"Is there another exit?" I asked.

The guard said, "No, sir. This room was constructed like your father's home. All the windows are impenetrable and immovable, and secured with spells. There are no exterior exits."

As the guard spoke, the butler's gaze shifted, just a little, to the side.

I turned to him. "Which window opens?"

He flushed. "The farthest on the right, sir. But only from the inside. I know your father insisted on the full security package, but Mr. Cortez..."

"Wanted a personal escape route."

The butler nodded. I knew there was only one reason he'd insist on an exit from this room, into which he could retreat, undisturbed, for hours. An escape route...to visit his mistress. Or I amended, as my gaze lit on a day bed, to sneak her in.

Mistresses were an expected part of a Cabal sorcerer's life, as in any situation where a man marries for duty rather than for love. But a secret way out also gave Hector an alibi when he needed one—his family insistent he'd been within the whole time, never daring to check.

Carlos had arrived at almost precisely the time my father's assassin had driven him into the panic room. He'd entered and left without anyone verifying that he'd actually spoken to Hector. Then he'd made it clear that Hector was not to be disturbed. Establishing a nearly ironclad alibi.

I turned to the butler. "When is the last time anyone saw him?"

"I spoke to him when he got home, around eight. But the cook brought his dinner in at eight-thirty."

I looked at the empty dishes on the desk.

"He calls when he wants them removed. If he's busy, we have to wait until he leaves. When he comes in here—"

"—he doesn't want to be disturbed."

I walked toward the window. It seemed to be ajar.

"Sir?" The guard was on the other side of the desk, looking down.

I saw a leather loafer protruding. I hurried around the desk, and almost slipped in a slick puddle. A pool of blood. Hector lay on his back, blood soaking his shirt front.

I dropped beside him and checked his pulse. I found none.

"Bring Paige in please," I said, as calmly as I could manage.

The butler started for the door, then I remembered another, more critical request.

"Do *not* let Emilio in. Stop him physically if you must."

"Yes, sir."

I crouched beside my brother's body. *My brother's body . . .*

My mind refused to process the thought. It was a trick. He'd faked his death—killed someone else and placed this impostor here, a man who looked like him, or a man under a glamour spell. Preposterous, of course, but it made more sense than the truth—that Hector Cortez, the ogre of my childhood, had been felled by something as ordinary as an assassin's bullet.

My brother . . .

"I'm sorry."

I looked up to see Paige. "Can you confirm . . . ?"

"Yes, of course."

As she knelt beside Hector, I took out my phone. There were steps that needed to be taken after the murder of a Cabal son, and I was not about to ask my father to take them. In fact, the first thing I did was insist that news of Hector's death be kept from him until I was there to break it.

An investigation had to be launched and a cover-up begun. The police could not be called. His wife could not even suspect that they'd needed to be called, a situation made more difficult by where he'd died. She had to be kept out of this room until his body could be removed, and to do that, we'd have to keep news of his death a secret until it was too late for her to rush in. If that happened, our only recourse was to claim suicide, an explanation that would raise almost as many questions as murder. Heart failure or a stroke would be easier, if it could be managed.

One call set the wheels in motion. I explained the situation succinctly, then said, "Until I inform my father, all calls regarding this matter are to come to me, at this number."

I expected some hesitation. But the chief of security agreed, and promised to keep me informed of all developments.

"Carlos," Paige said, coming over to me. "I never would have believed it. *Working* with Hector, maybe. But on his own? Something this complicated? Either we all seriously underestimated his intelligence, or this really was Hector's work—and Carlos just got greedy."

For a moment, I wondered what she was talking about. Then it hit me.

I sent one of the guards out to enlist the Cabal household staff to help tend to the family—and keep them out—then bring the butler to me.

"Did you admit Carlos earlier?" I asked the butler.

"Yes, sir."

"And the exact time?"

"Close to what Mrs. Cortez said. He arrived at nine-forty-five and left shortly after ten."

"And you're certain it was Carlos?"

He didn't take umbrage at the question. In our world, illusion and deceit are facts of life.

"I certainly believed it to be him, sir."

"And you didn't see Hector or admit anyone into this room after Carlos left?"

"No, sir."

Hector could have admitted someone through the secret window after Carlos left—but one thing was clear. We needed to find Carlos.

"What about William?" Paige said.

I hesitated. As much as I wanted to stop Carlos, I had another brother to think about—one who might need protecting. "William first. But before we go, I should . . ."

I cracked open the door and peeked out. The hall was empty, the staff having distracted the family or convinced them everything was fine. Should I find Emilio and tell him? He didn't know me. Should a stranger be the one to bear such news?

The butler spoke before I could. "I'll handle it, sir. Once Mr. Cortez is removed, I'll tell the widow, then let her break it to the boys. Stroke, was it?"

"Yes."

He nodded.

HOPE

UNWELCOME

"Have you spoken to your mother?" Karl asked as we walked to Cortez headquarters.

The question was so unexpected I could only gawk. "What?"

"Have you called your mother since you've been in Miami?"

I had the day I arrived, but since then had told myself she'd expect me to be busy with my story. Truth was, I'd been uncomfortable calling her while playing Faith Edmonds.

"Benicio can tempt you all he wants," Karl said. "You have a long way to go before he stands any chance of winning you over."

That's what he'd meant by the question about my mother. Would I ever stop being surprised—and maybe a little discomfited—by how well Karl knew me?

I took his point, but I only had to think back to those few minutes in the panic room to make me wonder how right he was. As long as my ties—to home and family, work and the council—stayed intact, I didn't have much in common with the young supernaturals in the gang. Yet, at times, like them, I felt alone and alienated by my powers.

I still mourned the perfectly open relationship I'd once had with my mother. There'd been a level of honesty there I'd never have again.

Even in the world of supernaturals, I'd never be truly understood or accepted. My powers were too different and disconcerting. Who wants to be around someone who can read their worst thoughts? Karl had worked around it, but I'm sure it hadn't been easy, which made me cherish his friendship all the more.

Still, I had a good life, especially compared to Jaz or Sonny. I wouldn't easily be swayed to a Cabal. That was Karl's point. But was he right?

In that panic room, my moral core had shut off. I'd looked at Troy and I hadn't even known who he was. I'd thought only of feeding off his death.

What if it happened again and I stood by and let someone die? I'd never be able to face my family again. I'd never be able to face the council. Wouldn't be able to face myself...

"Hope?" Karl was frowning.

"Sorry, I'm just—" I shook my head. "I'll be fine."

"You will. And I want you to call your mother in the morning."

"Yes, sir."

"I want you to invite her to... What's her favorite restaurant?"

"Odessa's in Philly."

"Invite her there to dine with us next Saturday night."

"Us?"

"Is that a problem?"

"It just sounds very... couple-ish."

"Is that a problem?"

I looked up at him. If it all did fall apart, there'd be one person who'd still be there, who wouldn't care what I'd done. Would he ever know how much that meant to me?

"Karl Marsten?"

We looked up to see Troy's partner, Griffin, walking toward us. Did his blue eyes frost over as they met mine? Probably my imagination. I was in the mood to see disapproval everywhere.

Karl extended a hand. When Griffin pretended not to see it, I *didn't* imagine the icy look in Karl's eyes. If he was going to make the effort, he didn't appreciate being repulsed by a glorified security guard.

"Have you heard from—" I began.

"This way," Griffin said, then headed back toward the building.

I hurried to catch up, but Karl caught my arm, his look reminding me that we were here to assist the Cabal, and damned if we were chasing after our escort.

"I'm sorry you were called away from home at this hour," I said, as Griffin looked back at us impatiently.

"You think I care about that?" His tone was so sharp I jumped. "My partner's lying on a hospital bed, fighting for his life. My boss was almost killed, and now he's guarded by security team flunkies I barely know. And I'm stuck playing escort for—" He stopped himself.

"A werewolf?" Karl said smoothly.

A grunt that could be a yes.

"I don't know why Lucas assigned you to us, but we had no say in the matter, and as soon as we find William, we'll be out of your hair," I said as we approached the front doors.

"Better yet," Karl said. "We could leave right now."

"You're not going anywhere until Lucas says so." Griffin yanked open the door.

Karl caught and held it. "I beg your pardon?"

"Lucas told me to guard you, and I will until I'm relieved of that duty."

"Is that Lucas's order?"

"I know my job."

In other words, Lucas had said no such thing. As we stepped inside, my cell phone rang. It was Paige.

"We just got to the office," I explained as I answered.

"Is Griffin there?"

I looked at the bodyguard, who glowered back at me. "Yes."

She gave a throaty laugh. "Is he giving you a hard time? Ignore him. He's a good guy. He just takes the whole bodyguard image very seriously. Not like . . ." A slight catch in her breathing.

"How's Troy?" I asked.

"He's in surgery now."

That's all she said. I guess it was all there was to say—that he'd survived long enough to get onto the operating table and we just had to wait and see what would happen there.

I could hear voices in the background. It sounded like an argument. Had they run into trouble?

"Anyway, I wasn't calling to pester you about your progress. I just wanted to say . . . be careful."

"Okay . . ."

"We just got to Hector's house. He's here in the study apparently, and has been all evening. Carlos was here an hour ago. So that's two pretty much accounted for."

I caught her meaning, one she probably didn't dare voice with others around. If Benicio's attacker had gone after one of the sons following his failure at the house, it would be William. If that attacker had managed to get into Cabal headquarters, he could be here now.

"Just be careful," she said. "Let Griffin take the lead. He's the professional."

GRIFFIN LED US past the young man at the front desk.

"Shouldn't we speak to him?" I said as we headed for the elevator. "He might know if William left yet."

Griffin grunted and kept walking, so I stopped. Karl did the same. Griffin reached the elevators, saw that we'd left him and strode back, passing us and walking to the desk.

"Mr. Cortez would like you to answer these people's questions."

The receptionist/guard gave him a discreet questioning look. Griffin's chin dipped a quarter-inch. In this business "tell these people what they want to know" could easily mean "tell them what they're *allowed* to know."

"Is William Cortez still in his office?" I asked.

"I believe so." He dropped his gaze to a display just below the desktop and tapped the screen. "His car is still in the garage, and I haven't seen him leave." Another tap. "Nor has he used his code on any of the other exit doors."

"When's the last time anyone saw him?"

I expected him to say, "How should I know?" but the guard tapped the screen a few more times. "He requested dinner at seven-thirty, and it was taken to his office at eight. He asked for coffee at nine."

"Has he had any visitors?"

"None that came through me, miss, and I've been on since seven."

We headed to the same elevator we'd been taken up in yesterday. As we waited, Griffin glanced over at Karl, eyes narrowing.

"Is that Mr. Cortez's shirt?"

Karl stretched his arms, the sleeves riding up past his wrists. "A poor fit, but the fabric and tailoring are superb."

"Where'd you get it?"

"I stole it, of course. While everyone was beating the bushes for assassins and trying to save your partner's life, I decided to do some shopping in Benicio's closet. I have a nice pair of diamond cuff links in the car too."

Griffin scowled, as if not quite certain Karl was joking. When we got onto the elevator, he covered the panel as he entered the code, just in case.

HOPE

OVERTIME

When we reached William's office, the door was open and there was no sign of an occupant. Griffin went in first, circled the room, then came out and said, "He's not here."

I stepped inside. Papers were scattered across an otherwise pristine desk, a briefcase sat on a chair and a suit jacket hung behind the door. Karl picked up the jacket. Griffin's eyes narrowed.

"I'm thinking of taking this too," Karl said. "You don't mind, do you?"

He gave the jacket a shake. At a jingle, he reached into a pocket and fished out a set of keys.

"So he hasn't gone far," I said. "Where's the nearest bathroom?"

Griffin walked to a closed door that I'd presumed was a closet, and opened it to reveal a dark and empty bathroom.

"Water cooler? Vending machine? Photocopier?"

He pointed to the cooler and an all-in-one printer. "There are no vending machines on this floor. If he wants something, he calls."

He crossed the room and picked up the phone, and I thought he was just being sarcastic—demonstrating—but he pushed a button and murmured something.

"Maybe he stepped out to stretch his legs," I said to Karl. "Can you tell?"

"Only that he's been in here recently. I could try tracking him, but he's been in and out of here so often that unless he went someplace he doesn't normally go, it would be difficult to find a fresh trail."

"Do you smell anything else?"

"Blood? No."

I closed my eyes, but all I could pick up was a general sense of unease and distrust emanating from Griffin.

"He left this floor at nine-thirty," Griffin said, startling me.

"What?"

"The elevator access records show he went down to the fourth floor at nine-thirty, but never came back up."

"What's on the fourth floor?"

"Lots of things."

He was out the door before I could get another word in.

"Karl?" I said. "Can you tell whether anyone else was in here with William?"

"I can try."

He walked to the doorway and dropped to his haunches. Griffin strode back as if just realizing we weren't behind him.

"Are you com—?"

Seeing Karl, he stopped and let out a snort of disgust. Karl ignored it, inhaled, then stood and brushed off his trousers.

"There seems to be a recent second trail, but that was probably whoever dropped off dinner."

"Are you coming now?" Griffin snapped.

Karl glanced over at him and smiled. "What's the magic word?"

Griffin stalked off, muttering a word under his breath.

"That's not it," Karl called after him.

Griffin's shoulders tightened as he realized he'd been heard, but he didn't stop.

WHEN THE ELEVATOR doors opened onto the fourth floor, it looked as quiet and empty as the other levels. Odd. I'd worked for corporations, and even on floors staffed by nine-to-fivers you could expect to see cleaners at night. But I suppose having cleaners—even your own staff—in a Cabal office, unsupervised, wasn't wise. Better to lock down the floors and monitor all access.

We followed Griffin until we reached the first junction. Then Karl stopped, his nostrils flaring, and veered down the adjoining hall.

We got about ten steps before Griffin's "Hey!" rang out.

"I thought I told you to stay with me," he said as he stalked up behind us.

"No, I don't believe you did."

"This is a Cabal head office. You can't just run off like that."

"Run?" Karl turned slowly, eyebrows arched. "I believe I was walking. I also believe you are in as much a hurry to get this over with as we are, but if I'm mistaken, then you go your way, and let me follow the smell of blood."

"Blood?" I said.

A faint wince—he hadn't intended to say that in front of me.

"Where?" Griffin demanded.

"I need to follow the trail to find the source. Now, if you'll allow me to do that..."

He continued down the hall. Griffin swung into his path. He moved so fast I stumbled out of his way, but it was nothing compared to how fast Karl moved. Before I could blink, Karl had the bodyguard pinned against the wall by his shirtfront.

"You want to take a pop at me?" Griffin said. "Go right ahead."

"I know you don't plan to hit him, Karl," I said. "But in case you're provoked, I'd strongly advise against it. He's a Ferratus."

Karl glanced at me.

"A half-demon who can make his skin as hard as iron. Hit him and you'll break your hand."

Griffin smiled. "Don't take her word for it. Go ahead."

"Once I have you pinned, you're no longer a threat. But before we continue this pleasant little venture, let's come to an understanding, Griffin. I don't trust you. You clearly don't trust me. Sudden moves of any kind can be easily misinterpreted as aggression."

He released Griffin's shirtfront. "Now, let's find the source of the blood. I doubt your employer would be pleased if you let a fellow guard bleed to death because you got into a pissing contest with a werewolf."

———

ANOTHER TWENTY FEET down the hall, Karl veered into a room and lifted a hand to ward me off. For once, I obeyed. I'd had enough.

Then the room went dark and I remembered that there was no sense blocking my eyes. The vision began.

A man stood with his back to me as he bent over an open filing cabinet drawer.

"Right where I said they were." He pulled out a folder. "I appreciate that you're putting in some overtime for a change, but if you're going to interrupt—"

The *pftt* of a silenced shot. The man fell back against the cabinet. I saw his face then. William. The folder fluttered from his hand as he stared, incredulous, at his shooter.

His mouth opened, but a second shot sent him reeling. He crumpled against the filing cabinet, then slid to the floor.

When the vision ended, I didn't jolt out of it. It just...stopped. And I just stopped. Like coming to the shocking end of a movie, sitting there, staring at the blank screen, unable to think, feel, move. Even the chaos vibes didn't penetrate.

"Hope?"

Karl's voice sounded miles away. I felt him grip my arms, as if through a thick winter coat.

"It's been too much for her," he said. "I need to get her out of here."

His words floated past, disconnected, meaningless.

"You're not going anywhere."

"The hell I'm not. Get out of my way."

I recognized the rising chaos, but it was like pouring wine in front of my face—I could see it, smell it, know what it was, but it had no effect.

"Hope? Can you hear me? Can you walk, hon?"

"Hon? I should have guessed. A werewolf thief. She must *love* you. Just dripping with chaos."

"Get out of my way."

"You do know that's all it is, don't you? That's all her kind care about. The chaos."

"Get the fuck out of my—"

My eyes snapped open and I gasped, as if breaking free of icy water. "William? Is he—?"

"Yes, and we're leaving."

"No, I had a vision. I can help. I want to."

"Oh, I bet you do," Griffin said.

"One last time," Karl said. "Get out—"

"Do you think Benicio Cortez won't figure it out, Hope? You fooled him for a while, and nothing I could say would change his mind, but if my partner dies because—"

Karl made a move, as if to brush past Griffin, but he stepped into our path again, and I plucked at Karl's sleeve, asking him to hold on.

"You think I shot Troy?" I said. "I was with Lucas and Paige, and if there's a better alibi than that—"

"You didn't need to pull the trigger. You had a whole gang of young men, just itching to do it, especially if there's a pretty girl goading them on, so she can sit back and enjoy."

"I didn't—"

"Mr. Cortez hates stereotypes. He thinks you should take the measure of the man, not measure him by his type. But in some cases, the type is all that matters, and I know all about yours."

"You know an Expisco?"

"Hope . . ." Karl began.

I wriggled from his grip and stepped closer to Griffin, consumed by the need to know, circumstances be damned.

"Are you still in touch with him? Could I talk to him?"

Griffin gave a harsh laugh. "Not without a necromancer."

"He—he's dead? How? No, just tell me. What was he like? Did he figure it all out? Did someone help him?"

"You want to know about Expisco half-demons? About yourself?" He stepped toward me. "Let me tell you about—"

Griffin staggered back, then collapsed to the floor. I wheeled to see Karl wiggling his fingers as if checking for damage. It took a moment to realize he must have clocked Griffin, the punch so fast I hadn't seen it.

I turned to stare stupidly at Griffin, lying unconscious across the doorway.

"Whoops," Karl said. "Benicio won't be happy about that. But I did warn him. No sudden moves. As long as he's out, though, no need to hang around."

He grabbed me around the waist and swung me over Griffin into the hall. I took one last look at the fallen Ferratus.

"Is your hand—?" I began.

"Just fine. The trick, apparently, is to hit them before they see it coming."

LUCAS

12

"THEY'RE ON THE FOURTH FLOOR," the guard said. "They went down about ten minutes ago."

I thanked him and headed for the elevators. Any would do. The fourth was staff level, meaning a simple card swipe or key code would allow us access.

As the car slowed, I stepped forward, waited for the doors to part and found myself nose to nose with Karl Marsten.

He had his arm around Hope, supporting her. Her face was drawn, and as her bleary eyes lifted to mine, she seemed to take a moment to recognize me.

I looked behind Karl. "Where's Griffin?"

"Taking a nap."

I must have looked alarmed, because he added, "I only knocked him out. But the man definitely needs to work on his people skills."

"And William?" Paige asked.

Karl's acerbity gave way to a look of genuine regret and he said gruffly, "I'm sorry, Lucas."

"Someone shot him before we got here," Hope whispered.

"Probably long before. The logs showed the elevator coming down a couple hours ago."

I thought I'd prepared myself for this. Hope went on, saying that she'd seen a vision of his death and that he'd been killed by someone he seemed to know, that he'd been getting a file and commenting on his killer working overtime.

Carlos...

"I can go back," she said. "I'll try again and maybe pick up more."

"No," Karl said. She shot him a look, not too tired to resent him speaking for her. "You've done enough."

"Karl's right," Paige said. "You need to get some rest." As he bustled Hope onto the elevator, Paige murmured, "I'm sorry for putting her through this."

"She wants to help," he said.

"I know, but we didn't mean to— We didn't know."

He nodded, then looked at me. "Your father did."

I felt the weight of that look. How many times had I seen it? As if they expected me to apologize for my father's behavior or at least explain it. I couldn't.

I promised to call Karl with an update in the morning. He pretended not to hear, and the elevator doors closed.

WE FOUND GRIFFIN in the doorway of a filing room, recovering from Karl's blow. He was convinced Hope was behind tonight's attacks, that she'd encouraged the gang to strike so she could enjoy the chaotic outcome.

I understood now that an attraction to chaos lay at the root of Hope's powers. I presumed it was similar to a demon's hunger for chaos, but it was difficult to transfer that concept from a demonic entity to a young woman, particularly one eager to *stop* trouble.

If my father knew of that chaos need, and brought her into a situation that would feed it . . . An issue to contend with later.

For now, I disabused Griffin of the notion that the gang was responsible for these attacks. The blueprints suggested they'd been involved, but only working under the real perpetrator—the one who'd supplied those plans. I did not, of course, speculate on the identity of that actor. Not until I had hard evidence.

When the security team arrived, I sent Griffin to the hospital to guard my father. Then I had to deal with William's body.

Two brothers dead; the third almost certainly responsible. Had someone suggested this possibility yesterday, I'd have agreed that such a thing could happen—the tensions and jealousies that had been simmering all my life could finally explode in a Shakespearean tragedy. But the admission would have been purely intellectual. To witness it unfolding? Beyond comprehending.

I STOOD OUTSIDE a hospital room in a small private facility run by supernaturals, funded by the Cabal for the sole use of their employees.

Two guards flanked the door, as immobile and expressionless as tin soldiers. I'd been standing here for five minutes and neither had acknowledged my presence. In light of the night's events, to speak would mean having to find something to say, and it was easier to stare straight ahead and do their jobs.

Paige had gone in first to get an update on Troy. He was out of surgery, still unconscious, but his condition had stabilized. My father was with him, Griffin having joined them.

When I heard Paige offer my father something to eat, I knew she was starting to stall. I had to get in there.

Oh God, how could I tell him?

I took a deep breath and walked in. My father, hearing my footsteps, pulled back the curtain.

"Lucas."

He reached out with one arm, the other hand clutching a coffee cup, cardboard rippling under his grip. One look in his eyes and I knew he already suspected what I was here to tell him. Maybe that should have made it easier. It didn't.

I walked over and embraced him.

A HALF-HOUR later I was sitting in the tiny Reflections Room with Paige. Two guards were posted at the door. I'd have preferred to stay with my father, but it had been his suggestion that we rest here for a few minutes. Someone had to find Carlos and supervise the intensive operations surrounding not only the investigation into my brothers' deaths, but also the notifications, the cover-ups and the arrangements, both private and public. It would be too much for my father. The duty fell to me.

And he had another duty, one that I could not help him with: telling Delores that two of her sons were dead and the third was missing.

I hadn't mentioned my suspicions about Carlos. As strong as my father was, that revelation might be too great a blow.

The search team had a report of Carlos dining at a restaurant he frequented. It had been hours since he'd been there, but it would be a place to start.

I was due to meet with the search team in thirty minutes. In the meantime, I was heeding my father's advice, resting in the Reflections Room. In a public hospital, this would be the chapel. While many supernaturals adhere to a religious faith, the Cortez Cabal is careful to keep such places nondenominational.

"I don't think I can do this," I said after a few minutes.

"You can."

"Investigate one brother for the murder of the other two? *My* brothers?"

"You can, but if you don't want to, he'll understand."

I shook my head. "It isn't a matter of want."

"Then you can."

I turned and she kissed me, barely more than a press of her lips against mine, but when she pulled back, I could still taste her. I lifted my hand to the back of her head, pulling her into me, and I wanted to lose myself in her, just for a moment, forget everything and—

My cell phone vibrated.

Paige sputtered a small laugh. "I'm going to guess that isn't your heart—or anything else—fluttering."

"Unfortunately."

"I'll go find coffees," she said. "We'll need them."

HOPE

DIAMONDS IN THE ROUGH

I dozed as Karl drove, waking, befuddled, when he pulled into a lot I didn't recognize. Then I remembered I couldn't go back to my apartment, and briefly wondered how I was going to brush my teeth before deciding it really wasn't that important.

Karl led me to an exit door. I felt a twinge of curiosity, but couldn't muster the energy to ask. We entered a quiet, carpeted hotel hallway. A glance up and down the hall, then he sat me in a plush armchair next to a window overlooking a pool.

"I'll be right back," he said. "Wait here."

"Where's here?"

"The Royal Plaza. I'm going to get us a room."

His lips brushed the top of my head. I watched him go, numb from my nap and number still from chaos exhaustion.

Why hadn't we come in the front door? I was sure this was a place with valet service, and surer still that Karl never parked his car when he didn't need to. One glimpse of my reflection in the window, though, and I realized I was in no state to endure curious stares.

I pulled my feet up, my shoes sliding off. I was almost asleep when Karl's hands slid under my arms, lifting me.

"Shhh, I've got you."

"No, I can walk."

So I did, shoes in hand, leaning against him for support. He let me get as far as the room door then scooped me up and carried me inside.

Even that brief trip to the bed, rocking against his warm body, was almost enough for me to drift off again.

But then, perversely, as I was finally lowered into the proper place for sleeping, the fog of the past hour parted and everything rushed back.

I saw Bianca's face as the gun fired. Her killer standing over her body. Benicio's guard, face destroyed, looking up at me, gaze empty. William reeling back, eyes wide with disbelief. Troy in a pool of blood.

I saw it all and I felt it all, the delicious chaos of destruction and death.

As I started to shake, Karl rubbed my arms, leaning awkwardly over the bed, then he sat and tugged me onto his lap. I huddled there as he whispered and stroked my hair. Was it only yesterday I'd silently cursed him for not knowing how to comfort me when Jaz and Sonny disappeared?

I let myself stay for a couple of minutes, then pushed away and wiped my eyes. As my vision cleared, I saw the last remnants of my mascara smeared across his white shirt.

"I hope you didn't want to keep that," I said.

He straightened his arms, the cuffs riding up his forearms. "Not really."

I looked at the ill-fitting shirt, tear-streaked and mascara-stained, and I didn't know whether to laugh or cry. In the last few hours, I'd yelled at him, kicked him, punched him and thrown up on him, and he was still here. Selfish? I'd never call him that again.

He pulled back the thick white comforter and sheets, and laid me down.

"I'm not really ready for bed yet," I said.

"I know. I'm just making you comfortable. I'd offer you a drink but..."

"Not the way I like to handle things. And probably not a good habit to get into."

"Agreed." He paused. "A bath?"

Any other time, that would have been the right answer. There was nothing like a bath for giving me time alone with my thoughts. But tonight even thinking about being alone, I started to shake again.

"I—I don't think I can do it, Karl." I looked up at him, my eyes filling. "If that's what it's going to be like . . . If it's only going to get worse . . . I don't think I'm going to make it."

The last words came out as a sob, cut off as Karl's lips pressed against mine. His hands went to my cheeks, holding me still as he pulled back just enough to break the kiss, his lips still touching mine.

"I—I'm sorry," I said. "I don't mean to—"

"Shhh. Here, focus on this."

The room went dark, a vision flashing, but I pulled up straight, shaking my head hard enough to scatter the vision and knock his hands from my cheeks.

"P—please. No more. I'm sorry. I can't handle any—"

"Shhh. Just look. It's okay."

The vision flickered and I tensed. Then, like peeking open one eye, I snuck a quick look.

I was crouched on a dark rooftop. At the distant roar of an engine, I walked to the roof's edge. Far below, car lights crawled along a busy road. A horn honked. I cocked my head but around me, all was silent.

A slow survey of the rooftop. Adrenaline still surged from a narrow escape. *Too narrow,* I chided myself. I was too cocky. Took too many chances and came too close to paying the price. But it felt good. So damned good. And I was good enough to pull it off.

A small laugh. Karl's laugh.

My clenched fist opened and I looked down to see a black-gloved hand and, nestled in the palm, a diamond bracelet glittering in the moonlight.

"Yes?"

Karl's voice, but disconnected from the vision, and it pulled me back into the hotel room. I was lying in the bed now, Karl stretched out beside me, his arm under my head, his face inches from mine, eyes as bright as the diamonds.

"More," I said.

He smiled. "Are you sure? You said you didn't want—"

"More. Please."

He took me back under, to the rooftop, diamonds in hand, the distant wail of a siren making my heart trip with exhilaration.

Simple chaos, but my favorite kind—that mix of danger and

excitement, devoid of moral quandaries. I was certain he hadn't found the bracelet lying in the trash, but he'd been careful not to show me where it came from, letting me enjoy the aftermath without guilt.

I stepped to the edge, so close my toes rested on air. The wind caught my jacket. It rustled and billowed. A strong gust rocked me, as if tempting me to take that final step. I smiled, and backed up a few inches to crouch on the edge and survey the street below. Lights flashed to the east. Coming from the same direction as the siren? Yes. Coming this way? Hard to tell . . .

The lights veered around a corner.

Yes, apparently so.

A fresh surge of adrenaline, telling me to move, but I lingered another moment, casually slipping my hand under my jacket, unzipping the inner pocket. I let the bracelet slide inside onto the small pile of others nestled at the bottom.

My pulse raced as the lights came closer, but I drew it out, waiting until the last possible moment—

The memory snapped off.

"Enough?"

Karl's face was inches from mine and I could feel his breath, smell it, and it reminded me of what he tasted like, and I wanted—

"Is that enough?" he repeated, lips twitching.

"No," I said hoarsely.

"You want more?" His hands slid down my shirtfront and started unbuttoning it from the bottom. "Maybe we should get you ready for bed. In case you drift off."

There wasn't a chance in hell of that now, and he knew it, his lips curving as my breath came in short pants. As he spread my shirt, his thumbs brushed my nipples, and I moaned.

"More. Please."

His hands went back to my breasts, cupping them, nipples squeezed between his fingers.

"Oh, you didn't mean *that*, did you?"

I hadn't, but I wasn't complaining. I writhed, trying to get closer to him, but he locked his elbows, his hands on my breasts holding me back. His fingers plucked at my nipples, hard and rough, sending shock ripples through me.

"More," I said.

"Of what?"

"Damn you."

His lips pressed against mine, his body still held back even as I strained to get closer.

"Don't worry," he murmured. "I won't make you choose."

The room dipped into blackness again as his teeth closed on my nipple and I hesitated, torn between the two worlds, perched on a rooftop, sirens growing ever closer, and lying on a decadently soft bed, feeling his tongue teasing my breast, hand sliding up my thigh. Then, slowly, they merged into one and I was on the roof, feeling what he'd felt, that delicious chaos, while his tongue and fingers and teeth satisfied the ache and stoked the fire ever higher.

The flashing lights stopped in front of the building and I knew there was no question now. Someone had sounded the alarm.

I loped across the rooftops to where I'd left the rope—

A flashlight beam pinged off the walls five stories below—in the alley, right beneath my escape route.

I surfaced from Karl's memory, gasping as he nipped the inside of my thigh. I arched back into the pillows, spreading my legs and lifting my hips, as if he needed directions. His laugh vibrated through me.

The vision pulled me under again and I was tugging up the rope as quickly and quietly as I could, all too aware that I was removing my only escape route.

Karl's tongue slid inside me and I called his name, my hands going to the top of his head. He chuckled again, the vibrations this time nearly sending me—

The vision surged stronger.

I had the rope. Now how to get off the roof...?

As I struggled for a backup plan, I surfed between the memory and the hotel room, wanting to see the escape to the end, lap up every bit of chaos, yet reluctant to miss one second of an amazing—

The vision yanked me back under, and this time I knew *he* was responsible, making the memory stronger whenever I was on the verge of deciding I'd rather immerse myself in the here-and-now.

I stood on the edge of the building again, this time along the side, between the street front with its flashing lights and the alley with its searchers. Someone shouted below, but I ignored it. The goal was to get off this roof before I *needed* to worry about what they were saying and the only way to do that was . . .

My gaze lifted to the building beside mine, then dropped to the fifteen-foot gap between the two. I laughed, and that laugh—half "are you crazy?" half "sure, why not?"— sent shivers through me. I surfaced from the vision, and those shivers turned into gasps and shudders, nails digging into the bed, his tongue and teeth doing things—

He pulled me under again and I barely had time to curse him before the vision took over.

I measured the distance between the buildings. A dozen feet? Fifteen? Miss and there was nothing to keep me from becoming a diamond-studded stain on the alley floor.

My kingdom for a backup plan.

If I splatted on the road, I'd have no one to blame but myself.

Perhaps if I returned the way I'd come up . . .

Another shout from below ruled that out.

I backed up ten feet, paused and made it fifteen. I stood there, heart hammering, straining to hear the voices from below.

Then I ran for the edge. At the last second, I launched. The other building seemed to loom an impossible distance away. I hit the height of my jump, started on the downturn and—

Oh, shit.

I wasn't going to make it.

The chaos was so strong I cried out as it hit me in waves, dimly telling me it wasn't chaos I was feeling, but I was trapped in the vision, falling, my feet dropping beneath the edge of the other building.

I'd missed—

Waves of orgasm cut off the thought. Then I felt the lip of the building cutting into my fingers. I braced before my arms jerked out of their sockets as my body came to an abrupt stop. I cried out, rocked by wave after wave, until I fell back onto the pillows, shaking. Even then Karl didn't stop, teasing every last shudder from me. When it finally ended, I opened my eyes to see him crouched on all fours over me, his eyes dancing.

"Done?"

I couldn't help feel a tingle of regret that it was over. I looked down, past his open shirt, to the bulge in his pants, and smiled.

I sprang so fast he let out a grunt of surprise. Flipping him onto his back, I crouched over him.

"Not done," I said.

His lips twitched. "More?"

I pulled his pants down just past his hips and straddled him. "Yes, more."

That same delicious laugh from the vision filled the room.

HOPE

LAYING THE BLAME

I lay on Karl, my head on his chest, his arms around me. His steady breathing said he'd fallen asleep. When I lifted my head and looked around, his eyes opened.

"Sorry," I said. "I didn't mean to wake you."

"I wasn't asleep. I thought you were."

"I should be but..."

"You aren't tired. Neither am I. How about that drink then?"

"Sure. I'll get—"

Before I could finish, he rolled me over and laid me down beside him, then swung out of bed. His pants were still around his knees and he reached down, as if to pull them up, then kicked them off and tossed them onto a chair, socks following. His shirt had disappeared at some point.

I propped myself up to watch as he crossed to the minibar, and remembered the first time I'd seen Karl shirtless. The morning after our night at the museum, I'd walked in on him fixing the bandage on his shoulder, his shirt half off. He'd jumped, pulling the shirt on as fast as a shy twelve-year-old. With Karl, it was the scars he was quick to hide—old bite and claw marks across his chest, the legacy of thirty years fighting other werewolves.

Those scars belied the smooth, sophisticated persona he cultivated, of a man who'd never stoop to anything as uncivilized as brawling. Tonight he'd shown that he was as quick with his fists as with his words, and he offered no apologies for that, but it wasn't how he liked to be seen. I suspected he'd conducted many an affair under cover of near-darkness.

So watching him, naked, I could appreciate that I was viewing a sight rarely seen. My tastes had always tended more toward reedy Bohemian types, but Karl made me admit that I wasn't immune to a more...masculine physique. No bulging muscles, but perfectly toned. Even the scars seemed to fit—a body for function, not show.

He crouched before the fridge and fished out bottles. As he turned, I resisted the urge to look away and let my gaze slide over him.

"You look...amazing."

He arched his brows in genuine surprise, then lifted the bottles. "You're supposed to say that *after* I get you drunk."

"Am I?"

He grabbed glasses, sliding the stems between his fingers so he could carry them. "Yes, because then you can blame it on the alcohol. Otherwise you risk inflating an ego that you know needs no help." He crossed back to me, setting the bottles and glasses on the nightstand. "And may I say in return that you look perfect."

I looked into his eyes and knew there was no sense lying to myself anymore. I was in love with him. More than that, I loved him. It had nothing to do with what Griffin said—a chaotic man for a chaos-loving demon. Karl knew when I needed to be set on my feet with a sharp word and a kick in the butt, and he knew when I needed someone to look out for me, and coddle me and tell me that I'm perfect.

I wanted to be that for him too. I had the first part down—keeping his ego in check—but I struggled with the second. Cooking him dinner, being there whenever he called, for as long as he wanted to talk, that all came easy. But complimenting him or even saying, "Thanks, Karl" was different. I'd worked so hard to keep things casual, so afraid of getting hurt that, even now, it was hard to drop my guard and let him know how I felt. I'd have to work on that.

I slid over to make room for him and he handed me a gin and tonic, then he got into bed, propping himself up on the pillows.

"Thank you," I said. "For the memories."

His brows shot up. "That sounds disturbingly like a brush-off."

"You know what I meant. *Your* memories. The ones you..." I struggled for a word. "Projected, I guess. I didn't know I could pick that up."

"Neither did I, but it seemed worth a try."

He lapsed into silence, his gaze going distant.

"I won't pry," I said.

"Hmmm?"

"If you're worried I'm going to ask about those early memories, I won't. I know you were just trying to find something to distract me."

"Ah."

More silence. He swirled the Scotch in his glass, frowning at it.

"Yes, you need ice."

A bark of a laugh. "No, that's not what I'm thinking. Good try, though. And ice *would* be nice."

"See? I wasn't reading your mind. I was predicting future thoughts. Even better."

A tiny smile. "As you are, apparently, still building your mind-reading skills, I'll have to tell you what I'm thinking. It *is* about that vision. I should tell you about it. Or maybe not so much *should* as *want*."

He went quiet again.

"You wanted to join the Pack," I said. "When you were young."

A slow nod. "Ironic that now, almost forty years later, I'm in it and uncomfortable with the idea."

"The instinct probably felt stronger at that age."

"At the time, it seemed obvious. That's how werewolves should live—as part of a Pack, growing up with Pack brothers, building a home and defending your territory. I blamed my father for dragging me from place to place, living in rooming houses and hotels. I blamed him and I hated myself for it."

I knew how much Karl had loved his father. Shortly after we'd met, I'd made the mistake of commenting on a father who'd raise his son to be a thief, and it had been the first time I'd seen Karl's composure ripple. He'd been as quick to his father's defense as I'd been when he'd commented on a mother who set her daughter up with blind dates. After that, we'd come to an unspoken agreement: taking potshots at one another was fine, but our parents were off-limits.

Karl's father had raised him as he thought best, into the only life he knew for a lone werewolf.

"That afternoon I showed you was the only time I actually saw someone from the Pack," Karl said. "We were in Vermont, working, at a resort, and the Pack arrived for a vacation. I only caught that glimpse before my father whisked us out of town. I don't think I'd ever been so angry with him. He'd always made them sound like monsters. That's why we had to keep moving—he said they'd kill us if we stayed. But seeing Jeremy and Antonio..." He shook his head. "They looked like ordinary young men, joking and teasing and hanging out. I saw that and I wanted it so badly. But, when I got older, I started to resent them because they kept us from settling down."

"From holding territory."

"Testosterone kicking in, I suppose. Joining them wasn't as important as showing them we weren't afraid. When I was sixteen, my father came to the motel we were staying in and told me we had to leave because a few Pack wolves were in town. But that day, I decided I wasn't going anywhere. I thought..." A bitter laugh. "I thought all my father needed was some encouragement. If I forced him to stay, he'd either see that his fears were ungrounded or he'd learn to fight for his place in the world. So I used the one stalling tactic I knew would work. I'd been Changing for a few months, and at that stage, it's very difficult. When the urge comes, it can't be denied."

"So you said you had to Change."

"I did. He took me into the woods behind the motel, and I did my damnedest. Eventually, it started, but even then it didn't go very far. My father stayed outside that thicket, encouraging me, for probably half an hour. Then he heard something and told me to stay still. A few minutes later, Malcolm Danvers found me."

"Jeremy's father."

"Malcolm found me, stuck in mid-Change. I don't know what he would have done, but helping me clearly wasn't on his mind. I heard my father calling Malcolm, luring him away. As I managed to Change back, I could hear Malcolm taunting my father. He kept trying to convince his two Pack buddies to challenge my father, saying no one would because he wasn't worth anything—he didn't have a reputation. Malcolm killed him. Snapped his neck, tossed him aside and went after me. I escaped. There was nothing else I could do, not at that age. Years later, when I was ready, I went back for Malcolm, but it was too late. Someone beat me to him."

I tried to think of something to say. I'd known his father had been killed by a werewolf and now I knew how. And, maybe, I knew why he struggled so hard with being in the Pack. Anyone who'd been involved with his father's death was long dead and no son could be less like his father than Jeremy, but still Karl had joined the group that killed his father. Accepted as Alpha the man whose father killed his. A death I knew he blamed himself for.

It would do no good to point out to Karl that he'd been young. I wouldn't be telling him anything he didn't already know. But what I'd felt in that glimpse inside him had been a cesspool of guilt and remorse—the memory he'd chosen when he'd needed to show me the worst one he had.

"I'm sorry."

It was the only thing I could say, but I meant it with all my heart, and he leaned over to kiss the top of my head.

"I want you to know," he said after a moment. "If I push you away, if I fight getting close, if I'm selfish, it's because that's the lesson I learned about myself. Let someone get close and..." He shrugged. "Maybe that's not a good idea with someone I care about."

"You were sixteen, Karl."

"I didn't say it was a rational fear. But the worst fears aren't, are they?"

He met my gaze pointedly.

"I don't think *my* fear is irrational, Karl. When I stood in that room, whatever would keep a normal person from wanting Troy to die was gone. Not buried. Not overshadowed. Completely nonexistent. It was like..." I cupped my glass between my hands. "I don't even know what it was like."

"Like a starving werewolf stumbling across dinner on two legs?" He took my glass and set it on the table. "What you're afraid of, Hope, is that someday, just for a few minutes, the thing that you are will overtake the person that you are, and someone will die because of it. A werewolf deals with that from the day he first Changes."

"But you can control it. You've never—"

"Three times. Twice in my teens, and I couldn't even tell you who

I killed. All I know is that I Changed and I woke stained with human blood. The third time, I was twenty, and I came to standing over the body of a man. Eating. Yes, most of the time, we can control it. It's like you with chaos. You can resist the urge to do something you consider wrong. My father did what he could to teach me that, but he never had the chance to finish the lessons. There's the instinct and it must be fed, and to the wolf there is no difference between a deer and a man. Both are prey. The wolf doesn't feel sorry for the man, doesn't consider the life he's taking, doesn't think of his wife and children, his mother and father. That's the human's job, and it's the werewolf's job to make sure the humanity in him doesn't disappear. When I came to my senses that day, and saw what I'd done, I knew I had to make a choice."

He shifted in the bed, turning onto his side, head propped up on his hand. "What happened to me happens to most werewolves at some point. They can decide that killing an innocent person proves they're a monster who must die. Or they can keep killing, blaming it on the wolf. Or they can understand the urge and avoid temptation. Don't Change in inhabited areas. Don't Change when you're too hungry. Don't Change when you've been drinking. And, just as important, sublimate the urge, that need to hunt, by going after rabbits or deer ... or diamonds.

"That's what you need to do, Hope. Avoid temptation. Avoid situations where it may be too much for you—like signing up to spy for a Cabal. And sublimate the hunger with chaos you can enjoy without guilt. I can help with that, but only to a degree. There are jobs I know you'd enjoy more than the little ones I offer. But I won't take you on them because later, you'd feel guilty. And, as you saw, sometimes I take risks myself. I have to, for the same reason you need to chase chaos. I can't ever bring you on a job like that and put you in that danger. Not after my father."

"I understand."

He studied me to be sure I did. Then he nodded. "I'll find more for you. Ones you can enjoy, guilt-free. The rest, you'll have to make do with secondhand."

I smiled. "I can live with that."

"Good." He sobered. "But remember, you'll never be perfect. With a werewolf, there's always the chance it can happen again. We cannot control every variable. I haven't killed a human in thirty years, but I have to accept that I could. And you need to accept that you could too. And, if you do, as horrible as you'll feel about it, and as much as you'll suffer for it, if you've done what you could to avoid it, it isn't your fault. You didn't choose to be half-demon any more than I chose to be a werewolf."

Silence fell.

After a moment, he said, "Have I put you to sleep yet?"

"No, not yet." I reached up and kissed him. "Thank you, Karl."

He pulled me closer, then turned out the light.

LUCAS

13

PAIGE RETURNED WITH COFFEES in hand, Griffin at her heels and a pained expression on her face.

"Your dad wants me to go with you," Griffin said.

I shook my head. "He needs you. Someone has already tried to kill him tonight."

"Yeah, but they failed, and no one's tried to kill *you* . . . yet."

I took the coffee from Paige. "I cannot imagine I'd warrant a place on anyone's hit list—anyone outside a Cabal, that is. I'd like you to stay with him."

"I know you would, but his orders trump yours."

I hesitated, and contemplated the possibility of giving him the slip. Paige shook her head, as if reading my mind, then glanced at her watch. She was right, of course. We were wasting time. So we set out, bodyguard in tow.

WE MET THE team searching for Carlos and compared notes to construct a timeline. After I'd seen him at the office, he'd visited the restaurant, then arrived at Hector's at nine-forty-five. Apparently, he'd been at the office shortly before nine-thirty, when he'd gone with William down to the fourth floor. Bella and the butler could easily be off by fifteen minutes, which would make the timeline tight, but plausible.

We needed to know exactly when Carlos had been at the office. A quick question to the guards had proved fruitless—they hadn't seen him—but querying the security system would reveal whether his access card had been used. That still wouldn't prove anything unless he'd gone to one of the top floors, which required his thumbprint.

I sent two of the six-member team to the office to check that. A further two would search and then stake out Carlos's apartment. The final two were to review the security tapes at my father's house.

When I finished outlining their assignments, the men looked at one another.

"Is there a problem?" I asked.

"No, sir," the leader—Carpaccio—replied in a tone that belied his denial.

I pushed back a stab of impatience. "Two of my brothers are dead. The third is missing and may be in the same danger. If you have a better idea for finding him, please say so."

The youngest—a half-demon named Pratt—spoke up. "Carlos— I mean, Mr. Cortez—"

"His given name is fine tonight, for clarity." The Cabal tradition on referring to all men of the inner family as "Mr. Cortez" was a ridiculously confusing conceit that annoyed me at the best of times.

"Well, Carlos, sir, he's never at the office past seven."

"Yes, I know. My brother isn't known for putting in overtime."

I realized the men were wondering why I was sending them to check two places where Carlos shouldn't be—the office and my father's home.

Paige took over to explain that, with men already checking places Carlos was known to frequent, plus the indisputable evidence that he'd been at Hector's earlier, it was not inconceivable that he'd also visited my father or gone to the office to see William. If he hadn't, there was no harm in reviewing the tapes and access logs, as it would need to be done for the investigation anyway. The men seemed to accept that, and left.

When they were gone, Griffin said, "You think Carlos killed them, don't you?"

I hesitated, then said, carefully, "I'm not ruling out the possibility."

Griffin nodded, seeming neither shocked nor skeptical.

I continued. "I don't want anyone except us to know that's what I suspect, which, coupled with the fact that the staff is unaccustomed to taking orders from me, could make this difficult. I would appreciate any help you can give."

"I'll back you up, but I'm not sure how much good it will do. If it was Troy..." The words drifted off and he shrugged. "They listen to Troy because they like him. They listen to me because I scare them. Together, it works great. Separate..." Again he let the sentence fade, as if realizing that the situation might not be temporary. "I'll do my best."

I DECIDED, SOMEWHAT belatedly, that we ought to join the search of Carlos's apartment. There might be clues to the crime, and the search team wouldn't know to look for them.

We returned to the car, which was no longer our inconspicuous rental but, at my father's insistence, a massive bulletproof, spell-proof, black SUV. On any covert mission, we'd have to park blocks from the destination and walk—which, to me, obliterated the safety value.

I was opening Paige's door when my cell phone rang.

"Mr. Cortez, sir? It's central security. Our switchboard just received a call from your brother."

My mouth opened to say "which brother?" before I realized I'd never again have to ask that.

"Carlos called?"

"Yes, sir. He sounded in some distress. We lost the connection before he could convey his message, but we managed to track the location of the call. Should we dispatch a team there now?"

"No, Griffin and I will take it. Could you please send the GPS coordinates to—" I glanced through the divider at Griffin, who lifted four fingers, "—car four."

"Yes, sir."

"And do you have a tape of Carlos's call?"

"Yes, sir. I'll play that for you now."

THE TAPE TOLD me little. Nothing, in fact, except that it *did* appear to be Carlos and not someone who'd found his phone and randomly hit speed-dial. He demanded to know why the network circuits were jammed and why a call to our father hadn't gone through. And he wanted to speak to "whoever was in charge there." Carlos wouldn't know the names of anyone "in charge" of the security center.

The operator then made the mistake of asking "Is this Carlos Cortez?" Perhaps she was unable to believe the subject of the intense manhunt that was jamming the circuits was actually calling in. Or perhaps she was simply following protocol, confirming his identity before passing the call along.

Her reward was a string of profanity, and a threat that she'd be jobless if she didn't transfer the call in five seconds. As for what happened next, I'm sure there would be an inquiry into the matter, and someone might indeed become jobless, because the line went dead. Carlos may have hung up. Or the flustered operator had made a mistake. Or the overloaded circuits disconnected the call.

The operator had called Carlos back, but only got his voice mail. Then she'd phoned me.

Had the call been a clumsy attempt to provide himself with an alibi? Pretend not to know why the circuits were jammed and our father unavailable, as if his ignorance would prove he hadn't been responsible? Or in light of my father's survival, might Carlos be trying to betray his comrades in the conspiracy to save himself? Or perhaps Carlos was not involved at all and was, this moment, at risk himself?

For my father's sake, I hoped for the last explanation and I hoped we would arrive in time.

THE ADDRESS TOOK us into southern Little Haiti, to a street that seemed to be trying to edge into the adjacent Design District. The art community had claimed about one quarter of the storefronts, and the "cafes and coffees" trend consumed another. In the remaining half, family-run Haitian businesses struggled to hold on, resisting the move to gentrification.

It was a commercial area and, at this time of night, the sidewalks were empty, the stores lit only for security. Even the cafes had long since closed. We shared the road with a single sports car, cutting through on its way elsewhere.

"One block over," Griffin said. "You want me to drive by?"

"In this monster?" Paige murmured under her breath. "Might as well have cherries on the roof."

"The vehicle is quite distinctive," I said. "To Carlos or anyone else associated with the Cabal. Just find a parking lot...or perhaps an empty lot will be just as obvious."

"Will it fit in an alley or service road?" Paige asked.

"I'll try."

He drove half a block, and wedged into a service lane so tight that Paige had to slide over and get out my side. I closed the door quietly, but the click still seemed to ring out like a gunshot.

If there was anything more obvious than driving a massive SUV through the empty streets, it was sneaking down them trailed by a six-foot-four bodyguard.

At the end of the service road, I lifted a hand to stop, then whispered, "Paige and I will look to the north and Griffin, you can continue—"

A slow shake of his head, arms crossed.

"I'll go north," Paige said. "You two continue—"

Another head shake. Paige and I exchanged a look, contemplating our chance of making a run for it. Tempting, but for a forty-year-old of his size, Griffin was surprisingly fast.

I was hoping to find a convenient alley that would lead us to our destination. Of course there wasn't one. As I considered the absurd problem of getting to our target, I was aware of time ticking.

"We can use blur spells," Paige said. "Griffin can follow with his armor intact. He'll seem to be alone, and he's safe from anything they can throw at him."

As we headed north, Griffin stayed close to the storefronts, hidden in shadow, his footfalls remarkably soft, his presence betrayed only by the occasional scuff on uneven pavement.

As we closed in on the GPS location, the street looked identical to the one behind us—lined with closed shops and no signs of life.

What would Carlos be doing here?

The signal had originated a half block east. I squinted in that direction.

Paige whispered, "An art gallery, a vegan restaurant and, I think, a boutique."

Clearly it was time to consider rescheduling that optometrist appointment I'd missed last fall.

"Someone really should circle around behind," Paige said, glancing at Griffin, standing with his back to the building so he could spot all comers. "He'll let me leave before he'll let you."

Not the solution I'd prefer, but she was right.

"Go," I said, before I could think better of it. "I'll be—"

"—watching out for me." She smiled. "I know."

LUCAS

14

THE GPS SIGNAL LED US to a narrow passage between an art gallery and a boutique clothing store. Halfway down, a service door stood ajar.

Paige was at the other end of the alley, hidden under a cover spell. I would have preferred to discuss that open door with her, but I was stuck with Griffin. I'd cast a cover spell over him, but it was less than perfect—because of his size or my lesser competence with witch spells.

"I hope you aren't thinking that door being propped open is a lucky coincidence," he said.

"In light of what's happened tonight, does Carlos think my father himself will come to his rescue?"

"Maybe. Or that maybe you will."

I hadn't considered that.

The door was barely ajar, enough to look accidental, as if someone hadn't noticed it didn't close behind him. Inside there could be anything from a lone assassin to a small army.

"I'm going in," Griffin said.

I caught his arm. "You might be impervious to normal harm, but you aren't immortal."

"Maybe not, but it's my job."

He tried to pull away, but I held on. "There must be another entrance."

I was breaking my cover spell to motion to Paige when the door flew open. I quickly recast.

A dark figure stepped out and eased the door all but closed, as if he'd left something jammed at the base to prevent it from shutting.

His build matched Carlos's, as did his dark hair.

My mind wanted to leap to the obvious conclusion and balked when I resisted. I could not make any assumptions.

Griffin had backed into the shadows. His eyes were narrowed, obviously doing the same thing I was—studying the figure with uncertainty. All we could see from this distance was that he was dark haired and clean shaven, like Carlos.

I looked toward Paige's end of the alley. When the man turned in the other direction, she peeked around the corner, breaking her cover spell for a look. Then she gave an exaggerated shrug, meaning she couldn't confirm his identity either.

The man lifted a radio to his lips, seemed to think better of broadcasting in such a quiet alley and reached for the door again. Before he had it half open, Griffin flew down the alley, grabbed him by the collar and threw him against the wall, his hands pinned behind his back.

I knew immediately this wasn't Carlos. My brother's snarls of outrage would have echoed through the night. Instead, the figure only struggled, kicking and writhing in Griffin's grasp. He yanked the man around to face me as I approached.

He was maybe half Carlos's age. "Who are you?" I asked in English, then Spanish.

He only looked at me, then at Paige as she approached, and finally up at Griffin. Griffin shook his head, to tell me he didn't recognize the young man. It was like being in a silent movie, no one saying a word, all too aware of the possibility that whoever was on the other end of the young man's radio was close enough to hear.

"Lucas?" Paige broke the silence. "Do you know him? Does he work for your dad's Cabal?"

Griffin glowered at her and even I wondered what she was doing . . . until the young man's gaze shot to me, his lips parting in a silent "Oh, fuck."

The first words out of the young man's mouth were, among postcapture utterances, second in popularity only to "I didn't do it."

"It wasn't my idea," he said.

"Where's Carlos?" I asked.

"If I knew—" His teeth clicked shut, expression closing down. "I want immunity."

Griffin's fist hit his jaw with a *thwack*. Paige covered a wince by looking away.

"Mr. Cortez asked you a question," Griffin said.

"I—I want immunity."

The demand fell into a plea, blood dripping down his chin. If he could still talk, though, the blow had been softer than it looked.

I waved for Griffin to hold back—pure theater, as he had no intention of hitting the youth again if it could be avoided. Then I nodded for the young man to continue.

"It's all gone to hell," he said, slumping in Griffin's grip. "He said it would be easy, but now the girl's dead and—"

"What girl?" Paige said before stopping herself. An apologetic look my way. "Sorry. You said the girl's dead and..."

He shook his head.

"Where's Carlos?" I asked.

"I don't—"

The young man stopped short, gaping at me. Then he slumped in Griffin's hands. Griffin jerked him upright again, but his head lolled, and when Griffin pulled back his hand, it glistened wetly in the dim light.

Something stung my shoulder. Then another blow, this one square in my back, so hard it knocked the wind out of me and sent me sprawling into the gravel.

"Down!" Griffin shouted as he shoved me.

"Paige!"

I saw her pale face, eyes wide, uncomprehending. I grabbed her legs and yanked her down. The bullet struck the ground a foot from Griffin's boot, sending up a geyser of dirt.

I reached for the door, but Griffin already had it open. He grabbed for me, but I dove through, shouting for him to get Paige instead. I slid across a carpeted floor, the pile burning my cheek, my injured shoulder colliding with a desk chair. I threw it aside and scrambled back to Paige as Griffin slammed the door.

"I'm okay," she whispered. "I just— I'm sorry. I didn't understand. A sniper?"

Griffin gave a grunt of assent and, for a moment, we all stayed there, in the dim light, our breathing the only sound. We were in a small office, with a desk, chair, filing cabinet, coffeemaker and nothing more.

Paige whispered and I moved closer to hear her, then realized she was casting a spell.

"No one's here," Paige said, voice still low. "Is he—? The boy. Is he dead?"

"Think so," Griffin said.

"Can we get him in here? To check?"

Griffin looked at me.

"Please," I said.

He waved us away from the door, peered out through a crack, then threw it open, grabbed the fallen youth's legs and yanked him inside. He tossed aside a wedge of wood used to keep it open, slammed it shut, and turned the dead bolt with a *thunk*.

Paige cast and a fiery light ball appeared over her hand. A flip of her wrist and it hovered over the boy as she examined him. He'd been shot through the chest. I pictured us in the alley again. Had Paige moved at that moment, she would have caught this bullet. Had I not pulled her down a moment later... I tried not to think of that.

The young man was dead. As Paige closed his eyes, Griffin called headquarters and ordered a SWAT team to our location, warning them of a sniper in the building to the south.

Then he gazed down at the dead youth. "How do our kids get mixed up in shit like this? Where are their parents?"

I knew Griffin was thinking of his son, Jacob, who would have been about this young man's age. Jacob hadn't joined a gang. His only mistake had been sneaking out on a school night when a killer had been targeting the children of Cabal employees. One would think that tragedy would have been enough to make a parent reconsider his employment, but Griffin had stayed on, his loyalty unwavering.

Paige had gone quiet and I knew she was thinking of Jacob too. She'd been the one to find his body, and had never forgotten it. She straightened, gaze turning my way.

"Your shoulder," she said. "Let me see it."

In the commotion, I'd almost forgotten the sting in the alley before

Griffin knocked me to the ground. I lifted my hands to my shoulder. My shirt was ripped, blood trickling down my chest.

"Just a graze," I said. "I'm fine."

"Right. Until you need to use your arm and it gives out mid-punch."

"We don't have time. We need to—"

"I'm casting a healing spell, Cortez, even if I need to have Griffin restrain you to do it."

I let her cast it as I looked around, wondering what had drawn the young man in here. The filing cabinet was locked—a thief wouldn't relock. The trash can was empty. While there was some minor untidiness, it didn't look as if the office had been ransacked.

Paige headed for the interior door. I bit back a "be careful."

As she reached for the door handle, she glanced over her shoulder and whispered, "Don't worry, I'll be careful."

I managed a wry smile.

She craned her head to look around, then shut the door again. "It's the gallery."

The young man certainly didn't look like an art thief. What were the chances of us stumbling over supernaturals conducting a burglary unrelated to tonight's events? In the very place Carlos had phoned from?

Griffin slipped into the gallery to search. He'd been gone for less than a minute when a crash sounded.

Paige peered through the door, but the noise hadn't been Griffin. He stood in the middle of the room, looking up. The sound must have come from overhead.

I eased past her. The gallery was a single room with only two exits—through the office or the front door. A third door, tactfully hidden behind a partial screen, stood open, revealing a tiny bathroom.

Paige looked up. "Storage space maybe? If so, how do they get there? I don't see a hatch and I didn't notice any door outside. Was there even a second floor? Or just an attic?"

I mentally replayed our approach.

"It's a complete floor, with barred windows. I believe there was a front door on the other side of this one. Leading to apartments, I would presume."

We looked up. If there were inhabited apartments overhead, then noises would not be unexpected.

"The question remains," I murmured. "Why come in here?"

My gaze traveled to the bathroom.

Griffin looked at me. "To take a leak? No offense, but..."

"Highly unlikely, I know."

The bathroom was tiny, and awkwardly set up, the toilet and sink facing one another, with barely enough room for knees. A poor design, but necessary—there was a second door directly across from the entrance. A closet with a deadbolt.

I slid the bolt, and pulled open the door to see a narrow hall ending in a staircase.

WE EXTINGUISHED THE light balls. Without them, the stairwell was pitch-black. We had to move up the stairs by feel as Paige cast sensing spells. When we reached the top, and her spells found no one lying in wait, she relit her light.

We were on a landing flanked by doors. The one to the right was unlocked. As I reached for the handle, Griffin shouldered me aside. I reminded myself that this *was* his job. If I was injured, he'd take the blame.

Griffin took out his gun, eased the door open a crack and stopped to listen. Paige motioned that she'd cast a sensing spell if she could get closer, but he pretended not to understand, threw the door open and wheeled in, gun raised.

After a slow look around, he waved telling us to stay put. When he'd turned away, I peered inside, then pulled back quickly. Beside me, Paige tensed, a spell flying to her lips. I shook my head. What I'd seen was no threat, merely something she didn't need to witness. But, of course, she would—there was no way around it—so I opened the door again. I held up a hand, warning her.

She peered around me. Her breath caught.

The door opened directly into a bedroom. There, on the bed, lay a young woman, naked and spread-eagled, tied to the bedposts, a belt around her neck. Even from here, we could tell that rushing in with first aid would be pointless.

LUCAS

15

"I SUPPOSE COVERING HER UP isn't a good idea," Paige said.

I nodded. Cabal security would be handling this, not the Miami police, but they'd still want the scene left intact.

Paige was unable to tear her gaze from the dead woman. I knew she was wondering who she'd been, what her life had been like, now reduced to this—a naked corpse exposed to strangers who were too busy with other concerns to mourn her passing or even care about the circumstances of her death, except as it related to those larger concerns.

I struggled to see her as Paige did. As a person. But tonight all I could do was assess the facts. Though she looked college age, the amount of smeared makeup made it hard to tell. Dyed blond hair. Faded track marks on her arms. A tattoo on her ankle that might aid in identification.

I turned my attention to the articles of male clothing strewn about the bed. Socks, shoes, underwear, a shirt...No sign of pants. Whoever had been with her had likely fled half dressed. Clearly not the young man from downstairs. But had he killed her?

I bent to examine the shirt. I suspected it belonged to Carlos. The young woman hadn't been hastily tied up by an experimenting amateur, but bound with leather straps. My brother's sexual proclivities were no secret in the supernatural community.

"She's been tortured." Paige had begun examining the young

woman. "There are knife wounds, but they look small and shallow, maybe from that." She pointed to a penknife lying beside a condom wrapper, then leaned closer to the girl's abdomen. "And I think these are . . . bite marks."

While this could indeed be evidence of torture, it was not necessarily the case if Carlos had been involved. But I saw no need to enlighten her.

A shadow fell over Paige. I reacted with a knockback spell, hitting the blur of motion before I could even tell what it was.

Carlos flew back into the open closet as Griffin ran from the adjoining room. Griffin tackled him and the two men went down.

"Get the hell off me, you oaf." A glare my way. "It's your *brother*, idiot."

It was the first time I'd heard Carlos call me that. He'd say mockingly a "little bro" or "baby bro," but in serious reference I was always his *half*-brother—if he had to admit to any relationship at all.

He struggled against Griffin's restraining hands, but he was no match for the bigger man. With one hand, Griffin tugged plastic wrist straps from his pocket and glanced at me. I nodded.

"What the hell are you doing?" Carlos said. "You're supposed to be rescuing me!"

"We need to escort you to headquarters," I said. "If you'll—"

"Headquarters? The fuck you are, you traitorous son-of-a-bitch. I wouldn't trust you to escort me across the road."

From brother to traitor in twenty seconds. If one angle didn't work . . .

"I need to take you back. Hector— Hector's dead."

"Hec—?" He lifted his gaze to mine. "Bullshit."

When I didn't answer, he searched my face.

"Ah, shit," he said. "What was it? A car accident? Heart attack? I know his heart had been—" His expression hardened. "If it was a heart attack, you better believe I'm holding you responsible, Lucas. You traipse into the office this afternoon, with no warning—"

"He was murdered."

His surprise seemed genuine.

"So was William."

His look turned to shock. "No way. No fucking way."

"I'm sorry."

"Yeah? I'll bet you are. I'll bet you're just rubbing your hands right now. Finally got rid of them, and now the way is clear. You can take over the company and run it into the ground, screw Dad over and call it a public service. Well, I've got news for you, baby bro. I'm still around. And while I am, you've got competition."

That was it. His shock and grief had lasted exactly thirty seconds before his true concerns took over.

Griffin made a move, as if to lead him away, but I shook my head. There was still one more test.

"They attacked our father," I said.

"Is he dead?"

There was no hope in his voice, but no concern either. I paused, giving him time to contemplate, to react, but his expression didn't change.

"He's fine."

"Oh."

"Griffin will escort you to headquarters."

Carlos lifted his bound hands. "Not like this."

"If you'll go willingly—"

"This isn't a request, Lucas."

My phone vibrated. It was the SWAT team. They'd already secured the area and were requesting permission to enter the building. I granted it and hung up.

"Lucas?" Paige nodded to the young woman on the bed and I realized, with no small amount of regret, that I'd forgotten all about her.

"Untie him, please," I said.

"Taking your sweet fucking time, aren't you? You like seeing me tied up?"

I was inclined to say *I* wasn't the one who liked seeing people bound and helpless. "No, Carlos, surprisingly, I have other concerns on my mind. Our father has charged me with seeing you safely delivered into protective custody. If I need to do so with you bound hand and foot, so be it. Before you go, though, I should ask what happened here."

"You think?"

We locked gazes.

"They came after me too," he said finally.

"Who?"

"Well, duh. Obviously the same people who killed William and Hector."

"You think?" Paige murmured, too low for anyone but me to hear.

"And the young woman. Is this your handiwork?"

I waited for him to object, outraged, but Carlos gave me one last unreadable look, then turned to Griffin.

"Home, Jeeves."

"Did they kill her to find you?" I asked.

"I gave you an order, Sorenson. Take me to my father."

"Did you see or hear what happened?"

He turned to me. "You're the detective, little bro. Detect."

CARLOS'S SURPRISE AT hearing of Hector and William's deaths seemed genuine, but he'd shut down when I'd hinted he might have played even a corollary role in tonight's events. In my experience, the innocent either proclaim their innocence or are too shocked by the allegation to intelligently respond. Carlos had done the Cabal equivalent of lawyering up—take me to my father.

I spent the next thirty minutes examining the crime scenes—the alley, the bedroom and the sniper's roost on a building a block over—and overseeing the technicians' work. They needed little guidance, but they indulged me, knowing I wouldn't contaminate evidence.

I focused on the young man. Identifying him and his role would help me understand what had taken place here.

He had no identification. He wore a cargo vest and pants, both with many pockets. When they were emptied, we had two cell phones, two radios, a handheld computer and two devices we couldn't recognize. The extra radios and cell phones seemed to be backups.

Paige took the handheld computer. "It's a homemade job. GPS maybe? Probably more. It's password protected and something tells me if he knows how to build it, he knows how to protect it. If I start trying to crack the password..."

"It could trigger a program to erase the contents."

"If I can use the lab at the offices, I can do more."

She checked one cell phone as I examined the other. All incoming and outgoing call records had been deleted. Both contained identical lists of eight contacts by initials only.

"GB," Paige said. "The gang leader is Guy Benoit, isn't it?"

I nodded.

"JD, SR, BS . . . The missing guys are Jaz and Sonny. The dead girl is Bianca. Maybe a coincidence, but something tells me if I press FE I'm going to wake up Hope."

"I suspect so."

With that one call we could almost certainly identify the young man. But if I woke Hope to send her pictures of a dead comrade—after the night she'd had—I could safely wipe Karl's name off *my* contact list.

I'd have the team run prints, photos and DNA of the victim against Cabal records. I was certain my father would catalogue such information. The completeness of those records was another matter—the gang members were a transitory lot.

My phone rang.

"Mr. Cortez? It's Tyson, at the hospital? Guarding Troy's room? You saw me there earlier?"

Ah, one of the silent guards. The inflections on his sentences told me this was a call he'd rather not be making and I braced myself.

"Troy's awake, sir."

I let out a silent sigh of relief. "How is he?"

"He, uh, seems fine, sir. He's, uh, asking me to— Well, I know you're busy, and he might be . . ." A lowering of his voice. "A bit confused."

The rumble of a voice came from the background.

"He, uh, wants me to ask you to . . . That is, if you think you should . . ."

The rumble grew, becoming Troy's voice, still too distant to be intelligible.

"I'm sure you have enough to worry about, sir, but he's concerned that—"

"Give me the fucking phone," I heard Troy rasp.

"He thinks you—"

"Give me the fucking phone, Tyson, or I'll be dead before you spit out the goddamned message."

"Better give it to him."

A hiss as the phone changed hands.

"Lucas."

"How are—?"

"Later. We've got a bigger problem. It was Carlos."

"Carlos...?"

"Who shot me. He came to the house, alone, wanting to talk to your dad, and I knew something was hinky, so I went to talk to him..." A soft grunt of discomfort. "Point is, it was Carlos. I woke up a while ago, but I've been playing possum, waiting for you to come back so I could tell you. I knew if I opened my eyes, the first thing your dad would ask was who shot me, and I sure as hell wasn't telling him."

"Good. I appreci—"

"Not so fast. He got a call that Carlos was at headquarters. I waited until he left, then asked Tyson to call you. I told him what to say, about Carlos. Then..."

His voice drifted off.

"Troy?"

"Your dad wasn't gone. He could probably tell I was faking it and hung around outside my door waiting to hear what I was hiding." He paused. "He knows it was Carlos, Lucas. And when he left here..." Another pause. "You need to get there before he does something he'll regret."

"How much of a head start does he have?"

"It took me five minutes to convince this numbskull I wasn't delirious and to call you."

Five minutes, and the hospital was an additional five minutes closer to headquarters, meaning my father had a ten-minute head start.

"I'm on my way."

LUCAS

16

I GRABBED KEYS and the location of a car from a shocked tech, and took off. As I drove along the quiet streets, Paige held on for dear life with one hand and called Griffin with the other.

Griffin was holding Carlos in the boardroom. My father had yet to arrive. Ideally, I would have had Griffin quietly relocate Carlos until we got there, but there was no way to do that without the other guards knowing, and no matter what I said, the first guard my father asked would tell him where to find his son.

I LEFT THE car at the front door and ran in, Paige jogging behind me.

"Is my father here?" I asked the desk guard.

"Y—yes, sir. Upstairs. With your—"

"How long ago?"

"Umm, two, three minutes?"

I threw the car keys on the counter as I passed. "It's outside. Have someone park it."

The private elevator would still be on the executive level, so we took the staff one as far as we could, then the stairs the rest of the way. Paige waved me on ahead—she'd catch up.

As I raced through the door, voices drifted from the other side of the floor.

"If you'll just wait, sir."

"Get out of my way, Griffin," my father replied.

"I need to update you—"

"Move, Griffin. Now!"

I knew Griffin would step aside. No one disobeyed a direct order from my father.

I broke into a run.

"Dad," Carlos said. "I heard—"

"You spoiled little brat."

A crash and a yelp from Carlos. I rounded the final corner to see the guards at the end of the long hall, clustered around Griffin.

"Griffin, stop him," I called.

"I can't—"

"Who did my father leave in charge?"

"Lucas, I can't—"

"I am in charge, and I gave you an order."

A moment of shocked silence then, as I drew close, Griffin nodded and went into the room.

"Mr. Cortez, you don't want to do this," he said.

"Oh, for Christ's sake," I muttered.

I yanked the guard blocking the door out of the way. Carlos lay on the floor, blood dripping from his nose, eyes glued to our father as he advanced on him.

"What happened, Carlos?" my father said, voice low. "Was it because I wouldn't advance you money to buy a new sports car? Or because I stopped buying off the whores you beat up? Or because you got sick of having to work for a living? No, not work. Just show up. Because that's all I asked of you."

"Papá—" I said.

"Stay out of this, Lucas." He didn't turn from Carlos. "I gave you every opportunity. An Ivy League education...and you wouldn't show up for class. A five-million-dollar trust fund...that was gone before you turned thirty. A VP's salary, with zero responsibilities... and you whine because I expect you here by ten every morning. I always knew you were a vain, vacuous, vicious brat, Carlos, but I blamed your mother's influence. I told myself you just needed guidance. I was wrong. Your *brothers*, Carlos..."

"Dad, I—"

"Your brothers!" he thundered.

His hands flew up in a spell. Carlos seemed frozen, making no move to cast back, as if he'd forgotten he could, as if this was a nightmare he couldn't escape even by simply diving out of the spell's path.

So I leapt into it.

The energy bolt hit my side and I convulsed, blacking out for a split second before hitting the floor and jerking back to consciousness. Consternation crossed my father's face, then vanished as his expression went blank.

"Lucas, get out of the way."

"Yes, Lucas," Carlos said. "We wouldn't want to see you get hurt."

I pushed to my feet and got between Carlos and my father . . . earning a shove between the shoulder blades for my trouble.

"You heard Dad. Get out of the way. You don't want to spoil his fun. He's been dying to do this for twenty years. Dying to beat the snot out of me. Tell me how he really feels."

"Lucas, get out of—"

"No."

"Oh, for fuck's sake," Carlos said. "You just can't help yourself, can you, Lucas?"

"Papá, listen—"

"Go save someone who needs saving," Carlos cut in. "He's not going to kill me. He might hate me. He might wish I was dead. He might wish he could do the job himself. But he can't. I'm all he has left."

"No," my father said slowly. "You aren't."

His gaze shunted to me. Carlos snarled in rage and I spun to stop him from attacking our father. His eyes met mine and I realized it wasn't our father he was after. Before I could dive out of the way, he kicked my feet out from under me. As I fell, his arm went around my neck, crushing my windpipe as he yanked me back onto my feet.

I opened my mouth to cast, but couldn't speak. When I jabbed my elbow into his chest, his arm tightened, cutting off my air.

"You're right, Dad," he said. "I'm not all you have left. But I can fix that."

With his free hand, he grabbed my hair and yanked my head back, letting our father watch as I wheezed and gasped.

"Do you know how easy it is to kill someone like this? How fast I can do it? Faster than you can cast a spell. But don't take my word for it, Dad. Give it a shot."

"Carlos, let him go. He only wanted to help. Let him go and we'll talk."

Carlos laughed. "Whoo-hoo. Listen to that. Who wants to play 'voice of reason' now? What's wrong, Dad?" His arm tightened so fast I gasped, eyes bulging. "Am I making you nervous? You should see your face, Papá. Sure, you'll grieve for Hector and William, but this—" He heaved me backward. "This one would *hurt*."

"If you—"

"Oh, that's the way. Threaten me. Come on, Dad. Tell me what horrible things you'll do to me if I hurt your baby boy. You say I don't pull my weight around here? At least I show up. This one spends *his* working hours trying to destroy us. He moves clear across the country to get away from you. Marries a witch. Adopts a Nast. You build him an office, and he uses his trust fund to buy it from you. Sets up shop fighting Cabals with your money. Anything to screw you over. But you keep chasing him, like a pathetic SOB who wants the one piece of tail that can't run away fast enough."

I kicked Carlos in the shin, hard enough to make him teeter. I grabbed his arm, but it tightened so fast I blacked out. When I came to, he'd gone absolutely still. I wedged my fingers between his arm and my throat, and still he didn't move. I looked up to see Paige across the room, her face pale with concentration.

"I—I'm having trouble holding the spell," she said. "Can you get away?"

My father stepped forward.

"Stay where you are, Benicio. Lucas?"

I pried Carlos's arm from my throat and managed a raspy, "I'm fine."

My father tried to move forward again.

"Not a move, Benicio," Paige said, "or I'll do the same to you. You know I will. Lucas, get away from him. I can't hold—"

The spell snapped as I lunged to the side. Paige hit Carlos with a knockback spell and he flew into the wall. My father lifted his hands. Paige turned the spell on him and he stumbled back.

The guards rushed into the room. Paige hurried to me. As she drew near, I could see she was shaking.

"I almost couldn't cast," she said. "The first one—"

"I'm all right."

Out of the corner of my eye, I saw my father advancing on Carlos, now restrained by Griffin.

"Papá. No."

"Didn't you learn your lesson, baby bro? Stay out."

"He would have killed you," my father said. "He killed Hector and William, Lucas. Murdered them in cold blood."

"We don't know that."

"Don't—?" He shook his head. "He shot Troy. Troy saw him. Are you saying he was mistaken? Lying?"

"No."

"I know what happened at Hector's. Carlos was there—the last person to see Hector alive. The butler and Bella both confirmed it for you. Are they mistaken? Lying?"

"We have no proof that Carlos shot Hector."

"You sent two officers back here after William's murder to look for evidence that Carlos had been here too."

"And they found none. His key code hasn't been used since he left."

"Do you think he's stupid enough to walk past the front desk? To use his own access code? For God's sake, stop being a lawyer, Lucas! This isn't a courtroom."

"Isn't it? You've judged him, found him guilty and now you're ready to carry out his punishment."

"He would have killed you."

"Perhaps, but you put me in charge of this investigation. You can't decide now that you don't want me acting like an investigator. I plan to see this through, and follow the letter of the law."

"Whose law?"

"Cabal law." I turned to Griffin. "Take him into custody. Not to the cells, but to the house arrest room. It's to be double guarded at all times. He's to have no visitors except those approved by me. None, including my father. He's to have no food except that ordered by me, delivered to me and taken to him by Paige or myself."

Griffin glanced at my father. He hesitated, back stiff, then he deflated and nodded.

"Lucas is in charge. Do as he says."

HOPE

RACKING UP CREDITS

The hotel room door opened with a click. Karl peeked around the corner.

"You're up."

I yawned. "Just stirring. Being lazy and enjoying it."

I was curled up in the king-size bed, propped on two pillows, with the rest strewn around me. On my morning bathroom trip I'd grabbed a robe—not for decency, but because it was thick and soft, too tempting to ignore.

"You look lost in that bed and that robe. Very cute." He smiled at me.

"Cute?" I sputtered. I undid the robe and spread it, then stretched out on top of the covers. "Better?"

His gaze slid down me. "I take it you don't mind a cold breakfast?"

I noticed the tray in his hands, steam billowing from the plate cover, and I pulled the robe shut.

"Damn," he said.

He set the tray down, handed me *USA Today*, then tossed the *Wall Street Journal* onto the other side of the bed.

"You really are spoiling me."

"No, I'm racking up credits. I suspect I'll need them."

He kissed my cheek as he leaned over to hand me a coffee.

"Speaking of credits," I said. "I called my mother while you were out. She said dinner Saturday would be wonderful. She'll make reservations."

"Too late. Done."

"You got reservations for Odessa's on a Saturday?"

His brows arched. "You think I don't know how to get a table at a popular restaurant? You forget who you're talking to, my dear." He set the tray between us as he climbed in. "Dropping your mother's name helped."

"I'm sure it did. She likes you, you know. For me, I mean."

"Good. Though I was on my best behavior that night, which may have skewed the results."

"I don't think so."

Our eyes met. He nodded. "Good."

I spread preserves on my toast. "She wants me to invite you to the spring regatta."

"Rowing? Are you competing?"

"I..." A shrug. "I'm out of practice, so it'll be strictly a social function for me."

"There's still time. Consider it a challenge. Get yourself whipped into shape by spring."

"Are you going to show your support at 5:30 a.m. practices?"

"Absolutely. From the comfort of my bed, I will be cheering you on wholeheartedly."

I laughed and took a bite of toast.

"I'll come out when I can," he said. "In return for breakfast afterward."

"Sounds fair."

"And you can tell your mother I would love to come to the regatta. I'm sure it will be a"—a sly grin my way—"glittering affair."

"Uh-uh. As my guest, you are forbidden to steal from my mother or any of her friends. I'll show you who you can steal from, provided a portion of the proceeds go to a charity of my choosing."

"A finder's fee?"

"You got it."

"Fair enough."

We ate for a few minutes. My paper rested on my tray; his on his lap, both still folded as we perused the lead articles, as if reluctant to open it and make that commitment.

"I made a few more calls this morning," Karl said.

"Did you phone Lucas? Did he say—?"

His glower cut me short, reminding me that we were leaving that aside until after breakfast.

"A couple of months ago, I talked to Jeremy about relocating."

It took a moment for me to understand what he meant. The bubble that was keeping last night's reality at bay also blocked any reminder that we were anything other than two ordinary people.

"Changing my territory," he prompted.

"Right, yes." As a Pack werewolf, Karl was allowed to hold territory. The others shared New York State. By choice, he got Massachusetts—a reflection on both his independence and his reluctance to fully join into Pack life.

"The calls I made today were inquiries into a couple of condos in Philadelphia."

He stopped there, and I had to replay his words before his meaning sunk in.

"You want to move to Philly? Relocate your territory to Pennsylvania?"

"Is that all right?"

"I suppose—I mean, yes. That's all right. Just...unexpected."

He reached to take a slice of bacon off my plate, using the excuse to study my expression. Moving territory wasn't something to be done lightly. Which meant he was serious. About me. About us. And I knew that, I guess. It was just...unexpected.

"It's really more of a home base than a home," he said. "I just thought Philadelphia would be more convenient, under the circumstances."

I nodded.

"I'm particularly interested in a new building about a block from your office."

I managed a smile. "Ah, the Renaissance Towers. Very classy. Did you know they tore down one of the city's oldest apartments to build it? Destroyed a heritage building?"

"I believe they preserved part of the facade."

"And evicted people who'd been living there their entire lives."

"It has a lovely view."

"I'm sure it does."

He sighed. "If I choose it, I'll donate five percent of the purchase price to a homeless shelter."

"That's not really the point."

"It has a lovely view."

I shook my head and finished my orange juice.

"Anyway, it would be convenient for *you*," he said. "A place for you to eat lunch, instead of brown bagging it at your desk. And a place to sleep if you work late or the weather's bad."

"That'd be nice."

He reached for my uneaten croissant. "You may find it more convenient, at some point, to stay there during the week, and we can spend weekends at your townhouse in Gideon."

I gave him a look.

"I said, 'at some point.' "

"I've never lived with anyone, Karl."

"Neither have I."

"I drool in my sleep."

"I know. It's cute."

As I opened my mouth, the phone blipped on my nightstand. A text message, which meant I didn't need to answer it immediately, but it made a good excuse.

"Who is it?" he asked, though his tone told me he had a pretty good idea.

"Paige."

As I skimmed through the message, my fingers tightened around the phone. "She says there was a shooting last night, while they were finding Carlos. They think it's a member of the gang. She's warning me that she's sending the photo separately, so I don't get a shock opening it, I guess." I took a deep breath and resisted the urge to check for the second message. "Troy's stable. And they did find Carlos. She says they're 'holding him.' " I glanced at Karl. "In custody? Do they think he's involved?"

His expression said he didn't care enough to speculate.

"She'd like me to call her. She probably has some questions about last night."

"Fine. Tell her you'll call from the plane."

"Karl..."

"Don't you see what he's doing?"

"Who?"

"Lucas. He's as sneaky as his father. I told him to call *me*."

"It's my help they need with the photo."

"He doesn't even call you himself, but has his wife do it, sending a text message so it sounds as if they're being considerate, not wanting to disturb you. Just watch. When you call, Paige will invite us out to breakfast, where Lucas will pounce, catch you off guard and talk you into staying to help him."

"And why shouldn't he? His brothers are dead, Karl. He'll do what it takes to find whoever is responsible. I know I would."

"Because you're close to *your* brothers. If Lucas was the dead one, Hector and William sure as hell wouldn't go looking for his killer. Unless it was to thank him."

"If Lucas thinks the gang is involved, then he needs my help and I'm going to give it. While he'd appreciate your nose, I can convince him you're otherwise engaged. So catch that plane to Philly, check the condos, take the keys for my place if you want to crash there . . ."

His look was enough.

"One day, Karl. Give me that, and if you want to help, I'd love that."

"Twenty-four hours. There's a flight leaving at ten tomorrow, and I'm buying tickets."

In other words, he'd expected this, and was just registering his protest.

"Thank you, Karl."

"Credits. I'm stockpiling 'em."

I OPENED PAIGE'S second message and braced for the photo. A young Hispanic man with shaggy hair and a tiny scar through his eyebrow seemed to sleep peacefully on a carpet. Rodriguez.

Jaz had said Rodriguez lived with his older sister in Miami, the one who'd called with the college news. Rodriguez was a half-demon, so his family didn't know about his supernatural life. Presumably his death was being handled by the Cabal. How could they let his sister know of his death, but deny her details or access to his body? Would they find a way . . . or just let him disappear?

When I called Paige, she sounded so exhausted I was sure she hadn't gotten to bed. Instead of her inviting me to breakfast, I offered to bring her one. But she brushed me off with thanks.

I aimed a glower at Karl, who could overhear Paige and had the grace to look mildly chagrined.

I told Paige who her victim was, and that I could only give a sur- name and sketchy bio.

"The tech guy, huh?" she murmured. "That makes sense. He had a lot of gear on him."

"Did the Cabal shoot him?" I tried to keep the accusation out of my voice. Wasn't sure I succeeded.

"I don't think so. We caught him in an alley and we were just about to get information from him. Obviously someone didn't want to take that chance."

"Someone from the gang?"

"We presume so."

I doubted it. Guy would trust Rodriguez to keep his mouth shut at least long enough for a rescue attempt.

More likely it had been a Cabal sniper who didn't dare admit his mistake to Lucas. If it had been the gang, they'd been aiming for who- ever was holding Rodriguez.

I didn't argue, though. The truth would come out. The Cabals might kill one of their own to keep him from talking, but I was sure the gang wouldn't.

"There's something else we were hoping you could help with," Paige said. "You may have heard the gang mention an off-site place where they keep supplies and such?"

"Yes, but I don't have any idea where it is."

"The Cabal has the address. It's a warehouse unit. We've had a team staking it out since three. At around four, two young men went inside. They haven't come out. We presume it's a rendezvous point and the others were already in there."

Others? With Rodriguez dead, there were only three members left.

"What about Jaz and Sonny? Have you found out anything? Is the Cabal still claiming they aren't responsible?"

A pause.

My heart hammered. "You've found them? Their bodies?"

"No, but Lucas is certain the Cabal isn't behind this. With every- thing that's happened, Benicio would come clean, if only because it could help solve the case. Lucas is—" A buzz of the phone, as if she was moving. "He's beginning to suspect they were never abducted."

"What?"

"I'll explain later. About the warehouse, though. Lucas wants to go in within the hour, and we thought you might want to be there just to, you know, negotiate. If things don't go as hoped, Lucas really doesn't want this to end badly."

That was her politic way of saying they feared if the gang resisted, the roust could turn into a massacre.

"We'll be there."

HOPE

PARTY TIME

Karl picked the lock of the unit adjacent to the one rented by the gang. Snipers covered us from the neighboring building. I knew that was supposed to make us feel safe, but it didn't, any more than the Kevlar vest I wore or the panic button in my pocket.

The door opened in to a cavernous, dark room filled with carpet rolls. I turned on my flashlight and we picked our way over the rolls to the far side of the room. Karl pressed himself against the wall shared with the gang's unit, listening. I knew what I should be doing—"listening" for chaos vibes or visions. But I was still raw from the night before, and spent the first couple of minutes just standing there, clenching the flashlight, braced against visions. When not so much as a stray chaos vibe pinged, I relaxed.

I glanced at Karl. He shook his head. No sounds from the unit either.

I took out my cell and called Guy. No one answered. Karl couldn't hear the ring from the adjoining unit. I hung up and tried Max. No answer. Same with Tony.

I left a voice mail message for Tony, asking where they were and what was happening. I could see them not answering my call—they had no idea whether I'd been kidnapped or had betrayed them, and if Guy wasn't there, they might not risk picking up. But they'd certainly discuss it or comment on it, and probably check the voice message. Still Karl heard nothing.

We went outside to find Lucas.

TEN MINUTES LATER, Karl was picking another lock—the door into the gang unit. This time he had not only snipers but two members of the SWAT team flanking him, one pressed against either side of the doorway.

Karl sampled the air, then checked with me. No chaos vibes either. The officers followed us inside.

This unit was divided into three sections—two rooms with closed doors plus a large open storage area. The officers passed us and swept the open area, then retreated to check the closed rooms. The first held two cots, a microwave and a minifridge—a place to hole up if needed. The room was empty.

One officer opened the second door, and they swung in. A grunt. Then a wave, telling us it was safe. It was not, however, empty. Max and Tony were passed out drunk at a dining table, a bottle of Glenlivet single-malt Scotch within reach.

I bent to read a note that had slid to the floor.

Party Time!
Yeah, it's the good stuff this time.
Guy

I whispered, "So what do we do?"

Karl's hand closed on my arm, and I thought he was telling me to be quieter. But he tugged me back and I realized he didn't want me getting too close. Smart—I didn't want to be within arm's reach if the guys woke up.

I turned to say something to Karl, then saw his expression and, at the same time, over his shoulder, Tony's. He lay on the table, arms askew, but his eyes were half open. Empty eyes . . .

I reached to grab his shoulder. An officer stopped me.

"D-dead?" I managed.

My gaze shot to Max. His head lay on his folded arms, face hidden. But his body was still.

No, it couldn't be. If they were dead, I'd feel it. I'd *see* their deaths. Nothing chaotic could have happened—

I saw the bottle again and flashed back to the night before. To the guard inside the house, looking as if *he* had just passed out, coffee cup by his hand. I hadn't felt so much as a twinge from his death. Because it had been unchaotic. Dead before he realized what was happening.

Karl leaned over the open bottle, being careful not to touch it, sniffed and nodded. One of the officers lifted his radio to his lips.

I walked back and crouched by the note. Someone must have planted it and made it look like it came from Guy.

The wording was perfect. "Party time." The joke about letting them have the "good stuff." Even the brand—the same kind Sonny had swiped from the stock at Easy Rider the night of the sweet sixteen heist.

After the rest of the team poured in and secured the building, Paige and Lucas joined us. Karl quietly asked whether I wanted to step out, but didn't argue when I refused. There was no chaos here to upset me, and I felt better staying with Max and Tony, so I could ensure they were treated as people, not anonymous casualties.

I couldn't cling to my naiveté any longer. Guy knew how to convince his people that he had their best interests in mind, but as much as I'd liked him he was, at heart, as power-hungry and ruthless as any Cabal sorcerer. He'd killed Rodriguez, Tony and Max, and maybe Jaz and Sonny.

Lucas must think Carlos was behind this, which would explain how the killer got easy access to his father's and Hector's homes, and lured William at the office. But he'd have needed help. He'd chosen Guy, a shrewd and ambitious gang leader with a reputation for discretion and caution, everything Carlos was not.

They'd hatched a plan, probably recruiting the Cabal security guards I'd seen. They'd used the guards to rob and beat Jaz and Sonny, planting the seeds. Then, with Jaz and Sonny gone and Bianca dead at the hands of the Cabal guard, Guy could whip the rest of the gang into full revenge mode. Having me disappear—presumably kidnapped—was a bonus he hadn't counted on, but had undoubtedly used to full effect.

The gang would help Carlos and provide him with an alibi—he'd been with a woman, and narrowly escaped death himself. But then these witnesses needed to be silenced. That's all Rodriquez, Tony and Max had been to Guy, despite his talk of brotherhood—tools to be used and discarded.

And Jaz and Sonny? Were they dead too? If so, why not display their bodies? Was Guy holding them somewhere, in case they still proved useful?

If we could find them, we might have our witnesses.

LUCAS'S PHONE RANG almost nonstop as he supervised the crime scene, and he was getting frustrated. With two brothers dead, the third in custody, his father in mourning and the entire Cabal in upheaval, the only man they could turn to was the one who didn't want the job.

I was shocked at how well he handled the pressure, especially under the circumstances and with no sleep. He might have never worked for his father, but he knew the organization and, it seemed, how to direct it.

Three calls came in succession as Lucas tried to supervise the removal of Max and Tony's bodies. Paige took the last for him.

As she listened, she frowned. "Are you sure about the time of death?"

Lucas glanced over sharply. She motioned for him to keep working.

"Yes, I understand," she said. "It's not an exact science, but it's definitely been more than twenty-four hours?"

A pause, then she looked my way. "I think I have someone who can make a positive ID."

I froze.

"I'll bring her down." She hung up and came over to me. "They found someone from the gang."

"Who?"

She shook her head. "Better wait until you see. Just to be sure."

DID THE BODY belong to Jaz or Sonny?

The question looped through my mind all the way to the Cabal morgue. I could have pushed Paige for an answer, but then Karl would see how important it was to me and I didn't want that.

Either way—Jaz or Sonny—this was going to hurt.

HOPE

POSITIVE ID

A young man in a suit that screamed "security detail" met Paige, Karl and me in the Cortez Corporation lobby and explained the situation as he led us to the basement, where the morgue and lab were located. The body had come from a contact in the city morgue.

"How does that work?" I asked.

"Mr. Cortez has friends everywhere and systems for everything. No one's ever going to come looking for this guy."

"The coroner said it was murder?" Paige prompted.

"Gunshot to the back of the skull. Right through the CNS. That's the central nervous system."

"Right."

"And it was a professional body dump too." He glanced at Paige uneasily, as if she might be shocked at the thought that someone could be a professional in such a thing. "It was pure luck that he was found so quickly. They ran his prints through their system, but he wasn't in it. He was in ours, though."

"So that's how you flag them," I said.

He deflated a little, as if I'd figured out the secret behind an illusion.

"But if his prints match the ones on file, he's already been ID'd," Karl said. "I don't understand why you need Hope."

"We have a name," Paige said. "Whether it matches this man is another question." She lowered her voice. "I'm pretty sure it doesn't."

The officer pushed open a set of swinging doors into the morgue. I've been in morgues before. Quite a few. One of Philadelphia's coroners was a past beau of my mother's, and when I'm on a story where a body is involved, he can usually make a few calls and get me in. He says it's because he trusts me to do a fair job, but I suspect he's still trying to earn brownie points with my mom.

A city morgue is usually pretty shabby. This one looked more like a slick TV show. No peeling paint or old textbooks propping up broken equipment tables. Everything gleamed and blipped and beeped. It was so state of the art that I wasn't sure what half the machines did.

I couldn't help but think we had indeed walked onto a set, that this was a fake morgue constructed to trick visitors and dispel the rumors I'd heard about how the Cabal really investigated suspicious deaths—by tossing the body into an incinerator and faking the reports.

A woman in a lab coat introduced herself as Dr. Aberquero. Late thirties, with a pinched face, no makeup and her black hair tightly drawn back. When she turned to shake Karl's hand though, a flash of consternation clouded her face as she stammered an introduction, probably regretting that decision to show up for work without makeup.

She cleared her throat and tore her gaze from Karl. "The, er, decedent shows no signs of trauma except for the gunshot, which entered at the base of the skull, killing him instantly . . ."

Karl slid a glance my way, and I shook my head. No chaos. Confirmation that whoever was on that table had, indeed, died without knowing what was happening to him, like Max and Tony.

Karl cleared his throat. "We appreciate the explanation, Dr. Aberquero, but I'm afraid anything beyond 'gunshot to the head' is wasted on us." A wry smile that had her fingers trembling on her clipboard. "We really just came to identify the body."

"Yes, yes, of course."

She stepped back, nearly smacking into me and blocking my approach to the table as she gave Karl ample room to move forward.

I stepped around her. Karl surreptitiously slid his hand against the small of my back, warm and reassuring. The doctor noticed and her disapproving gaze shot to me, another twenty-something dipping into her dating pool. I guess I'd have to get used to that.

She turned away and folded back the sheet. I let out a gasp, and could only stare, stupid with shock.

"Th-there's been a mistake."

"This isn't Guy Benoit?" she said briskly.

"Y-yes, but didn't you say . . ." I faltered and looked at Paige.

Karl answered. "You said he'd been dead over twenty-four hours?"

"I did," Dr. Aberquero replied.

"I'm sorry," Karl said. "But that isn't possible."

Paige nodded. "That's what I said. I thought maybe the fingerprint had misidentified him or that this wasn't the man Hope knew as Guy."

"It is," I said. "But I saw him yesterday. Talked to him."

The doctor flipped a page on her clipboard. "Then you must be mistaken."

"She isn't," Karl said. "I saw him as well. I'm sure we can get security camera footage from the club to confirm it. He was there yesterday afternoon meeting with people who knew him and saw nothing amiss."

"And as far as we can tell, he killed two people less than six hours ago," Paige added.

"Could the time of death be wrong?" I asked. "I know that under some conditions, the initial estimate can be off."

Dr. Aberquero sniffed. "*CSI* or *Law and Order*?"

"*The State of New York v. Edwin Cole*, 2005. Later evidence showed the victim's body had somehow been in a chilled state. Because that wasn't immediately detected, the time of death was wrong. As for the 'unidentified chilling,' it was postmortem freezing from a clever Gelo half-demon. I know this is the opposite problem, but in our world, changing body temperature isn't impossible."

"You're right. But we look for that here and there's every indication that this man has been dead at least twenty-four hours. I'd even say it's closer to thirty-six."

Paige thanked her. As we were about to leave, I saw Karl's gaze drifting around the room. Searching for something? Whatever it was, he'd have a better chance of getting it without me around, so I left with Paige.

A few minutes later, Karl emerged, dark blue fabric balled in one fist.

"Guy's shirt?" I said.

"Scent."

He waved for us to follow the officer to the elevator.

On the way upstairs, Karl said only that he wanted to return to the warehouse, presuming, I suppose, that we'd know he wanted to search for Guy's scent.

The officer took advantage of these last few minutes to tell Paige how happy he was that Lucas was investigating. How he'd heard such good things about his work. How he looked forward to working under him.

It could have been a show of support, but as Paige's fingers clenched around her purse strap, I knew she thought otherwise. With two brothers gone and the third accused, that left one Cabal son to inherit it all, and this young man was brown-nosing as fast as he could.

On the elevator, I touched Karl's elbow, hinting for him to work his magic, cut in and smoothly rescue Paige. I was surprised he hadn't already. But Karl just patted my hand, his mind miles away.

AT THE WAREHOUSE, Karl set about searching for Guy's scent. He found only old trails.

"But I know he was here yesterday," I said. "I heard him talking to Max about getting the equipment, and this is where they keep it. I suppose he could have waited in the car..." I glanced around the room where we'd found Max and Tony, now empty except for the table and chairs. "Where's the note and bottle? Taken into evidence I guess, but if you could sniff those, maybe you'd know who brought them."

"My sense of smell isn't that good."

"It *looked* like Guy's writing, and the wording was his." I knew I was grasping at straws. However impossible it seemed, Karl's findings only confirmed that Guy hadn't been alive six hours ago to kill Max and Tony.

"Dr. Aberquero thinks Guy has been dead since the night before last," Paige said. "But you and Hope both spoke to him past midnight that day, which means Karl was close enough to get a scent, right? *Was* it Guy?"

Karl lifted the shirt. "Is this the man I smelled the other night? I couldn't tell you. I think I faintly detected this scent, but there were others too, and he was wearing so much cologne, I couldn't be sure."

"Is there cologne on that shirt?" Paige asked.

"No."

I remembered thinking Guy must have been heading out on the town that night, because I'd never known him to wear a scent.

I glanced at Lucas. He was trying to listen, but his ear was attached to his cell phone, as it had been since we'd arrived.

"How could it be done?" I asked Paige. "Fake being someone else? And do it so well that it fooled his entire gang?"

Lucas hung up and pocketed his phone. "The most obvious explanation is the nonsupernatural. Guy has an identical twin."

I pulled out a chair and sat. "So, we have twins, playing the same man, fighting over what action to take with the Cabals. One wants to help Carlos kill his family, the other balks, the first kills the second. Very . . . Hollywood."

"Agreed," Lucas said.

"I don't think that's the answer," Karl murmured.

I glanced at him, but only got that distant look as his thumb rubbed his jawline.

"On to supernatural means, then," Lucas said. "The most obvious is a glamour spell. Under the circumstances, however, I can't imagine it."

"With a glamour spell, you have to *expect* to see someone else," Paige explained. "For example, if Lucas and I left and I said I was coming back, then cast a glamour spell to make him look like me, you'd see me walk into the room. But if I didn't say I was coming back, there's only a fifty-fifty chance it would work. And if you expected Lucas, you'd see right through it."

"It's a temporary illusion," Lucas said. "Prolonged use isn't possible."

"Especially if multiple people saw and recognized him, without expectations."

"That's the only supernatural solution I know of, but I'll go to headquarters and conduct the proper research. They have the most extensive files in—"

His cell phone rang. A line grew between his eyes as he answered it.

Paige lowered her voice. "He's not going to find the time. I'll do it. Do you guys want to come? Or, better yet, maybe you could check the scene where we found Carlos. If there are scents or visions, it might help fill in the blanks."

"Will do," I said. "Is the site still secured?"

"Discreetly. I'll have Lucas call ahead."

LUCAS

17

BY NOON I'D BEGUN TO WONDER whether it was possible for a cell phone ringer to wear out. If so, I prayed it would happen soon.

I couldn't complete a call without hearing the call waiting blip. If I managed to hang up, the silence would last less than ten seconds. My only choice was to let voice mail pick up for a few minutes by discreetly flipping the ring option to vibrate. I was becoming frightfully adept at operating that particular function. Not that it helped—I only had more calls to return and fell ever farther behind.

Some of the calls were case related—Simon with lab results, Dr. Aberquero with autopsy findings, a guard reporting from a scene. All expected and essential. But the others ran the gamut from "Should I cancel Mr. Cortez's lunch with the governor on Monday?" to "Hi, it's Bob in marketing, and I really hate to bother you, but your brother wanted to see my plans for the Wellspring campaign before I submitted the material to the printer." Part of me longed to say, "Do you remember who you're talking to and do you think I even know what the Wellspring campaign is, much less care?" But that wouldn't do, no matter how frayed my nerves.

I had to calm "Bob" down and tell him that if he'd been put in charge of Wellspring, then my family had every faith in his abilities and instincts. And if anyone complained, I would handle it. At this rate, I was going to be responsible for every problem from buying the wrong manufacturing plant in Missouri to a copier paper shortage at the Seattle office.

There were VPs capable of handling these problems, but the absence of the top three men crippled day-to-day operations. Ideally, we'd have declared a period of mourning and shut down Cortez Corporation, giving my father time to recover. But the majority of the company holdings were in the human sector. Telling the world two Cortez brothers had died of unrelated causes in one night would open the door to investigations, by the police, the press and the stockholders.

Somewhere between persuading my father not to kill Carlos and coordinating the stakeout mission of the gang's warehouse, I'd come up with a plausible story. Hector had died of a stroke. William, then, had to hop on the jet and fly to New York to salvage a merger orchestrated by Hector, which might, in the aftermath of his death, fall through. Somewhere between Miami and that meeting late this afternoon, William would suffer a coronary, brought on by his weight, jetlag, grief and worry over the merger. Awkward, but the best I could manage, running on stress and caffeine. So by tonight, the world could know that the Cortez Corporation had suffered a horrible tragedy, and would close operations temporarily to mourn. For today, though, it was all up to me.

Paige came with me back to headquarters. Once there, I moved on autopilot, my brain spewing commands, my body obeying, no time to pause much less think.

Yes, it's a horrible shock. Yes, my father is well, thank you.

No, I'm sorry, but I really can't look at that. No, I'm sorry, but I won't be at that meeting. No, I'm sorry, I don't know who's in charge of the special dispensations department now, but I will find out.

We met the guard I'd requested for Paige. I told him to take her to the research rooms, assign someone to guide her through the system, then stay with her until I joined them.

I said good-bye to Paige. Tried to ignore the worried look in her eyes. Kissed her forehead. Saw her onto the elevator. Caught the next one going down. Pushed "basement" for the morgue.

"Lucas!"

The use of my given name yanked me out of automode, and I grabbed the elevator door before it shut. A young man in a suit was jogging across the lobby. Everyone had turned to stare, but no one tried to stop him. His face was flushed from running, and his shoulder-length blond hair, usually neatly tied in a conservative ponytail, hung around his face.

"Sir?" Griffin said.

I raised my hand, saying it was fine. I let the young man onto the elevator and pushed the basement button again. He panted, his eyes bright from exertion, big and impossibly blue. The trademark Nast eyes. Savannah's eyes.

"Sean."

He clapped me on the shoulder. Griffin tensed.

"I'm so sorry, Lucas. I know you weren't close, but I'm sorry. How's your dad doing?"

"All right."

"And—" He turned to Griffin. "Your partner, right? Troy?"

"He's recovering, thank you, sir." Griffin's response was polite, but had a brittle edge. Nothing against Sean personally, but rather, who he was and what his appearance portended.

"Your grandfather is here, I take it," I said. "And your uncles."

"Yeah. I just ... I wanted to give you a heads-up."

"Because they aren't here to pay their respects."

"Well, they are, technically, but ..."

"But what really concerns them is not my family's tragedy, but what it means for the Cabals. Two Cortez brothers dead, the third ... un-available, the CEO in mourning and the bastard rebel son in charge."

"Um, pretty much."

I swore.

Sean's lips twitched. "I always thought that was the one word you *didn't* know."

"The last twenty-four hours have expanded my vocabulary."

The Nasts would be closely followed by the two other Cabals—the Boyds and the St. Clouds. All of them wanting reassurances that we were still the leader of the Cabal world. All of them ready to whisk the title out from under us if we showed any sign of weakness.

As the elevator touched down, my knees jiggled and, for a moment, it seemed as if the floor was about to vanish beneath my feet. A wave of exhaustion set my hands trembling.

I couldn't deal with this. I was in over my head. Out of my league. Choose your cliché.

This was not my world. I *fought* this world. And now I was being asked to save it from imploding. Everything in me said "let it implode." But if the Cortez Cabal crashed, the institution itself would not disappear. The jackals were already circling, ready to divvy up the corpse.

I stepped from the elevator and made a call upstairs.

"Members of the Nast Corporation will be arriving shortly. Please see that they are shown to the boardroom and served lunch. Have my cousin Javier attend to them during the meal and answer their questions, and I will be there within the hour."

"I'm sorry, Lucas," Sean said when I hung up. I knew he meant it. He might be a Nast, but he was Savannah's half-brother and the only member of her family who acknowledged her, much less attended to her. Over the last few years, his loyalties had shifted away from his family business—he was still a VP, but he was only going through the motions, eyes on the horizon looking for other opportunities.

"Is there anything I can do?" he asked.

I was about to say no, then glanced at the pad of paper still clutched in my hand. "The special dispensations department."

"What about them?"

"Who are they, what do they do and what other department head could I temporarily put in charge?"

He smiled. "Can't promise anything—the Cortez setup might not be exactly the same as ours—but I'll give it a shot."

I CHECKED IN with Paige before meeting the Nasts, an excuse to collect my thoughts. She gave me a brief update. Besides the glamour spell, she'd found only two explanations. Carlos could have been demonically possessed, which would explain why he denied being at the crime scenes. For Guy, the only answer was zombification, which would explain the use of cologne—to cover any stench of death. But a gunshot to the CNS would have meant he wouldn't have been able to walk normally, no matter what a necromancer commanded.

While she returned to her research, I tried to put the pieces together, but they only slid farther apart.

The lab had found no trace evidence to indicate Carlos had been at any crime scene except the one with the young woman. When I finally wrested a story from him, he claimed that he hadn't killed our brothers or attempted to assassinate our father. He'd never even been at Hector's. Nor had he spoken to Troy, much less shot him. Why tell such obvious lies when we had eyewitness accounts?

The death of the young woman was one murder he wasn't denying. He wasn't admitting to it either, but seemed to presume his silence answered my questions. He said she'd been a half-demon he'd met a few times, and that she'd lured him into a trap. I was left to assume that he'd realized he'd been tricked, killed her while trying to extract information under torture and hid when the others came.

If he'd caught a glimpse of whoever came after him, he was keeping it to himself. Suspicious, yes. But knowing Carlos, he'd have panicked, been unable to muster the courage to climb out a window and hidden in the closet using a blur spell. He wasn't about to admit to such cowardice ... even if it might help find his brothers' killers.

There was one piece of evidence that clearly spoke in his favor. The timeline. There was no way he could have traveled to all three locations in the time allotted, demonically possessed or not.

When I looked up from my notes, Paige glanced my way.

"I hate to give you one more thing to do, but have you called your mother?" she asked.

I must have winced, because she hurried on.

"I can do it. I just thought—"

"No, you're right. It should come from me." I really didn't want my mother to hear about the death of my half-brothers on the news.

"Oh, and I spoke to Savannah," Paige said. "She and Adam want to come down and help out."

"I'd rather—"

"They stay put and mind the shop. That's what I told them."

"Thank you."

I picked up the office phone to call my mother—I didn't dare check my cell and see how many voice messages I'd accumulated during my ten-minute recess. Before I dialed more than the area code, I heard "Sir?" and glanced up to see a middle-aged man in the doorway, clutching a file.

"Yes?"

"Warren from the lab, sir. We've never met."

"Warren?"

"Yes, sir. Warren Mills."

Normally I would have asked more, learning something about him, but today, committing his name to memory was the best I could manage.

"You sent down blood and DNA from an apartment. Not the one from last night. This was from..." He glanced at his notes. "Jaz and Sonny?"

"Yes, right."

"I think you need to see this."

HOPE

SCENT MEMORY

We went first to Jaz and Sonny's apartment. Karl didn't explain, but I knew he had to be second-guessing his memory of the scent he'd picked up from Guy and wanted to return here, where we'd seen him two nights ago.

The apartment was as we'd left it.

Karl inhaled. "Someone else has been here."

"I think Paige mentioned Lucas had techs come by and collect samples—DNA, fingerprints..."

He nodded and walked to the sofa where the jacket still lay.

"You said this was Sonny's?"

I nodded.

He sniffed it, and I realized that was why he was here—reacquainting himself with these scents.

"Let me grab you something of Jaz's."

He protested that he could tell Jaz's scent by elimination, but I hurried into the bedroom, eager to be doing something after a morning of following others around.

There were two twin beds in the room, and a laundry basket standing in for a hamper. At least 80 percent of the dirty clothes had made it in.

Lying on top was the shirt Jaz had worn after the sweet sixteen heist. As I lifted it, I saw him again, his eyes dancing with tequila, the fumes on his breath as his lips came toward mine, his hands pressed against my sides, eyes closing, inky lashes curling on his cheeks—

"Is that his?" Karl asked from the door.

I spun, raising the shirt as if to show it off, shielding my face. "It is."

He didn't respond. When I lowered the shirt, he was already gone. I grabbed a knapsack from the open closet, stuffed the shirt inside and hurried out. He put the jacket into a separate pouch, then wordlessly took the bag from me.

WE WALKED TO the car in silence. I fretted that I'd upset him, but he'd been quiet since the morgue. Making a big deal out of it would only confirm that this visit *had* affected me. That I was still thinking of them. Of him.

We were in the car before Karl spoke. "Sonny was at the warehouse."

"Probably. I was too new, but Guy trusted them. He'd have taken them there or sent them for supplies."

"I mean last night. His scent was as strong as the other boys'."

My heart thumped. "Maybe they were keeping him there."

"Maybe."

"Was there any trace of . . . anyone else?"

"Jasper? No." He paused. "I'm sorry."

THE WAREHOUSE WAS on the way to the apartment where Carlos had been found, and Karl wanted to confirm Sonny's presence—now that he had scent samples—and see whether there was a trail.

There was.

We expected it to lead to the street and disappear. Instead, the trail meandered down alleys and back roads. Despite the serpentine route, it was obvious Sonny had a goal in mind, and was detouring around major arteries.

"He doesn't want to be spotted," I said as we walked down a service lane. "Can you tell who he's with?"

"No one."

"He's alone? He must be escaping then."

Karl slowed, then looked over his shoulder at me.

My cheeks warmed. "I know that's not the only explanation, Karl. He could be—" I pushed the admission out. "He could have been at the warehouse of his own free will. He could be working with whoever is behind this. He could have delivered the bottle. I know all that. I just..."

I saw their faces: Bianca, Rodriguez, Max, Tony, Guy. Twenty-four hours, and almost everyone I'd met in the past few days was dead.

"It's just too much. I...need to hope."

He turned, stopping me in my path, and rubbed down the goose bumps on my arms. He leaned closer, and I thought he was going to kiss me, but he just leaned in, his voice lowering.

"I'm going to call Lucas and have them send a guard and a car. You should go to that apartment where they found Carlos, see if you can pick up anything."

"I'll be okay, Karl."

"I think you should—"

"It won't cloud my judgment. I promise."

One last squeeze. As we walked, he snuck glances my way. Looking for signs that he should insist on doing this without me.

The trail ended at a terraced garden, with notices that confetti and rice were prohibited. Presumably a popular wedding photo site.

Sonny's trail led across the gardens to the park beyond, which wasn't huge—maybe a couple of acres—with playground equipment and benches.

We stood in the shadow of a storage shed beside the garden. I wished I'd brought a jacket. A chill wind blew in from the north, and the sun kept ducking behind cloud cover. Miamians, accustomed to better weather, had forsaken the park, all except a single child and her nanny on the swings, and a man slumped on a bench.

I looked at the man. At his size. At his dark blond hair, ruffled by the breeze. My heart picked up speed.

"That looks like Sonny."

Karl crept to the garden railing, his head up, sampling the wind. He stepped back into the shadows with me.

"I think you're right."

The figure had his back to us, and was leaning against the corner of the bench, chin on his chest. "He could be sleeping."

"Possible."

I knew there was a more likely explanation. If Sonny had gone through all that trouble to avoid being seen, he'd hardly nap in a public park.

"I'm going to take a closer look," Karl said. "I need you to stay here, Hope."

"I will."

He glanced my way. "I mean it."

"I know. I'll wait here where I can see him, and if he moves, I'll hit my panic button to warn you."

"Good."

As he moved away, he stopped and looked back. His lips parted, but he shook his head. Before I could say anything, he was gone.

LUCAS

18

"SO WE ANALYZED THE DNA and blood samples." Warren kept his gaze on his notes, clutched in both hands. "Let's start with the DNA. The requisition says it's supposed to be from two magicians. But, well, sir, we didn't find any sorcerer genetic markers."

"They're human?" Paige said.

"Um, we aren't sure." He laid the pages down, his gaze lifting as high as my cheekbones. "We're running more tests. I wasn't comfortable bringing you preliminary results, but I thought..."

"I'd want to know this right away. Yes, thank you. So we have two samples, from possible supernaturals—"

"Probable, sir."

"Probable. Of one or more unknown types—"

"One, I believe. They share over 50 percent of their DNA in common."

"They're brothers?"

Paige pushed her chair back, getting to her feet. "Over 50 percent means *full* brothers, right?" She opened my satchel and took out a file folder. "Then I'd say we somehow got the wrong samples, because genetics can do some wonky things, but there's no way these two guys—" she put the kidnap photo on the table, "—are full brothers."

Beside it, she set the close-ups of their faces that I'd requisitioned from the computer lab. Even if one looked past the obvious coloring and ethnicity differences, there was nothing in the two young men's faces to suggest familial relationship.

"Hey, that's Jason." It was the younger of the researchers. She turned to the other woman and poked a finger at Jaz's picture. "Doesn't that look like Jason?"

The older woman glanced at me first. Only when I nodded did she walk over. She peered at the photo, then, after another glance at me and a reciprocal nod, she picked it up and studied it.

"It looks like him, but the eyes aren't right. Or the mouth. And the hair's curlier."

The younger woman took the photo. "Yeah, I see it. This guy's even hotter than Jason." An embarrassed giggle as she handed the photo back to Paige. "Sorry."

"Who's Jason?" Paige asked.

The younger woman opened her mouth, but her colleague beat her to it. "He worked in the library. Grunt work mainly—running books and reports around, filing them back on the shelves. Then he was transferred to . . ."

"Security division," the younger woman said with a sigh.

The other woman cast a knowing look at Paige. "Some of our younger staff were quite taken with him. Not that it did them any good. A sweet kid, but he kept to himself."

"Do you remember Jason's last name?" Paige asked as she swiveled her chair to the computer behind her.

"Dumas. But he isn't here anymore. He left about six months ago."

Paige paused, the human resources directory on the screen, and looked over at me. I was already on the phone. As I spoke to the HR department, I typed in the proper access codes.

A moment later, Paige was sending a page to the printer. She retrieved it and set it in front of the women.

"Is this the guy you knew as Jason Dumas?"

They nodded. The staff photograph showed a young man, perhaps in his early twenties, with a somber face, dark eyes and dark wavy hair, fashionably long.

This man was not Jaz. But there was little doubt he was a relative. A close one.

I moved the two head shots side by side. "Jasper and Jason."

"Jaz and Sonny," Paige murmured. She picked up the kidnap photo of

Sonny. "But there's no way, even with prosthetics, that this guy could be—" She pulled over her laptop. A minute of frenetic key tapping. "The answer isn't in there—" She waved at the books littering the table. "It's in here."

I moved behind her. On the screen was the interracial council database.

"Armen Haig," she said.

"Armen . . . ?"

"I have to call Elena."

HOPE

TRUTH

I stood as close to the railing as I could get without stepping from the shadows. I caught glimpses of Karl as he circumnavigated the park, approaching from the side opposite the playground. A couple of times he looked my way, even shading his eyes once, and I'd lifted my hand, but I could tell he hadn't seen me. The next time I'd slip into the light just long enough to reassure him. That is, if the sun would cooperate. It had gone dark again and—

"Hello, Faith."

My chest constricted at the voice, but I didn't move. Another auditory hallucination. Being here, seeing Sonny, triggered the memory, the voice, the words.

"You don't answer to that anymore? Hope, then. I think I like Hope better. Nuh-uh. Don't reach into your pockets. Hands up where I can see them, as the cops say."

As I pivoted toward the voice, I kept my eyes half closed. Bracing myself? Or denying the obvious as long as I could? Even through half-lidded eyes, though, there was no mistaking who stood before me, though his curls had been cut to just below his ears and his face was devoid of expression in a way I never imagined it could be.

I licked my lips and swallowed hard, trying to conjure up enough moisture to form words.

"Jaz."

The mask shattered then. He smiled, and it was that same smile I knew, slow and sexy, his eyes lighting up. Jaz.

My chest tightened again and my gaze slid down to his hands. To the gun pointed at me. He pulled it back, as if to hide it.

"Sorry, but I figured you might need a little incentive. And I might need a little protection. You may be tiny, but you're fast."

That jaunty tone was so familiar, so Jaz, that my fists clenched and I wanted to fly at him, to pummel him until I couldn't recognize him. The thought, the hate in it, made my bile rise.

"You're upset. I get that and I don't blame you. So here's what we're going to do. First, hand me your purse."

I did.

"Now, empty your pockets."

As he stepped toward me, my fists flew up, but he caught my arm and yanked me into the shadows.

"Let's back up," he said. "You saw Sonny out there, right? He's not sleeping. He knows exactly where your friend is, courtesy of my play-by-play into his earpiece. Last time I spoke to him, he set his watch for three minutes. If he doesn't hear back from me by then, he's putting a bullet through the werewolf. It's not silver, but I've heard that doesn't matter."

There was no animosity in his voice. No threat. Just Jaz, chattering away as always. Bile filled my mouth. I forced myself to swallow it.

"What do you want me to do?"

"Let me empty your pockets. Don't attack me or run. Then we'll walk that way." He jerked his chin toward the rear of the gardens.

"And then?"

"You're coming with me."

He sounded surprised that I'd needed to ask. As I lifted my hands, he stepped so close I could smell the citrus notes of his aftershave, and feel that low-level thrum of chaos, that aura that always surrounded him, that had drawn me in.

I took a deep breath and let him empty my pockets. When he finished, he paused a mere inch away, and I looked up to see his face over mine. His lips curved in that same almost shy smile that had set my pulse racing. I wanted to spit on him. But if I opened my mouth, I'd probably throw up instead.

I lowered my gaze. "Please, you don't need to do this, Jaz. Or whatever your name is."

"Jaz." His fingers slid under my chin, tilting my face up to his. "It's Jaz."

I looked into his eyes and, for just a second, that chaos sucked me back in. So pure. So absolute. How had I overlooked that? No, not overlooked. Dismissed. Seen what I'd wanted to see.

"Kidnapping me isn't—"

"I'm not kidnapping you." That easy smile. "I'm just taking you along. We have a lot to talk about and this isn't the place to do it."

"They won't care, Jaz. As hostages go, I'm useless. An employee, and an expendable one—"

He tapped his watch. I stopped.

"Sorry," he said. "I probably should have told him longer, but we're on a schedule. If I don't meet it . . ."

An apologetic shrug, as if the consequences of failing to make that call would be nothing more than mildly inconvenient. I glanced over my shoulder. Karl couldn't be more than a few yards from Sonny. Maybe he'd spring in time. Even if he didn't, could Sonny catch him off-guard? Karl already suspected Sonny was no innocent victim. If I—

"Hope." Jaz's fingers closed on my arm. "Fifteen seconds."

I couldn't risk it. I followed Jaz to the mouth of the alley. He took out a radio and told Sonny to hold off.

"Hold off?" I said. "You promised—"

He lifted his hand. "Sonny's going to walk away now and head for the street. We have one minute to meet him at the car. If we don't, he goes back and kills the werewolf."

Not "takes care of him" or "finishes things." Kills him. Blunt and unapologetic.

I let him lead me to the car.

LUCAS

19

PAIGE HAD JUST STARTED HER CALL when my cousin Javier, VP of technology, came to tell me the Nasts were getting impatient...and the St. Clouds had joined them. I checked my watch. I'd said thirty minutes, and it was going on thirty-five.

I caught enough to know Paige was asking Elena about the time she and other supernaturals had been kidnapped and studied by humans. While the Cabals had claimed no knowledge of the project, the Nasts had business ties with the financier—the late software tycoon Tyrone Winsloe—and none of the captives had been Cabal employees. Suspicious, but unrelated to the concern at hand which, from Paige's conversation, seemed to involve another captive, a man named Armen Haig who'd died before the escape.

I longed to stay a few minutes longer, but Paige and the council didn't need me and the Cabal did. A strange twist of priorities. An uncomfortable one.

I interrupted long enough to tell her where I was going, then followed Javier out, making the call to my mother on the way.

The meeting went exactly as I could have predicted. The Nasts and the St. Clouds offered their help in our time of grief. We only had to tell them what we needed. Of course, in telling them, we'd reveal our weaknesses, which is what they really wanted to know. It turned into a thirty-minute mutual reassurance session. *Thank you so much for the kind offer, but we're doing fine. No, really, we're fine. No, I mean it, we're fine.* Thirty minutes with my cell phone vibrating non-stop, messages piling up.

"I'm sorry," I said finally. "But I really do have to get back to the investigation. My father has put me in charge—"

"Of finding your brothers' killers?" Thomas Nast, the CEO, snorted. "Does he *want* the parties responsible found?"

Sean murmured something to his grandfather, who waved him off, making a face. But he didn't continue. Thomas had never been known for his tact, yet he was only saying what the others were thinking.

"Seems your father is putting you in charge of a lot," Thomas's son Josef said. "The Cabals are concerned about that. Investing so much power in someone who'd like nothing more than to see this institution collapse..." He tugged at his tie, clearing his throat. "It has us questioning your father's state of mind, Lucas. He's suffered a great trauma. There are provisions in the inter-Cabal manifest for this sort of thing, should a CEO be incapacitated and no one able to step into his place—"

"Nice try, Josef."

My father's voice came from the doorway. I stood to vacate his chair, but he waved me back down. When I hesitated, I could feel all eyes on me. I sat, but edged the chair to the side, giving him a place to stand at the head of the table.

Condolences filled the room. Any other time, my father would have received them graciously. He was better at this game than anyone. But today he cut them off in midsentence.

"As you can see, I'm not incapacitated. I have placed Lucas in charge of the investigation, using my staff and my resources. I expect when the situation is resolved, you will call an inquest into the proceedings, and I will fully cooperate. As for daily operations, those are also under Lucas for the time being, but all his decisions are being forwarded to me for final approval. Is that acceptable?"

He gave the final word a twist of sarcasm. The younger members shifted in their seats, casting glances at their superiors, who knew enough to remain stone faced.

"It seems you have the short-term situation under control," Thomas said.

My father's hand tightened on my shoulder.

"However," Thomas continued, "it is the long-term one that concerns us more."

"I'm burying two of my sons tomorrow—"

"And I buried one of mine four years ago. My heir. With nary a hiccup in the progress of daily operations."

"Have you felt a hiccup, Thomas? Because if you have, I'd love to know about it."

"We want to know your intentions, Benicio. As regards the naming of your *true* successor."

"You show me yours, I'll show you mine." My father's voice had slid into a faux breezy tone that for anyone who knew him served like a rattler's warning. "Who have you named heir in Kristof's place?"

"I have made my decision—"

"But won't tell a soul, because the truth is, you haven't made any decision." My father circled the table, walking behind the men. "It should be Josef here, who stepped up to the plate after Kristof's death and filled his shoes admirably . . . if incompletely. But you won't make it official because you're still holding out hope for young Sean, who shows every bit of his father's promise but, well, there's that touch of disillusionment settling over the boy. He's not quite sure this is where he wants to be. Not quite sure he believes in the Cabal anymore." My father clamped both hands on Thomas's shoulders and leaned down to whisper, loud enough for us to overhear. "I know what that's like."

He straightened, hands still on the old man's shoulders, fingers digging in.

"While I've enjoyed this chance to air our reciprocal concerns over succession, I have to wonder why the topic was broached at all. I've already named my heir. I did it years ago, as you well know."

I fixed my gaze on my father's chin, expression impassive.

"You can't be serious," Thomas said.

My father smiled. "I've always been serious. Lucas? I believe Paige was looking for you. She has something to share about the case."

When I went to stand, my knees seemed unable to flex, and I had to clasp the edge of the table to push myself up. Stiff-legged, I followed my father from the room.

"I'm sorry," he said as the door closed behind us.

"No need. It was a necessary maneuver. They will hound you for an answer until you give one and this will buy you the time you need to decide on an alternative course of action."

Silence. I didn't look at him. Couldn't.

"Paige *does* want to see you," he said after a minute. "But she's in the lab right now. As we head down, I'd like us to make a few stops. Just walk the floors. Let people see us. Reassure them."

I could scarcely afford the time, but I knew it was necessary. So I let him lead the way.

IT TOOK ALMOST an hour for us to complete the "rounds" . . . and that was with my father pressing forward as firmly but politely as possible. We finished in the cafeteria, where he insisted on buying lunch for me to take to Paige. That took another ten minutes, mostly dealing with more condolences, but he finally got through everyone and took me up the stairs to the executive dining room. It was empty. Not surprising. My father made it clear that he preferred the executives to dine with the employees, and few dared be caught doing otherwise.

"I really have to—" I began.

"Go. I know." He stopped at the window overlooking the cafeteria. "How many people does this office employ, Lucas?"

"Two hundred and forty-five, at last quarterly report."

"And the corporation? Excluding the sectors staffed by humans."

"Approximately four hundred and fifty."

"You know those figures without a second's pause, don't you?"

"I make it my business to know."

A slow nod. "Four hundred and fifty oppressed souls in need of rescue."

My jaw tightened. "Did you bring me up here to mock me, Father? Because I have—"

"—more important things to do."

I forced myself to look at him. "I don't see four hundred and fifty oppressed souls in need of rescue, but you know that. I see four hundred and fifty supernaturals employed by an organization that does not always have their best interests in mind."

"Because human corporations do," he murmured.

"Human corporations don't hunt down and execute former employees. Or torture those accused of corporate espionage. Or threaten the families of those suspected of espionage. Or use blackmail as a recruiting tool. Or—"

He held up a hand. "Point taken."

"Did I really need to make it?"

For a moment, he gazed out the window, watching his employees eat and talk.

"Of the Cabals, how do the Cortezes rank? In terms of 'human rights abuses'?"

"I won't answer that because you know the answer full well. To commend your standing is like praising a man who only beats his wife on Sundays."

"If this Cabal collapsed, where do you think these people would go? They're caged birds, Lucas. You don't just open the door and set them free. That would be a cruelty beyond anything you accuse us of. If the Cortez Cabal disappears, they will fly to the nearest place of shelter, to another Cabal, a worse—"

"Don't." The tray's edge dug into my thumb, and I realized I was still holding it—clutching it—and set it down. "This isn't the time—"

"No, it isn't. But it will soon be the time—"

"Carlos is alive—and probably innocent. Then there are my cousins..." I heard the desperation in my voice and cleared my throat. "There will be no need for you to make any determination for years to come."

"No? If the last few days have proven anything, it's that I don't have that time. We are going to need to talk about this."

I turned to him. "Please, Papá. Not now."

"When, Lucas? Tell me when I have to do this to you? Shatter your dreams? Make you become someone you should never have to be? Tell you it's your *duty*?" His voice caught. "When do I do this? Gain my heir and lose my son?"

"Not now. Please. I have—" My throat seized up and I had to force the words out. "I have to go."

HOPE

BIOLOGY IS DESTINY

Had I ever envisioned myself in this situation—taken hostage and being led to a car—I'd have foreseen my mind flying ahead at warp speed, eyes darting around, trying to find an opportunity to escape or at least to call public attention to myself.

But I just walked. Focused on putting one foot in front of the other.

Jaz strolled beside me, his arm in mine, chattering away. The gun was in his pocket. It didn't matter. The other gun—the one Sonny had for Karl—was more important. There are risks you'll take for yourself because you know that if your plan goes wrong, it'll be too late for regrets. But if you risk the lives of others and fail, you'll have a lifetime to regret it.

Jaz's plan rested on the presumption that Karl would have circled back for me rather than follow Sonny. I wasn't so sure. He could be tracking Sonny right now to our rendezvous point where he'd have a chance to—

"Here we are."

I teetered on the curb, and his hand yanked me back, jerking me from my thoughts. We were standing on a busy corner with no parking along either street.

"Where's the car?"

"There's one." He pointed at a truck zooming past. "And there's another, and another." He slanted a sidelong glance my way, as if honestly expecting me to appreciate the joke. "Oh, you mean *our* car. Let's see..."

He looked around, then leaned out and snapped his fingers. "Taxi."

A blue compact steered out of the line of traffic and pulled to the curb. Sonny sat in the driver's seat.

Jaz pulled open the back door. When I balked, he prodded me.

"Come on, Hope. It's a no-stopping zone."

I locked my knees and scanned the sidewalk, hoping...

"Jaz." Sonny's voice. Sharp.

"No problem, bro. Now, Hope, don't—"

He grabbed me around the waist, catching me off guard. I twisted, but he was already folding me inside. The back of my head smacked into the roof and I let out a yelp, louder than the tap warranted. No one around us even paused. A drama queen, making a big deal out of a knock on the head. And if my boyfriend seemed a bit rough? Not their business.

As I hit the seat, I scrambled around, hands balling into fists, Jaz's gun pointed at me.

"Hope. Please."

I considered my options and saw none I liked.

In the front seat, Sonny grabbed his hair and pulled it off. A wig. He tossed it onto the seat and ran his hands through his hair—dark and wavy.

The light ahead turned yellow. Sonny slowed, earning a honk from the driver behind. As we waited, he rubbed his hands over his face, brisk and hard, as if he had indeed been sleeping. I glanced at Jaz, but he was looking out the side window.

The car started forward again. Gripping the wheel were hands as dark as Jaz's. I blinked and looked out the window, expected to see the sun gone again, but it still blazed brightly.

I strained to get a look at Sonny in the mirror. For a moment, I saw nothing. Then he moved and I bit back a gasp. It looked like Jaz's face in the mirror. At the next light, he turned, and I saw that the dark eyes weren't as deep-set as Jaz's, the lips fuller, mouth not as wide, the face thinner, and somber in a way that was as "Sonny" as Jaz's infectious grin was him.

"Hope, meet Jason," Jaz said, startling me. "My little brother. He prefers Sonny, though, so you can stick with that."

Sonny raked his fingers through his hair again. "I hate it when it's this short. And I swear it feels like straw. Dye it blond. Dye it back. Can't be good."

"Bitch, bitch, bitch. It's going to be a *lot* shorter soon."

"Don't remind me."

Jaz looked at me. "Hair's a problem. Small changes in color, texture, length, we can manage. Otherwise, it's dye and wigs. Build is even worse. Again, small changes only. Lifts, posture, clothing, it can only do so much. If a guy is five foot eight? Six foot four? Forget it. Luckily, people aren't that observant. If you're off by an inch or ten pounds, no one notices."

All this he relayed as conversationally as he'd tell me how he got to work each morning. When he finished, he eased back in his seat and scratched his jaw, gaze slanted my way, expectant.

He did it. *They* did. Killed them. Their gang. Their friends. And now he sat here, chattering away, same old Jaz.

As I listened to him, the bile threatened to return. I sat as still as I could, ignoring his hopeful glances.

He adjusted his seat belt. Squirmed in his seat. Tapped his fingers against his leg. Once he reached over as if to touch me, then pulled back.

He wanted me to ask questions. He wanted to tell me more. I was disappointing him.

Good.

If I could push him far enough, maybe I'd piss him off. Then the mask would crack and I'd see what lurked beneath. I knew that wasn't safe—I should be mollifying him, not thwarting him. But I couldn't help it. I needed to see the monster. I needed to stop seeing Jaz.

"Glasses?" Sonny said after a few minutes.

"Oh, right."

Jaz reached under the seat and pulled out a bag. Inside were oversized dark sunglasses with side pieces. He handed them to me.

"Put them on, please."

And what if I don't, I thought.

But common sense won out and I took the glasses. I'd play the game while I looked for my chance to escape.

No, not escape. If I ran away, we'd lose them. If they could do what I'd just seen—a supernatural power, not a trick or disguise—

then they could hide anywhere, as anyone. I had to stay with them until I could get help.

I put on the glasses and the world went dark.

"WATCH YOUR STEP."

Jaz took my arm. I resisted the urge to shake him off and let him guide me up three steps. The glasses were blacked out on the inside, as effective as a blindfold.

The click of metal on metal. Keys. Or lock picks. Jaz's thumb beat a tattoo on my upper arm as we waited. I caught a whiff of garbage left in the sun too long. The pressure of Jaz's fingers on my arm warned me we were about to move, then, "Okay, one more step up."

I presumed we were at a hideout until I walked through the doorway and a wave of chaos memory hit. The crack of buckling metal, as a figure leapt onto a car hood. The stink of burning streamers. The flash of a demonic dog's head rearing up in a doorway.

"The banquet hall," I murmured.

"You're good." Excitement crept into his voice as his fingers tightened. "What do you see?"

I shook my head. He led me forward at least twenty feet.

"If I know where I am, I can take off the glasses, can't I?"

"Not yet."

He stopped. The chaos in the air seemed brittle. Tension. A moment of silence, then Jaz broke it with a small cough.

"I'll..." he began.

"Take it from here," Sonny said.

"Yeah."

Strain tightened Jaz's voice. All traces of excitement gone. Cold fingers of dread crept up my spine. I desperately sent out feelers, but I couldn't read him. I never could. It was as if his nonstop chaos vibe interfered.

"Guard the door, okay, bro?" he said. "I'll be down after I... take care of this."

Take care of it?

I wheeled, fists lashing out in the direction of his voice. One made contact. Jaz gasped. Blind, I kept turning, veering toward the door, hand flying up to wrench off the glasses—

Cold metal pressed into the base of my skull.

"Stop, Faith."

It was Sonny, his voice as cold as the gun barrel. I pictured Guy on the gurney. Heard Dr. Aberquero's voice: "Single gunshot to the base of the skull, through the central nervous system." To my shame, I let out the first note of a whimper.

He withdrew the gun. "Go with Jaz."

As Jaz led me away, I kept hearing his words: *I'll take care of this.* I felt myself move across the room, up the stairs, his hand on my elbow, heard his murmured directions, but none of it seemed real, as I floated, numb.

Get him away from Sonny. That was the key. Away from Sonny...

"Duck your head. It's a low opening." He chuckled. "Even for you."

The smell of stale cigarette smoke hit me and even before he tugged off my glasses I knew I was in the room where we'd waited for the heist to begin.

"Remember this?" He backed up and waved at the spy hole. "Us? Watching the party?"

He took my hand and sat cross-legged, pulling me down in front of him. My gaze ran over him, looking for the gun. I needed to know where it was before—

"Do you still have the watch I gave you?"

He had to repeat himself before I understood, and even then I didn't understand. Didn't know what possible significance it could have to this moment. I shook my head.

"That's okay. It's probably at your apartment. We'll get it when all this is over."

We'll get it? As in him and Sonny? Retrieve the valuables after he "finished this"?

"Remember when you first came to the club?" he said. "Sonny and I heard the new recruit might be an Expisco and we thought 'Oh, shit.' Definitely not good for our plans. When I went to that door, we'd already decided how we'd get rid of you. But then I opened it and...bam."

He grinned. "One split-second and everything changed. Of course, Sonny wasn't too happy, but he came around when he saw how useful you could be."

"Useful?"

He squeezed my hand, then uncrossed and recrossed his legs. "Yeah, that doesn't sound good, but that's how Sonny is. The practical one. I'm the dreamer, he's the doer. It's..." His pupils dilated and his color rose, and he looked like he had that night after the heist. Drunk on adrenaline and tequila. "I can't even begin to explain it, Hope. Sonny and me—we can do anything. And now, with you, it's only going to get better."

I should be relieved—he wasn't going to kill me—but I could only stare at him. He squeezed my hand hard enough to hurt, apologized, rubbed his thumb across my knuckles, then uncrossed and recrossed his legs again, as if he couldn't sit still. His face glowed and I swore I could see a barrage of thoughts ping-ponging around behind his eyes as he struggled to release them in some semblance of order.

Another hand squeeze, pulling himself closer with the motion. "You'll see, Hope. You'll see. And when you do..."

His eyes rolled back, pure bliss, the tip of his tongue sliding between his teeth. Even through my fear, I felt the waves of chaos rolling off him, that pure chaos, so intense that for a moment, I just wanted to let go, to share that high.

I slid back and disengaged my hand from his.

He sighed. "Yeah, I know. You're not too happy with me right now. You liked them. Hell, *I* liked them. Guy, Rodriguez, Tony, Max. Even Bianca wasn't so bad. But there wasn't any other way, Hope. You'll see that soon. You can't worry about other people. They'd do the same to you. You can't let anything block you from your goal."

Another shift, this time stretching his legs, letting them rest against me. "Sonny and I, we've been given a gift. To not use that gift would be wrong. You have one too—something that makes you better than any Cabal sorcerer. So why should you work for them? Grovel to them? Why should they hold all the power? Biology is destiny, Hope. It's time for you to seize your destiny."

I could only stare at him, searching his eyes for the fever of madness. What glowed from his face was the fervor of conviction. Was it the same thing?

"You killed Bianca, didn't you?" I said finally. "It was you, in the hall. You impersonated that Cabal guard—the one you claimed robbed you. You killed him and the other one, staged their homes and 'became them' to kill Bianca."

A soft sigh. "It wasn't supposed to go down like that. I leaked Guy the identity of the guard, thinking he'd take me for the break-in and I'd show them evidence to prove the Cabal was a threat. But he cut Sonny and me out. Fortunately, we had a backup plan."

"Killing Guy and impersonating him."

"Oh, *that* was always part of the plan. Had to be. It didn't work any other way."

"You were Guy that night, in your apartment. It was Sonny the first time—taking me there to point out the evidence that you'd both been kidnapped, so I'd support the story for the others. But later, when I went back, you're the one who showed up as Guy."

He smacked his open palms on his thighs, setting his whole body rocking. "Yes! You knew it."

"I didn't—"

"No, no, you didn't understand it, but you knew it. See, that's what Sonny was afraid of. When we saw you and the werewolf in the apartment—there's a camera, got it from Rodriguez with some other stuff, such a sweet kid, I really hated..."

His voice trailed off, then he smacked his palms on the floor, so hard I jumped. "Gotta be done, right? First thing you learn. You *cannot* hesitate. Anyway, the camera. We see you and your friend..."

Again, he faded. His gaze jumped to mine. "He's in love with you, you know. Useless, of course. He has no idea what you need. Anyway, we figured out what he was when he waltzed out as a wolf. Cool trick."

He said it with a mix of admiration and condescension, the way one might praise a child who's learned a simple magic trick.

"So we see him and you and we figured out you weren't who you said you were. Sonny thought you might be a threat. He wanted to get in there, suss out the situation, grab you or..." His fingers tapped against his knee. "Or something. I convinced him to let me go in as Guy, get you away from the werewolf and kidnap you if I had to, so you wouldn't get hurt. Sonny didn't want me doing it 'cause he thought you'd recognize me. But I knew it would be okay. You wouldn't understand what was going on, but still, I knew you'd know it was me. Deep down, you'd know."

He rubbed his hand over his mouth as if trying to wipe away his grin. His eyes danced.

"Remember that night on the building?" he said. "You understood *that*. What I was saying. About the Cabals. That's what I'm talking about. What all this is about."

"It wasn't Guy selling you on his theories, was it? You weren't listening to him; he was listening to you."

"Sure, but I let him pretend it was his idea." He flashed me a grin. "That's the key to working with people like Guy. The seed's already there. You just need to water it, nurture it, let them think it's all about them, their ideas and then—" He shook his head. "We can talk about that another time. We'll talk about a lot. But right now, I need a favor."

"Favor?"

"Something I promised Sonny I'd talk you into doing. A show of your loyalty." He lifted his hands before I could speak. "I know, I know, I haven't won you over. Far from it. But Sonny needs this reassurance now. And you'll see this is the best way to do it anyway. The least..." A wrinkle of his nose. "Messy. We've had too much of that shit now, and Sonny would rather do it this way. So would I and, I'm sure, so would you."

"What is it?"

"We need you to call Paige Cort— Shit. Winterbourne." He rocked back with an exaggerated wince. "I gotta remember that. Anyway, your werewolf friend will know you're with us, so now you're going to call Paige and tell her you've made a big mistake. You'll say you came along with me willingly, but you didn't realize what you were getting into, yadda, yadda. Now you want out, but you're scared of Lucas and the Cabal, so you want your council boss Paige to mediate, 'cause everyone knows she's good at stuff like that. You tell her you want to talk to her. You'll set up a meeting for tonight."

My mouth hardened. "So you can kill her? I will not—"

"No, no, see, that's what I mean about messy. All we want to do is kidnap her. The idea with Carlos only took us halfway, and now he's a write-off, so we need to move to plan B."

"Which is...?"

"Lucas, of course."

LUCAS

20

ARMEN HAIG. The human chameleon. That's what Elena said they'd called him in the compound. He could alter his facial features, not much, just enough to be unrecognizable. The parapsychologist at the compound had postulated—accurately, it would seem—that Haig was a forerunner of a new supernatural race. He'd also hypothesized that in a few generations, Haig's descendants might not only be able to change their features enough to escape a police officer, but to kill that officer, *become* him and walk away undetected.

Elena had recalled that statement with a rueful laugh, because she could imagine few people less likely to need to evade the police than Armen Haig. A quiet and thoughtful psychiatrist, he'd been biding his time, planning his escape and trying to decide whether he could trust Elena enough to accept her help. Then the man financing the operation, Tyrone Winsloe, played one of his sadistic games—the sort that made Carlos look like an amateur.

He'd told Elena that Armen had escaped and tried to force her to hunt him. When she'd discovered it was a setup, he'd given her an ultimatum—hunt and kill Haig or be killed. Haig had saved her from making the choice by killing himself. The ultimate act of selflessness, committed for a stranger.

Apparently genetics was the only thing that ran in the family.

There was little doubt Jaz and Sonny had killed my brothers and exterminated their own gang to cover their tracks, just as there was little doubt they'd fulfilled that parapsychologist's prophecy. They could become someone else.

There was no mention of the Haigs in the corporate files, but the Cabal had access to public, and private, records in the human world, with a search system that impressed even Paige. We found Armen Haig easily. He'd disappeared in the summer of 2000. Missing. Presumed dead.

We also found Jasper and Jason Haig. Born 1980 and 1981 respectively. Mother: Crystal Haig, niece of Armen. The boys shared a father, identity unknown, but from the DNA profiles, the lab suspected he'd been Crystal's close relative. The third generation of a supernatural mutation, with both parents in the same bloodline, further accelerating development.

When the boys were preschoolers, their mother had started traveling and hadn't stopped until her death, after a stint in a mental institution. Her records showed a diagnosis of paranoid schizophrenia. She'd had one overwhelming delusion—that her sons, who she claimed had "superpowers," were continually threatened by shadowy organizations known as "cabals," which wanted to kidnap and experiment on them, like they had her uncle.

There was no indication the Cabals knew anything about Crystal or her sons. But if they had, her fears would have been well grounded. The Cabals fought bitterly for custody of rare supernaturals. For a new mutation like this? They'd have destroyed everything—and everyone—in their path to get these boys. The fact that they *hadn't* only proved they'd known nothing about them.

What stories had Crystal told her boys? What hatred of the Cabals had she instilled in them? It didn't matter. Whatever environmental factors had gone into creating Jasper and Jason Haig, they weren't children anymore. They were brilliant and ruthless killers, able to take on the form of anyone. A threat unlike any we'd ever seen.

I was working through the implications with Paige when a commotion sounded in the hall. I opened the door to see Karl striding down the corridor, smacking an open palm into the chest of a guard who stepped into his path. Griffin tried to elbow past, but I blocked him.

"Why the hell aren't you answering your cell phone?" Karl snarled, advancing on me.

"My cell—?" I pulled it out and saw the ringer was still turned off from earlier.

"Where's Hope?" Paige asked.

"That's what I was calling about." He planted himself in front of me, lips parted, teeth showing. "They took her."

JASPER AND JASON had kidnapped Hope. It was easier to think of them that way, to divorce them from the image I'd already formed of "Jaz and Sonny"—harmless young men who'd been unwitting pawns in a battle between the gang and the Cabal.

Karl had been tracking Jason. As for how or why, he wasn't about to waste time on explanations. He'd left Hope behind, and when Jason got into a car in a crowded lot, he'd noted the license and make, then hurried back for her. She was gone, and the spot where he'd left her had been rife with Jasper's scent.

Karl's black mood only darkened when he realized this revelation—that Jasper and Jason were alive, and coconspirators—did not surprise us.

Griffin said, "So Hope left with this guy and you know she was kidnapped because . . ."

"Because I know Hope."

"Are you sure?"

Karl swung on Griffin. Griffin's cheek twitched—the "tell" that he was activating his armor.

"There are other reasons Hope might go with Jasper," Paige said.

Karl stiffened, and I knew Paige had been right about the nature of Hope's developing relationship with Jasper Haig.

"She wouldn't," Karl said.

"What I meant is that she might have seen him and followed for a better look. Or maybe he approached her claiming he needed help and, still believing he'd been kidnapped, she went with him. Or maybe she realized he was behind this, and thought playing along was the best way to stop him."

"She wouldn't be that stupid."

Paige flushed and I knew she was thinking of the times she'd done something "that stupid" trying to stop a crime.

She hurried on. "Whatever the reason, she's with him and we need to find them."

"No one's even going to bring it up, are they?" Griffin said. "Maybe he—" a thumb jab at Karl, "—doesn't see it, but we can't go rushing in to rescue the girl without considering that she might not want to be rescued. Or that it's a trap."

"Hope isn't involved," I said. "Now, we need to make a list—"

Griffin strode in front of me. "Did you ever hear what happened with Dean Princeton, Lucas?"

"Yes, I did."

"So you know? And that doesn't change anything?"

"No, it does not."

"Who's Dean Princeton?" Paige asked.

"It's not imp—" I began.

"Expisco half-demon," Griffin cut in. "The only one who's ever worked for a Cabal. When he was Hope's age, maybe a few years younger, he was the nicest kid. Wanted to be a bodyguard, but everyone told him he wasn't tough enough. He worked at it, though. Took a job in security. Got promoted to backup guard for Lionel St. Cloud. Then they started finding the bodies."

"Dean Princeton has nothing to do with Hope Adams," I said. "And to draw an analogy based on racial type is nothing short of prejudice. You cannot—"

"His racial type is what turned him into a killer! Are you saying that's not relevant? Hope Adams is Lucifer's daughter. She's a chaos demon. Did you actually read the reports on Princeton, Lucas? Did you see what he did to those people? Hear all the witnesses testify about what a sweet kid he'd been once? Maybe you're right, maybe this girl's demon is still sleeping, but it's going to wake up, and I'm not sure we should be in such an almighty rush to save—"

The last words were a strangled cough. Karl had Griffin by the throat.

"Hope is not Dean Princeton," Karl said, his voice barely above a whisper. "I could trot out twenty man-eating werewolves for you. Does that mean all werewolves should be killed at birth...just in case? Where Hope is concerned, you stay clear. You don't spread your stories about Dean Princeton, especially to her. If you don't want to help find her, then don't. But I'm going to and you won't stop me."

"*We're* going to help you," Paige said, laying her fingertips on Karl's arm. "He's thinking of us, not Hope, and we understand that. It doesn't change—"

A cell phone ring. I murmured an apology, then realized it was Paige's.

She frowned at the display. "A pay phone? Probably a wrong number. I'll take this outside."

HOPE

VISIONS OF MADNESS

Joan of Arc saw visions of God. Believing she was the messenger of the Almighty she mustered the will and the passion to rally the French against the English invaders. Touched by God? Or by madness? History is filled with tales of visionary madmen, and I had no doubt Jaz was mad, with a fire that burned through self-doubt and moral qualms.

A few days ago, I'd reflected on that impulsive side of Jaz, how he pursued what he desired without fear. I'd chalked it up to a charming lack of self-doubt and self-consciousness. It was a lack of something all right . . .

Listening to Jaz, I remembered those moments in Benicio's panic room, where I'd been unable to comprehend that Troy's death would be wrong. I'd wanted it. It would serve me. Therefore, it should be.

The demon in its purest form. Ego ruled by id. That was Jaz.

I remembered too my thoughts on first walking into his apartment. I'd reflected on how his cheerful, impulsive nature was kept in check by cold sense, leading him to save money while he had it. That observation, too, came back to haunt me now.

For most people, that lack of self-doubt and conscience would be their undoing. The first time their goal exceeded their reach, they'd do something foolish and die pursuing their mad dreams. But not Jaz. He was crazy enough to hatch impossibly grandiose, destructive schemes and brilliant enough to carry them through. And if he went too far? He had Sonny to pull him back in line.

This hadn't been the slapdash plan of two brazen young supernaturals. They'd been plotting this for years, taking a job at the Cabal and studying Carlos—the brother least likely to succeed, but the one they could best impersonate. Then they'd infiltrated the gang, seducing Guy with Jaz's wild visions, swaying them into allies and, finally, into tools to execute their plans.

Kill the most prominent members of the Cortez Cabal family, then take the place of the remaining one?

Madness.

What if Benicio hadn't planted me in the gang? What if Karl hadn't called in Lucas? Would Jaz and Sonny have still failed? Even in failure, they'd achieved half their goal, and had a backup plan for the remainder.

Brilliant madness.

Lucas was their new target. They'd kill him, impersonate him and find Carlos guilty of the murder of his brothers. Then they'd let Benicio hand over Cabal power to his beloved youngest son, as Lucas "saw the light" and renounced his former crusade. When the transition was solidified, the old man would die in his sleep.

Lucas was as good a target as Carlos—maybe even better. His age, coloring and physical size were closer to Jaz and Sonny's. Add lifts in their shoes for a few weeks until people wouldn't notice the difference. Wear looser suits until they could lose some weight—or have Lucas bulk up. An easy transformation.

Like Carlos, Lucas would be expected to know little about the inner workings of the Cabal, so no one would question his ignorance. He was even more an outsider than his brother, and far less known in the Cabal, making him easier to impersonate.

The only sticking point was Paige.

They couldn't fool her. So, wisely, they wouldn't try. They'd kidnap her and keep her out of the way while "Lucas" took over the Cabal. In the meantime, he'd continue searching doggedly for his wife—suitably heroic and sentimental. By the time he found her, she'd notice he wasn't himself, but her protests would be chalked up to post-traumatic stress. Besides, he *had* changed—she'd left "Lucas Cortez: Cabal-fighter" and returned to "Lucas Cortez: Cabal leader."

Whatever Paige's reaction, Jaz assured me the path was predetermined. Divorce.

"Irreconcilable differences. Completely understandable under the circumstances. She'll get a nice settlement, and I'll be free to marry you." He grinned. "It'll be perfect. Lucas and Paige, estranged by tragedy and circumstance, parting civilly, and then, after a suitable period, who does he turn to? The beautiful half-demon who helped him find his wife, catch his brothers' killer and save his father, then stood by his side through it all. A fairy-tale ending."

The only thing left was for me to call Paige. And I would, because here was the fatal flaw in Jaz's plan.

Two years ago, when I thought I'd been working for the council, I'd pictured them as a powerful group overseeing perhaps dozens of field agents. That was the perception many supernaturals had . . . and one the council knew better than to dispute, because it was far more intimidating than the truth: the delegates did all the work themselves. Jaz had heard enough of my conversation with Karl that night in the apartment to figure out I worked for the council. So, to him, I was one of that presumably vast network of operatives.

If that were true, and Paige knew me only as an employee, then the story he'd concocted seemed plausible enough. I'd been seduced into Jaz and Sonny's scheme by my demon side, but now my real nature was asserting itself and I wanted to make amends. The person I'd naturally turn to was the one outside the Cabal. The one who was powerful in her own right. And the one with a reputation for being unrelentingly fair and merciful.

Had I really considered betraying the Cabal, then changed my mind, Paige was indeed the one I'd turn to. And she would help me . . . if she believed me capable of such a thing. Between Paige and Karl, they'd know this was a trap. She'd never accept my invitation at face value and show up alone. No matter how careful Jaz and Sonny were, they were only two men. No match for a Cabal SWAT team.

So I called.

"CAN YOU FEEL it?"

We stood in an office building alcove, tucked into the shadows. Jaz moved behind me and put his hands on my hips, leaning against my back. When I stiffened, he only chuckled and bent to kiss my neck.

"Not so fast, huh?" He rubbed my hips. "That wasn't a problem before. We both felt it. Fast wasn't nearly fast enough. It was like..."

He rested his chin on the top of my head. "I can't even describe what it was like. I'm at a loss for words. Can you believe that? It'll be like that again, Hope. I know, right now, you're probably thinking 'fat chance, you son-of-a-bitch,' but you'll see. We'll pull this off and I'll serve you the Cortez Cabal on a platter." His arms slid around me. "Yours, mine and Sonny's. All the power you've ever wanted. All the power you deserve. It'll be..." A shiver ran through him. "Perfect."

For just a moment, feeling that rising lick of chaos, I saw his dream glittering before me.

He was right. We did have something. I was a half-demon starving for chaos, and he was a chaos feast. Maybe if I was what I feared I was, I'd hear the rumble in my belly, urging me to partake.

I did feel a rumble, but it was only my stomach churning. Minutes to go. Could I pull this off? I had to.

I glanced around, searching the shadows alongside every darkened building. Looking for Karl, even as I hoped he wouldn't risk coming so close.

Paige had agreed to meet me. She'd been smart enough not to give anything away on the phone, in case Jaz or Sonny was listening, just like she'd been smart enough not to press for details. But I could tell by her tone that she understood.

And so, as we waited for her, the Cabal SWAT team would be taking up position two blocks away, near the meeting site.

Jaz gave another low laugh, and his fingers traced a line under my left breast. "You *do* feel it. Your heart's racing."

His voice dropped, breathing accelerating as his fingers slid over my breast. He squeezed my nipple. I wrenched out of his grasp and wheeled. He backed up, hands raised, palms out.

"Sorry, sorry. I didn't mean that, Hope. I'll never— I won't push. I swear it. I just..."

His gaze traveled down me, eyelids half closing as his lips parted. Then a sharp, full-body shake.

"Damn, damn, damn. We were so close. It would have made a dif-

ference. I know it would have. I wanted you so badly and you—"
Another shake, harder, then a roll of his shoulders. "Okay, okay. Not
the time, I know. Right now, we need to ..."

His lips pursed as if he'd lost his train of thought.

"I need to meet Paige in five minutes," I said.

"Duh, yes. Sorry. Let's get moving."

I WAS SUPPOSED to meet her at a parking lot. From there, we'd walk
to a newly opened club a block away. This area of downtown Miami
was peppered with office towers and didn't see much of a nightlife.
Scores of lights illuminated every building, but the sidewalks and
roads were nearly empty, giving the street an eerie, deserted look. I
shivered and blamed the cooler night air. The Metromover whirred
past, making me jump.

As we approached the parking lot, Jaz spoke. "So you're okay
with the plan, right?"

"Meet her out front and cut down the laneway to the east. If she
balks at taking the service road, circle the block and you'll grab her
from the other end of the lane."

"Good, good."

Another half-block, then he laid his hand on my arm. "Don't do
anything stupid, okay, Hope?"

"I'm not—"

He stepped in front and lowered his face closer to mine. Worry
creased a line between his eyes. "I mean it. Please, please, please, don't
screw this up. I made a deal with Sonny. He's not happy about bringing
you in, but I swore you'd be smart, and if you aren't ..." He rubbed his
throat and cleared it. "Just don't. Please, Hope. Sonny will have you
guys covered the whole time. If he sees anything go wrong—you devi-
ate from the plan, Paige takes out her cell phone ... He's a crack shot."

"I know."

He nodded, squeezed my arm, then sent me on my way.

RIGHT ON SCHEDULE, Paige emerged from the dark depths of the lot. As
she approached, her gaze tripped along the street. Every few seconds,
a car passed, more when the lights two blocks down changed. Across

the road, a couple walked, presumably heading to the club. Jaz had been meticulous choosing this location. Empty enough to avoid witnesses. Busy enough that it wouldn't spook her.

I'd worried whether the parking lot itself would be a problem. It was almost empty, and only sprinkled with lights, as if they didn't do enough business after dark to warrant more. For a guy, not a problem. A woman might think differently.

Paige blinked as she stepped from the shadows and the streetlights hit her.

"I hope you locked your car," I called as she approached.

She started and pulled up short. Lost in her thoughts?

"Your car," I said. "Did you lock it?"

"Um, right. Yes."

Her voice was pitched higher than her usual contralto and her gaze kept darting along the road. Nervous, and not doing a very good job of hiding it. I told myself I was projecting my own tension on her. But as she drew closer, I could feel her anxiety, the chaos tickling along my nerves. I caught snippets of her thoughts. Random worries that she was making a mistake, that she never should have agreed.

I longed to lean closer and whisper reassurances, but Sonny was out there, watching. I had to play this cool. Especially if she wasn't.

"The club's this way," I said.

She fell into step beside me. I pointed out the couple across the road, commenting on their clothes. She said little. I yammered on, filling the dead air, hoping to calm her. Ahead, the couple crossed the road and went down the side street. We were approaching the service road.

"Bet that's a shortcut," I said. "Let's take it."

She didn't resist and I didn't expect her to. Getting off the street would give the Cabal team a chance to swoop in.

We started down the narrow road. It was dimly lit, but not dark. Paige walked briskly, with renewed confidence. The end was in sight, her nervousness fading. It seemed, though, as if I'd caught it. Sweat beaded along my lip.

I focused on the door ahead.

It was about eighty feet away now. I knew it should be cracked open, but from here it was impossible to see.

When I got closer, I was supposed to steer her that way, then as we passed, Jaz would throw open the door, grab Paige, then grab me. He'd pull us both inside and throw me aside. I'd pretend to hit my head and pass out. That was critical to his plan—that Paige have no idea I was involved, so she couldn't finger me later. I had to be a co-victim until Lucas was dead and I could be "freed" while Paige remained a captive.

None of that, though, would ever come to pass, because between here and there, I had every expectation of rescue. Would they come while we were still in the lane? Or wait until Jaz pulled us inside? Either way—

Something moved to my right, the blur of a figure seeming to leap from the wall itself. I swallowed a yelp and wheeled, expecting to see a tactical team member rappelling down from the roof.

Instead, I saw an open door and a dark figure within it. Paige shrieked. Fingers clamped down on my arm. I opened my mouth to tell my rescuer that Jaz was farther down, waiting. But it was Jaz standing there. Holding me.

Paige gibbered in fear, and I had an insane urge to shout at her to stop because I couldn't think with her chaos waves so strong, and I needed to think, but the moment I *could* think, I realized that help wasn't coming, that she wouldn't be screeching and clawing at Jaz if it was.

He flung me into a tiny room, his arm flying up as if with the momentum of the throw, but it was little more than a shove. As I stumbled, I remembered the plan. My first thought was "to hell with the plan." But before I could catch my balance, I realized I'd be a fool not to play along.

So I let myself fall, my head hitting the concrete floor hard enough to knock Paige's chaos waves from my head. When I closed my eyes, though, they returned, washing over me, and I let them dull the fear, whet my senses.

Across the room, Paige's cries had fallen to stifled whimpers. Jaz was talking to her, his voice low and soothing.

"I'm not going to hurt you," he said. "I need you, Paige. Think about it. You're no good to me as a hostage if you aren't healthy."

I cracked open my eyes. Paige had her back to the far wall, pressed against it, Jaz holding her forearms, but standing far enough away not to spook her.

She'd gone still. Lulling him before she cast a spell? I thought about getting her attention, but if she looked my way, so would Jaz. Better for him to forget I was here...

I measured the distance to him. Could he see me from this angle? I wasn't sure. I couldn't risk it.

I needed to move fast and bring him down so Paige could cast her binding spell. As I drew my legs in, preparing to spring, Jaz crouched, pulling Paige lower until she was sitting on the floor.

"Okay, now you wait here. I'm going to check on Hope."

I half closed my eyes. He started to turn. I quickly caught Paige's attention and mouthed "cast!" Her brow furrowed.

Cast. Cast, damn you! Why aren't you—?

He moved again and I shut my eyes, then cracked them open. He had his back to me. His hand was under his jacket. I saw that, and I knew.

I flew to my feet and ran at him. I saw the gun. An explosion of terror, almost knocking me off my feet. Beautiful terror. Sweet and pure chaos. So perfect...

He raised the gun.

No!

I clamped down on my lip and the burst of pain wrenched my thoughts free. I threw myself at Jaz. I hit him. The gun fired. And then, as we hit the floor, I felt it. A second chaos blast, this one so strong I blacked out.

The waves rocked me and that was all I could think about, all I could feel. And that was okay, because as long as I felt them everything was fine. Everything was—

The waves began to ebb. No! I clung to them, holding tight, but they were slipping away now, gentler, rolling over me, the edge of terror and pain gone, only the blissful aftermath remaining.

I lifted my head. Struggled to focus. Everything in me pleaded with me to relax, just lie back and enjoy it. Don't spoil—

I saw Paige. Crumpled against the wall. Her pretty face twisted with horror. A bullet hole through her forehead.

I screamed. As the sound ripped from my throat, it changed into a roar, the chaos bliss hardening into something that filled me, burned me, seared my eyes, my brain, my gut. Through the blaze, I saw Jaz. Only Jaz. On his feet. Coming toward me.

I lunged at him, kicking, clawing, screaming in a voice I didn't recognize as human. I smelled blood. I felt its heat. I tasted its sweetness.

Something jabbed my arm. The prick of pain only spurred me on, but Jaz had wrenched from my grasp. I wheeled. Through the blood haze, I spotted his dark form, and I tried to launch myself at him, but I just kept turning. Turning. Turning. My knees gave way and I spiraled to the ground.

The last thing I saw was Paige's dead eyes, staring at me.

HOPE

CRASH AND BURN

Twice before, I'd watched my life crash and burn.

The first time had been my last year of high school. In the midst of SATs, training for a regatta and struggling through the first serious fight with my high school sweetheart, I'd started seeing visions. Convinced it was stress, I'd been furious with myself for showing such weakness and determined to "fix" myself before anyone found out and shipped me off to therapy. I'd fought it so hard that I had a breakdown, I lost it all—the SATs, the regatta, my boyfriend—and spent my prom night in a private mental hospital.

It took years to recover from that, but I did. I learned what I was. I established contacts in the supernatural world. I graduated from college. I found the "council" and got my job with *True News*. From debutante to tabloid-reporting, gun-toting, chaos demon spy girl. Not exactly what my mother had in mind, but I'd been pleased with myself. It was like going to bed an ordinary girl and waking up a superhero.

More like super-chump. I'd discovered that my new life was built on a lie. I wasn't protecting the innocent; I was delivering them to the Cortez Cabal. My self-confidence took a beating that it still hadn't recovered from. But with Karl's help I'd bounced back and became exactly what I thought I'd been before—a council operative.

Now, with a single bullet, my world had shattered again. This time it wouldn't heal.

Paige had believed me. I said I'd needed her help and she'd taken me at my word. How many times had I heard the council tease Paige about her impetuousness? They told stories of her running headlong into danger, mind fixed on a soul that needed saving. But such tales were rooted in the past, and even Paige laughed at them. She was older now. More experienced. More cautious.

Yet hadn't I seen the worry in Lucas's eyes when she set out on a dangerous assignment? I'd always told myself he was just concerned for his wife. Now I realized that Paige was, at heart, the same person she'd always been, one who'd throw herself into a bullet's path to save a friend.

I'd called for help. She'd listened.

I'd begged her to tell no one. She'd listened.

After arriving, she'd had misgivings, but I'd played it so cool she'd told herself she was wrong. And followed me to her death.

She'd trusted me. She was dead. It was my fault.

Benicio Cortez would chase me to the ends of the earth, now, convinced I'd been part of the conspiracy against his family. Who would I turn to? For justice? For mercy? Lucas? The council? I'd killed Paige. No one would help me now.

I would not recover from this. Could not.

And yet, even as I thought the words, they were only words. I didn't care what happened to me. All I could see was Paige's face. Her dead eyes staring at me.

My greatest fear had been that, faced with the death of a friend, I'd be so overcome by the chaos that I'd stand by and watch. Now I knew I'd been wrong. I'd faced the chaos and overcome it. I'd tried to stop Jaz. Tried to save Paige. Did it matter? No. Because I'd still been responsible for her death . . . and I didn't even have the demon to blame.

I LAY IN the back of a car. I had no idea how long I'd been there, trapped in my thoughts, smelling vinyl and vomit, feeling the rumble of the tires, hearing the sharp words of an argument. It all washed over me, muddled by whatever drug sloshed through my veins.

Even when the voices became coherent, I listened, aware that what I was hearing was important, connected to me, but unable to *make* that connection. Just disembodied voices floating through the ether.

"You have to do something about her."

"Everything's fine."

"Fine? Look in the mirror and tell me everything's fine, Jaz. She attacked you—"

"I shot someone she liked. What's she supposed to do? Run over and kiss me?"

"Kill you more like."

"She wouldn't do that."

"No? Well, judging by those scratches, she sure as hell tried. I hate to see what you'd look like if you hadn't shot her with the sedative."

"You don't understand."

"No, Jaz, I don't."

Silence.

"I need her, Sonny."

"Need? You met her a few days ago. Days! And now, all of a sudden, you can't live without her. I'm starting to wonder where that leaves me."

"Right where you've always been. My brother. *Nothing* is more important to me."

"Nothing?"

Silence.

"You want me to choose, Sonny? Is that what this is about? You're feeling threatened so I need to make a choice?"

"I never said—"

"Here, take this."

"What the hell are you—?"

"Go on. Take it."

"For God's sake, Jaz. Stop being such a fucking drama queen. I—"

"Take the gun. Fire it. Because if you're going to make me choose, you might as well put a bullet in my brain right now."

"Goddamn it! You're crazy, you know that? As screwed up as—"

Silence.

"As Mom?"

"I didn't mean that, Jaz. You know I didn't."

"At least I come by it honestly."

"I didn't mean—"

"It's okay, bro. Maybe I am a little fucked up. Maybe a *lot* fucked up. But you know what's really nuts, Sonny? I know that, and it doesn't make any difference. I look at Hope back there and I think 'Goddamn it, man, what are you doing?' But it doesn't change anything because I *feel* it's right. It's what I'm meant to do. Just like all this." Pause. "Have I ever steered you wrong?"

"No, Jaz."

"As crazy as my ideas are, have they ever been something we can't manage?"

"No."

"Then trust me."

"I do."

"I know you're tired of this, bro. I know you want it over with. Me and my mad dreams. But we're almost there. Remember when we were little, and Mom would say we had to move again, and you'd cry and cry. What did I promise you?"

"That someday we'd stop running."

"And when you were older, she'd say we had to move and you'd try to reason with her, and you'd get so mad because she never listened. What did I promise you?"

"That you'd stop it."

"The only way to stop the Cabal—really stop them—is to become them. We're close, Sonny. So close. Just a couple more months, then, when everything's in place, you can go back to being you. Free."

"And what about you?"

"I'll be fine. I'll get used to being Lucas and I'll have Hope."

"What if she doesn't . . . come around?"

"She will. This is a lot for her to absorb. You can't blame her for being freaked out. But she loves me. I know that. She'll come around."

"Not like she has much choice now."

Silence.

"That wasn't how I wanted it."

"I know, Jaz. But now she'll have to see what it's like from our side."

When all went quiet, my thoughts folded back into themselves, and I was lost again.

I GROANED AND clutched my stomach. Jaz caught me by the shoulders, steadying me as I sat on the seat edge. Another seat, another car. Sonny had dropped us off in a parking garage, where a second vehicle waited, then he'd left to ditch the first a couple of blocks away.

"Just crawl in and lie down," Jaz said.

"I—I—" I heaved, slapping my hand over my mouth. "Oh, God. I need air."

He hesitated. It was safer with me in the car. "The air's not much fresher out here. Worse even. All the carbon monoxide."

I looked into his eyes. "Please."

A pause. Then, "Yeah. Okay. But just for a minute."

Mission accomplished.

He led me over to a pillar near the railing, far enough back so I wouldn't be seen, but close enough to catch the breeze.

"Sonny's going to come out right over there. Any minute. Then I'm getting you back in that car before he finds out."

I nodded. He kept one arm around my waist, the other holding my arm, supporting me as I leaned against the pillar.

"I'm sorry, Hope. I really am. It was a helluva thing to do to you, but I had to. If I'd let you know what I planned, you would have been an accomplice in Paige's death. I wouldn't do that to you."

And you think I'm not an accomplice now? I brought her to you.

He fingered the gouges on his cheek. "I deserved every one of them. And more. But once you get past this, you'll see there wasn't any other way. She's gone to the other side now, and she's okay. All those good deeds she did here? She's in the best place they've got. And Lucas will be with her soon, and they'll be happy. Do you think she'd really prefer it the other way? Kidnapped, terrified and alone, finally rescued only to discover that the man she loved has changed into someone she doesn't recognize? She's better off."

There was no pleading in his voice. He honestly believed Paige was happier dead, and that it was only a matter of time before I "came around."

I resisted the urge to push him away and stand on my own feet. I could. Almost as soon as I'd awoken, the effects of the drugs had worn off. I'd gotten him out here, alone, and now I had to . . .

To what?

Run away? Where? Kill him and drag him, like a trophy, back to the Cabal? Throw myself on their mercy?

To my shame, there was a fraction of my soul that didn't want to do anything. That just wanted to throw up its hands and go along for the ride. Abdicate responsibility. Overthrow conscience. Join Jaz and believe in his mad dreams.

It was a tiny part, but it had to be acknowledged. That's what Karl had tried to tell me last night. I couldn't keep pretending that part didn't exist. I had my demon, and it wasn't evil any more than was his wolf. It just wasn't human. It lacked the ability to comprehend the conscious lives of others. It hungered and it desired and it knew nothing else, strove for nothing else but the satisfaction of those hungers and desires.

The human in me would never pass a car accident and see a covered body without feeling a jab of grief for a life lost. The demon could see only what it could take from that death: chaos. Likewise with the wolf, who would see only a meal already brought down. Not evil. Just not human.

When the demon whispered in my ear, telling me it would be easier to give in to Jaz, accept the chaos feast he'd set at my feet in offering, I couldn't be horrified by the impulse. I had to listen, refuse and move on.

"Oh, there he is. Let's scoot you back in the car."

My chance was evaporating. Was I strong enough yet to knock him out? Was I *ever* strong enough? The element of surprise. That was my only hope.

I let him lead me toward the car. I saw his gun on the front seat, where he must have laid it while trying to get me into the back. If I could swing the door open, hit him, grab the—

The flash of fangs. A growl that skittered down my spine. I went rigid, a name on my lips. Karl. I looked around, but of course, he wasn't there. A vision. Meaning he was close.

"Hope?" Jaz's voice. His hand squeezed mine, the other still around my waist.

Where is she? The snarled question reverberated through my head. A crack. Blinding pain. Only I didn't feel pain. Just chaos, rippling through the air, floating up from . . .

My gaze flew to the railing.

"Hope? What do you—?"

Jaz followed my gaze. A small noise. An odd noise. Like a tiny chirp of fear. He dropped me and ran for the railing.

"Son—!"

The word cut off with a strangled cry. He ran back to the car, pushed me aside, clawed at the door, finally getting it open.

Where is she, you son of a bitch?

Karl. I swore I could hear his voice. Impossible from thirty feet below, but it was as clear as if he was beside me.

I walked to the railing. Seemed to float, pulled along by the tethers of chaos.

There, on the street below, Karl had Sonny on the ground, one knee on his back, hand wrapped in his hair, head pulled back so far that with the barest tug, his neck would snap.

Karl slammed Sonny's face into the pavement.

Where is she?

I opened my mouth to shout. Then I saw Sonny's hand, sliding from under his jacket. Karl didn't notice, too focused on his task, the chaos waves even from this distance so sharp and hard they stopped the breath in my throat. Sonny's hand slid out. His gun in that hand.

"Karl!" I screamed.

Jaz shoved me aside. He aimed his gun. It was too far. Too dangerous. He let out a strangled cry and jumped onto the railing, as if ready to leap off it.

A growl. A shot. A snap.

The last somehow seemed loudest, though I heard it only in my head. Heard it. Felt it. Saw it. The whites of Sonny's eyes, rolling as his neck snapped. His face going slack. Head falling to the pavement.

HOPE

DEATH WISH

"No."

The word was barely a whisper. Jaz tottered on the railing. One lunge and I could have pushed him off. He toppled backward, half falling, half stepping down.

"No."

He collapsed where he was and sat there, clutching the railing bars, Sonny's name on every breath. His grief washed over me, so strong it blocked the death and held me as tight as any binding spell, unable to move.

I looked at the gun on the ground, dropped beside Jaz. I looked back into the parking garage.

"Don't," he rasped.

He still sat there, clutching the bars, face pressed to them, watching his brother's body below.

I took a step back.

"They're coming." He rubbed his hands over his face, swiping at the tears. "Don't leave me here." He picked up the gun by the barrel and held it out. "Finish it, Hope."

"You—you want me to—"

"I killed Paige. Killed Guy. Killed Bianca. Helped kill Rodriguez and Max and Tony. You want to do this."

I stared at the gun.

"And if revenge isn't enough . . ." He met my gaze. "Maybe pity is. I want to go with Sonny. Don't let the Cabal take me. Please."

I took the gun. Wrapped my fingers around the stock.

"Through the mouth. Or the back of the head. That's the quickest." A tiny, tired smile. "Maybe not the most chaotic, but if you get something from this—" His eyes lifted to mine. "Take what you can, Hope. My last gift to you."

If he wanted to die, all the more reason to say no. Punish him. Turn him over to the Cabal. Make him stand trial. Let them execute him. But standing here, looking into his face, I still saw Jaz, and I still felt something. Maybe only pity, but it was enough.

He opened his mouth. I put the gun in.

"Step away from him now!"

I jumped so fast the gun barrel slammed against the roof of Jaz's mouth. Two men in tactical uniforms approached from my left. Two more from my right. All with guns trained on me.

"You have five seconds to step away from him!" one barked.

Terror filled Jaz's eyes, pleading with me to pull the trigger. For a second, the chaos swirling around me was too much and I stood there, dazed. Then I moved my finger.

"One second!"

A dark shape smashed through the two men on my left, knocking them aside like bowling pins. I saw Karl's face. Saw his terror, felt it, as sharp as Jaz's. He tackled me. I crashed down under him. Heard a shot. Heard him grunt in pain.

The tactical team rushed in, stepping over us to get to Jaz. When my head stopped spinning from the chaos, I realized I was still on the ground, Karl stretched over me, not moving.

I remembered the shot. Felt the weight of him, pinning me down. And then, a tiny whimper, bubbling up from my throat.

"Don't move."

His fingers gripped my shoulder, mouth moving to my ear.

"Wait."

I let out the breath I'd been holding, then found myself flat on the pavement, lungs compressed by his weight, gasping—

"Sorry."

He lifted up, giving me breathing room. Then he slid off me, his gaze fixed over my shoulder, watching the tactical team, as if expecting our first sudden move would bring a gun barrel swinging our way. But they had Jaz cuffed now. Cuffed and gagged as he writhed and struggled, eyes blazing. Then he saw me and went still.

Our gazes locked.

He jerked his head so fast the gag slipped. His gaze swung to Karl, catching his attention, making sure he had it, then turning to me.

"I'll come back for you," he mouthed.

With a snarl, Karl was on his feet. Two officers lifted their guns. I pulled him back down beside me.

"He wanted that," I said. "He wanted you to kill him."

I felt the chaos swirl from Karl as they took Jaz away. Not jealousy but fear.

They can't hold him, Karl thought. *He'll escape. He* will *come for her. She'll never be—*

He cut the thought short. His arm slid around my back and he pulled me onto his lap and we sat there, watching them take Jaz away.

"Why didn't they let me kill him?" I whispered. "Do they want to put him on trial? Make him stand judgment?" I looked quickly at Karl. "They don't understand. He can *become* anyone."

"They know."

"That's why—" I swallowed. "They were under orders to bring them in alive."

I shivered and he rubbed my arms, pulling me against him, sitting on the cold pavement, leaning against some stranger's car—

"Paige." The name burbled from my throat and I scrambled up from Karl's lap. "Oh, God. You don't know. They don't know." I looked up into his face. "She's dead, Karl. Jaz had me lure her in and I thought she'd bring backup, but she didn't and he—"

"Hope?"

A soft contralto voice echoed through the parking garage. I turned and my knees gave way. Karl caught me.

"It's okay," he whispered. "*She's* okay."

I watched Paige walk toward me, her face tight with worry and guilt, and I knew then that I was dreaming. Still drugged and lying in the back of that car, lost in my thoughts. In my dreams.

"I'm so sorry, Hope," she said. "I'm so, so sorry."

"It wasn't her idea."

Another voice. I looked over Paige's shoulder to see Lucas.

"It was Benicio's plan," Karl said, a growl underscoring his words. "If I'd known—"

"But he didn't. Yes, it was my father's idea, but I agreed with it and I talked Paige into it." Lucas stopped beside me. "We couldn't see any other way, Hope. It was a cruel ruse and I sincerely apologize."

"We had to stop them," Paige said.

I shook my head. "No. I saw you. The hole— That was real. You were dead."

"A glamour spell," Lucas said. "Cast on a Cabal prisoner await-ing execution for murdering her parents. My father—" He inhaled. "*We* offered her a deal. If she went along with it, and it succeeded, she'd be granted a pardon. If it didn't . . ." He let the breath out and, in that second, seemed to age a decade. "Then the writ of execution was carried out."

I looked from him to Paige. To sacrifice a life—even to stop a killer—would have taken a lot of soul searching and, from their ex-pressions, the decision still didn't rest easy. For most people, the choice would be simple—the woman had been condemned to die so her death might as well serve some higher purpose. But Paige and Lucas weren't most people.

"You're right," I said. "It was the best way to get to them. The only way probably. It was fair. She'd earned her death and you gave her a chance to beat it."

Neither spoke and I could tell, as sincere as my words were, that they didn't really help.

"Speaking of executions," Karl said. "I trust Jasper Haig is going to be taking that woman's cell, and her slot on the schedule."

Lucas pushed his glasses up and pinched the bridge of his nose.

"You know Benicio's plans, Karl," Paige said. "Lucas argued strenuously against them, and he'll continue to argue—"

"You can't let him live. The man can impersonate his jailer. His lawyer. His doctor, for God's sake. If he comes into contact with any person—"

"I don't think it's that simple, Karl, and we will take every precau-tion and security measure—"

"He's already pissed on all your security measures! He got into your father's house. Shot his bodyguard. Killed your brothers—"

"Because we didn't know what we were dealing with."

"Do you really think it's going to matter? He's an accomplished thief who can steal any identity. He will escape. And when he does, the first place he's going is—" He glanced back at me and stopped.

"Paige is right," Lucas said. "I *will* fight this, Karl. I could not agree with you more on every point you've made. Jasper Haig should be treated as a criminal, not as a research subject." His voice dropped. "But getting my father to agree, even under the circumstances, may be beyond even my influence."

ЯND, FOR NOW, it was.

Lucas argued. Paige argued. I argued. Karl threatened. Benicio would not budge.

All this had begun with one woman's paranoid delusions, convincing her sons that they had to spend their lives running because, if they stopped, the Cabal would pounce on them and they'd live out their days as laboratory rats. In trying to escape that fate, Jaz found himself living it. For now...

Would he stay locked up? Karl didn't believe it. Neither did I. Jaz would never throw up his hands and say "guess you got me." While he could draw breath, he'd be plotting his escape and his revenge. Karl had killed his brother. He'd never forget that.

Lucas had promised to keep us updated on his situation and we'd continue fighting for his execution. For now, though, that had to wait, and I had to concentrate on getting back to the life I thought I'd lost. My job, my family, my home. It was all waiting for me. And Karl. Most of all, Karl.

Hours later, Karl and I stood outside Cortez Cabal headquarters, staring up at the morning sun.

"Another sunny day," Karl said.

"I'm tired of sunny."

"I hear Philly's expecting a snowstorm tonight."

"Good. We'll be just in time."

His hand cupped mine. "Are you sure? You still have a few days. We can get away. I'll take you anyplace you want to go."

"I want to go home." I looked up at him. "I want to go visit with my mother and tell her you're moving to Philly. I want to tour over-priced condos that displaced impoverished seniors, and needle you about it mercilessly. Then I want to take you home, hole up for the storm, then go back to work chasing alien abduction stories and Hell Spawn sightings."

"Are you sure?"

I lifted onto my tiptoes and kissed his chin. "Absolutely."

LUCAS

21

I WATCHED JASPER through the one-way glass. He lay on a king-size bed, eyes glued to a handheld video game. MTV flashed on the plasma screen affixed to the wall. A take-out pizza box rested by his elbow.

This was how the Cortez Cabal treated the man who'd killed two of its top executives and attempted to kill its CEO. This was how my father treated the man who'd murdered two of his sons and plotted to kill the rest of his family.

I knew the room was actually a jail cell. A life sentence with no chance of parole, kept alive only because he could prove useful. But it wasn't enough. For his crimes, and for the threat he posed, I wanted him dead.

My father had decreed mercy. I'd argued for capital punishment. Did I ever think I'd see that day?

I had weighed the factors and decided Jasper Haig should not be allowed to live. How often had my father made that very decision and I'd condemned him for it?

Only twenty-four hours ago, I hadn't hesitated to condemn another criminal. When my father had suggested sending a convicted murderer to meet Hope in Paige's place, I'd agreed, knowing I was sending that woman to an almost certain death.

I'd weighed the factors, analyzed the risks and made my decision.

Whatever I felt about the outcome, I still believed we'd made the right choice.

"Sir?"

Griffin gestured toward the door, impatient for me to get this meeting over with so he could return to my father's side. I lifted a finger and checked my cell phone. Three text and two voice messages. None of them from Paige.

She was back at the hotel, working. Work she could have done from any office in the building. But since yesterday—since I'd agreed with my father's plan—there'd been a distance between us that I knew I wasn't imagining.

I'd text messaged her an hour ago, asking her to join me for lunch. No answer yet.

I closed the phone and motioned for the guard to open Jasper's cell.

Jasper sat up, legs swinging over the bedside. Two guards darted past me, flanking him and motioning for him to stay seated. As he settled back onto the bed, one fingered his gun, the other readied his powers.

Jasper's lips curved, amused by the thought that he presented such a threat. If he wanted to strike at me, he'd hardly do it in front of three Cabal guards. Jasper was a plotter, not a fighter.

Even as he reclined against the pillows, smirking, I could feel the weight of his gaze on me, assessing me, then shifting to the guards, judging which he could best impersonate.

I made a mental note to speak to my father about that, and ensure all guards assigned to Jasper were as far from his physical type as possible. That would slow him down, but it wouldn't stop him. My father had bought his docility by promising a necromantic visit with his brother's ghost, but the respite would be only temporary. It had taken Jasper years to plan his attack on the Cabal. He would be in no rush to escape from the consequences. But we could never forget he was planning that escape.

I stepped forward. "You wished to speak to me?"

"I asked for your dad, but you'll do just fine." He scanned me, measuring, assessing, noting my expressions, my idiosyncrasies.

"How's Paige?" he asked after a moment.

I tensed, but he only sat there, expectant, as if simply making friendly conversation, not reminding me that he'd tried to kill my wife.

"That was a clever trick," he said. "The glamour spell. Really clever."

Again, no mockery in his voice. Nothing but genuine admiration, as if complimenting a fellow chess player who'd made a brilliant move. That's all this was to Jasper. A game. And I was only a competitor. Or a pawn.

"You wished to speak to me?" I repeated.

"Hope," he said. "I want to see her before she goes."

"She left this morning."

"Did she say anything? Leave me a message?"

"No."

Dismay flickered, but he bounced back with a smile. "She's still mad. That's okay. She'll come around. She just needs time. When she does want to talk to me, you'll let me know, right?"

"I'm sure you'll be informed."

"Thanks. I'd appreciate that."

As he grinned, I almost expected him to pass me a tip, as if I were a concierge at his new five-star hotel.

"Is that everything?" I said.

"Yep. Thanks."

I started to turn away.

"Oh, sorry," he said. "One last thing."

I slowly turned back.

"About the werewolf. Karl, is it?"

I said nothing.

"Could you pass along a message?" A slow smile. "Tell him I'm thinking of him."

I WAS WALKING from the cell when Carlos strode past the hall door. I resisted the urge to step aside before he saw me.

"There you are," he said, shoes squeaking as he wheeled. "You're a hard man to find these days. I'd almost think you were avoiding me."

"Hello, Carlos."

"We missed you at the funeral today. Mom was hoping you'd show. She really wants to talk to you."

"I'm sure she does," I murmured.

Carlos laughed. "You know my mother. She takes a big interest in your health."

"If you'll excuse me . . ."

"Not yet." He stepped into my path. "Someone else has been avoiding me. Dad stood beside Mom and me during the service then he took off. That was the only time I've seen him since he accused me of murdering my brothers and tried to kill me. Think maybe he's feeling bad about that?"

"It was a very difficult situation and—"

"Stuff it, Lucas. Rumor has it he wants to buy me out. Have you heard that?"

"No," I lied. "Where did you—?"

"I have my sources. They tell me he's been asking about my debt and my expenses, trying to figure out how much it would take to make me walk away. So how about I help him out with that? I'll name my price. You give him the message."

"If you wish."

"Oh, I do." He stepped nose-to-nose with me. "Tell our father he doesn't have enough to buy me off. By Cabal law, I am entitled to a seat on the board and stock shares, and my birthright is not for sale. I'm not going anywhere, baby bro. Maybe you don't think I pose much of a threat. With Hector and William around, I knew I didn't stand a chance of sliding into the big seat. But now . . ." He eased back, teeth bared in a grin. "Now everything's changed."

WHEN CARLOS WALKED away, I didn't follow, but retreated into the room outside Jasper's cell, returning to his window, watching him.

Jasper had no idea what he'd done.

I had no idea what I'd do about it.

"It doesn't matter how hard you stare; unless you've learned a spell for laser-vision, you can't make him disappear."

I turned to see Paige, her face drawn, eyes underscored with dark smudges.

She managed a wan smile. "Still on for lunch?"

"Yes, certainly. I wasn't sure . . . I thought you might want to be alone."

"I don't. Not anymore." She stepped up to the one-way glass, looking at Jasper. "I had a lot to think about and you have too much on your plate already."

I must have looked worried, because she touched my arm.

"We're okay," she said. "I'm just ... struggling with the choice I made."

"You didn't make—"

"Of course I did. I didn't argue very hard. There was no point. Your dad had made up his mind and if I fought it, I'd only be trying to absolve myself of guilt. If I'd *had* the choice, would I really have said 'Oh, no, please send me instead of the convicted murderer'?" She shook her head. "I just wish we hadn't needed to make that decision. And I have a feeling it's not going to be the last one." A small laugh. "I did say I wasn't going to bother you with it, didn't I?"

"I'd like to hear—"

"Later. After we're away from all this." She swept her hand across the room. A pause, then she said, "I saw Carlos. Did he speak to you?"

"He knows about the deal. He's not taking it."

A slow nod. A moment of silence. "Everything's going to change, isn't it?" she said quietly.

"I don't know."

Her hand slid into mine, fingers entwining with a squeeze. "Whatever happens, whatever you decide, now, later ... I'm not going anywhere. You're stuck with me, Cortez."

I leaned down to kiss the top of her head and murmured, "I hope so."